The Pool of Unease

Catherine Sampson

W F HOWES LTD

This large print edition published in 2007 by
W F Howes Ltd
Unit 4, Rearsby Business Park, Gaddesby Lane,
Rearsby, Leicester LE7 4YH

1 3 5 7 9 10 8 6 4 2

First published in the United Kingdom in 2007
by Macmillan

A CIP catalogue record for this book is available
from the British Library

ISBN 978 1 40740 934 4

Typeset by Palimpsest Book Production Limited,
Grangemouth, Stirlingshire
Printed and bound in Great Britain
by Antony Rowe Ltd, Chippenham, Wilts.

For Mai Jiesi

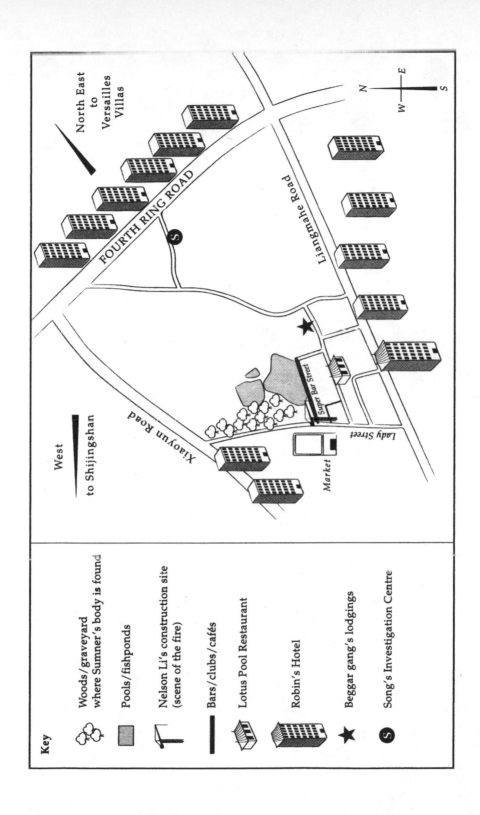

Key

🌳 Woods/graveyard where Sumner's body is found

▦ Pools/fishponds

🏗 Nelson Li's construction site (scene of the fire)

▬ Bars/clubs/cafés

🏢 Lotus Pool Restaurant

🏢 Robin's Hotel

★ Beggar gang's lodgings

Ⓢ Song's Investigation Centre

FOURTH RING ROAD

North East to Versailles Villas

Liangmahe Road

Super Bar Street

Lady Street

Market

Xiaoyun Road

West to Shijingshan

N
W — E
S

CHAPTER 1

Song watched and waited miserably in the small car, his long legs jammed painfully under the steering wheel, chin buried in his scarf, as the snowflakes tumbled from the night sky and settled on his windscreen. Beijing's snow was desert snow, desiccated and fine, like the yellow sand that would blow in from the Gobi when spring came. Song's hands were rammed deep into the pockets of his sheepskin, his fingers stiff around a digital camera. The temperature had dropped to eight below zero. Normally he would have kept the engine running and the heat on, but for the sake of his mission he was attempting to become a non-person – the non-driver of a non-car. He concentrated for a moment. He could feel nothing from the waist down. His legs had become non-legs, his feet non-feet.

He tried wiggling his toes but he could sense only a distant twitch. He was risking frostbite for the client who had given him his orders in a voice like nails dragging across a blackboard.

'They say you're clever; well, don't get clever

with me. Just follow my husband like a dog follows a bitch.'

So here he was, faithful bloodhound Song pursuing the faithless husband, who had disappeared twenty minutes earlier into a brothel, waiting in a car parked opposite a public toilet. The outer wall of the toilet had turned into the unofficial neighbourhood dump and rubbish was overflowing from the pavement into the gutter. In this weather even the stench was frozen solid, along with the crap and the snot and the maggots. The cold had driven almost everyone off the streets to huddle inside, but a scavenger – a man – was picking through the mess, a basket over his shoulder. He glanced up at Song with fear in his eyes, then looked away. Song remembered how, during the summers of his youth, he and his neighbours had slept on makeshift beds in the open air to escape the stifling heat of their homes. Now the world was full of strangers and paranoia was rife. Neighbours had been uprooted by order of the city government and replanted at opposite ends of the city. They installed steel security doors and bars at their windows to fend off burglars, real or imaginary. Official notice boards in the streets warned women not to go out alone at night. In the past few weeks, tales of rape and murder and theft had spread across the city. No one knew what was true and what was not, and now everyone looked at strangers with . . . well, like the scavenger had looked at him.

'I'm up to my eyeballs in shit too, brother,' Song muttered. Matrimonials stank of treachery and deceit, the clients stank of it and the husbands stank of it, and Song could smell it on himself. Usually he turned matrimonials down, but this month he needed the money more than ever because his father was in hospital receiving treatment for bladder cancer, and the imported medicines and the doctor's bribes were bleeding the family dry. The final tally, whether his father lived or died, would be more than one hundred thousand *yuan*. Which happened to be more or less what Song had borrowed from his father to set up the agency a year before. Neither his father nor his sister had mentioned it, but Song couldn't help replaying in his mind how his father had queued outside the bank to withdraw his life savings, money scrimped and saved from a scrawny income. His father had pressed wads of notes into his son's hands, and Song had accepted with gratitude, never dreaming how badly his father would need the cash, and how soon.

Song looked back towards the brothel, determined not to miss the husband. In Chinese, the massage parlour was called the Fragrant Companion. It had an English name too, and Song sounded out the letters one by one under his breath, 'O-r-g-a-s-i-n,' then tried the whole word: 'Orgasin.' He didn't recognize it, but then he'd had only a couple of years of English in school and his teacher had had less than that. He noticed that a black Santana with a white police number plate was parked on the other side of the road further down. It looked unoccupied, but given the dark street and the tinted windows he couldn't say for sure.

Inside the glass-fronted brothel, two girls sat on a sofa in the glow of pink neon. It was a slow night. They huddled, chatting and knitting, around an electric heater, its red bars almost touching their shins. Each wore a white down-filled jacket and high-heeled white boots that came to their knees, but underneath Song could see cleavage and thighs exposed. Their cheeks were rouged, their lips glossed purple, their hair dyed yellow: a rainbow of bravado. He wondered whether the women were frightened of their customers. Did they pay heed to rumour, or did their work require the quashing of imagination?

Song was afraid that if they spotted him loitering in the car they might come and extract him, like a snail from its shell, then carry him across the street and have their way with him whether he liked it or not. Once, on a business trip to Hainan Island, he had answered a knock at his hotel room door at midnight, thinking there was some emergency. He'd found a woman standing in the hallway. She had pressed herself hard up against him and attempted to kiss him – he'd been too sleepy to be interested and too sleepy to resist – then, when he refused to invite her in, she had demanded two hundred *yuan* in payment for services rendered, although of course he had required none and she had rendered none. Song had refused to pay and she had threatened to shout rape. In the end, he'd haggled her down to one hundred *yuan*, paid her off and returned to his bed.

Tonight, Song had already snapped a series of pictures for the client's album – the husband getting out of his car, pushing open the glass door of the brothel, a girl rising from her seat to attach herself to his arm, pushing and pulling him, while he laughed and pretended to protest, through the heavy velvet curtain into the back room. But he knew what every client really wanted – a photograph of genitalia gave an aggrieved wife excellent leverage.

The two girls were looking out at the car now and giggling. One of them got to her feet, tugging her skirt down over her thighs. She pulled open the door and, hunching her shoulders against the cold, picked her way across the icy street and straight for him. She stopped by his car and rapped on the window. Sighing, he turned the key in the ignition, pressed a button and the window hummed down. The woman bent and leaned in so that her face was just inches from his and he could smell garlic and rice and cheap scent.

'Want to come and play?'

Song shook his head. 'Aren't you afraid? Some men would pull a knife on you.'

'Are you threatening me?' Her voice – uneducated,

heavily accented – was loud and challenging. Her eyes ran over the long body folded into the driving seat, the broad shoulders, the long bespectacled face and the shaved head. She smiled. 'I know you. You're the man who lives on Alley Number 10. I've seen you around. I'll give you a discount.'

'I've never seen you before in my life,' Song snapped. But she was right, of course. He lived on Alley Number 10, on the east side of the lake, in a one-storey brick building with a yard out front and a wall that enclosed the small compound. It doubled as his office. There was even a brass plaque by the tall iron gate: Sherlock Investigation and Legal Research Centre. Its neighbours on Alley Number 10 were a fruit stall and a tattoo parlour.

The Communist Party didn't much like to admit that private detectives existed or were necessary. But then the more the politicians talked about a 'harmonious socialist society', the less the country looked and felt like one. The economy was booming, and the necessity for private detective agencies was booming in line with what people perceived to be a rise in extramarital affairs, kidnapping, petty crime, violent crime, ID theft, insurance fraud, corruption and trickery in every facet of personal and commercial life. In many cases the police were in it up to their necks, and the justice system had teeth but no backbone. If private detectives had not mushroomed in this dark and steamy environment it would have been a socialist miracle.

Song had decided to be diplomatic and to name his agency in a euphemistic way in order to avoid unwanted political interference. 'Investigation and Legal Research' put him at the pale end of a spectrum that consisted only of shades of grey.

'So why are you sitting here in the cold talking to yourself?' Irritation had crept into the prostitute's voice. She'd left the comfort of the brothel and braved the freezing air outside to honour him with the offer of her body, and he'd rejected her. It was an insult. She glanced over towards the brothel, where the husband was still closeted, then back to the car, and Song saw in her eyes that she had worked it out. She banged her fist once on the hood of the car and stalked away from him, her high-heeled boots slipping and sliding on the ice.

He swore softly to himself. If he just sat here, she'd go inside and tell the husband that there was a man sitting outside watching him. He might as well follow her in, barge in on the husband in the act, at least try to get the photos the client wanted.

He pushed open the car door, still cursing. Paper trails were his thing – paper trails and internet searches and knocking on doors and watching and listening, and hearing what people said, not just with their words, but with their voices and their eyes. He hated matrimonials. It would all be a horrible mess, it always was, everyone would howl and shout, and the husband would give chase, and at the end of the day Song would have nothing to show for it but a digital image of an anonymous toe or an elbow.

He stepped out of the car, the smooth soles of his boots slipping on the ice. Then, as he took another step, a scream scythed through the air and shocked him to a halt.

The scream – female, high-pitched, terrified, breathless, a wordless, formless plea for mercy – arrived from silence and was cut off, abruptly strangled, leaving a gurgling echo in its airy wake. Song stopped still, listening for more. The scream jabbed at his memory and his memory expelled another scream. His earliest memory, one he'd tried to bury for four decades. His mother, hounded by a vicious mob of former pupils, pushed from the third-floor window of the school building, scream reaching Song in an adjacent courtyard. His father grabbing him, holding him back, whispering urgently in his ear that he must not run to her, not yet, or they would turn on him too.

This time he could run, no one was holding him back. And he did, he ran, dimly aware that the husband had reappeared from the back room of the brothel and that the girls were turning towards him, flirting and joking with him. Song half slid, half stumbled on numb legs down Likang Alley, which cut away from the main road, towards the lake and the scream.

When he reached the back of the Red Flag Hotel he came to a gasping halt, staring around him, but there was no one to be seen. The strip of bars and nightclubs that ran along the south shore of the lake was mostly dark, and Song thought they had closed early for lack of custom. But the dull glow of the city cast everything in an orange half-light.

The boiler that served the hotel was belching steam. Kitchen detritus, mainly gelid cabbage leaves, was piled next to a mound of bricks and a stack of cement bags, all dusted with snow. Until recently a maze of alleys had backed onto the Red Flag Hotel. They'd been torn down by an army of men wielding hammers and picks, and a cavalry of donkeys had arrived to cart the bricks out of the city. A few ragged brick walls still stood, but mostly there was a Siberian landscape of snow-covered rubble. A spotlight placed on a squat metal stand illuminated the entrance to the construction site, where a hoarding showed a golden sun rising over a red horizon. Where once there had been peasant homes, soon another of Nelson Li's luxury real-estate projects would thrust skyward, a potent symbol of the ambition of both the man and the city.

Song strode across the loose stones and bricks, the snow crunching underfoot. Ahead of him lay the dark lake, which became solid ice most of the winter, thawing partially when the sun appeared, its surface pitted with puddles of water and ragged

9

at the edges, then freezing hard again, new layers of ice forming over old.

Song stopped and sniffed the air. He smelled smoke. In front of him an army-issue tent had been erected as a night-watchman's shelter. Outside the tent, a spotlight was aimed at the stretch of construction site that bordered the lake, and in the distance Song saw a figure hurrying along the path that skirted the water, pushing a heavily laden cart. A wail of fear rose from inside the tent, a childish voice, and a different terror, a different kind of call for help. This sound, unlike that first awful scream, still held a germ of hope for salvation. In the same moment, he saw flames licking their way up the side of the canvas.

Song ran to the tent and pulled open the flap, standing clear, fearing that flames would billow out. He secured the canvas, twisting it around a pole, then pushed at the metal stand underneath the spotlight, manoeuvring it so that the light shone, intense and white, into the interior of the tent. Only then, covering his nose and mouth with his hand, did he peer inside. The stove had fallen or been pushed against the tenting and flames were advancing up the back wall. In the glare of the spotlight he could see something sprawled on the ground to his right.

He grabbed a handful of snow and then another, grinding it into the wool of his scarf and securing it across his mouth. Then he cursed, got down on his hands and knees and crawled into the burning tent, taking his first breath of scaring smoke. He peered down – the light was too bright and the smoke burned his eyes – and stretched his hands towards the shape, bracing himself for the weight of a body. But instead his hands clutched what felt like empty skin, a slimy film which slithered from his grasp. He exclaimed in horror, pulling his hands back sharply, confusion overwhelming him. Then, bracing himself again, he reached out and pulled the skin towards him. Now he saw that it was discarded clothing, fabric not flesh.

Song grunted with relief, laughing at himself, then stared at the dark sticky substance that was coating his hands and dripping onto his clothes. In alarm, without thinking, he rubbed his hands on his trousers. Then, squinting around him with eyes almost blind from the smoke, he saw other pieces of cloth soaking in a pool of this same dark liquid that stretched across the canvas groundsheet. A woman's shoulder bag lay where it had fallen or been hurled. What had happened here? A woman had died violently – the conclusion was instinctive and instantaneous – but who, and at whose hands? He grabbed at the bag, stuffing it inside his jacket pocket. Tears rolled down Song's cheeks, and his lungs rebelled, telling him to get out. He glanced up. Above him the roof was burning fiercely.

Behind him he heard coughing and he wheeled around, still hunkered down, to find a knife held at his throat. The knife shook, waving dangerously.

Song's eyes followed from the blade, which was covered in blood, to a tiny hand on the metal handle, an arm that trembled as the ragged boy who held it coughed and gagged, eyes swollen and weeping, legs collapsing underneath him. Song snatched the knife away from the child, who cried out in fear and confusion. He scooped the child up, clutching boy and knife against his chest.

Dizzy now, with blackness seeping into his vision, he pulled the burning canvas aside where it had fallen across the entrance. The flames leaped to his right arm and started to feed on his sleeve, and then began to consume his skin. He propelled himself away from the fire and collapsed, rolling on the snow to extinguish the flames. The child fell away from him.

Song lay on his back on the snow, gagging and coughing, then eased himself onto his hands and knees until he could breathe again through a windpipe scorched raw. A stripe of agony burned from his right elbow to his hand, which still gripped the knife that he had snatched from the child. He scrambled to his feet, and as he did so a ball of muck rose from his lungs and he doubled up and spat it into the snow, retching, shredding the delicate tissues of his throat. Next to him in the snow lay the child, small and filthy, hair long and matted, huge eyes wide with terror, breathing rapidly, unnaturally.

From the street came the sound of voices, and Song sensed figures emerging from the shadows.

The spotlight that illuminated him was also blinding him and he could not see their faces. Sobbing with the pain from his arm he took a step backwards and realized that the child had flung himself forwards and was clinging to him, a skinny arm wrapped around his leg. Song tried to shake him off, but the child was stuck like glue, his face transfixed in terror. Song bent down. The only way to free his leg was to hoist the child up again, and this he did, with his left arm, his good arm. He thought about dropping the knife, but then he decided he wanted it for self-protection, in case they tried to lynch him.

'Let him go,' someone shouted.

'He won't let go,' Song attempted to shout, but nothing came out, not even a whisper. His throat was as dry as sandpaper, his tongue swollen, not a drop of saliva in his mouth. His heart was banging against his ribs. Was he about to have a heart attack? He began to panic. He moved his tongue awkwardly around his mouth, but still he could not speak, could not explain himself. He had been struck dumb, he was covered in a dead woman's blood, with a dead woman's bag in his pocket, he was brandishing a murder weapon. At best he would face hours of interrogation, at worst a murder charge, an injection of poison into his veins or a bullet in the back of his neck.

'He set fire to the tent!' one voice shouted, and another called out, 'He's covered in blood – look at his clothes.' A third voice started a chorus of

13

fear that turned rapidly to accusation. 'He's got a knife . . . He's a killer . . . He's going to kill the child . . . Murderer!'

Song tried to retreat, but the child's arm was locked tight around his neck, so when he fled, making for the woods that bordered the west shore of the lake, he ran with the child still in his arms, and the knife clutched awkwardly in his hand.

He carried the boy through the woods, forcing his legs to keep moving one ahead of the other, his feet sinking into the snow, his lungs begging for him to stop, his thirst – the need for moisture in his mouth – almost unbearable. It was his heart, labouring against the smoke that still billowed in his lungs, that nearly brought him to the ground. He held the boy's thin body like a stick of wood against him, and the child moaned and spluttered and retched in his arms, then spat onto Song's jacket.

Lights from the buildings around leaked between the trees, and Song could see just well enough that he was able to dodge between them and the mounds of dirt that were graves. He had never had reason to enter these woods before, but he knew that this was the graveyard for the village that bordered the lake. The city was encroaching, high-rise towers all around, but still the earth was dug here, in between the trees, for the dead from the village. Once he thought he heard a voice behind him and he turned in fear, knowing that a murderer might share these woods with him. When he saw no one he halted to heave air into himself and expel, or this was how it felt, the lining of his lungs. The child stank. He must have lost control of his bladder in the tent, and now the urine-soaked rags that clothed him were freezing stiffly onto his body. Well, he would have to fend for himself. Song began to disentangle himself and then, with shock – one shock on top of all the rest – realized that under the rags the boy had only the one, sinewy, arm. The other shoulder was a stump. Song dumped the child on the ground and stepped away from him. The child, too weak to get to his feet, lunged after him on his knees.

Song thrust the knife inside his clothing and felt it slice through the fabric. He broke into a staggering run and the point of the knife jabbed against his thigh as he ran, faster now without the burden of the child. Then he heard the child coughing. Song slowed, turning around, nursing his right arm against his body. In the gloom he saw the child huddled on the ground, heaving and sobbing, shoulders hunched, head turning this way and that, and it seemed in that moment that their pain was inseparable.

He watched for another moment. Then he returned to the child and crouched down beside him.

'Come on, then, you little runt,' he hissed, which was all the sound he could manage. He hoisted the child onto his back and hurried towards the road. It was clear now that none of the men and women by the lake had dared to follow him into the woods. But the police would arrive soon, and they would have no such qualms.

Just yards away the night-time streets were still busy with cars but he could not risk a taxi, not if the police were out looking for a blood-covered arsonist with a child in tow. He could not go home or to the office. If the woman from the brothel talked to the police, they would know where to come looking for him.

Eagle Run Plaza loomed above him, its mirrored glass reflecting the opaque sky. He lowered the boy from his back and took a good look at him for the first time. His body was as light as a five-year-old's, but his skinny face looked older, perhaps seven, even nine years old. The child's eyes were dark with fear, his mouth working to take in oxygen.

Song breathed a curse. Where could he hide a boy with one arm?

He dug in his pocket for his mobile phone, punched in a number with cold, clumsy fingers. The voice that answered was sleepy, protesting. Song started to interrupt, but all that came was a hail of coughing.

'Song?' His friend Wolf's voice came down the line, worried now. 'Song, what's the matter?'

Song moved his tongue around his mouth again, tried to summon some saliva.

'Bring the van,' he wheezed. 'I'm on Tianze Road, on the edge of the wood. Bring blankets.'

'What's happened?'

'Just get your arse over here.'

Song hung up. He thought he might pass out from the pain in his arm. He could hear a siren in the distance, getting closer. He waited, squatting, leaning his back against a tree, curling his body around the boy's to keep him as warm as he could. He could feel his heart pounding against the boy's chest.

CHAPTER 2

When I awoke the plane was lurching over mountains. Gently I withdrew my arm from the armrest, where my obese neighbour's gut had come to rest like a gigantic jelly on top of it. I lifted the shade and peered out of the window and saw the first streaks of dawn fall on white peaks. My watch was still on British time. It was midnight in London, where I had extricated myself from the twins' farewell hugs the day before and closed the door behind me, wiping my eyes. Leaving them felt like tearing off a strip of my own flesh, but I knew they would come to no harm. At that moment they would be tucked up in bed, their poses even in sleep an uncanny echo of each other's, both either curled in fetal position, or on their backs, limbs flung wide. I closed my eyes and thought of them, wishing I was there with them. I did not know what awaited me in China, and I felt the pull of home strongly across all the miles I had already travelled.

Finney would be alone in our double bed, snoring. Even on a Saturday the twins would wake him at six. Next week he would have to get them ready for school. We'd run through the morning routine as though it was a military manoeuvre, but there had been no time for a practice run, and I was worried by the fact that Finney seemed to think there was nothing to it. Finney's not the twins' father – their father's dead – and it doesn't come naturally to him to be the alpha and the omega of parenting, even for a few days.

I adjusted my watch. It was eight a.m. in Beijing, where we would land in a couple of hours. I'd endured seven hours already, suspended thirty thousand feet in the air, cramped in row thirty-nine next to the man with a vast belly, who was clad in a red and yellow kaftan. Now he stirred and leaned over me to peer out of the window, and I had to press myself back into my seat to avoid getting squashed. I smelled sweat, but then nobody is very fragrant at the end of a long flight.

'Pretty bumpy out there, huh?'

I made a non-committal sound. Around the time his head had flopped onto my shoulder, he and I had got about as familiar as I wanted to get.

'First time in Beijing?'

'Uh-huh.'

'Business or pleasure?'

'Business,' I replied.

Perhaps the truth would shut him up: a man's been beheaded, I have to investigate. But I didn't say it. The bloody brutality of Derek Sumner's murder had soaked the headlines of the British papers for the past twenty-four hours, and any mention of the murder was as likely to stimulate conversation as to kill it. Instead I resigned myself to a friendly chat, and I heard all about my companion's business plans, and his family, and the state of his marriage, and his cats. It's the journalist's curse and her blessing, too. There must be something about my face which says, 'Please tell me your life story.'

Only when the captain switched on the seat-belt signs to signal twenty minutes before landing did my companion fall silent.

At last I turned my attention to the files. I could have recited their contents verbatim, but this is what I always do when I am reporting on a story, and what Finney tells me he does too, when he is investigating a crime. I read and read again, in case something which escaped me the first time – some fact or comment or circumstance – strikes me with new significance.

Derek Sumner had grabbed headlines even before his throat was cut by an unknown assailant. He was the Beijing representative of Kelness, an independent integrated blast furnace and steel mill, which exported high-quality steel to China for use in its booming automotive industry. China was a car manufacturer's dream, a nation of 1.3 billion feet itching to press down on an accelerator, a nation racing from zero private car ownership to gridlock on the roads. Each one of those cars, its chassis, axles, hubs and gears, contained a good-sized chunk of high-grade steel that China had to import. But even with customers like those in the Far East, who were hungry for feather-light steel sheeting, for finely forged joints and seamless piping, back in the north of England the Kelness mill was going bankrupt, struggling under the weight of a £10 million bank loan for new machinery. Which was why, when a Chinese entrepreneur called Nelson Li quietly suggested to Kelness that he would like to buy the steel mill if it came at the right price, he found a cautious welcome.

Derek Sumner, therefore, found himself recalled to Kelness and given a new commission: to steer a course through secret negotiations with Nelson Li.

When news of the negotiations leaked in Britain, as was bound to happen, the Kelness workforce erupted in outrage, accusing their bosses of gross naivety. The financial press did nothing to allay their fears. Correspondents described Nelson Li as a 'ruthless dealmaker' who had built his $1.4 billion fortune on the back of property speculation and the entertainment industry, including a string of nightclubs. He was, the papers noted, 'a complete newcomer' to the steel industry. Profiles painted him as a colourful figure who shopped for big-ticket items like luxury cars, yachts and a private jet. He was a nationalist who spoke proudly about the growing power of China in world trade, but who had a fascination for things foreign, and

21

particularly European. He had adopted his own English name as a tribute to the British naval hero. His daughter he had called Pearl, a direct translation of her Chinese name. His son he had named Nixon. This, said Nelson Li, was in honour of Richard Nixon, who had broken through the ice of the Cold War to visit Beijing in 1972, recognizing that China was such an important power in the world that America must engage with her.

Nelson Li was a big spender, but he was not a fool. Pointedly, the press asked why Nelson Li would dig deep into his pockets to pay a wage bill for British workers that would be tens of times what he would have to pay in China. Flamboyant or not, Nelson Li remained tight-lipped on his plans, except to issue a brief statement praising Kelness workers for their skill and expressing the hope that 'we will be able to learn from you' – words that business analysts interpreted as a portent of doom.

One might have assumed that Derek Sumner was chosen for the delicate job of chief negotiator because of his superior diplomatic skills. However, just days after returning to Beijing to pursue the negotiations he had attended a private banquet hosted by Nelson Li where he allegedly uttered two sentences which were shortly to be immortalized:

'You've got no real trade unions, so you've got it made. You should dismantle Kelness, fire all the staff, ship it out here, and get some peasants to stick it back together out in the countryside.'

Sumner surely did not know that night that there was a local journalist sitting across from him. There were, after all, more than a dozen Chinese at the big round table. Sumner and his colleague, Karen Turvey, were the only non-Chinese present, and since everyone was there at the invitation of Nelson Li, he assumed he was among friends.

The next day, however, Sumner must have begun to realize he'd put his foot in it. Not at first, perhaps, when the quote surfaced in the Chinese press as evidence of yet another Western businessman excited by China's business environment. But by the time the remarks, now restored to their original English, had made it to the international news agencies, they began to take on a different flavour. By the time they reached Kelness, five thousand miles away, Sumner's alleged comments were toxic.

'Brit Turns Native, Mauls British Workforce' trumpeted one British tabloid. Inside the paper there were references to Sumner's eyes 'narrowing to slits when he talked about firing the men who sweat in the furnaces of hell to pay Sumner's wages'.

'Kelness: A Chinese Takeaway More Sour Than Sweet' one financial newspaper posited, reminding readers that in 2001 another Chinese entrepreneur had bought a steel mill in Dortmund in Germany. A thousand Chinese had arrived and, in less than a year, working twelve hours a day, seven days a week, had dismantled the whole lot, packed it up and shipped it off to a site at the mouth of the Yangtze River, where it had been rebuilt.

At this point, protests turned into riots. When Richard Toms, the CEO of Kelness, tried to say that Sumner had been misquoted, bottles of imported Chinese beer – already empty – were thrown at his house.

Others expressed themselves more eloquently. 'They ship the plant over there, they should ship us with it,' one steelworker said. 'I'll go with the wife and the kids. There'll be nothing for us here.'

I visited Kelness twice in all, making documentary pieces on the debacle for the television series *Controversies*. The first time was just days after Derek Sumner allegedly made the comments in Beijing. I interviewed one of his colleagues, a man called Angus Perry, who toed the management line, saying Sumner had been misquoted. I'd been told by the press office at Kelness that Perry worked with Sumner in Beijing, which made it sound as though he should know exactly what Sumner had or hadn't said. But when I asked Perry on camera whether he'd actually been at the banquet, he'd had to admit that he hadn't. Perry must have known how bad it would look on television, and I think he took my question as a personal humiliation. I felt bad for him because Kelness had put him in an impossible position, presenting him as a witness to what Sumner had said when in fact he had not been there.

Then, two weeks later, when the unrest showed no signs of abating, I'd returned to Kelness to film a follow-up. When I tried to find Angus Perry to ask him some more questions, I was told that he had already returned to Beijing to work alongside Sumner on the negotiations with Nelson Li. That was when the news of Derek Sumner's death broke. That day I was eager to get my last interviews done and head back to London. To be honest, I'd seen all I wanted to of Kelness. The place had an angry, depressed feel to it, as though years of financial difficulty had taken a toll on personal relationships too. My cameraman had filmed grim housing, run-down pubs and boarded-up shops to illustrate the economic devastation that Kelness had already suffered over the past decade as the steel mill had shrunk and laid off workers.

I was literally just about to step into the office of CEO Richard Toms when his ashen-faced secretary rushed past me and slammed the door in my face. Ten minutes later, four security guards appeared from nowhere and escorted us from the premises. It was clear something was up, and instead of heading back to London we hung around to find out what that something was.

Later, when Derek Sumner's death was made public, the news spread through Kelness like a sudden draught of frigid air, paralysing all who came in its path. It was the nature of his death, malicious and quick and sickening, that stopped us all in our tracks.

Derek Sumner's headless body had been found in a shallow grave in a patch of woodland just off a road known as Lady Street. This was all the information the Beijing police had seen fit to release.

In Kelness, I conducted a few miserable interviews. It was the kind of reporting that made me want to hand in my notice: catching people on film in the grip of emotions that television simply wasn't sophisticated enough to handle. There were men who'd been bad-mouthing Derek Sumner as a traitor who were now appalled at his fate. No one would have wished this on him, but you could tell from the shocked way they spoke that they felt almost responsible, as though their bitterness had travelled halfway round the world and taken shape on the blade of a stranger's knife. Those interviews, and the murder itself, weighed horribly on me. I remember driving back to London with a sense of dread.

My friend Jane is the editor of *Controversies*, but she had just had her second child, a boy, and was on maternity leave. I'd been urging her to get back to work as soon as possible. She was barely out of labour, but I didn't care for her stand-in, Damien Wondell, or the Boy Wonder as Jane and I knew him. He was nearly a decade younger than either of us, which was offensive in itself.

Unconstrained by children or spouse and, it seemed, spectacularly unencumbered by friends, Damien was powering his way up the Corporation management structure. He was always in the right place at the right time, licking ass, kicking ass, as appropriate, and all with an infuriating boyish earnestness. But he also seemed to me to be constantly on the verge of losing it, and that was what made me nervous.

'You have to follow the story to Beijing,' Damien said. We were walking down a corridor in the Corporation, and I had lengthened my stride to his, our shoes hitting the carpet together with military precision. Damien always issues orders on the run, as though he has somewhere to be, although we always seem to end up in the same place we started.

'Derek Sumner was in the wrong place at the wrong time,' I argued. 'It was the work of a madman, nobody believes it has anything to do with the Kelness deal.'

Damien shook his head.

'I disagree. He was murdered in Beijing, so the story's there, not here. We look lazy if we do it from here.'

I knew Damien was right, but he always puts me so much on the defensive that I find it difficult to agree with him.

'Okay,' I conceded after a moment, 'we need a Beijing angle.'

To state the obvious, *Controversies* prides itself

on being controversial, which is why it uses its own dedicated correspondents. There was no way the Corporation could have the same journalists stirring up trouble on *Controversies* and then re-arranging their faces into a mask of objectivity on the ten o'clock news. The other *Controversies* trademark is that the same correspondent follows one story from week to week so that whoever the correspondent is, he or she knows the story inside out. Kelness had been my story from the moment it broke, which meant that if we needed a Beijing angle I would have to be the one to supply it, not some other *Controversies* journalist, and not the Corporation's bureau in Beijing.

'You need a tourist visa. The Chinese will refuse you a journalist visa if they're embarrassed by the death of a foreigner, which they are, of course. Anyway we can't afford to hang around while they're making up their minds. So if you go to Beijing say – where are we, Wednesday? Okay, you get your tourist visa tomorrow, you fly on Friday. Take a MiniDV camera with you – if you start sticking a full-size camera in people's faces, you'll be kicked out quicker than you can say politburo. Wrap up the piece there by Friday next week, and we'll schedule it to air on the Saturday.'

I took a deep breath. Damien has a chip on his shoulder about working mothers, and the fact that he was filling in for a maternity leave seemed to have turned him into a walking glob of testosterone.

'The twins . . .' already I could see his face darkening and his eyes seemed to develop an ominous gleam, 'they have their school concert on Monday afternoon . . .'

He stopped walking, his hand on a door with a stick figure painted on it, and I realized we had come to a halt outside the men's toilets. I wondered whether this was where we had been heading all along, a symbolic ending for my career.

'What are they going to do, sing "All Things Bright and Beautiful"?'

'Come on, Da—'

'No come on, Robin. Can't their dad go to the concert?' Damien didn't know me very well, or he'd have known that their father, Adam, had been murdered when the twins were just months old. Finney, who had been living with us for the past year, was doing his level best, but to call him 'Dad' was stretching it.

'It's not that simple,' I said, trying to hold my ground. But we all knew that Damien's stint on *Controversies* was just a staging post to senior management, where he would hold our careers in his twitchy hands.

'Robin, this is your story.' He gave the door a tap for emphasis, and pasted concern onto his face. 'I can give the story to someone else if you really want me to, but if you back out it's not going to make you feel good about yourself, and it's not going to make me feel good about your level of commitment. I know you and Jane go back

29

a long way but, you know,' he grimaced, 'Jane's going to have to make a few hard decisions about her priorities too.'

I opened my mouth to protest, but he held up a hand to stop me. A man I knew slightly – Jim something – walked between us and into the men's room. When he had gone inside, Damien spoke quietly.

'You know what they say: if you can't stand the heat, get out of the kitchen.' He pushed open the door and turned to go inside, then looked back with a smug smile on his face. 'Or in this case, of course, if you can't stand the heat get back in the kitchen.'

I stared at the door as it banged shut behind him. Then I shoved it open to follow him. My heart was pounding against my ribs with fury.

'Hey!' The Jim-something guy was standing at a urinal, his head twisted towards me. 'You're not supposed to be in here.'

I ignored him, saw feet below a cubicle door.

'Damien, are you in there?' My angry voice bounced off the tiled walls and came back at me.

'Robin, what the hell are you doing in here?' The feet did a startled jump.

Jim muttered furiously to himself, zipped up his flies and headed for the door. Failing to wash his hands, I noticed.

'You cannot say things like that,' I said loudly. 'Don't you understand that?'

'Are you threatening me?'

I wondered how long I could be angry with a pair of feet beneath a toilet door.

'No, Damien, I'm not threatening you. I'm just giving you some advice.'

There was a moment's silence. I realized just how ridiculous the situation was. Then I turned and walked out, letting the door close behind me.

I went to look for Sal Ghosh, and was relieved to find him in the office we'd shared before I started working for *Controversies*. You can't ever be sure Sal is in the country, let alone the office. Sometimes he goes for months without a war zone, and he'll slump around the Corporation claiming to be glad he's not under fire in some godforsaken corner of the globe. Then, out of the blue, he'll get the call and he'll curse and he'll flap but his face will come alive, and he'll flourish his passport and be gone. I could see him through the glass door, the only living thing in the middle of the great chaos that is his office, the precarious piles of magazines, the overflowing shelves of tape and film, the tangle of wires for a playground of technological gizmos. He was swinging disconsolately on his office chair, punching at his computer keyboard, black eyebrows lowered over black eyes, frowning, sensuous lips puckered against olive skin. I pushed the door open. He glanced up, his face broke into a grin, and he lumbered to his feet, arms outstretched.

'Goldilocks – ah, your hair has grown, at last,

31

you look almost feminine, you appear like a . . . like a goddess in the festering pit of tedium we call our place of work.'

Goldilocks was the name he'd given me on the day two years before when, after a stint in the Middle East, he'd walked back into his office to find I'd taken it over. I was sitting in his chair, at his desk, and if he'd had a bowl of porridge I'd have been eating it.

I allowed him to hug me, then pulled away. You don't want to get caught for too long in Sal's arms.

'Why don't you tidy the place up a bit?' I suggested. 'Then it won't fester.'

He ignored me.

'You're here to pick my substantial brain on Beijing, I presume, to dip into my well of knowledge?' He sat back down and waved me towards what used to be my own office chair. 'When do you leave?'

'How do you know I'm going?'

'Of course you're going.'

I pulled a face, but I couldn't expect Sal to understand. He had no children of his own, and he rarely asked after mine.

'Get what's-his-name to look after the kiddies. What is his name? Pinny? Plod . . .'

'Sal, don't do that.' I sounded sharp, unamused, but it had been a bad day and I had no patience with his petty jealousy of Finney.

'You're such a spoilsport,' he said. 'My point is simply that if you want a career, and you do, then

32

you have no choice. Here . . . here is the extent of my wisdom . . .' He scrabbled around on his desk and then he handed me a card. There was a name, Blue Tang, the word 'interpreter', and a mobile phone number.

'What kind of a name is Blue?'

'She's a dynamo,' he said. 'She looks about sixteen, five foot tall if she's an inch, but she has the smartest head on any pair of shoulders in the East. Get her into trouble and I shall hang, draw and quarter you.'

'Why would I get her into trouble?'

'I'm assuming, given the nature of the story,' he said slowly, 'that you're not sitting around twiddling your thumbs for three weeks while the Chinese government decides whether or not to give you a journalist visa.'

'No.' I was impatient with his air of superiority. 'I'm getting a tourist visa, it takes a day.'

'So,' he dragged it out again, 'every piece of reporting that you do inside China is illegal. You do know that?'

'Of course I know that. I'll keep my head down, I'm not a fool. The worst they can do is throw me out.'

Sal tipped his head to one side and gave me a long look.

'You might get a tad roughed up. We had a camera team who were strip-searched . . .'

'Oh, shit . . .'

'But my point is that you must make sure Blue

keeps her head down too. Anyone you employ as an interpreter is aiding and abetting you in an illegal activity. At the end of the day, you'll survive because you have a foreign passport and white skin. Blue Tang has a Chinese passport; if her delightful government wants to throw her in jail for a decade, they can. It's their country.'

His phone rang.

'You should get that,' I told him, standing. 'I need to go.' What I actually needed was time to sit and read and think. My head was so full of the complications of leaving the twins that I'd given almost no thought to what awaited me in Beijing.

He reached for the phone, raised a hand in farewell and blew me a kiss.

At home, to keep the children at the table while they ate their supper, I got out the atlas.

'This is Asia, it's a continent thousands of miles from Europe,' I told William, who peered politely at the map, a piece of pizza sticking out of his mouth, jaw chewing. He had been playing outside in the cold wind, and his cheeks were bright pink. 'And this is China.'

He nodded, and repeated the word 'China' obligingly, spitting pizza all over the atlas.

'And here is Beijing,' I said, wiping specks of tomato from the capital city.

'Why?' asked Hannah. She stopped eating and raised her left eyebrow sternly. You could hardly see the eyebrow beneath her curls, it rose so high, but I knew the expression well, and it always made me nervous.

'What do you mean, why?'

'Why are you telling us this?'

'No reason. I'm just showing y—' I faltered, deciding on total disclosure. 'I may have to go there for a few days, for work.'

Hannah and William exchanged a look.

'Who will look after us?'

'Who will look after us?' William echoed. He spoke with pathos unlike his sister who had been accusatory. His eyes were huge under soft brown hair that fell in a fringe. 'Who will look after us?' he groaned again. Once Hannah had established a linguistic theme it was always William's job to embroider it with expression, and to repeat it again and again until it reached its full dramatic potential.

'Carol,' I said firmly, 'Carol and Finney will look after you. Carol will put you to bed and Finney will get you up in the morning and take you to school.'

They stared at me. William's chin began to wobble. Hannah frowned.

'That's a bad idea, Mummy,' she said.

'It will be just fine,' I replied. I couldn't take it any more. I stood up and reached for their empty plates. 'Who wants ice cream?'

Finney came home at eight, when the twins were in bed. He looked wiped out. He smiled at me, but it was a weary echo of the smile that had stunned me when we first met. He touched his lips to mine, but distractedly, then pulled open the refrigerator door, reached inside for a beer, and sat at the kitchen table, his head in his hands. Finney was abandoned by his mother at birth and he doesn't depend on anyone, including me, for comfort when he's down. I try not to depend on him, either, because my life before I met Finney taught me you can't rely on men, although I'm now having to rethink this in a radical way. Brought up in a children's home, he feels comfortable in institutions, which is probably why he joined the police, and his loyalty to that flawed organization is something I have struggled to understand. But then, he's as cynical about the media as I am about the police force.

'How was your day?' I asked.

'Not exactly edifying,' he answered drily. For the past six months he'd been working on the Met's computer crime squad. It was wearing him down. Days sitting in front of a monitor sapped his energy, and then there was the garbage he had to look at. Some of it was almost laughable in its grimness, but he'd given up laughing after the first week. He had told me he felt overwhelmed by the sheer size of cyberspace, by the fact that vice and fraud and nastiness could crawl into an infinity of dark pockets, every one of them outside national boundaries.

'What about you?' he asked.

I pulled up a chair and sat opposite him.

'I think I have to go to Beijing the day after tomorrow,' I said, screwing my face into an expression that I hoped conveyed deep apology.

He gazed at me, pushed his hand through his unruly greying hair, and sipped his beer. I thought perhaps it hadn't sunk in.

'Beijing,' he said blankly.

'Derek Sumner's been murdered there,' I said.

'Oh, Christ.' He ran his hand over his face.

'I'm sorry,' I said. 'It's only for a week. I tried to tell Damien I couldn't go, but he wouldn't listen.'

He closed his eyes and shook his head.

'Carol will pick up the twins after school.' I wanted him to know I had it all worked out. 'She can feed them, I can ask her to stay later so she can put them to bed and wait till you get back. It's just the mornings . . . But look, if I can't go, I'll just say so to Damien; what's he going to do?'

He raised his eyes to mine.

'Do you want to go?'

'I don't want to leave . . .'

'Forget the kids for a moment . . . it's a week, how much damage can I do?'

I nodded, not liking to reply.

'I want to go because it's my job to go,' I said slowly.

'Obviously.' He looked exasperated. 'But?'

'But . . . for someone to kill like that . . . it makes my blood run cold . . .' I frowned, not liking

37

to concede this. 'I don't mean I'm scared of the man with the knife . . .'

'God forbid.'

'I'm reluctant, that's all. I'm not sure I want to get swept up again in the kind of hate that's involved here. I'm reluctant to – I don't know – to . . .'

'To look evil in its face,' Finney supplied. Evil is not a word I like to use, but Finney uses it when he encounters sheer malice.

'I didn't even know the man,' I tried to reassure myself. 'It's not as though I'll get involved.'

Finney gave me a look that was unreadable. He went to the fridge, took out a box of eggs, broke four of them into a bowl, then whisked in a splash of milk. I watched as he turned on the gas and poured the eggs into the frying pan. Finney was the chief investigating officer when my former lover, Adam, was murdered, and I was Finney's prime suspect. My desperation had driven me to investigate Adam's death aggressively, to the point where I had almost (and would have, were it not for Finney) died. In the years since, I had shored up my life, my family was secure, and Finney had joined us. All of these things had brought me deep happiness. But Finney knew that Adam's murder was still a raw nerve for me. I still had nightmares about that period, when my whole life had seemed to shatter in front of my eyes. A year or so after Adam's death, when a colleague of mine disappeared, I had become involved again, losing all sense of personal danger in the investigation that had become an obsession. Finney was the one who'd ended up in hospital. I'd scared Finney and I'd scared myself.

'You'll be fine,' Finney said as he tipped the omelette onto a plate, 'and we'll be fine here while you're gone. Everything will be just fine.'

We ate the omelette watching the news on television, cursing companionably at politicians, and afterwards I sent Finney to bed while I cleared up. By the time I followed, just minutes later, he was fast asleep. Lying there, with the stresses of the day gone, his face looked ten years younger. What would have happened if we had met ten years before when things were simpler, before he had met his wife and been divorced, before I had Adam's children? I would have liked to share my children with him, but I didn't think that was ever going to happen. I crawled in next to him, kissed him goodnight, and soon I slept.

First thing in the morning I called my mother and my sisters, Lorna and Tanya, and Tanya's husband, Pat, and I enlisted them all to go to the twins' concert on the Monday afternoon, in case work called Finney away. And actually to supplement him even if he made it to the concert, on the principle that one common-law stepfather, a grandmother, two aunts and an uncle ought to

39

just about compensate for one absent mother. Then I fought my way through the Christmas shoppers and went and stood in line at the Chinese embassy for a visa.

CHAPTER 3

Wolf turned the key in the lock, pushed open the door and Song stepped inside, the boy in his arms. The walls were bare brick and the glass in the high window was broken. The room belonged to one of Wolf's friends who had left town and given the keys to Wolf in case he came across anyone who wanted to rent it. Wolf's friend had used the room as a car repair workshop and it still smelled of oil. It was empty except for a cold stove, a bare light bulb and a grimy bed mat rolled in the corner. There was no running water and it was bleak and dirty, but it was a refuge of sorts.

As soon as they were inside, the boy stopped clinging to Song and instead seemed bent on escape. He squealed and grunted like a frightened animal and hurled himself at the door, even though his lungs were so choked from the fire that he had to keep stopping to cough and spit. Wolf, his silver-dyed hair flopping, blocked him effortlessly each time, lifting him up as though he was a puppy.

Song retreated into a corner of the room. He

watched the boy. It was the first time he had seen him in the light but still he could not put an age to him with any accuracy – between six and nine, he thought. The boy had the dark skin of a peasant, with rough red patches high on his cheeks from extremes of sun and cold. The peculiarly adult set of his features spoke of undernourishment. Song looked away from the boy and extracted the knife from his pocket. The knife had cut a gash in the jacket and in his trousers, and his leg was raw and bloody.

'Give me a hand,' Wolf said, and Song turned to see that his friend had unrolled the bed mat on the floor and that the boy had collapsed onto it, wheezing. Carefully, weighing it in his hands, Song placed the knife on the concrete floor. It was streaked now with Song's blood as well. He looked down at it. It was a knife built for precision, perhaps thirty centimetres long, including the handle which fitted smoothly in his palm. The blade was an elegant curve, about six centimetres wide at its fattest point. Song peered more closely at it. There was lettering etched on the blade, not Chinese characters, something foreign, and a logo. There was a chip in the blade, about three centimetres along from the point. The point of the knife had been blunted, too, and he thought that it might have been dropped point down. But when Song ran his fingertip along the blade a bead of blood oozed immediately. Someone had sharpened the knife, grinding it down until it cut effortlessly through flesh.

'Hey,' Wolf said again

Together they stripped the boy's foul clothes off and wiped him down as well as they could, using hot water from the thermos that Wolf had brought with him in the van, and they pulled an outsized sweatshirt and jeans over his skinny limbs, because Wolf hadn't understood that he must bring clothes for a child. Eventually the boy fell asleep, huddled on the mat on the floor, his breath rasping, racked with spasms and coughing fits.

'You should have let the vicious little bugger go,' Wolf said, nursing a bruised ankle. Song didn't reply. He remembered how he'd dumped the child in the woods, and how the child had flailed around in panic. Now he regretted going back for him.

Wolf looked at his friend, and for the first time he saw the blood-soaked trousers, the burned sleeve, the raw pain in his friend's face. Song was shivering.

'I'll get some coal for the stove,' Wolf said, and he went out into the street. He would steal some, of course, from the pile outside a neighbour's door. Song thought Wolf made a strange lawyer. He seemed to have no sense of private property.

Song reached for the thermos. He tore a strip of cloth from one of the blankets Wolf had brought. He cleaned his leg and was pleased to see that although the knife had skinned a large area of his thigh, there was no deep incision. He was lucky, he thought. Song took off his jacket, and – biting

43

his lip lest he shout out – he peeled the burned sleeve away from his scorched arm.

Wolf returned with a stack of coal briquettes. He glanced at Song, who was sitting cross-legged, head lowered, in the corner, his red burned arm resting on his knee. For a moment Wolf just stared, shocked by the injury. Then he squatted by the coal stove, lit it, and fed the coal inside. Soon there were flames, and then, slowly, there was heat.

'You know if they arrest you for stealing coal, you'll be easy to identify in a line-up,' Song said, his head still bowed. The pain had diminished enough now that Song could speak, and he wanted to show Wolf that he could. 'It's not wise to turn to a life of crime when you've got your nickname tattooed on your forehead.' Wolf grinned, and his fingers went to the black character, *lang*, for wolf, that he'd had etched onto his forehead ten years ago in a burst of youthful rebellion. The tattoo was just four centimetres square, but back then he'd worn his hair short and the mark stood out bare and bold on his face, the only tattoo on the university campus. The tattoo got him suspended. He'd had to beg and bribe his way back in so that he could take his final exams, and it had effectively ended his chances of working for a prestigious firm after graduation. No one wanted a lawyer who had labelled himself a wild animal. His mother wept when she realized that he'd brought ruin on himself. 'You say it's only a small tattoo, but your brain is as small as a pea,' she scolded him.

44

After a few minutes, Song struggled to his feet and went over to the fetid heap of discarded clothing. Using only his left hand, his jaw tensed against the pain and the effort, he grabbed the boy's jacket and wrapped the knife in it. It was too late to start thinking about evidence bags. The knife was contaminated anyway now, with Song's blood mingled with that of the victim, Song's fingerprints with the boy's and with the murderer's. To hand that kind of DNA and fingerprint cocktail to the police would be to invite confusion. The rest of the clothing he fed into the fire. The boy's stuff went in first, then his sheepskin, charred and bloody.

'The boy should go to a hospital,' Wolf said, watching him, 'and so should you, your arm will get infected.'

Song shook his head, face pale. The cold in the room was numbing the pain slightly, but not enough. Soon the skin would peel away and his flesh would be raw. He felt drained at the prospect of so much pain.

'It looks worse than it is. Doctors ask too many questions, I might as well hand myself in.'

'You haven't done anything.'

'Tell that to the witnesses who saw me brandishing a knife covered in blood,' Song said sharply. 'The girl from the brothel knows me. My car is parked right there.'

The car, a modest Volkswagen Gol, was ideal for stake-outs. An unfaithful husband, his head full of lust, had never been known to give a Gol a second glance, whereas a BMW or a Buick might have distracted him.

'Explain what happened, it's quite reasonable.' Wolf spoke over his shoulder while he unbuttoned his shirt. When he had stripped to his thick long-sleeved undershirt, he soaked his outer shirt in water from the thermos, letting the excess splash onto the floor, where it steamed into the cold dry air.

'You mean throw myself on Detective Chen's mercy?' Song gave a harsh bark of laughter.

Wolf said nothing. He held the wet shirt to cool for a moment, and then he went to his friend and wrapped it carefully around Song's burned arm, gratified to hear his friend's sigh of relief. Wolf had heard – although not from Song – about the day Song had beaten up Detective Chen's henchman, Psycho Wang, how he had cursed Detective Chen to his face and walked out on his position in the serious crime squad. How, a year later, Song had topped that offence with another, by walking out on his wife, who was also Detective Chen's daughter. After all this, instead of staying well out of Detective Chen's way, which would have been the prudent course of action, Song had set up shop advertising himself as an investigator, as though he was directly challenging his former father-in-law. It was perhaps hardly surprising Song would not throw himself on this man's mercy.

'There was no body in the tent, just blood, do

46

I understand correctly?' Wolf sounded more legal-istic now.

'That's what I told y—' Song, impatient, was cut off by Wolf.

'So then, without evidence of a crime, what can they accuse you of?' Wolf looked triumphant.

Song stared at him.

'There's a body somewhere . . .' He tried to think through what had happened, but the pain from his arm was hard to ignore. 'The killer must have removed it . . . There was a man with a cart by the lake . . .' His voice trailed off. He had assumed the cart was laden with restaurant slops or scrap metal, but maybe it had laboured under-neath some other cargo.

'My point exactly,' Wolf said. 'The killer must have removed the body. Why, then, would you kill someone, remove their body, and subsequently return to the scene of the crime to wave a murder weapon around in front of witnesses?'

For the first time, Song felt the stirring of hope. Wolf was right. Why would a killer, having removed the body which incriminated him, return to the scene of the crime? He worried over it, knowing that Wolf had a habit of persuading him that everything was all right when it patently was not, and then the answer came to him in horrid clarity.

'Because of the knife! They'll say I went back because I'd forgotten the knife! Or because I was going back to kill the boy, the witness.'

There was silence for a moment. Wolf frowned.

'The girl from the brothel,' he spoke slowly, 'she knows you were outside when the scream came . . . and after the scream there wouldn't have been time for you to leave the car and get to the tent and kill a woman and dispose of her body and get back there . . .' Wolf stopped speaking. Song was shaking his head.

'None of them heard the scream but me,' he said. 'I was the only one outside.'

For a moment they stared at each other. Song bent and, wincing, used his good left hand to pick up the woman's bag from the floor. He crouched and propped it on his knee, so that he could look through it one-handedly.

Wolf hunkered down next to him and looked queasily at the bag as Song turned it over, examining it. It was white plastic, splashed with dried blood, with a zip that must have broken long ago, because the owner had rigged up a piece of string to keep it closed.

'She couldn't afford a new bag,' Wolf said.

Song reached inside and, grimacing, drew out a brown plastic comb with tiny flecks of scalp still sticking in between the teeth, and a long black hair clinging to it.

'Plenty of DNA there,' Song said, 'if anyone reports her missing.'

'Better for you if they don't. If no body shows up perhaps they'll decide that nothing happened in there.'

Song dug in again and brought out a lipstick that had lost its lid and was almost entirely used up.

'I wonder whether she used it.'

'She must have been a prostitute,' Wolf said.

Song looked up at him sharply, annoyed at the way his friend jumped to conclusions.

'Just because she was out at night and had half an old lipstick in her bag? Perhaps she fished it out of someone's trash can and liked to carry it around.'

Again Song's hand vanished inside the bag, and this time he pulled out a plastic bag containing small denomination cash folded carefully. Song counted it out.

'Nine *yuan.*'

'Just pennies.'

'He didn't kill her for her money.'

Song examined the bag the money had been in, but it was wafer-thin plastic, unmarked, and it crumpled into nothing in his large hand, the sort of bag handed out in their thousands and millions by convenience stores.

'She's a migrant worker,' Wolf opined. 'No native Beijinger is that poor. Like the other women who were killed. They were prostitutes.'

Song was irritated. 'It's all rumour – plagues, earthquakes, serial killers – there are no such things as facts in this city. We whisper and we whip ourselves into a convulsion of excitement.'

★　　★　　★

49

The child stirred. His eyes opened, fixing on the blood-spattered white bag and widening in alarm, his head jerking back as he scrambled to a sitting position.

Song hauled himself to his feet, still nursing his arm. He hobbled over to where the boy sat – his leg was beginning to throb now, where the knife had skinned it – then he crouched down next to the boy.

'What's your name?'

The boy coughed and twisted his head to spit on the floor. His eyes seemed to grow bigger, and the rest of his body to grow smaller inside his vast clothes, like a scarecrow, one sleeve hanging limply at his side. His head swung restlessly, setting his shoulders in constant motion, his eyes never settling.

'We want to help you,' Wolf said, and the boy's eyes darted towards him, then beyond him.

'There was a woman,' Song said. 'What happened to her?'

The boy opened his mouth but no sound came out. He looked idiotic with his mouth hanging open, head jerking to and fro.

'Who was she, who was the woman?' Song pressed him. He tried to smile. He remembered from dealing with his own son that looking angry made children clam up. He tried to reproduce the kind of grin he'd seen on the face of a teddy bear.

'Who else was in the tent?' Song tried to keep the smile on his face, but he could hear the frustration in his own voice and the boy cringed away from him, as though Song had dealt him a blow.

'Why were you in the tent last night? Who was there?' With every question Song's voice got louder.

The boy began to keen, and the high-pitched noise scythed through Song's head. The boy rocked backwards and forwards where he sat. His head bashed against the wall behind him, first by accident and then harder and harder, on purpose, and the howling turned to full-lunged shouts of pain. Song felt the pain as though it was his own head bashing against the bricks. Unable to bear it any longer he grabbed the boy and pulled him forwards, and shook him.

'Shut up!'

Suddenly still, the boy gazed up at him with eyes gone blank.

'You crazy child, I should have left you to burn!' Song spat the words out and stalked to the door. A few moments later, Wolf followed his friend. Outside the room was a small private yard where Song was smoking a cigarette, his face creased with anger that was turned on himself.

'I'm a fool. The whole neighbourhood must have heard me.' He kept his voice low. This street, the main thoroughfare through Anjialou, was as noisy as a funfair in the day, with dogs barking and neighbours yelling and washing their hair in the street, and hanging their laundry and meat out to dry, and gridlocked cars honking their horns. The eastern end of the street was devoted to taxi repairs, and this was where they had taken shelter. Song's office was several streets away, surrounded by vegetable sellers and pancake stalls. Anjialou was originally an old village street lined with farmhouses, but the city had grown up around it and now it boasted sex shops, cheap restaurants and convenience stores. The peasants had taken advantage of their prime location to rent out their crumbling brick cottages to migrant labourers who slept whole families to a room with toilets halfway down the street. Now, at night, the street was quiet, but the neighbours might be awake and listening. People here lived crammed in like cooked rice, the individual grains all swollen, stuck together in a pot. There was no privacy.

'How old do you think he is?' Song asked. 'Six, seven?'

Wolf took the pack of cigarettes from Song and helped himself, the lighter flaring in the dark. 'You're the one with a son. I have no experience of kids. All I know is he's stinking the place out.'

'We can't keep him here,' Song muttered, then doubled over, shaken by a fit of coughing.

'We should let him go,' Wolf replied quietly, when Song had recovered. 'He's a street kid, he'll find his way back. He must have lodgings close by.'

'What happens to him then?'

'The beggar gang will take him back. One-armed boys can't be that easy to come by, he must be quite a money-spinner.'

Song dropped his cigarette on the snow-covered ground and extinguished it with his boot. His lungs, still clogged from the fire, were protesting at the smoke. 'What if he knows the man who killed her and the boy saw what he did? He's a witness. The killer will come looking for him.'

'So hand the boy over to Detective Chen,' Wolf suggested again. 'If he saw anything he can tell the police what happened to the woman and he can exonerate you.'

'You want to hand anyone to Detective Chen, *you* hand him in, you say it was *you* who was there,' Song muttered. He remembered how Detective Chen got information from suspects, and sometimes from witnesses too. What if the boy, like Song, had happened on the crime scene by accident? What if he just wanted a warm place to sleep? What if he didn't know the woman, and had slept through the attack? What if he had not seen the attacker and could not exonerate Song? What if the boy simply babbled and bashed his head against the wall?

'Say, just say, you or I hand him in to Detective Chen,' Song said softly, 'what happens then, after they've got what they want from him? They chuck him back on the street, or send him back to whatever shit-hole he came from?'

'We can't worry about that.' Wolf peered through the doorway into the room. The boy sat on the mat, rocking backwards and forwards, his mouth working silently, his eyes still staring. 'You're the

53

one who's always telling me the agency isn't a charity. We can't afford to pick up every kid we see on the scrap heap.'

'You're right, of course, I wasn't thinking, we can hardly support ourselves, much less him. He's a liability.' Song fell silent for several minutes. When he spoke again his voice was hard and unnatural, as though he had braced himself to be cruel. 'Tomorrow we'll kick him out. He can look after himself. I've got enough on my plate without a stinking crippled kid to look after.'

CHAPTER 4

I recognized Blue Tang from Sal's description – she was the shortest person in the hotel lobby except for a blonde-haired girl running in circles around a vast Christmas tree. We had communicated by email and Blue had agreed to work with me for the week that I was planning to be in Beijing.

'When we meet I will carry a copy of the *China Daily*,' she had emailed, 'or you will not see me. I have no excellent features. I am not pretty or tall, and I do not wear rich clothes.'

Sure enough, there was the *China Daily*, folded, under her arm. I approached her, saying her name and extending my hand. She took it and looked me up and down. Her hand was as light and lifeless as a feather but there was energy behind her eyes. She wore her hair long and straight. It hung to her waist, emphasizing her short stature. The padded green jacket which reached nearly to her ankles didn't help – she looked as though, if she toppled over, she might roll round and around the lobby in perpetuity.

'I'm Robin,' I told her.

'I know that. I'm Blue.'

'I didn't expect the Christmas decorations.' I indicated the tree, which reached high into the domed ceiling of the lobby. It was fake and heavily decorated.

'You should not be surprised,' she told me with a serious expression on her face. 'Beijing is very Western now. Christmas and Valentine's Day are important festivals here.'

'And Easter?'

She gave me a quick glance.

'No.'

'Why not?'

'People don't give presents at Easter.'

'But they eat chocolate.'

She pulled a face.

'Chocolate is not so interesting. People can eat chocolate any time, but you need a reason to give a present.'

I nodded at the logic of it, but the nodding made me wince. Since getting off the plane I had showered and lain down for a nap. I'd set my alarm for my meeting with Blue, but I must have fallen into too deep a sleep, because when it went off it set my head pounding. The Christmas carols that were being pumped over speakers into the lobby were only making things worse, and the pounding had become a needle of pain that seemed to extend from my right eye back into my skull. Frankly – although I did not want to admit this to Blue – I felt entirely disorientated;

56

I had only a rough idea what time of day it was, and had to keep reminding myself I was in China.

'Let's take a walk,' I suggested. 'I want to see where Sumner's body was found.'

She looked me up and down with a critical eye. 'You should wear more clothes.'

'I'll be fine,' I told her, already irritated by her bossy tone. 'My boots are warm.'

'You should wear a hat.'

'I never wear a hat.'

For a moment we gazed at each other coolly, and I realized that I had morphed into Hannah, my four-year-old daughter, standing in the hallway with her chin stuck out, refusing resolutely to put her coat on. The thought of my daughter made me long for her.

We headed out through the glass doors that led to the street. She was dwarfed by the willowy hotel staff who stood at the entrance in fur jackets over silk cheongsams that were slit to the thigh, their silky hair gathered in chignons atop their doll-like heads, their feet perched on platform slippers like stilts.

'Do women still wear those clothes? They can't be comfortable.'

'Only for the tourists,' Blue said, and although her tone was even, her eyes conveyed a sneer.

Outside, the air hit my lungs. It was razor cold, with the texture of grit and the taste of sulphur.

'It's very dry in the winter,' Blue said, zipping up her down jacket so that only her eyes peeked out from beneath her hood, 'and it's cloudy.'

'This isn't cloud,' I protested. 'It's pollution.' All around us the air was a grey haze. It veiled the buildings and leached the colour out of the sky. It didn't move like mist, nor was it patchy like fog. There were no clouds, no differentiation in the colour of the sky.

I looked up and down the street, considering our options. The road was solid with cars. In one direction it joined an expressway. In the other it stretched straight until it vanished in a dusty cloud that seemed to be kicked up by the relentless procession of traffic. Neither direction was enticing.

'Follow me,' she said, and set off, confidently striding across six lanes of traffic, dodging cars. I hurried after her, worrying that Sal had finally drunk his memory away, and that he had recommended the wrong person. 'Oops,' I imagined him saying, sitting by my hospital bed, 'did I say Blue Tang? She had a death wish. I meant to say Fuchsia Tian.' A fat blue Buick came within inches of me, blaring its horn. When I stopped midstream to let it pass, a green Jeep nearly clipped my heels from behind. It was a foolhardy exercise – sheer luck got me to the other side alive.

My companion took a turn to the left, and I tried to strike up conversation.

'Why did you choose Blue as your English name?'

'Everyone asks me that. It is my favourite colour. I feel happy when I see the colour blue. Also, sometimes I feel blue, so I think it is a very honest name. Your name is Robin.'

'It is.' But more was clearly needed, so I added lamely, 'A robin is a small red-breasted bird that appears in the winter in England . . . I didn't choose the name. It was given to me by my parents.'

'You could change it if you choose to.'

'Legally I suppose I could. But I've grown up with it, I like it. I wouldn't want to change it now.'

'In China we change everything all the time. New things are always better, but then they get old too and we need to change all over again. It is very tiring.'

I glanced at her face, wondering whether this was a joke, but her expression remained dour.

We turned right. There were construction sites on both sides of the road, cranes stretching their long necks, loads balanced precariously. Everywhere was the dust that comes of knocking things down and building them up. She was right. Nothing looked old, nothing looked what I thought of as traditionally Chinese. The sea of bikes I'd half expected from old television footage was gone – perhaps the cars had run them all over.

'There is the Lotus Pool restaurant.' She pointed down a lane to our right, to a two-storey structure of slate and glass. 'In the newspaper article that you emailed to me it said that was where the British man ate his dinner before he was killed.'

'That's right.' I paused. 'Come on, let's take a look.'

The staff scurried to their posts as we walked in, greeting us and bowing. Blue scowled at them. I looked around me. The dining room was vast, subtly lit, and its centrepiece was a waterfall that fed into a pond, upon which floated golden lily pads. One wall had been turned into a grotto, with hundreds of golden statues of Buddha, each one placed in its own hollow.

'Upstairs there are private rooms,' she told me, nodding towards a staircase. 'That's where the British man ate.'

'I'd like to take a look,' I said.

A supervisor accompanied us through a maze of corridors, each lined with doors, one of which she opened for us. Inside, the carpet seemed to be about six inches deep. The dining table was polished to a high gloss and dark wood cabinets lined the room. The dining table was set with silver chopsticks and crystal wine glasses. By the window was a settee upholstered in red and gold brocade, presumably for taking a rest between courses.

'It's beautiful,' I said to Blue. 'Have you ever eaten here?'

'My family doesn't have so much money. We don't eat in restaurants like these.'

'Maybe one day you'll get rich enough to bring them here,' I suggested.

But you'd have thought I'd said something deeply offensive.

'I will never get rich,' she spat the words out. 'I am only one metre forty-eight centimetres tall and I am not beautiful, so no one will give me a job. I could only go to a second-class university because I am so short, and there are many jobs I cannot apply to like bank clerk and teacher and air hostess. If I have no job then I should marry a rich man, but that will not happen. I had a boyfriend. He was not so rich, he was poor like me, but still his parents made him break up with me because they told him my family has no money, and if I have a baby with him the child will be too short and he will have no future.'

I stared at her, appalled.

'And he broke up with you,' I asked, 'because of what they said?'

She nodded mutely. The supervisor who'd led us to the private dining room was watching us, bemused, and I thought Blue was about to burst into tears, so I nodded my thanks, retreated from the room and led the way back downstairs and out onto the street.

'If he broke up with you just because his parents told him to, then you're too good for him,' I told her as we emerged into the chilly air outside. For a moment I didn't think she had heard. Then she threw me a grateful glance, smiling at me for the first time. She started talking to me about her family. Like I said, it's the journalist's curse and a blessing.

Her parents were both factory workers in the

north-east, hard-working people who had scrimped and saved for her education. In the economic reforms of the past decade both of them had been laid off. Her mother was now working as a seamstress in a tailor's shop, and her father had become a taxi driver. She said he'd had to borrow from aunts and uncles to pay the rental on his taxi, and that the owner of the taxi company took most of her father's turnover. Blue was an only child. She didn't say as much, but it was clear from what she said that she was the only one in her family with huge ambition and a vision of a better life. It was clear to me, too, that whatever it was that set her apart, she'd had it since the day she was born.

I listened as attentively as I could to what she was telling me. But the scale of everything, the acres of roads, the inflated buildings, the wilderness of the construction sites with their earthen dunes, their gaping foundations – and all of it retreating into soft focus behind the smog – added to my sense of unease. I was reminded of a dream that I had had as a child, when it seemed that the world had expanded around me so that I was reduced almost to nothing.

'The street we are on is known as Lady Street,' Blue was explaining, 'because ladies like this street. There is a clothes market where ladies like to shop. Not only ladies, of course. Some men shop there, and some foreigners . . . If we go down here,' she turned into a narrow alley leading off to the right, 'then we get to the lake where the British man was killed.'

I stopped on the corner.

'Hang on a minute. Where's his office?'

She pointed straight ahead, past the clothes market.

'You see that tall building on the corner?' she asked. 'I think the Kelness office is on the fifteenth floor.'

I thought about it for a moment, my brain still foggy from the flight.

'So if he was killed where his body was found, in the woods,' I said slowly, 'that means he was making a diversion. He didn't need to go into the woods even if he was going back to the office.'

'And if he was going home, he would just get a taxi outside the restaurant,' Blue agreed.

'Perhaps he wasn't killed there,' I murmured to myself. So far neither the Chinese police, nor the British embassy, nor the family, had made public any autopsy findings. For all I knew, Sumner might have been killed elsewhere and his body dumped in the woods by the lake.

We turned off the main street, and immediately the feel of the place changed. The pavement disappeared and cars navigated slowly but carelessly through the mass of pedestrians, honking their horns. Smoke and the smell of roasting mutton rose from a streetside barbecue. A gob of mucus landed at my feet as a man blew his nose onto the ground.

A ragged woman approached me, her hair

hanging in rat's tails around her face. She held a pole, and on the end of it was a fishing net like the one the twins used on the beach. She waved it in front of me, effectively blocking my path. For an instant I just stood there in front of her, defeated, as she waved the net under my nose. There were grease stains on her grey jacket, which was bloated by layers of clothing underneath. She was saying something to me and stupidly I tried to understand, standing there with my head on one side. Blue's hand descended on my arm. She yanked me to one side, and we proceeded.

'There are beggars everywhere now,' Blue said. 'In the streets it is easy to sidestep them, but the clever ones are at the bus stops. You can't get away from them unless you want to miss your bus. Sometimes the Communist Party orders the police to clear them out of the city.'

'Who are they?'

'The newspapers say that they belong to gangs and they are tricking people and that really they are rich. But in the countryside we have too many poor people. They come to the city because people are richer here.'

We passed a shopfront, and I stared at the row of women sitting on a sofa on the other side of the glass as if they were lined up for sale. Only slowly did it dawn on my jet-lagged brain the significance of the shop's English name which, if I read it correctly, was 'Orgasin'.

An old man limped into my path, a hand

outstretched, but this time I was ready for him. I stepped aside, as Blue had advocated, but as I passed by I glanced at his face and saw that one side of it had been burned, the skin stretched tight over the bone, his lips all but gone.

'Blue,' she was a step ahead of me, and I reached out to touch her shoulder, 'can you help me ask this man what happened to his face?'

She glanced at him, then looked away.

'He's burned,' she said.

'Yes, I can see that. I want to know how it happened.'

She spoke to the man. As I stood there, with the crowds passing us by, watching Blue engaged in conversation in this language that I could not even begin to understand, I began to realize the complexity of our alliance. I was her boss by virtue of the fact that I was paying her $100 a day, yet she was the one with the power. I had no way of knowing whether she was translating my words faithfully, or whether she would report what was said honestly. I would simply have to trust her, and trust not only her linguistic skill but her goodwill. It seemed, right then, like too much to ask of our relationship. I hardly knew her.

Blue turned and spoke.

'He says he was working in a plastics factory in his village and there was an explosion. He was burned down one side of his body, his face, and his arm and his leg. He can't work any more, so he begs to pay for his son to go to school.'

'How old is he?'

'He is forty-nine.'

He looked not a day under seventy. I dug in my bag for the money I'd changed at the hotel, pulled out a note with the figure '50' written on it and pressed the note into the man's hand. He looked at it, placed his palms together and bobbed his head in thanks.

I turned to Blue but she was distracted, her gaze directed towards a white van with official markings and a black unmarked sedan, both parked by what seemed to be a pile of ash at the edge of yet another construction site.

'Police,' Blue said. 'There has been a fire.'

There was a board at the entrance to the construction site, decorated with a red and yellow logo that depicted the sun rising over a red cityscape and the words Sunrays Property in English.

'This construction site belongs to Nelson Li,' Blue explained. 'He has many important friends, so he is very successful.'

We were approaching the lake which had featured in all the reports of Derek Sumner's death, conjuring up a picture of tranquil beauty. In fact the 'lake' was a series of grubby ice rinks reflecting the overcast sky, their surfaces pockmarked, and peppered with fishermen with rods who sat on stools by holes they had dug in the ice. Their bicycles were abandoned nearby, as though they had slid and toppled and been left

66

where they had fallen. On the far side, a group of kids tested the strength of the ice by lobbing bricks onto it. Here and there, in a patch of sunlight, or where the fishermen had been particularly active, the ice had thawed through, and I could see the murky water beneath.

'It's used for breeding fish, not for swimming.' Blue turned away. 'It is too dirty.'

I walked to the water's edge. Shabby bars and nightclubs with rickety terraces were propped precariously along the shoreline. On the far side of the water were ramshackle houses, behind them much taller tower blocks lined up like gigantic advancing infantry.

A sonorous belch issued as the water heaved up against the ice.

'This way.' Blue led the way towards our left, along a dirt path strewn with rubbish. There was a corrugated-iron fence at the edge of the path, plastered in sheets of white paper that bore a cross and black Chinese script.

'What are they?'

'They are advertising medication for sexually transmitted diseases,' she explained. 'It is very popular now.'

I wondered whether she meant that the medication was popular, or the disease, or just sex itself.

Blue stepped through a man-size opening in the fence, and we found ourselves among trees. Here and there, underneath the umbrella of branches, were mounds of earth. When the newspapers reported that Sumner's body had been discovered in a 'woodland cemetery' I had envisioned an area of cultivated parkland in the city, not this scruffy patch of land that time forgot huddling beside a polluted fishpond in the shadow of skyscrapers. The ground was littered with old plastic bags, odd shoes, empty food packaging.

Blue had come to a halt, and as I did the same I shivered. It had been cold even in the sun but here, in this tenebrous half-light, it felt arctic. There were ragged patches of snow on the ground.

'What's a graveyard doing here? Actually, what's a wood doing here?'

'This is a village.'

'But we're in the middle of the city.'

'Yes, but this is a village,' she insisted. 'The city didn't reach here before.'

'We're surrounded by tower blocks.'

'Soon they will build tower blocks here too.'

I approached one of the graves. The white flowers on top were made from tissue paper and held in place by a brick.

'What on earth was Sumner doing here?' I asked the question of myself, but she answered.

'I don't know, I didn't see it in the newspapers.'

'Neither did I,' I told her. I had been shocked by the paucity of information that could be gleaned from the Chinese newspapers, even with the aid of interpreters in London who knew what they were looking for. One or two of the business papers had reprinted Sumner's comments about

68

rebuilding Kelness in the Chinese countryside, alongside approving editorial comment. But there was no mention of the controversy surrounding the buyout, or the protests in Kelness, and nothing about Sumner's death.

'They will write about it when the crime is solved,' Blue said.

Further in we came upon a grave dug but not filled, as though it was waiting for its future occupant to die. Crimescene tape had been tied from tree to tree around the depression in the ground, and the dirt around it seemed to have been churned up by a great number of people. Some five yards away there was another, smaller, area of rough dirt taped off.

'This must be it,' she said. 'Two places: one for his body and one for his head.'

I put the thought of it out of my mind, tried to concentrate on what my job required. I needed pictures. The light was terrible, but I wasn't sure when I would be able to come back or whether the light would be any better then. Blue watched as I took the MiniDV camera from my bag.

'It's very small,' she said doubtfully.

'The pictures are pretty good, though. We use it when it's impossible to carry a big camera around, or where we might get in trouble for filming.'

'Like here.'

'Like here,' I agreed, and Sal's warning about not getting Blue into trouble came back to me.

'You know,' I said to her, 'all I'm going to do is to take a few minutes of film, then I'm going to walk back to the main road. I can meet you there. You can leave me to do this on my own.'

She braced her shoulders against the cold, and thought for a moment.

'No,' she said, 'I'll stay with you.'

'I mean it,' I said, thinking that perhaps she didn't understand. 'It will be safer for you. I'm here without permission, I'm on a tourist visa. Sal told me if the authorities get angry with me they'll simply put me on a plane out. But if you help me they could put you in jail.'

'I know that,' she said. For a moment our eyes locked, and I thought I had rarely seen such stubborn determination. There was something else there too: an undercurrent of anger. Now was not the time to pursue it – the frigid conditions meant that we'd end up with frostbite if we lingered – but I wondered whether, by the end of the week, I would know more about the rage that was simmering under her skin. I didn't particularly want to be on the receiving end of it.

'You know what? If you're sure you're going to stay, could you film me doing a piece to camera? You know what that is?'

'Sal told me. You talk to the camera.'

'Pretty much.'

So she held the camera and pressed record, while I stood in front of the grave and spoke.

'Last week, Derek Sumner ate a final dinner with

70

his colleagues in a Beijing restaurant near here.' I moved slightly to one side and gestured to the depression in the ground. 'It's believed that this is where police found his murdered body lying on frozen ground the next day. So far, the investigation of his death has been conducted in near-total secrecy by the Chinese police. There are basic questions still shrouded in mystery: was Derek Sumner killed here or somewhere else? If he was killed here, *why* was he here, and *who* was he with?' I broke off. I felt like a ghoul and a fraud.

'What?' Blue was surprised.

'That's enough, the light's terrible,' I told her, taking the camera back from her and packing it away in my bag, bending over so that Blue could not see my face. When I stood up straight again, she was frowning at me.

My joints were getting stiff and slow with the cold, my ears were hurting, and a wave of jet-lagged exhaustion had broken over me. The sky was thickening now, a bitter wind was moving through the skeletal trees, and I was filled with a sense of foreboding.

As we emerged from the woods there was an excited shout from the other side of the lake, and then another, of alarm. I looked across. A couple of youths at an open-air pool table by the water's edge were looking in the direction of the shouts. Still carrying their cues they ran towards the gathering crowd on the edge of the smallest pond.

'I'm going to see what's up.' I turned to Blue, and was surprised by the look of fear on her face. She shook her head. I left her standing there and hurried across the causeway of packed earth that separated the large pool from two smaller ones. The smallest pond seemed to be even more of a rubbish tip than the rest of the area, a rainbow of plastic bags cascading down the bank. The pond was shallow. At points, brown earth or larger items of trash – an old office chair, an ancient suitcase – rose above the level of ice.

I pulled my scarf over my hair, which is red with a thick blonde streak (that is to say, a white streak dyed blonde) that falls over my eye. In London my appearance was unremarkable. In Beijing I was beginning to realize that my hair, combined with my pale, freckled skin, was a liability. I didn't want to draw attention to myself, but from the back of the crowd I could not see over people's heads. There was a lot of pushing and shoving going on, and I elbowed my way to the front for a better view. Immediately I regretted it.

'Oh dear God,' I whispered.

In the pool of dirty water by the shore where the ice was thawing, a human hand was visible, tangled in weeds. Some of the people around me were pulling away in revulsion. Others were shouting at each other. One elderly man had grabbed a pool cue and was leaning forward, prodding at the hand. It swayed to and fro in the water, and an arm emerged. There was more shouting, and the pool players pushed through the crowd. Standing on the bank, they grabbed up bricks and brought them down hard, shattering the ice. One of them leaped onto the surface where it was still firm, and leaned over to dislodge a great block of ice that had been loosened by the blows, and as he did so the head came into view and a horrified exclamation swept through the crowd. Three of the pool players hacked and heaved at the ice, clearing it slowly away, and the body came more fully into view. A girl, fifteen or sixteen perhaps, long black hair fanning around a head that had been almost severed from her torso, the great gash washed clean of blood. Her eyes were closed, the mouth open, skin and lips pale. Torn clothing clung to her upper body, below that she was naked. This last fact, in front of the crowd, seemed as indecent as her wound. With the movement of the men on the ice, the head moved gently back and forth, grotesquely alive.

'You must go away.' A voice spoke in English at my ear and I turned to see Blue, her eyes wide with horror. She jerked her head towards the causeway and I realized for the first time that I could hear a siren. The black police sedan we had seen parked by the construction site was heading towards the lake, a flashing light on its roof. It was making slow progress on the uneven ground, but either the car or its occupants would be with us in seconds.

I thought of my camera, still in my bag. I looked

again at the dead girl. A dark birthmark extended from her left eye to her cheekbone. I could see her ribs. The siren sounded again. If they found me here, with a camera in my bag and film of the grave-yard, then I would be put on the first plane out. I allowed Blue to take my arm and pull me away from the crowd. She led me away from the causeway, towards the maze of houses, still grip-ping my arm. We entered a narrow alley with low brick buildings to either side of us. People were coming to their doors, alerted by the commotion. I glanced inside, and saw tiny dark rooms and chil-dren padded thickly with clothes. One after another they caught sight of me and stared. There was no hostility, just curiosity, and I realized that my hair had come loose and was hanging around my face. I wrapped my scarf tighter and tucked my hair away. Behind me I heard a voice through a loud hailer.

'The police are telling people to move away,' Blue muttered to me. Her pace quickened. 'You must not be detained as a witness. You would have trouble.'

And so would you, I thought.

A few minutes later, by the roadside, we passed a man holding a live chicken down on a trestle table and chopping at its neck with a cleaver, blood dripping to the pavement. He and his customer were concentrating on the struggling mass of feathers in his hands. Neither of them seemed to be aware, yet, that anything had happened, and I

74

realized that we had walked far enough that they had not heard the alarm raised.

'Where are we?' I asked.

'I don't know, none of these streets even have names, they just have numbers.'

'You knew,' I said to her, in a low voice, hurrying beside her. 'When they started shouting you knew what they had found. I could see it on your face.'

A mongrel appeared from a gap between the houses, and started to follow us, sniffing at our heels.

'I didn't know,' she said, 'but I was afraid. I heard that the lake is a bad place, I heard that it is cursed, that there is a monster who is preying on women. I heard about it, but I wasn't sure if it was true. Now I know it is . . . oh . . .' She moaned and stopped for a moment, wrapping her arms around her stomach and doubling over, spitting bile into the filthy gutter. I waited for her to feel better.

'Why didn't you tell me?'

Blue straightened up and we hurried on.

'It was only a rumour,' she said. 'Sal told me journalists aren't interested in rumours.'

Normally I would have laughed out loud at the thought of Sal not being interested in rumours, but I had rarely felt less like laughing.

'Well, you can take it that I'm interested in rumours. It seems to be the only kind of news you get in this country.' My shock turned into anger. 'If someone's killing women why isn't it in the papers?'

Wanly, Blue shook her head. She didn't know. Or rather we both knew.

'What kind of country is this?' I ranted stupidly, as if she could help it, too shaken by what I had seen to control myself. 'It's criminal. If women don't know, how can they protect themselves? If our government covered up like that, it would be a national scandal.'

Blue was silent.

'People hear things,' she said eventually, 'they tell each other.'

We seemed to walk for hours through the maze of shacks. Everywhere I turned I saw families struggling against dirt and the bitter cold and poverty. I saw mangy dogs and children with red wind-roughened faces and runny noses, and woks covered in thick black grease in the kitchens, and stoves belching out thick black smoke. The sky was rapidly darkening, and as lights were switched on inside I could see bedding rolled and stacked against walls to make space for living during the day.

'Are these families all villagers?' I asked Blue. I was so cold that I could barely speak by now. I could not imagine trying to find comfort in these grimy homes.

'I think most of them are not from Beijing,' she said. 'They come here to find work, and they rent rooms from the peasants because the rent is cheap here. The locals don't trust them. Many people say that is why there is more crime now, and they blame the migrants for these murders.'

We emerged, finally, from the alleys onto a main road, and within seconds Blue had hailed a taxi.

Feeling ashamed at my outburst I invited Blue to eat with me in the hotel, although I myself had no appetite. She shook her head miserably and said her mother would have cooked her dinner. She looked pale and tired, and if she had looked dour before, now she looked downright scared. I wondered whether she would back out of our arrangement, but she wanted to check the time that we should meet the next day, and I suggested twelve-thirty.

'I am very sorry,' she said, as we parted outside the entrance to the hotel.

'Sorry for what? You've been a great help.'

'I am sorry that this is your first impression of Beijing,' she said, near tears. 'Beijing is my city. It has many problems but there are also many wonderful places to see.'

'I'm sure there are.'

'That girl, I have never seen anything so terrible in my life . . .'

'Nor I,' I said.

As I entered the opulence of the hotel I had the unnerving sensation that I was passing through a portal into another galaxy. The Christmas tree was all lit up and the doll-headed mannequins were whispering amongst themselves. A pianist in a tuxedo was playing in the lobby bar, where well-dressed men

and women, Western and Asian, were sipping cock-
tails. I had an urge to stand in the middle of the
lobby and shout at the top of my voice that a girl
lay slaughtered and naked not a mile from where
they sat. But measurements in miles are sometimes
irrelevant. I was as far, here, from that scruffy village
as I was from London.

I took the lift to my room, removed my boots
and coat and padded over the thick carpet to look
out of the window. It was dark by now, and the
grey dust of the city was invisible. In its place
there was a sea of fairy lights and neon signs, as
though the day's brutal realism had to be countered by a night-time of fantasy. There were
flashing peacocks, shimmering rainbows and
incandescent butterflies, all picked out in lights.
Some of the signs were in English with the words
'karaoke' and 'massage' illuminated. There were
vast advertising hoardings too, some of them set
on towers high above the streets. I stared blankly
at the signs. My head hurt, and jet-lagged exhaustion had drained me of the ability to think straight.

I went into the bathroom and washed my hands,
soaping them and running them under hot water,
then soaping them again. For some reason I had
the sensation that I had knelt and touched her
cold dead skin, although I knew that I had not.
At least, I thought not. I stared at myself in the
mirror. My eyes seemed huge, and I felt that the
image of the dead girl in the lake must be etched
onto my retinas because the sight of her had been

so physically shocking. I washed my face, rubbing at my eyes. I towelled my face dry, then looked into the mirror again. Perhaps a bath, I thought, would wash it all away from me.

While the water was running I picked up the phone and looked at my watch. It was six Beijing time, ten in the morning in London. I dialled Finney at work. The ring tone sounded familiar, as though I was calling from Charing Cross to say I'd be home late. After a moment Finney picked up.

'Hi,' I said, forcing a cheerful voice, 'I'm here.'

'You mean you're in a five-star hotel room perusing the room-service menu?' It was so good to hear his voice. I wanted him to keep on talking. I didn't want to have to say anything, I just wanted to listen. But he was waiting for me to speak.

'How are things at home? How was the kids' day?' I pressed the buttons on my mobile phone until I had a picture of Hannah and William in front of me. If he talked to me about my children, and if I could look at their faces as he spoke, then I didn't have to think about the dead girl . . .

'I got them off to their play dates. Hannah couldn't find her shoes, but we found them in her bed. We were even on time.'

'In her bed . . .' I was finding it difficult to concentrate. Politely I echoed his words.

'It's a long story . . . Is there something wrong?'

Everything was wrong: the careless nudity, the twist of her head on its remnant of flesh, the sliced skin, the swimming legs. Finney mustn't know, I thought. He mustn't know. I must pretend.

'Nothing's wrong. It's just that I told you I didn't want you to keep coming to my rescue,' I said, aiming for a light, jokey, tone, 'and now here I am asking you to look after my children.'

His voice, miles away, was bemused.

'So what am I supposed to do about it, say no?'

He waited for me to respond, but I was silent, and he went on, 'Is everything okay? What about you, how was the flight?'

'The flight . . .' I took a deep breath. 'I can't believe I got here just this morning . . .'

'Robin?' His voice was concerned.

'I'm here. Oh, Finney . . .' I couldn't hold it back. 'This afternoon I saw a murdered girl, they were pulling her body out of the lake. Her throat had been cut, they were bashing at the ice with rocks, and . . .'

'Are you all right?'

'I'm fine.'

'You're not fine.'

'I have such a headache,' I said, my voice catching, 'and I'm so tired I can't even focus my eyes.'

There was a moment's silence on the line. I tried to pull myself together.

'A Chinese girl?' Finney asked.

'What?'

'Was it a Chinese girl who'd been killed?'

'I suppose. I can't be sure. She looked Asian.

80

Apparently – there's a rumour, I should say – there have been other women killed.'

'Did you talk to the police? What do they say?'

'I can't talk to anyone, most of all not the police. I'm not even supposed to be here.'

'Love, you don't mess with serial killers.'

'Not a serial killer. Apparently a monster, a curse . . .' I produced a mirthless laugh. 'Look, don't worry, I shouldn't have said anything. But is a killer who preys on women going to kill a man? Could this have anything to do with Derek Sumner?'

'There are no rules,' Finney said. 'There's no point in speculating, you don't know enough about the scenes of crime or about the circum-stances.'

'This one was pretty much in my face . . . They both had their throats cut, I know that. Perhaps Sumner's murder was a copycat killing, someone taking advantage of the other killings to get rid of him?'

'Sumner's head was severed, that's one step beyond . . .'

'Perhaps he had more time, or perhaps he felt differently about Sumner, or . . .'

'Or perhaps they're completely unrelated.' Finney's voice was taut with concern. 'Robin, you're not on your home ground . . . promise me you'll keep at a distance.'

I could promise no such thing, of course. I would learn nothing if I kept my distance.

'Finney, I need to sleep,' I told him. Another

great wave of exhaustion had come crashing over me. 'I'll call you tomorrow.'

I went into the bathroom to turn off the water. But before I had even undressed I lay down on the bed thinking perhaps I would close my eyes just for a moment. Warmth and exhaustion conspired to send me hurtling towards sleep. As I lost consciousness I knew that my last thought would be my first on waking: What did it mean, this woman's savage death, so close to Sumner's shallow grave?

CHAPTER 5

The exhaust fumes from the gridlocked traffic seeped into the taxi and played around Song's nostrils. The fabric of his trousers rubbed painfully against his leg where the knife had skinned him. His head hurt, his lungs ached, and his arm throbbed. Wolf had gone to the pharmacy and brought back a tube of yellow unguent that Song had smeared on his burned arm. It smelled foul, like rancid sesame oil, and had streaked his raw flesh green.

His knees were jammed up against the seat in front, and the driver had the heater on at full blast. On the radio the weatherman was telling listeners that the temperature would drop to ten below overnight, and that if they were venturing out they should put on at least one pair of long johns underneath their clothes and should not forget to wear a hat. Song felt claustrophobic inside the taxi, and he had an awful sense that things were about to get worse. He was taking a big risk. If the police had staked out his ex-wife's apartment, he was finished. Wolf had been dead set against him going.

'Lina's like a sponge,' Song argued. 'She sucks

up everything her daddy tells her. I need to know what the police know. Besides, I can see my son any time I want.'

'You don't want to see your fat kid,' Wolf said. 'You want to taunt her father.'

'I want nothing to do with him.'

If only he'd stayed away from the daughter it would have been all right, he could have made a clean break. But he might as well have married the man, he saw that now. Nine years in the same office as Detective Chen, seven of those as his son-in-law as well as his protégé. He'd been charmed by Detective Chen at first, everyone was, taken in by the handsome face, the quick wit, the spotless uniform, the way he knew everyone and would help his friends out of sticky situations. Then Song noticed how, after these incidents, the friends came to thank Chen, and to bring him gifts: cigarettes, bottles of brandy, invitations to dinner, tickets to a show, a Rolex watch. Soon they came with envelopes of cash. Society was changing so fast. There were people with money, people who could pay to influence the outcome of investigations. Detective Chen was not the only one, of course, who was soliciting tokens of respect and gratitude. A police officer earned so little, just about a thousand *yuan* a month, so it made sense to take a bonus. But there were others, like Detective Fang, whom Song had observed steadfastly refusing gifts and bribes.

Detective Chen's good deeds became grotesque.

A man, a distant relative of a provincial mayor, was detained on suspicion of murder and released without explanation. After this, Detective Chen was invited to a dinner so alcoholic that he was sick on the table and still the waitresses brought the food, ferrying dishes of crab and abalone and shark's fin and placing them in the pool of vomit. A few months later, an elderly man was beaten by the sons of a high-ranking soldier. The sons were identified by witnesses, but they were never even detained, much less charged. After that, Detective Chen was said to have enjoyed several nights at a bath house run by the People's Liberation Army in the arms and bed and body not of one woman, but of many. When a new officer was discovered to have a record for causing grievous bodily harm that man – Psycho Wang – far from being fired was taken to Detective Chen's bosom.

That was around the time Song met Chen's daughter, Lina, with her tiny waist and almond eyes, and he'd let her caress his brain down to somewhere around his groin. Stripped naked, placing his hands on her body, she'd spoken in her soft voice of how her father had never shown her love, how he had never spent time or money on her, how she had never had presents and had been the most deprived of children. At that point an alarm should have rung out noisily since Lina showed no signs of deprivation but, burning in the heat of desire, Song heard only what he wanted to hear, that she shared his dislike of her father, and he rejoiced. Soon – very soon, because she fell instantly pregnant – they were married. Only then did Song discover that the daughter, who swore revolt so convincingly against her father, was in fact going through nothing more than a passing phase. Song never did find out exactly what treat her father failed to provide to cause her temporary rebellion, but father and daughter were soon reconciled. Soon Song began to realize that she was besotted by her father, and that she measured love in the same material terms that her father measured respect and gratitude. It became clear to Song that his wife's relationship with him was dependent on her relationship with her father. As long as Lina was angry at her father she lusted after his most vocal critic, who was Song. Once returned to the warm embrace of her father Lina turned against her husband.

When the child – Detective Chen's grandson – was born, gasping for air, the cord twisted around his neck, Song could have sworn that the cord was around his own neck not the child's. But now he had a son, Doudou, to bring up, so he tried to carry on as normal. For six years he tried to ignore Detective Chen's egregious behaviour and his wife's coldness. He tried until the day he could endure no longer, and his fist smashed into Psycho Wang's ribs and he cursed Detective Chen and slammed the office door behind him. Lina, leaping to her father's defence, berated Song. She accused him of being disloyal and of being spineless. A year later, Song walked out on his wife and Doudou, who was seven.

Song visited his son, but irregularly, baffled by the impossibility of being a father in this situation.

Mostly, he tried to forget them all. For a year he took freelance security work, usually as a bodyguard, but between contracts he was broke. His life was going nowhere. Then one evening he found himself at a family gathering, seated next to his second cousin, Wolf, whom he hardly knew. He had heard about the tattoo, of course, and expected it to cover the whole of Wolf's forehead, it loomed so large in family lore. Neither Song nor Wolf was good at family conversation, and so they found themselves talking to each other, shoulders hunched over their beers, while vast amounts of food were consumed around them and toasts of clear rice liquor were drunk. When the meal was finished, the table piled high with platters of half-eaten food, Wolf's father leaned across the table to address them. His cheeks were red from the alcohol. 'The two of you, you're both failures,' he said, slurring slightly, 'you should set up shop together.' They protested, of course. But the idea was not a bad one, since both of them were unemployed and Wolf's legal training complemented Song's investigative skills perfectly. Within a year, they had set up the agency.

Then came the day Detective Chen huffed his

way into Song's office and sat himself down without an invitation. These days Detective Chen's handsome face was beginning to show the ravages of food and drink and whorehouses.

'I can have you shut down.' He leaned forward. 'A word in the ear of the commercial department, and your business licence is withdrawn like that,' he snapped his fingers.

'I operate within the law,' Song muttered, hardly raising his head, as though one glance at Detective Chen could turn him to stone.

'The law is irrelevant,' Detective Chen said. 'The chief of the commercial department owes me a favour.'

'I'll fight you in court.' Song's voice strained with the effort of containing his temper. He could not understand what he had done wrong that the day should bring Detective Chen through his door.

'In court,' Detective Chen laughed contemptuously, 'with your punk lawyer?'

When Song did not reply he continued to sit there. After a moment the grin left his face.

'If you can convince me you are beneficial to society I may be able to save you,' he said.

Song licked his lips. This was worse than he had thought.

'How would I do that?'

'I have encountered a scoundrel, an anti-social element.'

Song said nothing. Detective Chen hesitated for

a long moment, his face twitching with indecision, his foot jiggling up and down nervously.

'Every week I play mahjong,' he began eventually. 'One day at the game I met a man called Manager Yu . . .'

Manager Yu had boasted of how he had made a fortune playing the stock market. When Manager Yu invited Detective Chen to his office for a game, Detective Chen had been impressed to see that Manager Yu worked at the Stock Market Education Council. No wonder, he thought, that Manager Yu knows how to work the system. Detective Chen suggested to Manager Yu that he might invest some money on his behalf, and Manager Yu happily agreed. In the space of a month, Detective Chen handed over ten million *yuan*, the proceeds of many years of corruption, at which point Manager Yu promptly disappeared. When Detective Chen returned to the Stock Market Education Council and asked to see Manager Yu, the staff there said he was not their manager, the title was simply a nickname. The man, indeed, had nothing to do with the Stock Market Education Council, and had simply rented a room there which he had used to play mahjong. When Detective Chen's story came to an end, Song sat in silence, savouring it. Then he spoke.

'You were very stupid,' he said.

'He seemed credible.' Detective Chen's face was puce and sweating.

'Get your own officers to investigate,' Song

snapped, knowing very well that this was the last thing his father-in-law could do. 'Or would they ask you where the cash came from?'

'It's more appropriate that I pursue this personally.'

'Then pursue it personally. I won't rescue your blood money for you. I applaud Manager Yu for his contributions to society.'

'You'll do it or I'll close you down,' Detective Chen said, and he sat there for some minutes as Song came to terms with the fact that he had no choice.

It took Song two months to track Manager Yu to a town in the north-east, where he was playing mahjong in the local government offices. Back in Beijing, Song told Detective Chen where to find his nemesis.

'You get your money back yourself,' he said, 'that's an end to my part in it. I've found him for you, you can set your own goons on him. I'll not be your muscle.'

Detective Chen grumbled, but they both knew that Psycho Wang would do a better job than Song. This – the physical extraction of cash – was what he was best at.

'Send me your invoice.'

'There's no charge, I don't want your dirty cash.'

Detective Chen did not like that. His eyes glanced nervously around the office.

'Then what's the price of your silence?' he muttered.

Song said nothing.

'I'll take the paperwork,' Detective Chen said, grabbing for the file.

Song made no move to stop him.

'Remember, I can ruin you,' Detective Chen hissed, as he retreated through the door.

'And I can ruin you too,' Song murmured to himself, for he had spent the previous evening scanning all the paperwork onto a removable hard disk that was now hidden in a box of his personal effects stored on top of the wardrobe underneath a pile of junk. Until this day, Song had thought of that disk as his insurance policy, but it would carry no weight against a charge of murder.

The taxi drew up outside Prosperity House, a thirty-storey residential block with Greek columns at the entrance and a golden statue of a gladiator on guard outside. The developers had tried to create an impression of exclusivity in spite of the unfashionable address, miles from the city centre in the strip of land between the fifth and sixth ring roads.

Song paid the driver and got out into the cold, zipping up the coat he'd borrowed from Wolf. It was black wool and double-breasted, military in style. Wolf fancied himself a rebel in it but, catching sight of himself in a window pane, Song thought it made him look like a fascist. He felt uncomfortable, so he lit up a cigarette and inhaled slowly, then coughed and stubbed it out on the gladiator's foot. He'd always maintained that cigarette smoke was better for the health than the Beijing air, but since the fire his tolerance for cigarettes seemed to be woefully reduced. He stood for a moment, looking up towards Lina's apartment. He had not told her he was coming, in case she had time to alert her father. He leaned in close to the intercom and tapped in Lina's apartment number.

'It's me,' he said, when she answered. 'I've come to see Doudou.'

She buzzed him in without saying anything. He asked himself whether her silence was suspicious, but thought she was probably just being unfriendly, as she usually was.

The lobby was empty. Song remembered a concierge at the desk, but now it was unmanned. The lift was waiting, open, and Song walked into it and pressed the number twenty-three, but as soon as the lift door closed he began to panic. He could still change his mind, he told himself. He could stop at any floor and get out and walk away. The lift ascended. He cursed himself. Perhaps he should have walked up the fire escape, they would not have been expecting that, but he could not face the thought of walking up the stairs with his injured leg. When he arrived at the twenty-third floor and the door opened, he braced himself for an attack. He stepped out onto the landing, and then thought that perhaps *they* were waiting in the fire escape, and that the fire door would burst open. But he crossed the space without a challenge and reached the heavy metal security door to Lina's apartment and pressed the buzzer.

It took her a while to undo all the locks and latches, but eventually she opened the door dressed in a flannel dressing gown and slippers, her elfin face bare of make-up. Her hair was cut in feathers around her face.

'I was expecting Daddy,' she said, as if he should apologize for disappointing her.

Song stared.

'He's coming here now?'

'Maybe,' she shrugged, 'maybe not. He said he might drop by, but he's so busy now. Why are you just standing there letting the cold air in? I thought you wanted to see your son. Take off that ugly coat, I'd forgotten what bad taste you have.'

Song took off Wolf's coat carefully, trying not to show how much his arm hurt as he pulled it from the sleeve. And then he had to take off his sweater, which meant more pain, or he'd have melted clear away, the apartment was so hot. A bundle of orange fur appeared, ran at Song and then scattered away from him, barking.

'What's that piece of vermin?'

The dog was setting Song's teeth on edge with its yapping, running back and forth between the sofa and the front door.

'Don't say that. He's my fuzzy baby, he's my chow chow. He just doesn't like strangers.'

'He'll grow as big as a lion, and you'll have to put him down,' Song said.

'Oh! Don't say that,' she protested. She knelt next to the puppy and covered his ears with her hands, as though he could understand.

Song stepped past her and pushed open the door to the bedroom quickly, so as to take whoever was inside by surprise, still half expecting an ambush.

He found his son lying in shorts and a T-shirt on the bed, his eyes fixed on the television, a packet of chocolate biscuits beside him. Doudou looked like a beached whale, his fat legs ending in big bare feet that seemed to form flippers, his stomach resting all around him. He raised a hand in greeting at his father, his jaw chewing lazily. Lina followed Song into the room.

'My darling loves the ads,' she said proudly.

Song glanced up at the TV. A woman in a bikini top was thrusting her chest at the screen and suggesting that viewers should take a handful of pills every day if they wanted breasts as big as hers.

'He's ten years old,' Song protested.

'Don't be silly, he doesn't understand. He likes the car ads better. What's that smell?'

Song could smell it too, the paste on his burned arm was melting in the heat of the apartment and giving off fumes.

'I just ate,' he said.

Song turned and left the room. He was beginning to feel sick and he wasn't sure if it was the

94

heat, or the sight of his son like this, or the sense of helplessness that overwhelmed him every time he visited. He had tried to write his son off, to distance himself from the whole situation, but when he stayed away it built up in him like nausea, so he kept coming back, thinking he could change things. Six months ago he'd persuaded Lina to send the boy to a camp for fat kids, and the camp counsellors had chased him round a race track, and laughed at him while he tried in vain to touch his toes, and fed him raw vegetables. The day he came home, Lina had rung Song in tears. 'He's a skeleton,' she'd wailed, 'he's fading away.' She had fallen on him with sweets and with jars of sugar-packed yoghurts, and it hadn't taken long for Doudou to get his old figure back.

'He needs to exercise his mind and his body,' Song said, pulling a chair up to the kitchen table, lighting a cigarette and pulling a fancy ashtray towards him. He inhaled, but the smoke made him feel sick and he stubbed it out. 'For heaven's sake, the child should not be in bed. He should be working hard and resting hard if he's going to make something of himself.'

'Make something of himself like you did?' Lina asked. The puppy sniffed around Song's ankles and he kicked it away, harder than he might have, because he knew what was coming next.

'Yes, like me,' he said wearily.

'So he can be a big success like you?' Her voice had the glistening sheen of quicksand. 'A big-shot swimming champion who trains for years then drops out of the final for no reason? A police officer who's everyone's golden boy but who picks quarrels with his superiors? Two times you could have had it all, and two times you've thrown it away. What's wrong with you? Look at you now, a private eye spying on unfaithful husbands. You can hardly make ends meet. You're pathetic. You try to pretend you're a detective, like Daddy. You advertise yourself as though you can compete. What did you think, that he'd be scared when you set up your little office? Well, he's not scared of you. He laughs at you.'

She looked up at him innocently, her perfect dainty face slightly thinner than he remembered, lips slightly parted, flawless skin.

'Lina, this isn't about me, it's about Doudou. He can't rely on your father for his future. He has to learn to rely on himself. Who knows whether your father will be able to maintain his position? You haven't done a day's work for years.' He snatched up her manicured, soft-skinned hand by the wrist and shook it in front of her face until she wrenched it out of his grasp. 'But Doudou has no choice, he has to make his own way because one day all your daddy's friends will desert him. I hear the gossip. People are talking about him, about his mistresses, his villa in Tongxian. The politicians have to get rid of people like him, or the people won't stand it, there will be chaos. You must hear how the leaders talk on the news, they know they must root out some of the corrupt ones, or they'll all be finished.' Still she wouldn't look at him, and he felt an uncontrollable urge to scare her. 'You think they don't know how he lines his own pockets? They keep him there as long as he's useful to them, and the day he's more trouble than he's worth, he'll have a bullet in the back of his head, and you'll be on your own and in disgrace.'

'Then you'll have to support us,' she retorted quickly, 'instead of flouting your responsibility. What you give us doesn't even pay the rent on this dump.'

'What I give you probably doesn't keep the boy in sweets,' he snapped back.

She gave him a contemptuous look. He shook his head. He should never have got into this. If he had aimed to charm information out of her, he had failed. And he was wasting time. If Lina's father had said he might come by, he could be there any time. He needed to build bridges, and fast.

'Lina.' He lit up again. Being with Lina always made him feel as though he needed a cigarette. He coughed as his lungs protested and stubbed the cigarette out next to the other one in the ashtray. 'I'm sorry. I speak so bluntly only because I care, and because we're close enough that we can be frank. I'm only concerned that you're real-istic about the future. I care too much about the boy to let him go through political trouble. You know what's in my background. I won't let that happen to him.' He reached out and gently turned her face towards him so that he could look into her eyes. 'And I won't let it happen to you.'

She reached out and put a hand on his burned arm, and a flame of pain shot up through the nerves to his neck. He tried not to cry out as her fingers massaged his shirt, the cotton grinding against his raw flesh. He looked down at her hand. Her fingers were perfectly manicured, her nails polished purple, each with a rose painted in tiny white brush strokes. Sweat seeped from the skin above his mouth.

'I know you still care for us,' she said, 'but you are too sensitive.'

Song removed her hand from his arm and held it in his large palm. She seemed to take it as an encouragement.

'Daddy doesn't do anything wrong,' she said. 'He adapts to his environment. There are people who need his help, and he helps them, then they repay him in any way they can as a mark of respect and friendship. It's what they call the free market. I'm like him, I adapt well. But you don't. You're inflexible to the point of stupidity. You abandoned us because of what you called ethics, but in fact you lost us because of your oversensitivity and because of your curiosity about things that don't concern you. You're a simpleton, and you left me with no choice but to rely on Daddy.'

Song nodded, fixing his face in a facsimile of humility. It was all he could do not to slam her hand down against the table top and argue with her. But he could not afford to. Instead he patted her hand and tried to chuckle.

'I know your father does important work. He must be under pressure at the moment. I keep hearing about the murders by the lake.'

'One of them was a foreign man,' she told him, 'and dead foreigners are terrible trouble, they cause such diplomatic awkwardness. The foreign ministry is pressing him to make progress on the case, they say it's too embarrassing to have it unsolved. They talk about harming economic growth in Beijing, and about endangering the public security environment at such a sensitive time. If my father is forced to bear the blame for that, his career will be finished.'

'And apart from the foreign man . . . ?' Song prompted, wanting a full picture.

She glanced at his face, her interest piqued by his curiosity.

'Today they pulled a girl, a teenager, out of the lake and Daddy had to rush over there. She'd had her throat cut. That makes three in as many weeks.'

'Three?' he blurted out, then again, 'Three?' If he kept saying the number then she wouldn't know that his head was filled with the memory of fresh blood on his hands and on his clothes. Unthinking, he glanced down at his hands. He had scrubbed them until the skin had broken. If they found blood on him now it would be his own.

'But this time they saw the man, a big brute,' she told him, 'like a yeti. He was running away and he took a child with him.'

Song was seized by an urge to push aside his chair, make a break for the door and run. Had she been playing with him all this time? Were the police waiting for him outside the door? Surely even Lina would not arrange for him to be arrested in front of their son. He had to clench his muscles to stop himself jumping to his feet.

'Who is this man, this brute?' he managed to ask.

She shrugged. 'I expect they will learn more from the witnesses.'

Song realized that he had let his head slip into his hands in an attitude of despair. He pulled himself upright.

'Three of them, you say,' he repeated again, still clutching at the number. 'Were the women raped?'

'Why else would anyone do it?'

Was she speculating or was there evidence? Song did not dare to ask her outright.

'No one needs to kill for sex in this city.' He was thinking aloud now, trying to quiet his panic with reason. 'Three,' Song counted. 'That's a girl pulled out of the lake today, and the foreigner last week . . .'

But she wasn't inclined to list them for him. 'Daddy's tried to keep all of it quiet. He's kept it out of the papers. The editors have all been silenced.'

'They should be warning people there's a maniac about.'

'The people who live there are peasants. They become hysterical too easily.'

'Better to be hysterical than to have your throat cut.'

She gave a snort and sat back in her chair contemplating him, her lips twitching in a smile. 'What do you think? If they catch the big man, what sort of creature will he be?'

Song could bear no more. He stood up abruptly, pushing his chair back.

'I'll say goodbye to Doudou.'

She followed him through to the bedroom, but the boy had fallen asleep and was snoring loudly. Lina came to stand beside him and they looked down at the boy they had conceived. Lina took hold of Song's hand.

'The day he was born I'd never have believed he could look so gross,' Song murmured. 'He was such a skinny baby, like a beansprout.'

'Perhaps he could do with some exercise,' she conceded. 'I'm thinking of arranging golf lessons for him.'

'Golf is a rich man's sport, not exercise for fat children,' he protested. Golf was a sport for the corrupt and for the powerful. Was this what she wanted for her son?

But he glanced at her and saw that in her eyes there was, at least, still love for her son. Something occurred to him, and he looked around.

'You share this bed?' he asked.

'He likes to be close to me,' she said, leaning over to pinch the boy's fat cheeks. 'He's my Buddha baby.'

Song said goodbye, grabbed his sweater and Wolf's coat and took his leave. In the lift, he stared at himself in the mirrored walls. A big brute of a man, like a yeti? He had never considered himself brutish. He examined his reflection. He was big, of course, his shoulders could have pulled a plough, or they would never have chosen him to swim. He'd done a stint in the army after that. When he became a policeman his colleagues teased him that he looked like a professor because of his long thin face and his spectacles. Then he'd had his head shaved, which had put an end to that; no one had dared to tease him about anything at all. Still, he was bemused to be described as a brute. When he peered into his eyes in the mirror he saw no violence, only confusion.

The lift arrived at the ground floor and the door opened. The lobby was still empty. Song stepped out into the night. After Lina's apartment, the air was glacial. The fug in the apartment had clouded his head, and he decided that despite the pain in his leg he would walk for a while before he took a taxi.

He had gone a short way down the street when his mobile phone rang, and he pulled it from his pocket. It was Lina already, in an angry whisper.

'What have you done?'

'I don't know what you mean . . .'

'Daddy's here, in the other room,' she said. 'He wants to know when I last saw you.'

'He's there?' Song looked back. He was barely a hundred yards from the gladiator statue. Detective Chen must have been going up in one lift while he was coming down in the other. He swallowed the urge to laugh.

'He's in the kitchen but I closed the door. I don't want him to know I'm ringing you.'

Song frowned. Lina had spent their entire married life playing father off against husband like this. She was well schooled in deception. What could he tell her that she would believe?

'He wouldn't tell me why he wanted to find you, so you have to tell me,' she whined, still whispering, 'or I'll be forced to tell him you were just here.'

Song almost sobbed with the frustration of it. Why was it that his brain, usually so good at coming up with prevarication, was frozen with fear?

'I did some work for him,' the fat white lie started to ooze out of him. Best to keep as near the truth as possible, he thought, it was a principle of his investigation work. 'I did some work for him and he wants me to do some more, but it's too risky for me and he's not going to pay, so I've been keeping out of his way. Can you do me a favour? Can you tell him you haven't been in contact with me?'

There was silence on the line, a silence thick with suspicion. There was a click as she hung up. Song tucked his phone inside his jacket, looked up and down the street and then started walking as fast as his injured leg would allow, his hand stuck out to hail a taxi. The euphoria he'd felt at escaping Detective Chen was already a thing of the past. He must cover his back, cover his face, cover his tracks. First he had to lose the boy, and then he had to lose himself.

CHAPTER 6

The girl in the lake raised an arm from the water, pulled her head back onto her neck so that it was set only slightly off-kilter, and walked onto the shore. I shouted out loud, waking myself up. I reached out and switched on the bedside light to banish the apparition. I lay there for a few minutes, blinking, trying to sort out what was reality and what was nightmare. The reality was bad enough. There was no way I would get back to sleep, and anyway I felt so awake that I assumed it must be morning.

I got out of bed, padded barefoot over to the window, and pulled back the heavy curtains only to find that the sky was still black. There was no sun, only the illumination of the street lights and the flashing neon billboards. The road was still busy with a steady stream of taxis. Frowning, I squinted at my phone. I shook my head, checked again. It was ten p.m. I'd been asleep for all of three hours.

Groaning, I turned the light out and went back to bed. I lay there for what seemed like an hour, staring at the ceiling, willing myself back to sleep.

I filled my mind with Hannah and William, thinking they would comfort me. Instead I just worried. Would Finney remember all that I had told him? He hadn't written any of it down. When I looked at the time only five minutes had passed. I read for ten minutes. After that I was more awake than ever. In the end I gave up on sleep. I went and looked out of the window again, in the direction of Lady Street, where a mass of lights blazed from the cafes and clubs by the lake. I remembered the crowds milling around and imagined that it would still be busy – it was only late evening, after all. There had been other Westerners in the restaurants, and they were unlikely to have heard about that afternoon's vile discovery. I would not be on my own there, and I would not stand out. I reminded myself that Sumner had died there in the night. Perhaps if I retraced his steps I would begin to understand what it was that had taken him there. Perhaps I wanted to show myself that I could overcome my fear, and that I could return to the icy lake even in the dark.

I showered and dressed, and then I went downstairs to the lobby. Cocktail hour was long over, but a straggle of hard-core drinkers kept the waitresses from their beds. A board by the reception desk informed me that the temperature outside had now dropped again to minus ten degrees Celsius. Halfway through the revolving door, an arctic gale hit me. I almost carried on going 360 degrees straight back into the lobby, but then I was outside, and the doorman – a man of about fifty, rigged out in livery worthy of Henry VIII – was asking me whether I wanted a taxi, and I was saying yes.

'Very cold,' the doorman said in accented English, making a shivery action, hugging his arms around him.

'Very cold,' I agreed. I didn't envy him spending the night in the open air.

When the taxi came my new friend asked me where I wanted to go, and when I showed him on the map there was a bit of toing and froing with the driver, who I guessed didn't want to go such a short distance. But the doorman had the kind of build you didn't argue with, and eventually the taxi driver let me climb in. He stopped to let me out when I spotted the turn-off to the lake and charged me all of about seventy pence, which I guessed must be the minimum fare. The alley where the beggar had stopped me with her fishing net was lit with an advertising hoarding that welcomed visitors, in English, to 'Super Bar Street'. I walked the way Blue and I had gone earlier that day.

The crowds of Westerners I had expected to see were simply not there. The few pedestrians who were around seemed to be heading away from the bars and out to the main street. The bar touts were desperate to get punters through their doors. I began to regret coming here – the place had a more aggressive feel to it than it had during the day. The pleasant evening stroll I had envisaged in the comfort of my warm hotel room was not an option out in the bitter cold. I glanced at my watch and realized that it was nearly midnight.

I hadn't eaten for hours but I wasn't hungry, which was just as well because most of the restaurants seemed to have shut up shop. Further along the street the strip of clubs looked deserted, although there was no way of knowing. There were no windows, only heavy black doors and the distant thump of music.

'Come inside, lady, have drink, dance.' A wiry young man, not much more than a boy, approached me, blocking my path and gesturing comically at a concrete bunker with a steel door that advertised itself as 'Fashion Club'. My first instinct was to push on by, but I checked myself. I was freezing cold, I was learning nothing out on the street, and the boy had a sweet grin, clowning around with his friend like a kid.

I nodded and he led me inside, practically skipping with excitement at his success. Once my eyes got accustomed to the dark I could see why he might be chuffed by the arrival of a paying customer. There was a cloud of dry ice pumping onto an empty dance floor, and a young Chinese DJ in T-shirt and jeans swayed behind a mixing deck, his fingers busy. My guide showed me to a low sofa by an even lower table and handed me into the care of a waiter. I peered at the rumpled drinks list, ordered a glass of what called itself 'local' red wine and sat back.

There was a waitress behind the bar, and a teenager slumped on a sofa not far from me, one leg propped on the other knee, white-sneakered foot moving relentlessly with the throb of the music. He was skinny, and he had the kind of fine cheekbones that define a classical Chinese face, an effect accentuated by long sideburns that ran to his jawline. As if he felt my gaze upon him he looked up and caught my eye. He nodded at me, and then just looked at me until I turned away in discomfort.

The waiter brought me my glass of wine and the bill, and waited while I got out my money. I paid, took a sip, and winced.

'No customers,' I shouted over the music, gesturing at the empty space all around us.

'Dance?' He gestured at the dance floor.

I shook my head.

'Football?'

'What?'

'Football,' he repeated, pointing to what I now saw was table football, in front of the dance floor.

'Why not?' Table football is our household's favourite sport.

He gave me the thumbs up.

I followed him over to the table.

'Why don't you have any customers? Are they afraid?' I asked.

He pulled a face that suggested he didn't understand. And when I mimed being afraid he still didn't get it, or didn't want to get it. His eyes went nervously to the young man with the sideburns, who was still reclining on the sofa, foot twitching. The waiter saw my eyes follow his. 'The boss,' he said.

'He looks too young to be anyone's boss,' I said, but my footballing companion didn't reply. We knocked the ball to and fro. If it hadn't been for jet lag I would have thrashed him, but after a few minutes he claimed victory. We shook hands and I thanked him for the game, then headed for the exit. As I left, the lights went out behind me. Someone had clearly taken an executive decision that there would be no more customers that night.

Outside, the street had emptied. The bar touts had given up and gone home, and most of the lights had gone out. I came upon a group of men. By the look of them, they were locals. They were moving down the street and talking animatedly, and one of them was clasping a stack of handouts to his chest. As he passed me by, he pushed one into my hands. It was a sheet of flimsy paper, folded like a letter. I peered down at it in the light from the bar, but it was covered in Chinese characters, and I put it in my pocket.

I headed back the way I'd come. Behind me, the men's voices had fallen silent. Ahead of me, the street was patchy with pools of light and areas of impenetrable shadow. I walked fast. On my right I passed the construction site where

Blue and I had seen the police investigating a fire.

On my left was the lake, and I heard the water groan against the ice, and the ice shift and crack. I remembered what I had seen that afternoon and I shivered, wishing I had never left my bed. I heard footsteps behind me. Coming to a halt, I spun around, adrenalin pumping. A man was on my heels, and I almost shouted out in alarm. He nodded at me and said, in stilted English, 'Good evening,' and I recognized him as the young boss from the nightclub.

I watched him walk towards a huge car that was parked on the pavement. He pulled open the door on the driver's side, climbed inside, and pulled the door closed. Then the car – a Hummer – roared past me, and he honked his horn either in greeting or in a warning to get out of his way. A few moments later I reached the main road and a stream of taxis.

Back at the hotel I checked my email. There was a brief note from Finney, who had sweetly transcribed the children's greetings to me. William wanted me to bring him a panda, and Hannah wanted a very, very, very beautiful purple dress. Finney told me again to be careful, and not to get too involved. He also wanted to know where I remembered last seeing the remote control for the TV and where the delivery menu was for the Chinese takeaway.

There was an email from Damien.

✉

Press reports that Sumner victim of serial killer. Do we have this? If not, why not? Story re possible radioactive contamination at Kelness. Need yr input. Rgds D

I stared, frowning in utter incomprehension. Radioactive contamination? My input?

I'd thought I was tired, but I couldn't have slept then. I spent the next hour at my laptop, hitched up to the hotel broadband, trawling through the British papers. Google offered me a raft of stories about the negotiations between Kelness management and Nelson Li, and I found what I was looking for in the *Financial Times*.

Negotiations about the future of Kelness are taking place behind firmly closed doors. But explosive allegations by the Chinese side that there was an incident of radioactive contamination a month ago at Kelness have nevertheless leaked out. Sources close to the negotiations said yesterday the Chinese side claims it is in possession of a memo documenting a cover-up by Kelness management and possible contamination of steel workers at the bankrupt mill.

Radioactivity is a known hazard at steel mills, where shipments of scrap metal are imported from unknown sources in Russia and Eastern Europe for use in the smelting process. After a handful of high-profile incidents in which radioactive steel has been recycled into radioactive furniture and jewellery, most mills have invested heavily in expensive screening systems to alert managers to radioactive shipments.

The wires had already picked up the story. Facts were thin but speculation was rife. This was a scare tactic by the Chinese side, one analyst suggested, to beat down the price of the plant. But several correspondents agreed that if it was an invention it was an outrageous one, and doomed to failure. Logically that led most editors to assume that there was at least a kernel of truth in the story, although they all tiptoed around saying it overtly, clearly terrified of lawsuits.

As I navigated from site to site, foraging for scraps of information, I saw a new Reuters story had just popped up, and I clicked on it and read.

The Kelness press office issued a statement today saying that it was 'not in a position to answer any questions about "an alleged incident of radioactive contamination", or about the monitoring of radioactivity at Kelness'.

One industry insider said the company was 'hauling up the drawbridge, going into defensive overdrive'.

I opened up Damien's message again, clicked on Reply, and sat staring at the screen. Exhaustion finally trumped adrenalin. My eyelids closed of their own volition, and when I jerked myself awake my brain simply wouldn't function, all rational thought drowning in a syrup of nonsense. I forced myself to type: 'I'll ring you tomorrow,' each letter a struggle. I hit Send, collapsed onto the bed, and fell immediately asleep.

CHAPTER 7

After his visit to Lina, Song didn't want to return to Anjialou at all – it was too close to the lake, too likely that people would recognize him – but he could hardly abandon Wolf with the boy.

When he reached Anjialou he stopped at the Good Neighbour Cheap Meals stall for three take-away bowls of noodles. He was so hungry that he chose to ignore the fact that he should not be seen near here. As he spooned chilli sauce into the plastic containers, the man who served Song seemed to take an unnecessarily long look at his face. 'Where do you live?' the man asked. Song pointed vaguely in the wrong direction, then hurried on as soon as he could, walking first one way, then doubling back, trying to move normally, although balancing three plastic containers, three pairs of disposable chopsticks and two bottles of beer made his arm scream with pain.

When at last he pushed open the door, he saw the boy was sleeping on the thin mattress and Wolf was sitting on a box, reading a newspaper. Wolf looked relieved, scrambling to his feet.

'You see?' he said cheerfully. 'They're not even looking for you. They don't know it was you who was there.'

'Oh, they're looking all right.' Song looked grim. He handed Wolf the plastic containers and peeled off the heavy black coat. 'I missed Chen by the skin of my teeth.'

Song glanced around him, trying to distract himself from the gnawing pain in his arm. Wolf had made some home improvements. Three wooden crates, upended, had become table and chairs, the stove was burning fiercely, and an enamelled bowl, complete with flannel and towel, constituted the bathroom. This was one good reason to have Wolf around. Song could sleep on a peasant *kang*, hard concrete under his back. Wolf needed a sofa on which to take a rest, he liked a low table on which to rest his teacup or perhaps his feet. He would make some woman a fine husband. But amidst all the domesticity, something was missing.

'The knife,' Song demanded, 'where's the knife?'

'Here.' Wolf picked up a plastic carrier bag, and when Song looked inside he saw the boy's jacket. He prodded at the filthy material, and felt through it the knife's hardness.

They sat on the boxes and started to eat their noodles. Song tried to do like Wolf, to scoop them greedily into his mouth, but the truth was that his arm hurt so much that it had dulled both his brain and his appetite.

'My mother keeps messaging me,' Wolf told Song, embarrassed. 'She's set up a date for me tomorrow night. She wants to know where I am, wants me to promise I'll be there.'

Desperate to marry her son off, Wolf's mother spent her mornings attending gatherings of similarly anxious parents in the park. She had a note pinned to her jacket listing Wolf's qualities, so that the other parents – who had similar adverts for their marriageable offspring pinned to their own clothing – could see what was on offer. She had never listed the silver hair, or the tattoo, but after Wolf's first date word got round. Now she had to depend on newcomers, those who hadn't already heard, to give Wolf a chance with their daughters.

'She says the daughter has bad eyes, but she's got a job in an American company. I bet she's got a squint, or she's cross-eyed. That'll be it, or glasses as thick as Coke bottles. Still, if she takes them off . . .'

Wolf sneered loudly at his mother's attempts to marry him off. He said he could not understand why anyone would want to take on the duties and expenses of a family. Once Song asked him why he went along with it and Wolf replied that a date was a date. What he meant was that sex was sex.

Song was not listening to Wolf's nervous prattling. He had escaped Detective Chen by seconds. The neighbours would explode with nosiness within twenty-four hours. Song could stay in

Beijing no longer. They could give refuge to the boy no longer.

'You're better off without me,' Song said, interrupting Wolf. 'If they come looking for you and they can't find you, they'll know you're with me, and it will make it worse for you. I'll get rid of the boy tomorrow morning and then I'll leave town. You can take over the office and in the evening you can date the blind girl.'

'Where will you go?'

'If I don't tell you, you can't tell anyone else.'

'What if I need you?'

'You can handle yourself in a fight if one of the husbands gets nasty.'

'It's not the husbands I'm scared of, it's the clients. They're all so angry.'

Song jabbed his chopsticks in Wolf's direction.

'Pat them, like you'd pat a dog, be nice to them so they feel better, but don't sleep with them, or they'll want us to work for free. And we don't work for free under any circumstances. Anyone tells you a sob story, you give them a bill for the time it took you to listen, and then you bill them for the tissue you give them to wipe their eyes.'

Wolf nodded. It was usually he who gave Song this talking-to. They were as bad as each other. They would have to learn to be ruthless if they were to make good money from the agency.

'What about your father?' Wolf asked.

'My sister will look after him. I'll have to get

118

cash to her . . . You're going to need cash too,' Song said.

Wolf grinned.

'So I can send you cigarettes in jail.'

'Tell you what,' Song was blunt, thoughts of his father sobering him, making him intolerant of Wolf's jokes, 'you can pay for the bullet in the back of my head.'

The grin died on Wolf's face. He scrambled to his feet.

'Don't talk like that.'

Song lowered his head into his hands. The pain drained him. Human company was almost more than he could bear, and yet he did not want to send his friend away. He raised his head.

'You must prepare yourself. The police will come and find you. You must think about what you're going to say to them.'

'I'll tell them the truth. I'll tell them you haven't hurt anyone. I'll tell them you saved the boy from the fire.'

Song heaved himself to his feet and stood facing Wolf. His face was dark with pain and worry, and Wolf looked up at him with concern.

'They don't give a fuck about the boy, remember that. They need to make an arrest. You're a lawyer, you must work out your defence as carefully as if you were in court. Don't protect me if it comes at a cost to you, but don't dump me in the shit if you can avoid it.'

Wolf opened his mouth to speak, then closed it

119

again, his boyish features creased by a rare frown. Good, Song thought, I have worried him.

Gently, with his one good arm, Song pushed his friend towards the door. He reached out for the plastic bag that contained the jacket and the knife, and he made Wolf take it, saying, 'You must hide this, you know where.' Even once he was outside in the yard, Wolf delayed, turning and walking slowly backwards, so that he faced Song even as he retreated. 'You should be watching your back,' Song told him, laughing softly. 'You walk blind like that and you'll walk smack into their arms.'

When Wolf had gone, Song went back inside and sat by the fire. He felt uneasy, but he could not identify a single cause. So many things were going wrong. He pulled his mobile phone from his pocket and dialled his sister's number. When she answered her voice was thick with sleep.

'Why are you calling so late?' she complained, then, anxiety hitting her like an electric shock, 'Did the hospital ring you? Couldn't they reach me?'

'No, no, not the hospital,' he reassured her, 'it's not Pa. At least, there's no emergency that I know of. It's me. I have to go away . . . can you tell him?'

'He wants to see you all the time.' There was no emotional blackmail in her voice, just a stating of the facts as they both knew them. 'How long will you be gone?'

'I don't know.' Song sighed. 'I have to keep my head down, I . . .'

'You're in trouble?' She was alarmed now, and Song regretted letting it slip, making her anxious when she had their father to worry about. It was Song who breezed into the hospital to sit at his father's bedside for half an hour, his sister who cooked soup for him and bathed him, and made sure he had water by his bed, and helped him to use the toilet. It was she who negotiated with the doctors.

'No, no. It's nothing. Tell him a few days . . .'

There was a pause, and Song thought: she knows that I am lying.

'Brother, I don't like to raise it . . .'

'There's a bill to pay.'

'I'm sorry. They are trying new drugs imported from Germany . . .'

'How much?'

'Six thousand *yuan* . . .'

'I'll take care of it, I'll make sure it gets into your account. You shouldn't be worrying about money,' Song said. He ran his palm over his face anxiously, wondering whether he had this much cash to hand. How could he transfer the money without making a visit to a bank?

'He's anxious in case you're not there,' his sister was saying. 'In case something happens, he wants you there.'

For a moment Song could not speak. Then he said, 'I know, I'll try to be there.'

After he said goodbye to his sister, he realized why Wolf's departure had made him so uneasy,

121

but it made him feel no better to have worked it out. For the first time in his life, he thought, perhaps Wolf will betray me, just as I am abandoning my father, not because I want to, but because I have no choice.

Song did not sleep well. He did not know where to go. He could go and stay with friends in any one of half a dozen cities. But if the police really wanted to find him they would track down his friends, and then they would be in trouble too for harbouring him. He could go anywhere the length and breadth of China and stay in villages or towns where no one knew him. But any stranger attracted attention in small towns, and besides, he feared that the tedium of small town life would kill him as surely as a firing squad.

Before dawn, pulling his boots onto his stockinged feet and Wolf's coat tight around him, he stepped outside – he needed to use the public toilet, and he wanted to get there before the morning rush. When he returned to the room, the door was ajar. Cursing, he scanned the dark street and caught sight of movement. When he gave chase, he saw the child disappearing into an alleyway just yards away and within seconds had the boy by the scruff of the neck.

'Where are you going?' he hissed. But the boy twisted his head away. Song swung him nearly off the ground in his frustration, and was shocked again by how light the child was.

It struck Song that he was an idiot. He'd wanted to get rid of the boy, and the boy had got rid of himself. Why on earth had he gone after him? Angry at himself, he turned and marched him back towards the van. He opened the door and pushed the child inside, then clambered into the driver's seat and revved the cold engine, trying to ignore the pounding pain in his arm every time he had to bend it or move it so that it came in contact with clothing.

He pulled out into the street. The sky was still dark, and as they drove snow started to fall again in slow flurries. The child was not hysterical as he had been the day before, but he was restless, unable to be still, his body jerking and twitching. He kept turning his head, first to look out of the window, then back at Song, then out again. Song made no effort to talk. If he communicated with the child, if they talked, it would be more difficult to dump him back on the street. They reached a junction, and Song brought the van to a halt, then gestured at the child that he should decide which way they went. For a moment, his eyes darted around in confusion, and then he seemed to get the idea.

The boy directed Song to a street where he had seen the long-distance buses unload their cargo of migrant workers from the provinces. Set back from the road there was an unoccupied luxury apartment complex with uniformed guards at the gate. Then a line of run-down shacks with official

123

plaques – the local Greenification Bureau, a branch of the Public Order Patrol. Song pulled into the kerb where the boy indicated, and like a flash the boy had opened the door and was out and running, his heels disappearing through a gate.

Cursing again – the boy for his unpredictability, himself for pursuing the boy – Song locked the car and followed, jogging through the snow so he didn't lose him, wincing at the pain in his injured leg. He saw the boy disappear through a door, and he followed. In front of him, the boy pulled a cord and the room was illuminated by a single light bulb hanging from a flex in the centre of the ceiling. Voices cried out in protest. As Song's eyes adjusted to the light he saw that most of the small space was taken up with beds – hard wooden pallets that created shelving three-deep against the walls. On each of these, small bodies were squirming angrily, hiding their faces against the sudden light. The room reeked of unwashed bodies and cooked cabbage.

The boy stood in the middle of the room and shouted excitedly, the words that had been dammed up for the past twenty-four hours now spewing out of him. Song's ears were not attuned to the dialect, he couldn't keep up, but he knew just from listening that the boy was from Hebei Province, the province that encircled Beijing, and which had pockets of dire poverty. Song counted six children, then saw another face emerge and realized that one of the bunks housed two chil dren. They huddled on their beds hugging their clothes around them, big thick jackets, scarves still wrapped around their necks, listening to the boy, whispering anxiously to each other, the smallest child crying.

Apparently alerted by the noise, a man walked into the room – he did not at first see Song standing in the shadows by the door – and yelled at the children, who fell at once into a fearful silence. Seeing the absentee boy there, he lunged towards him and slapped him hard across the head so that the boy fell to the floor clutching his scalp and crying. At which point Song stepped out of the shadows. There was a shocked pause, and then the man grabbed a metal rod from the floor and swung it at Song's head. Song – stunned by this turn of events so early in the day but with his sense of self-preservation intact – ducked under the rod and grabbed at it with his left hand. He caught and held the bar so that the man – who was clearly vicious but also small – could not use it as a weapon. After a few moments, during which the man tried to wrest the rod from Song's grasp, he gave up and let go. Which left Song armed. It was not what Song had intended, but considering the situation it was not, he thought, necessarily a bad thing.

'Who are you?' the man demanded, reduced to a kind of snarling civility simply by virtue of Song's superior strength, and by the metal rod in

Song's hand. His Chinese was heavily accented and ugly, the kind of Mandarin a peasant spoke when he had to. He looked like a peasant too, dark skinned, with hair that had not been cut in a year, an ill-fitting suit bulging over a twisted spine and layers of padding.

'I found the boy. Who are you? Where are you from?'

The man spat on the floor.

'Where's the boy's sister?' he demanded.

'His sister?'

The boy scrambled to his feet and burst again into a flood of speech, and after a moment the man's face dropped, his jaw hung open. Song stood and watched him, ill at ease. His ears were beginning to pick out meaning from the alien dialect, and what he heard frightened him. Now the man seemed to be questioning the boy, both of them agitated. Several of the children began to moan and cry. The man yelled at the boy, and Song thought that he was accusing him of lying.

'You,' Song prodded the man hard in the shoulder with the metal rod, 'tell me what he's saying.' The man gaped and blinked at Song, as though the boy's story had wiped out all memory of this rod-wielding stranger in their midst.

'Nothing, he's saying nothing,' the man muttered, casting Song a look of abject fear.

'My sister's dead,' the boy howled, sinking to his knees, and this time the words were unmistakable.

For a moment, Song stared at the boy in horror.

This, then, explained the depth of his distress. He had witnessed his sister's murder. Again the twisted man spoke angrily.

'He's lying,' he said, 'he's making it up.'

'The boy's telling the truth,' Song said quietly. 'I saw the pool of blood where she was slaughtered. Yesterday they pulled her body from the lake.'

At this news, the boy started to sob uncontrollably. A woman appeared now in the doorway, looking from Song to the man, to the boy. She was almost square, her shoulders as wide as her legs were long. Her hair came to her shoulders, framing a plump face with small dull eyes. Without saying anything she crossed to the boy, who was still on his knees, and tried to pull him to her, but he pushed her away, and she took a step backwards, putting her hands on her hips.

'What's going on?' she demanded of the man. When he didn't answer, she addressed the boy, who was weeping hopelessly now.

'Did your sister run off to Mummy? Well, she can explain to Mummy why there's no fucking money coming at the end of the year. Or did she find a man to take care of her, the little whore?'

The man opened his mouth and closed it again.

'She'd never seen so much money . . .' the boy wailed. 'He showed it. He was going to give her five hundred *yuan* . . . five hundred . . . he said he would give it to her, he showed it to her.'

'You went with her?' Song crouched down on

the cement floor, so that his eyes were on a level with the boy's. The boy gabbled, but Song was getting used to the dialect now, picking out the vital words, fitting them together.

'She was frightened. She'd never done it before, she didn't want to, she was frightened, but he showed her the money, she was scared.' The boy's huge eyes were raw. 'I hid so that he wouldn't see me, I went with her . . .' His voice gave out, and his head slumped forward to the floor and his shoulders heaved silently.

'Who was he? Did you see him?' Song murmured the questions in the boy's ear. Then he nearly fell forward as a foot landed on his backside. He steadied himself by putting his hand down and realized his fingers were in the man's spittle.

'Who are you?' It was the woman. 'Get out of here.'

Song shifted, wiping his hand on the floor, ignoring her. He leaned over the boy again, speaking close to his ear.

'Who was he? Did you see him? Would you know him again?'

Again the woman's foot jabbed at him. The boy was still prostrate, but he shook his head to and fro. No, he seemed to say, no he had not seen the man.

The woman got hold of Song's ear and tried to pull him away from the boy. Angrily he batted her hand away. He stood and his gaze swept the squalid room. The man was muttering to himself, his mouth appearing to work involuntarily, 'Dead. Murdered. She's dead.'

'Dead?' The woman echoed, sharply. 'The girl's dead?'

She saw the answer on their faces, and her jaw slackened in shock.

Song's mouth was dry. He looked at the children. They were huddled together. The younger ones were still crying, noses thick with snot, some of the older children talked agitatedly in low voices. He looked down at the boy, squirming miserably on the floor.

'You,' he walked over to the man. 'You're his boss.'

The man stared at him, then nodded, running his tongue over his lips.

'And this woman is the sister's boss, right? Who is she, your sister? Your wife?'

There was no response but a flicker of the eyes.

'Just you and the wife? With so many kids to watch?'

'And my brother, three of us.'

'You're from Hebei,' Song said.

Again the jerk of the head.

'Where does the boy's family live?'

Behind him, Song heard the woman's voice: 'Shut up, you half-wit, don't tell him anything.'

'Didn't you hear? She's dead,' he snapped, casting her a venomous glance. He took a breath. 'The boy's mother lives in a village called Xiaoshanzi in Longhua County, in Hebei. His father's in jail.'

'How much does the boy get from you?'

'A hundred a month,' the man breathed softly, his breath foul, 'to be paid into the hands of his mother once a year at Spring Festival. The same for the sister. We take care of food and board.'

'I can see that. You're very generous.'

'It's a better life than they have at home.' The woman's voice was sharp, defensive. 'This is their big chance. They get to know the business, they'll have a future.'

'That's what you told their mother, is it?'

She didn't answer, except to spit on the floor at his feet.

Song pulled his wallet from his pocket. He took out a business card, and all the cash he was carrying, which was a few hundred *yuan*, trying to look as though there was plenty more where that came from. The man made a grab for it, but Song snatched it out of his grasp and held it in front of the man's face.

'This goes towards your train tickets. Take the boy back to his mother, and tell her what happened to her daughter,' he said. 'Bring proof that the boy is with his mother to my office, along with receipts for your travel expenses. I'll pay them all, and you'll get an extra five hundred on top.'

He folded the money around the business card, and the man seized it, gabbling, 'I'll do it. I'll take the boy home. His mother must have her son back. I'll bring you a photograph. The boy can telephone you. He'll tell you I have fulfilled my responsibilities. We know where to find you.' He shoved the notes in his pocket and held the card reverently in his hands.

At once, Song regretted giving this man his business card, his name, his address, a way of finding him. But he told himself that the man had no more interest in talking to the police than he did. And what else could he do? Song could feel the boy's eyes on him, and he turned away. His mouth tasted bitter, and he felt dread sitting heavily in his stomach.

He spoke to the woman.

'If the boy stays in Beijing, he'll be a liability to you,' he said. 'The police are looking for him to help with the murder enquiry.'

She did not reply, but he saw the word 'police' register, and the words 'murder enquiry'. She was not stupid. She was a monster, but her monstrosity lay in the cold calculation of profit and loss, and in the computation of risk. In that lay the only hope for the boy.

He turned his back on them and walked away. Outside, the snow was still falling, slow and heavy. Song was surprised to find himself stricken with despair. He could barely lift his feet to move across the dirt yard, and there was a band tight around his chest. He could not fool himself. There was no hope for the boy. There had been no hope for the boy since his mother bore him into penury then sold him into beggary. There was only the reality of cash. A few hundred *yuan* placed in the hand of the boy's boss was like money burned. It would not be spent on a train ticket. Song might get a phone call, he might get a photograph, he might even get a wad of receipts thrust into his hand. But receipts could be bought and sold, and photographs faked. The boy would not see his mother again. Song could feel their eyes on his back. He kept walking, because he could not for the life of him think what else to do.

CHAPTER 8

Next morning I awoke to find snow falling from a congested sky. I took a taxi to a residential compound to the south-east of the city centre which went by the unlikely name of Post-Modern City. When I stepped out onto the pavement I had to tip my head back to look up at the stark white apartment towers which seemed to vanish into the smog at around the fifteenth floor. It looked plain modern to me.

I'd found Derek Sumner's home telephone number in my notebook, scribbled by one of his colleagues whom I'd interviewed about the Kelness negotiations before the murder. Derek Sumner's grieving widow, Zhuli, had answered the phone to me herself, her voice small and bewildered. Her English was fluent, but I wasn't sure she understood that I was a journalist, and that I wanted to interview her for television. She agreed to see me, but I put the phone down feeling dirty, as though I was taking advantage. She should have someone else answering her phone, I thought, protecting her from people like me. I would talk to her first and make sure she understood what she was agreeing to before I produced a camera.

I found Tower B, took the lift to the twenty-first floor, rapped on the door to apartment D, and waited apprehensively, delving in my bag for lipsalve. In the space of twenty-four hours the Beijing air seemed to have extracted all moisture from my skin and lips. I rapped again, and after a moment the door opened and a young woman appeared. Zhuli's black hair was cut neatly around her face. Her eyes were pink-rimmed and almost swollen shut. Underneath a white smock I could see the curve of her belly where her baby lay curled inside her. She frowned at me, perplexed.

'I'm Robin Ballantyne,' I held out my hand, 'we spoke on the telephone.'

Recognition dawned in her eyes and she reached out and touched my hand, her fingers barely brushing against mine, then stood back, opening the door wider, and murmured, 'Yes, yes, please come in.'

I stepped inside the apartment and found myself in a double-height space, with floor-to-ceiling windows. Beyond the glass the air was thick and grey, the snowflakes like a veil. Way below my feet the faint outline of south-east Beijing lay like an architect's model, flat as a board, all straight lines and block-like buildings. It took a moment for the sensation of height to hit me and then I thought I would fall with the snow, that my body would pass through the illusion of glass, and that I would plummet twenty-one floors to the ground way below. I grasped the back of a chair and turned away. How could anyone choose to live up here? I was annoyed with myself. I had thought I'd brought my vertigo under control years ago. But the events of the past few days had unnerved me.

'I'm sorry,' I said to Zhuli, who was watching me apprehensively, 'I'm afraid I'm not good with heights.'

She nodded, lowered herself carefully onto a sofa that looked more Swedish than Chinese, and sat twisting her hands nervously in her lap. I chose to sit in a matching chair close to her although it faced the window. I saw that Zhuli's eyes were fixed on a framed black-and-white photograph that hung on the wall.

I recognized Derek Sumner from the British newspapers – he had a broad friendly smile with dimples that carved swathes through his cheeks, and bright eyes under heavy brows. His hair was spiky and messy. He looked like a lot of fun. He was thirty-five years old when his head was severed from his body. In the photograph he had his arm around Zhuli, and both of them were dressed in down jackets. Behind them was a log cabin, and climbing the sheer mountainside above that was something even I could identify as the Great Wall.

'Where was that taken?' I asked.

'It's a place called Huanghuashan,' Zhuli said.

'Huanghuashan,' I echoed, trying to copy her

pronunciation of the strange word. 'It looks beautiful.'

'Nelson Li has a house there. He invited us for a weekend. We were very happy there.'

A powerful memory overwhelmed me. In an ex-council house a world away, my twins six months out of my belly, I had sat and looked at a similar photograph, and known that the man in the picture was dead. I sat silently with Zhuli for a few moments. It seemed the most natural thing in the world to reach out and take her hand, and she gripped me tightly. She seemed terribly alone. Together we watched the mesmerizing descent of the snow. After a while she let go of my hand.

'I'm not sure how well I explained why I'm here—' I started to say, but she interrupted, speaking quietly.

'I'm sorry I have wasted your time. When you telephoned me I thought you just wanted to talk to me to write about Derek in the newspaper, but my friend explained that the Corporation is a television company in England. I meant to ring you to cancel because . . .' and here her composure began to desert her, her chin shuddering violently, 'I cannot . . . speak on television about Derek.'

'I don't want you to,' I said, suddenly sure that I meant it. I was losing my nerve, I thought. Damien would be sitting here sweet-talking her into an on-camera interview, whereas I was beating a rapid retreat. 'It's me who should be apologizing. I shouldn't have intruded. But perhaps . . . could I just talk to you for a few minutes? I mean, not for attribution, I won't quote you. Just for background, so I understand about Derek's life here.'

She scrutinized my face with her teary eyes, then nodded. I hesitated. I didn't know where to start. She lifted her hands from her lap and rested them on her tummy.

'When is your baby due?' I asked.

'In six weeks, but I think maybe the baby will come early, because of what has happened.'

'I'm so sorry about your husband,' I said. 'Do you have someone here with you? Someone to help you?'

'My mother came at once,' she said. 'She is out buying groceries. Derek's mother will arrive tomorrow. She wants to take his body . . .' Her jaw shuddered. 'It is still with the police . . . they are . . . investigating . . . his body. There were rats . . .' She fixed me with a stare of such painful intensity that I could not bear it and I had to look away. 'They won't let me see him. Rats were eating his body . . . his eyes . . .'

Then her poise gave way completely and her eyes flooded with tears which ran down her cheeks, and her mouth opened in silent agony. Her pain was tangible, it flowed from her and gathered around her and filled the room. The tidal wave of her emotion engulfed me and I found myself unable to speak. I reached out to touch her shoulder but this time she pulled away.

'I'll make us a cup of tea,' I whispered. Blindly, distressed by Zhuli's grief, I pushed open doors until I found a bright, airy kitchen. I stepped inside, took a deep breath, and was startled to find a Chinese girl in there already, wiping down the worktops, her long hair tied back in a pony-tail. She looked up, startled, and with a jolt of horror I realized how much she looked like the girl in the lake. She even had a small blemish under her eye. She looked about sixteen, and terri-fied. She too must have felt and feared the sense of tragedy that pervaded the apartment.

'Tea,' I murmured, and mimed sipping, and she looked relieved. She filled the kettle, and opened cupboards, bringing out boxes of teabags, and a teapot and cups, putting them on a tray in front of me. I said 'thank you' in English, because I didn't know how to say even that in Chinese, and she gave me a nervous smile, picked up a mop, and left the room.

I waited while the kettle boiled, unwilling to go back into the other room. I tried to detach myself from Zhuli's pain. I concentrated on the kitchen. It was a lot neater than mine, where the walls were plastered with paintings Hannah and William brought home from school. There was a notepad stuck to the fridge door, pencil attached, and someone had scrawled on it in a masculine hand, 'dinner party – Sunday'. Sunday was today. I inspected the boxes of tea. I thought that perhaps Zhuli would like to drink Chinese tea, and I spent

138

a few moments scrutinizing a paper bag full of what looked like dried flowers, but I didn't know what to do with them so I settled for Tetley's.

When the tea had brewed I carried the tray through. Zhuli was curled on the sofa, a tissue balled in her fist, her face drained of all colour. I placed the tray on the coffee table, poured the tea, and handed her a cup. She looked surprised.

'There was a girl in your kitchen,' I said, 'and she helped me to find things.'

'That's our *ayi*, our maid, she cooks and cleans for us.'

'She looks very young.'

'She told me she's eighteen,' Zhuli said. 'Peasant girls look younger than city girls; they are more innocent.'

I wished then that we could have sat and talked about her *ayi*, or about anything at all except murder.

'Where did you meet Derek?' I asked.

Her eyes, tired and sad and unwilling, sought out my face.

'We worked in the same building,' she said eventually. 'I am an accountant, I work for a German company. My office is on the same floor as Derek's. We met in the lift, and in the canteen, and then we became friends. I told him my job was very boring, all numbers, and that I liked hiking and camping, and when he said that was what he liked too I thought he was joking, but he wasn't. I used to take him to the countryside . . .'

She paused for a long moment then continued, 'And I took him to Hangzhou to meet my family. My parents thought he was very funny, they liked him very much. We were married a year ago.'

Her mouth worked and her forehead creased with the effort of holding back tears.

'Can you tell me about the night he was killed?' I asked. I felt brutal, but I had to ask.

'There were visitors from his company in Beijing for the negotiations,' she said, 'and they went to the Lotus Pool. It's very smart, very expensive. I don't know . . . they ate their food and then they left . . .'

Her voice trailed off. She was staring into space, and the misery on her face had been replaced by bitterness.

'None of his friends can tell me which way Derek went,' she said, her voice hard. 'Ever since he got in trouble for saying those things about rebuilding the steel mill in China his friends have been angry with him. They gave him the cold shoulder for no reason. He was so embarrassed, so humiliated, and his friends, they did not support him . . .'

'Not one of them saw which way he went when he left the restaurant?'

'Nobody knows if he was coming home to me, or if he was going back to the office – sometimes he eats and goes back to finish something off, he is so conscientious . . . I think this is what you should do, you should ask them yourself, Colin and Owen and Angus and Karen: Why did none of you share a taxi with him? Derek loves to be with people, he would never choose to be on his own. Why didn't he get into a taxi with them? I don't believe he walked off on his own. Why would he do that? I think he would go for a drink with them, he would drop them at their hotel and then come back to me . . .' She shrugged helplessly.

'Did he have enemies, had he argued with anyone?'

'How could a good man like that, a man like Derek, have enemies, someone who would do something like this?' Her voice was full of anguish. 'The police tell me nothing, the embassy tells me nothing . . .'

She could manage no more, and I could push her no further.

'Where can I find Derek's colleagues, the ones who were with him that night?'

She shook her head.

'I think Owen and Colin have gone back to England already. They are based in Kelness.'

'What about Angus Perry? I spoke to him once when he was in Kelness.'

'Angus spends almost all his time in Beijing now. He has a serviced apartment in the Rainbow Hotel, and Karen lives in the Grand Canal building on Guanghua Road.'

I got her to write down Karen Turvey's address for me – I had to put the paper in front of her and place the pen in her hand. My visit had drained what little energy she had.

I got up to leave and she struggled to her feet to see me to the door. She had her hand on the door handle when her mobile rang.

I suppose I could have let myself out, but I didn't.

She pulled her phone from a pocket in her smock and took the call.

'Yes, yes, I am Zhuli . . . Hello, Mr Nash . . .' She listened intently, her forehead creasing. 'I see . . . I understand your meaning. Can you repeat his name? How do you spell that?' She closed her eyes in concentration. 'I don't think . . . no, I don't remember Derek ever talking about a man with this name . . . I will, of course, I will give it some thought. Please will you let me know what you find out? Yes, of course, thank you. No . . .' Her eyes went to me, and I thought that Mr Nash, whoever he was, had warned her against speaking to journalists. She said goodbye and hung up, her face an awful mixture of confusion and hope and fear.

'Are you all right?' I asked.

She nodded briskly.

'Mr Nash is trying to help me find out what happened to Derek,' she said, 'that's all.'

'Is he from the embassy?' I hazarded. There had been something in her tone that suggested officialdom.

She nodded once but said nothing, reaching out to open the door. I pressed my card, with the number of my Beijing mobile scrawled on it, into

142

her hand. 'If you think of anything you feel I should know, please telephone me,' I urged.

When she had shut the door behind me and I could walk away, I felt the burden of catastrophe rise slightly from my shoulders, but it did not go away completely. Instead it hovered around me, like a dark winged shape, so that I could sense its presence constantly, just at the corner of my eye.

Karen Turvey didn't answer the door of her apartment, but a Chinese neighbour returning from a workout told me in good English that I'd find her in the gym on the third floor of the building across the road.

I walked into the marble lobby, took a lift, and ignored the young woman at the gym's front desk, who addressed me with a heavily accented, 'Can I help you?' The place was busy, with young well-dressed Chinese men and women wandering in and out, and that must have kept the receptionist occupied, because no one chased me and demanded to see my membership card.

Inside, the gym was as big as a football field, and well supplied with machines, each wired up to a personal TV monitor. I scanned the room. There was only one Caucasian, long auburn curls tied back from her face with a bandanna. She was running on a treadmill, a towel flung over the bar, her forehead dripping with sweat. I could hear her grunting breaths. I approached her.

'Hi,' I shouted over the drone of the machine.

She glanced down at me, her brow creasing in irritation.

'What?' she shouted back.

'I'm looking for Karen Turvey.'

She punched the buttons on the machine and it gradually slowed to a walk. 'What do you want?'

'I'm really sorry to interrupt like this. My name is Robin Ballantyne, I'm a journalist for the Corporation. Zhuli Sumner told me where to find you, she said I should talk to you.'

Her face darkened and she carried on walking, her long legs taking great strides. If I hadn't mentioned Zhuli I know she'd have had me thrown out then and there.

After a moment she gave a huge, explosive sigh and switched off the machine, snatching at the towel and mopping her forehead and her neck.

'What do you want to talk to me about?'

'About Derek,' I told her. 'Zhuli said I should speak to you.'

'You've seen Zhuli?'

'This morning.'

'Is she okay?'

'Not really, no,' I said.

'No,' Karen said brusquely, 'well, how could she be? I don't know why I asked. Look, I don't know whether I should be talking to you.'

'Just on background, not on film,' I said, my heart sinking. It was clear to me that Karen Turvey wouldn't agree to be interviewed on camera, certainly not right away, but a television documentary needs pictures. There was a limit to how many interviews I could write off before I would end up limping back to London empty-handed.

'There are some things I don't understand,' I said.

'Welcome to the club. Look, I'm not going to say anything on the record, I'll tell you that up front. If you want to come and get a coffee with me, that's up to you.'

I hung around while she showered. When Karen reappeared, her hair still damp, we went to the ground floor where there was a Starbucks cafe set back from the lobby. I ordered an Americano, and she had the same, and we settled at the only vacant table. I looked around at the dark green sofas, and the laptops on tables, and the glittering lobby beyond.

'We could be anywhere in the world,' I said.

'Globalization,' she said with satisfaction, waving her hand towards the smartly dressed Chinese who sipped lattes and frappuccinos, 'and the new middle class.'

I thought about the maze of alleys by the lake-side, the migrant families crushed into slums, and the stench from the gutters.

'When Derek Sumner talked about rebuilding Kelness in the countryside and employing Chinese to work there, I'm guessing he wasn't talking about the people you go to the gym with,' I said.

Karen looked taken aback.

'He did say it, didn't he?' I asked gently. 'You were there. If you say he didn't, I'll believe you.'

She looked away from me, down into her half-empty cup.

'It's very sensitive . . .' she said eventually.

'With all due respect, it's difficult to ask anything about Kelness these days that isn't sensitive,' I said mildly. 'I suppose I could ask you about radio-active contamination?'

She shook her head and for an instant she closed her eyes.

'Of course he said it,' she said dully, 'the poor stupid guy.'

'He said all of it? About how Kelness should be dismantled and rebuilt in the Chinese country-side?'

'He said it sarcastically.' She kept her voice low and her eyes flicked around the neighbouring tables. 'Derek was capable of saying stupid things when he'd had a couple of drinks. Like most people. And at these banquets you get force-fed alcohol – have you tried *baijiu*?'

I shook my head.

'It's like lighter fluid, it's served in tiny glasses like thimbles. But they keep filling up your glass, and to be polite you're supposed to empty your glass every time there's a toast, which is every other minute. It's calculated to put you at a disad-vantage.'

'But Derek must have been to banquets before. He must have known what he was doing, surely?'

'Of course. He'd developed a technique. He'd hold the *baijiu* in his mouth and spit it into his water glass, pretending that he was taking a drink of water.'

'So why didn't it work this time?'

'Nelson Li spotted what he was doing and called him on it. He turned it into a big joke. So Derek not only had to drink the stuff, Li forced him to catch up with them and drink all the toasts he'd spat out. Derek had already had a gin and tonic before dinner. So he got drunk and he got careless, and he got pissed off with Nelson Li for forcing him to drink. So he drank more, until instead of being the company man he usually is, he made this sarcastic crack about how great it would be to dismantle Kelness and rebuild it here, and how wonderful it was to be able to exploit the workforce. And then two days later it blew up in his face. He was mortified.'

For a moment I said nothing, struck by her choice of word. Mortified. Killed by humiliation.

'Kelness backed him,' I said. 'They said he'd been misquoted.'

She gave a small, humourless laugh.

'This is all off the record, right?' She waited for my nod, then went on, 'Okay, off the record they had to, didn't they? What else could they have said?'

'They could have replaced him.'

'Nelson Li likes him – liked him – really liked him. Derek had been round to his house with

147

Zhuli for a private dinner, Derek knew the whole family. Li's daughter, Pearl, is a really smart kid. She works for her father and I'm sure the son, Nixon, will do the same. It's a family business. You can't beat the kind of personal relationship Derek built up, not here. Kelness management knew if they got rid of Derek they'd blow the deal. Not to mention that if the management replaced him it would have been as good as confirming that he'd said what the newspapers claimed.'

'If the management had replaced him it might have reassured the workforce that they weren't being sold down the river.'

She pulled a face.

'The workforce will believe what they want to believe. Maybe they'll keep their jobs, maybe they won't. Something was going to make the penny drop. If it wasn't what Derek said, it would have been something else.' She nodded towards a woman in a beige uniform who was mopping the floor, then at another who was wiping down the mirrored walls of the lift lobby, and a third who was wiping down tables. 'Look around you. Labour's cheap. I pay my *ayi* about a hundred quid a month, and for her that's a fortune. She's left her kid in the countryside with her parents so that she can come to the city to earn that kind of money. Those women mopping up over there are probably getting half that. They work all month for the kind of money we'd spend on a bad meal out. It's all very well to be superior about it, but where do you think all the cheap stuff in the super markets back home comes from? All the clothes, and kids' shoes, and their toys? Cheap Chinese labour, women like those, earning fifty quid a month. And why? Because if they stayed in their village they'd more likely earn fifteen quid a month. Their fields are all dried up, or their land's been taken by the local officials to build a golf course, so they come here or to the other big cities. To them, the streets are paved with gold. Kelness is no better or worse than any other company – they live or die by the market, and in a global market there's no such thing as a minimum wage. If that means taking advantage of cheap Chinese labour, so be it.'

'You were at the dinner on the night he died too.'

'I was.' She sighed. 'It goes round and round in my head.'

'Zhuli is upset that Derek was on his own at the end of the evening, she can't understand why he didn't leave in a taxi with someone else, or go for a drink. She says you'd all been giving him the cold shoulder.'

Karen stared again at her coffee cup, and this time her expression was one of devastation.

'If I could change it, I would,' she said.

'Is Zhuli right, were you freezing him out?'

Karen took a deep breath.

'He'd made things difficult for all of us. Not just that. I was there at the banquet, so I know he was being sarcastic, but a couple of my colleagues who weren't at the banquet think he was seriously suggesting dismantling Kelness and firing all the workers. Angus and Owen, for instance, they've both lived in the town most of their lives, if the mill goes, their friends and families go under.'

'But why would they think Derek would do that?'

She gazed at me for a moment.

'Angus said to me he thought Derek was sucking up to Nelson Li, hoping for a job with him here. He had a Chinese wife, they'd bought an apartment here, they were going to have a kid. Angus thought maybe they wanted to make a life here.'

'Do you think anyone hated him enough to kill him?'

'I don't know anyone who hated him, full stop.'

'You said people at Kelness had cooled towards him.'

'I said cooled. I didn't say they killed him.'

'That night—'

'Look, I don't want to give you the wrong impression. People may have been feeling a bit pissed off with Derek, but we're all grown-ups. We had dinner together, it was perfectly civil. The food was great, the restaurant was gorgeous, we had a private room, and I had a go at them because they all wanted to watch football on the telly. Nobody argued, nobody so much as raised their voices at each other. When we'd finished we went outside and the lads let me have the first taxi, so I didn't see what happened after that, but no one was in such a snit at Derek that they'd have refused to share a taxi with him.'

'Can you think of any reason he was in that woodland?'

She shook her head.

'Not one.' She glanced at her watch. 'I need to get going, this has taken far too long.'

'I'm sorry, I'll let you go, but just now you said that Angus thought Derek was sucking up to Nelson Li, and you told me yourself how much Li liked him, how he'd had him to dinner at his house. Might it be possible that Angus is right, that Derek was trying to secure a future with Nelson Li, and that it was Derek who was passing company information to Nelson Li?'

'I think that's ridiculous,' she said firmly.

'Is this the first leak?' I asked. 'Or have there been more, things that haven't got into the press?'

Karen's face went white. She pushed her chair back from the table and stood up.

'Look, it wouldn't have been my choice to speak to you at all, but Zhuli sent you so I've told you everything I know. Don't you dare twist it so that it looks like Derek Sumner was some kind of traitor selling dirty secrets. He was a decent man, and that's all that Zhuli and her kid have left.'

'You didn't answer my question,' I said.

151

She looked around her in exasperation, then came and leaned over to speak quietly in my ear.

'If you start to fuck with his reputation,' she said slowly and clearly, 'I will personally find you and fuck with yours.'

CHAPTER 9

Song's taxi pulled up opposite the train station. Below the monumental pillars of the Stalinist facade the forecourt was heaving. 'It's easier if you get out and walk.' The driver nodded towards the pedestrian bridge over the six-lane highway. Song handed him the fare then got out of the car, looking up at the overpass. It was thick with people weighed down with bags and bedding rolls and food making their way through the snow to the station. Song's guts twisted with anger that he should be forced to join this exodus from the city.

He started up the steps, moving with the flow of people. It was like riding an escalator: you couldn't stop or even slow down or there would be a pile-up, you couldn't race ahead or you'd have someone spit curses in your face. Song had no luggage, not even a change of clothes. He hadn't bathed properly since the night of the fire, and even the clothes he'd borrowed from Wolf felt stiff and stale. The long black coat had gathered dust from the floor of the beggars' hovel. In his wallet he had an ID card, an ATM card, and he'd

153

had Wolf bring him the stash of petty cash from the safe in the office.

He kept his head down, because his height attracted immediate interest. The train station was always crawling with police on the lookout for trouble. He spotted a plainclothes cop on the far end of the bridge, and then one halfway along, standing still against the tide of humanity, watching. He didn't slow down, because to do so would be to draw attention to himself. Better just to shuffle on with the crowd, join the queue in front of the ticket office, join the queue at the platform, take a seat if there was one, stand in the aisle if not, never break ranks.

At the far end of the bridge he moved down the spiral staircase that led to the station forecourt, still keeping his place in the formation, his feet hitting the metal steps in time with those in front and behind.

Then, as he reached the bottom of the staircase, a shot of pure pain hammered into his side below his ribs, jerking him backwards, jolting his muscles into spasm, paralysing his voice even as he tried to shout out. He collapsed clasping at his side, gasping.

Hands grabbed him and pulled him onto his knees, and a voice jeered in his ear, 'Bit of a shock to bump into me, eh, fucker?'

The voice flooded Song's blood with hatred. He twisted to face his attacker, a young man whose belly had already begun to swell with beer and whose neck looked too thick for anyone's head, but especially for his own, which was tiny, with eyes like raisins and a flat nose like a button. The face, the raisin eyes – Song had last seen them all in police uniform. Psycho Wang was flanked by two thugs who moved towards Song, cutting off escape. Around them, people watched from a distance or moved on. Several of them had seen what Song himself had discovered, that all three men clasped the rubber handles of short electric truncheons. Silently Song thanked the heavens for Wolf's thick coat that had spared him from worse pain.

'We've got a car waiting.' Psycho Wang's voice was thick with malice. 'Your father-in-law wants to see you.'

Song roared and lunged at him from his knees, but Psycho Wang just stepped aside and laughed, so that Song fell forwards on all fours. Around him he heard people tittering. Song saw Wang's feet step towards him, then the electric baton appeared in front of his eyes, just an inch from his face. Snow fell softly on his head. He heard Wang's voice in his ear.

'You get into the car, or I'll shove this up your arse.'

The car was a black Audi with shaded windows, no number plates, and a siren that shrieked. They had jammed Song into the middle, pressed up against Psycho Wang, who leaned heavily against him as the car swung back and forth across three lanes of traffic, the driver's foot pressed down on the accelerator. On the other side of him one of the thugs picked his ears with his fingernail.

Song closed his eyes. He remembered how it had felt when his fist entered the soft pillow of Wang's belly. For so long he'd tried to banish the memory, the pleasure of causing pain had been so intense that it had frightened him, but now, with Wang hard up against him, he couldn't help himself. The woman was a migrant worker in her forties, one of hundreds, carrying her bedroll on her back at the railway station, arriving in the capital to look for work. Wang had offered her thirty *yuan* – a day's wages – to carry a plastic bag of heroin to an address in the south-west of the city. There, Wang and his officers had lain in wait for her, grabbing her, finding the heroin, charging her with trafficking. This was a favourite pastime of Wang. The point, of course, was to boost Wang's quota of drug busts. But instead of being crushed by the enormity of the injustice that had befallen her, the woman had cursed and sworn and yelled about him from the cells. Song heard the noises. He went to see what was going on and found the woman on the floor, curled into a ball, trying to protect her face, which Wang was kicking, his foot moving back and forth with mechanical regularity. Song had entered the cell. He remembered how satisfaction had burst through him as his fist connected with Wang's gut, remembered the feel of knuckle in fat, the look on Wang's face, the moue of the mouth and the explosion of air as the fist drove through to the muscle, to the diaphragm.

Memories like these were best kept buried, Song thought. If he began to take pleasure in them he would become an animal, no better than Wang. Song focused on his heart rate, willing it down. If Detective Chen's intention was to arrest him for murder, he couldn't use hired muscle. It didn't look good on the paperwork, and that was one thing Chen and he shared: they liked their paper-work in order.

If, on the other hand, Detective Chen planned to leave Song half-dead in a ditch with his teeth scattered in the snow, then goons would be perfect for the task in hand. Through half-closed eyes Song followed the route. They were travelling out of town towards the east, weaving from lane to lane, moving dangerously fast, leaving the traffic behind them. Around them, the landscape was all dried-up farms and stray dogs. Snow coated the trees and lay thick across the fields and swirled as they passed.

They came to a halt. Wang pushed Song out of the car, just as he had pushed him in, and as he straightened up Song saw that the Audi was parked outside a grimy three-storey building which stood on its own in the middle of fields. The windows were boarded up, but faded hoard-ings were painted with pictures of blonde women in bikinis advertising karaoke, business facilities, and massage. The name of the place, the Lucky Valley Pleasure Palace, was spelled out in dusty golden characters above the doorway, which was framed in plasterboard Greek columns. Song remembered the name. It was a private club which, two years before, had become notorious in a corruption case involving a city official who had famously been discovered to be keeping twenty-nine mistresses stashed around the city. Since his disgrace, the Lucky Valley Pleasure Palace had fallen on hard times.

'Move!' Wang ordered, shoving him towards the entrance. Song ignored him, turning slowly to look to east and west and south and north, seeking a way out, but there was nowhere to run. The land stretched open and flat and uncompromising in every direction. There was no forest to give him cover, no village in which to take refuge, not a soul who would witness his fate. Too late, he realized his delay had pushed Wang beyond reason.

'Move, you fucker,' Wang shrieked, his arm with the cattle prod reaching towards Song. Again the electric shock kicked through him, the current searing his muscles, burning his head momentarily clean of all thought.

The Lucky Valley Pleasure Palace was dark and cold. Weakened now by Wang's attack, and flanked by the thugs, Song followed Wang through a ball-room, past a stage curtained in heavy red drapes

158

with stone pillars carved in the shape of naked women on either side. A glittering disco ball turned silently over their heads. They made their way through a shadowy bar, bottles of liquor ranged in front of a mirror, the glasses smudged. Their footsteps echoed in the empty space. They climbed a staircase, its carpet grubby and threadbare, and processed along a corridor lined with doors to what looked like guest rooms. Wang stopped outside room number fifty-eight, and rapped on the door. There was a grunt from inside, the door opened, and a young woman in a short waitress's dress emerged, glancing in embarrassment at the delegation of men. She scurried off down the hallway, arms wrapped around her chest.

Wang muttered an obscenity and shoved Song at the door.

Inside, Detective Chen was sitting on a sofa, hunched forward over a plate of sliced fresh fruit on the coffee table. The room smelled of mould. There were lights on in here, a fluorescent desk light and a wall fitting above the sofa. At the far end of the room was a kingsize bed. It faced a large flat-screen television on which a pornographic film was frozen, coitus interruptus. To the left of the sofa a door opened onto a bathroom, and Song saw a sunken jacuzzi. Lina's father looked up, his face lit ghoulishly by the fluorescent light.

'I'm glad you accepted my invitation.'
'Is this the new police headquarters?'

'You could say these are my private offices,' Chen said. 'There are too many prying eyes around the police station. This is my personal business, yours and mine.'

He waved Song to an upholstered chair, but Song shook his head and remained standing. Detective Chen had been a good-looking man, clean cut and handsome, but the ruddiness of the complexion could no longer be put down to good health. Good food and alcohol had turned boyish cheeks into jowls. His hair, dyed jet black and as dry as straw, was bouffant above his lined forehead, and his eyes were rimmed with red.

'Did you kill her?' Chen's voice was heavy with contempt, and his anger rose even as he spoke. 'That's what I need to know. Did you kill her?'

Song didn't trust himself to speak. His fist itched to bury itself in Chen's belly.

'The tart in the massage parlour told our officers that you were there. She didn't know your name, but she knew where you lived.' Detective Chen spoke rapidly, looking up at Song. 'Your car was parked there, it was listed on the police report. You think I don't know your cheap sardine can of a car? You think I don't know your licence plate? The witnesses described a tall man, broadshouldered, with a shaven head, brandishing a knife and carrying a boy. Did you think I was stupid?'

'You always know exactly what you're doing.'

'Did you kill her? Did you screw her and slit

her throat and dump her in the lake? Is that how you get your kicks now you don't have my daughter?' His voice weakened and took on a whine. 'Are you trying to ruin me?'

'To ruin you?'

'My own son-in-law.'

'Ex-son-in-law.'

'The father of my grandson. Would you ruin your own son?'

'I don't kill women,' Song said quietly. Detective Chen looked away, towards the door, then back to Song.

'What were you doing there, then?'

'I was staking out the massage parlour, that's all. I was in the wrong place at the wrong time. I heard a scream, I saw the tent on fire. There was blood in there and clothing. No body. I saved the boy from burning.'

'Why did you run?'

'They were shouting at me that I was a murderer. I wasn't thinking straight.'

'Why take the boy?'

'I couldn't get rid of him. He wouldn't let go of me.'

'Witnesses saw you waving a knife around.'

'I took it from the boy. He must have found it on the ground. He was terrified, he didn't know what he was doing. He'd have had my nose off with it if I hadn't taken it from him.'

'What happened to the knife?'

'I dropped it in the woods.'

Detective Chen reached for a pack of cigarettes and lit one. He put it in his mouth and inhaled.

'We didn't find it,' he said.

There was a moment's silence.

'If you send me to the firing squad,' Song said, 'the killer will keep killing.'

'You think I want to send you to the firing squad?' Detective Chen took the cigarette from his mouth and raised his head to glare at Song. 'I have a daughter and a grandson . . . I have myself to protect. It will ruin me to send you to the firing squad.' He hunched over his cigarette, muttering to himself, 'And it will ruin me not to send you to the firing squad . . .'

'What do you mean?'

His former father-in-law turned his head this way and that, and he scratched his cheek. At last, reluctantly, he confided, 'The foreign ministry is breathing fire down my neck. There's a slaughtered foreigner, women with their throats cut. I have to give them someone. Someone has to pay.'

'Are you sure it's the same killer? A man who preys on women and then who breaks the pattern, killing a foreign man? What's the evidence for that?'

Detective Chen didn't seem to hear him. He chewed his lip, gazing into the ashtray.

'I need to ask you something. I've seen where you were parked that night. Who else was parked there?'

Song frowned, thinking back, seeing the lights of the brothel, the women inside, and on the street outside . . .

'A black Santana with police plates.'

Detective Chen stared at him, then swore violently. He pushed himself up from the sofa and started to pace.

'Did you get the number?'

Song shook his head. In fact Song thought he could recall most of the digits of the licence number, and even the order in which they came. But he had seen Detective Chen manipulate partial evidence to fit a suspect, and he would not volunteer it.

'It's a cop gone bad, that's what they're saying,' Detective Chen told Song. 'A black Santana with police plates was parked nearby when the first woman turned up, on the rubbish heap by the public toilets behind the bars. No one took the number, but they're willing to swear they were police plates.'

'Police plates can be stolen and sold on, or faked. All you need is the right friend in the right place.'

'I know that,' Detective Chen sneered. 'I'm not a fool, although I'm being treated like one. They're talking about setting up a special serial killer squad, to come in over my head.'

'A serial killer squad?'

'It will be run by little boys with university degrees who think if we describe the bastard's mother, or discover that he wet the bed, he'll walk

163

through the door and introduce himself and say, "Yes, officer, you're so right, I wet the bed, I torture cats and kill them and film it and put the pictures on the internet, and I knew you'd find me because there are only thirteen million people out there on the streets.'"

'He tortures cats?' Song grimaced.

Detective Chen waved his hand as if it was unimportant. 'Cats!' he said dismissively. 'We think he may have been attacking women in Shijingshan, near the steelworks. One woman has disappeared, another was mutilated, but she escaped.'

'Are the victims raped?' Song asked.

'The bitch on the scrap heap near the lake was a prostitute, she's full of DNA. Did the same man fuck her and kill her? You tell me.'

'What about the boy's sister? Was there DNA on her?'

Detective Chen gazed at Song. He smiled unpleasantly.

'So that's who she was, the one in the lake, she was the boy's sister?'

Song gave a curt nod, angry at himself for telling this man anything at all.

'His sister . . . so . . . that's very interesting. His sister, then . . . the two of them from out of town?'

'I don't know,' Song lied.

'Here with their parents, I'll bet? Their father working on a construction site, children begging and stealing during the day?'

Song gave a small shrug.

'They must be staying in some slum somewhere near the lake.'

Song said nothing. Detective Chen gazed at him, a muscle of annoyance working in his jaw.

'The girl, the sister,' he said eventually, 'if there was rape we might have got DNA from the vagina although she was in the water. The pathologist didn't find any, but it doesn't mean much, it may have simply washed away. There might have been semen caught in the clothes, but everything below the waist was gone . . . You say there was clothing in the tent?' He looked up at Song.

Song nodded, lips tight.

'So the clothing must have burned in the fire.'

Chen came and stood in front of Song, and Song could smell his sour breath.

'I had the tart from the massage parlour sent back to Wuhan. Your car's in the pound. I've done what I can. I'm the only one who knows it points to you.'

'You're protecting me?' Song almost laughed.

'What I have done I can undo.'

Song thought about that.

'What do you want from me?'

'You know what I want. I want the boy. He's my witness. He must have seen the man who killed his sister, he can identify him, he'll find my murderer.'

'I don't have the boy . . . He ran away.'

'You let him go?'

'He ran off in the woods.' The lie came easily, fluently. 'I couldn't follow him in the dark.'

Chen stared. His face turned grim. He sat back down and reached for his cigarette.

'He told you the girl was his sister, you had a conversation, and then he ran away? You're lying. You are obstructing justice, and I won't have it. I'll throw you to the dogs, you and the boy, wherever he is. You'll find the boy,' his voice was low, 'or Wang will find him first. And when you find him, bring him straight to me, or I'll let Wang have you both.'

CHAPTER 10

Adrenalin had kept me awake through my meetings with Zhuli Sumner and Karen Turvey, but exhaustion hit me the moment I walked away, and I had to drag myself back to the hotel. What with jet lag, my late-night bar crawl and Damien's email, I was short of sleep. All I wanted to do was ring Finney and speak to my children, then curl up in a freshly made bed and sleep for eight hours. Instead I found Blue waiting for me in the hotel lobby, sitting disconsolately on a sofa by the Christmas tree and still wrapped in her sleeping bag of a coat. I hurried over to her, looking at my watch. It was one o'clock.

'I'm sorry, I know we said twelve-thirty.'

'It's okay,' she said glumly, as though she had expected no more of me, which might well be true, because she'd worked for Sal and he was rarely on time for anything.

She agreed to a sandwich in the coffee shop, and we found a table by the window. Outside, a frosty garden had been turned into Santa's grotto. Inside, the heating was turned up high.

'You should take your coat off,' I suggested. 'Aren't you hot?'

Awkwardly, Blue peeled off her coat and handed it to a waitress with a look of deep suspicion. Under the coat Blue was as skinny as the hotel staff, if considerably shorter.

We ordered – a BLT for me and Singapore noodles for her. Then I dug out the flyer I'd been handed outside the bar the night before.

'Can you tell me what this says?' I asked, pushing it across the table to her.

She took it and read silently, then looked up.

'It's about the murders,' she told me. 'It says several women have gone missing in the past six months near the lake and the police don't investigate properly – it says they are lazy and corrupt. It says women walk in the streets in fear, and after the death of a foreign man there is no longer any guarantee of safety for anyone, rich or poor, and the economic life of the area is put at risk. It says the police do not care because the women are not rich or famous, they are poor migrant women and they are working in menial jobs. It suggests there is –' she fished for the word – 'a covering.'

'A cover-up,' I corrected, and she nodded, frowning at her own mistake.

'It doesn't matter,' I said gently. 'I'm not criticizing – your English is excellent – I'm only correcting you so you know next time.'

'I am only annoyed with myself,' she said, unsmiling. 'I should study harder, and then my

168

English will be perfect and I can get a better job.'

My instinct was to tell her to relax, not to worry, but I feared it would sound as though I was belittling her ambition.

The waitress arrived at the table with our food, and in a flash Blue had pulled the flyer from the table so that it was out of sight. The waitress left, and Blue resumed her translation without comment. I started picking at my food. I'd thought I was famished, but now I found all I could do was nibble some salad. It was the meat that I had real problems with, the slices of bloodless flesh reminding me of the wound on the girl's throat.

'It says they have formed an action committee and they will gather opinions on protest action.'

'Who are they?' I gave up, pushing my food away. She looked at me in confusion.

'Who wrote this flyer, you mean? It is signed by . . . they call themselves the Residents' Safety and Justice Action Committee. But I don't think they are a real committee.'

'Why aren't they real?'

'They can't just make their own committee. They need permission to form an organization.'

'Maybe they got permission.'

'Nobody gets permission.'

'What do they mean by "protest"? Will they have a demonstration?'

'I don't know. Demonstrations are only allowed with permission, but . . .'

'Okay, I get it, no one gets permission. If they go ahead and demonstrate anyway, how will the police respond?'

'They'll tell them to go home.'

'And if they don't go home?'

'I don't know. Maybe they will promise the people they'll try harder to catch the killer. Or maybe they'll find out who the ringleaders are and make them keep quiet . . . It depends on the situation. If they still don't go home it may be dangerous . . .' She shook her head, at a loss. 'These things are too complicated for you—'

I glanced up at her and interrupted.

'What do you mean, too complicated for me?'

'China, what happens here . . . I don't think you can understand.'

Blue was right, of course. I felt totally at sea, but I didn't like having her tell me so.

'Why not?' I challenged her. 'I mean apart from the language, which is why I've got you.'

'China is . . . very special. Its history is very long, its culture is very strong, its people . . .'

'Do you think people here are any different from people anywhere else?'

'Well,' Blue seemed stunned by my question, 'of course.'

'I don't,' I said. She frowned across the table at me, and I shrugged apologetically. 'Deep down it seems to me that people are pretty much the same the world over – they care about the same things and worry about the same things. What one thing do you think makes Chinese people different?'

She thought for a moment, and then said, 'We Chinese care very much for our families.'

'And so do we English,' I said. I smiled at her and she half smiled at me, unconvinced.

'Do you want to see pictures of my children?' I asked her, and she brightened immediately. I showed her the pictures on my mobile phone, and she clapped her hands with delight at William's huge eyes and Hannah's curls. Finney was in one of the photographs and she breathed, 'So handsome.' She commented on the size of the house, although I'd always thought of our Victorian terrace as cramped. She also commented on how many toys the children had.

When we finished eating, I told Blue I had some emails to catch up on, and that I wanted her to spend the afternoon at the lakeside bars. I wanted to know anything she overheard about the deaths of Sumner and the women, and anything more about the protest.

'Be discreet with your questions,' I advised her. 'Avoid the woods and make sure you leave the lake by nightfall – we should assume that it's not safe there.'

She took her coat from the waitress, put it back on. She turned to me.

'When I look at the photographs I think my life is very different from yours,' she said, 'and my parents' lives are very different from your parents' lives, I think. I do not understand how people can be the same if all their experiences are not the same.'

She turned again and walked away from me, her big green coat making its way between the tables. I was surprised by her forthrightness and surprised at my own disappointment. It was true that I found her company oppressive, but I had believed we could find some common ground. Perhaps I was being naive.

I sat at the desk in the hotel room, looking out over the expressways that criss-crossed and twisted below my window. There were roadworks, but still the traffic squirmed and pushed around the obstruction. Snow had piled in filthy ridges at the roadside.

I reached for the phone. Sal had given me Sean Benton's name and mobile number as a useful Beijing contact. 'He's a spy, of course,' Sal had said to me. I had no idea whether he was joking, you never do with Sal. Spy or not, Benton was the only contact I had in the embassy, and the phone call I'd half overheard at Zhuli Sumner's apartment that morning had made me think the embassy knew something.

Sean Benton tried to wriggle out of seeing me, but when I mentioned Sal's name he gave in, as everyone does. Men in particular always have good memories of the time they've spent with Sal in bars and restaurants. Then I called Nelson Li's secretary, relieved that she answered her mobile on a Sunday. Her name was Jade, she had text-book English and promised to call me back when she'd spoken to Nelson Li about seeing me.

I trawled the news again for more on the Kelness story about radioactive contamination, but it was Sunday, which is always a slow news day, and not even Reuters seemed to have come up with anything new since the night before.

When I couldn't dig up anything more I lay down on the bed and closed my eyes. The ring of the telephone dragged me back into conscious-ness exactly one hour later. Nelson Li would see me the next day at half past ten, Jade said. After I'd put the phone down I spent the next hour phoning around the freelance cameramen who worked in Beijing. I'd read enough about Nelson Li to know that he would not be impressed by my MiniDV camera. I needed a camera the size of a tank, and lights bright enough for a football stadium to make him feel that I was taking him seriously. If I gave him a stage he might perform.

I looked at my watch. It was four in Beijing, eight a.m. in London. I felt cheered by the prospect of speaking to Finney and the twins.

'Yes?' Finney sounded impatient. I could hear the twins in the background, their voices raised in argument.

'It's me.'

'Good. Here, talk to your children. Tell them to stop messing about and eat their breakfast.'

He passed the phone to Hannah, who greeted me happily enough and then lapsed into one-word responses. Yes, she'd slept well. Yes, she'd had a lovely play in the park the day before. Yes, she was eating her breakfast. Then she lost interest entirely and handed me to William, who kept asking when I was coming back and then pretended he couldn't hear when I told him. 'I can't hear you, Mummy, say it again. I can't hear you, Mummy, say it again,' he chanted. I told him I'd bring him back a present and miraculously his hearing was restored. Then he must have put the phone down on the table, because there was a thunk and I could hear Finney, exasperation in his voice, urging them to eat. Eventually he must have seen the receiver lying there, because he picked up.

'Hello?'

'I'm still here. It's not a good time, is it?'

'They've got no sense of urgency.' Finney sounded as though he was at his wits' end. 'They wander around half dressed as though it's a Saturday.'

'It's Sunday,' I said, mystified.

'It's . . . Sunday. Damn, what's wrong with me?' Finney fell silent for a moment, and when he spoke again his voice was sheepish. 'You're right, it's Sunday. I've got them sitting here in their school uniforms waiting for Carol so I can go to the office.'

'I'm guessing you'd rather be there?'

'Well . . .' Finney hesitated. 'What on earth am I going to do with them all day? I took them out yesterday . . . You mean Carol's not coming in at all?'

'She doesn't usually on a Sunday.'

Finney muttered something under his breath.

'I might have to call her in for a couple of hours,' he said. 'I've got work to do today. Something's come up on a case . . .'

I was unsettled by Finney's confusion.

'Why don't you give Ma a call?' I suggested. 'Or Tanya. I'm sure they'd help out.'

'Hmm.' Finney sounded reluctant, and it occurred to me that he didn't want to ask my family for help, that he wanted to show us all he could do it on his own.

'We usually see Ma at some point over the weekend,' I said gently. 'I think she'll miss the twins if she doesn't see them.'

'I suppose I could give her a call,' he said. He was sounding a bit happier by the time I put the phone down, but I had a sudden and powerful urge to get on a plane and fly home to hover quietly in the corner of the kitchen just to see that they were all okay. I felt uneasy as I put the phone down, but I was four thousand miles away and there was nothing I could do. I had to trust Finney.

The restaurant was tucked away in a narrow alley lined with low, cramped houses. Snow had replaced the coating of grey dust that I saw every-where. Like the dust, snow put every line into soft focus, so that buildings blended into the sky above and the earth below.

The restaurant was set back from the road with its own parking lot, which was full of black Audis. Chauffeurs dozed inside their vehicles, their seats reclined. I pushed open the doors, and found myself in a fug of cigarette smoke, the noise of conversation almost deafening. A wait-ress approached me and I gazed around anxiously, looking for Benton. I had managed to bluff my way as far as the restaurant armed only with an English approximation of its name and an imaginary pair of chopsticks with which I had shamelessly mimed eating. But how on earth did one mime 'Have you seen a British diplomat called Sean?'

A sea of Chinese faces greeted me, some of them raised towards me in polite curiosity, but for the most part too engaged in their meal to pay me any attention. There were a few Caucasians dotted around, most of them in groups. The waitress gestured that I should look around the corner, and there was my man – at least, I assumed he was mine – waving me over, a genial pale face, shiny balding head and half-moon spectacles. He stood and shook my hand, and I apologized for being late.

'Never mind, never mind, I went ahead and ordered.'

In the centre of the table there was a plate of shredded white meat sitting in a pool of yellow oil.

'It looks good,' I said politely.

I took off my coat, put it over the back of my chair, and sat down. A waitress pulled a nylon cover over both coat and chair, then she picked my bag off the floor where I had put it and placed it on a chair next to me. I looked enquiringly at Sean. His face was younger than the balding head suggested, with pockmarks on his forehead from acne long gone.

'The cover's to protect your coat from oil splashes,' he explained, leaning forward and raising his voice over the noise of conversation around us, 'and you shouldn't put your bag on the floor unless you want it to become mysteriously sticky.'

'I won't make the same mistake again. This place looks popular.'

'Every provincial government has a representative office in Beijing,' he told me, as a procession of waitresses arrived, each bearing a different dish, 'and every one of those offices has its own restaurant. This is the restaurant attached to the representative office of the Sichuan provincial government; a lot of the people eating here are officials dispatched from Sichuan to work in the capital. They like home cooking. Even the cooks are sent from Sichuan.'

'And the official cars outside,' I said, 'all those

Audis, I suppose the perks of working for government are the same the world over.'

'Exactly. And yes, my car is outside,' he smiled, 'but I drove myself. We Brits are democrats at heart.'

'You choose to do without your immunity from prosecution for traffic violations, then?' I asked.

'Good heavens, no.' He laughed. 'I'm a democrat, but I'm not a masochist. You surely can't expect me to pay a Chinese parking fine. Just as you can't expect me to live with my regulation one child in a shoebox a few metres square. The British taxpayer provides me with a nice suburban house. Thank you very much for your generosity, by the way – I assume you're a taxpayer.'

'I am indeed, and honoured to support your lifestyle,' I said.

I smiled, and Benton smiled back. He had a dimple in his chin that gave him a slightly self-mocking expression, as though he could see the joke even if he was the butt of it. He seemed to me, despite his slight pomposity, to be one of the new breed of diplomats who were at least capable of seeing the vanities of the foreign office for what they were.

'Tuck in,' he urged, 'this is cold shredded chicken marinated in sesame paste, a classic Sichuan dish.'

I picked up my chopsticks and tried to look appreciative of the food, which he had clearly chosen with care. There were prawns deep fried in their shells hiding in a mound of red chilli, lightly sautéed leafy greens scattered with garlic, and noodles doused in an evil black paste. Benton ate with relish, pulling the heads off prawns, brown juices oozing from their brains, popping them into his mouth whole, chewing, then spitting the shell out. It was a gory process. He looked up expectantly.

'What is it that you want to ask me about?'

'All right. The day I arrived – yesterday, in fact – I went to take a look at the lake where Derek Sumner was found, and I saw them pulling out the body of a girl. She'd been murdered.'

Benton put his chopsticks down on his plate. He was not shocked or repelled. He was, simply, all at once intensely interested.

'Are you sure she was dead?'

'She was submerged under the ice and her throat was almost completely severed. She was dead.'

He picked up his chopsticks, then put them down again.

'Beijing is not without its problems,' he said vaguely.

'Is Beijing awash with bodies, then?' I challenged him, annoyed by his diplomatic evasion. 'Tourists just trip over them, do they?'

Benton's eyes flicked to mine, then away. He licked his lips, and when he spoke he was choosing every word.

'It's always been a remarkably safe city.' He thought for a moment, wiping his mouth with a paper napkin, then qualified his statement: 'Certainly for the expatriate community. A lot goes on among the Chinese that we simply don't hear about. The newspapers are . . .'

'Rubbish,' I supplied.

His mouth twitched in a smile.

'They fulfil a different function, let us say; their primary purpose is still propaganda. Although even that is changing.'

'I've heard that other women have been killed near that lake.'

Benton's eyes rested on my face. He waited until the waitress had refilled our teacups with bitter black tea.

'I think it's fair to say,' he said, weighing every word with what seemed to me extraordinary caution, 'off the record, of course, that we have been aware of rumours about a serial killer operating not just by the lake there, but across the city – unless there is more than one. You are the first eyewitness we've had, and I don't of course dispute what you saw, but there are always rumours here . . . if it's not serial killers it's earthquake or disease. Rumour flourishes where there is no real provision of information.'

'But this isn't just rumour, is it?' I said. I took a deep breath. I was about to wing it. 'Zhuli Sumner was called by the British consul today, and she was asked whether her husband had known someone, a man who I'm assuming has been arrested in connection with Sumner's murder—'

180

'No,' he cut me off sharply. 'Not in connection with her husband's death.'

'Then . . . in connection with what?'

'I'm not going to comment.' All traces of boyish naivety had gone from Benton's face.

'You just commented, you confirmed that a suspect has been detained.'

'No.' He picked up his chopsticks and reached for his bowl of noodles. 'You misunderstood. No one's been detained in connection with anything, I don't know what you're talking about.'

I watched him raise the bowl almost to his face. His chopsticks scooped the noodles up in one smooth movement to his mouth, the sauce splattering softly around his lips.

'If there's no link to Derek Sumner's murder why would the British embassy even be involved?' I murmured. His eyes flitted towards me, but he didn't answer, just kept hoovering up the noodles.

'There's going to be a protest about the murders,' I told him.

He looked up at me, eyes sharp, mouth full. He swallowed, and removed a sliver of something green that had got stuck between his teeth.

'When?'

I took the Action Committee's photocopied letter from my pocket, and he actually reached out for it, but I pulled it clear of his fingers and held it just far enough away that he could see the scrawled black characters.

'Can we agree,' I said, 'that the only reason a

British diplomat would be interested in a protest about the serial killings is if there's some British connection, which means either that there's a link with Derek Sumner's death, or that you suspect some British guy . . . that's it, isn't it? There's a British suspect?'

Benton looked exasperated.

'Look,' he took a deep breath and leaned further over the table towards me, his face so close to me that I could see purple veins around his nose, 'you must keep your speculation to yourself. Do you understand? A British man was arrested last night after he allegedly attempted to rape a Chinese woman at knifepoint in the woods by the lake. The police are investigating whether he might be linked with the deaths of the women, or of Derek Sumner. That is all – and I mean *all* – that I can tell you.'

'Who is he?'

'I can't give you his name.'

'What was he doing in Beijing? Does he have anything to do with Kelness? Did he know Derek Sumner?'

Benton held up his hand. 'Stop right there. I've told you what I've told you to shut you up.'

'To shut m—'

'I'll explain. But first I want to take a look at this.'

He snatched the Action Committee's flyer from my hand, his eyes running easily over the tiny characters. Eventually he looked up and flourished the piece of paper at me, looking worried.

'Can I take this?'

I shook my head. It had names and addresses on it, Blue had told me, of people we might need to interview. He flicked the flyer against the table top in annoyance, then bent his head over the paper again, apparently trying to commit as much of it as possible to memory. At last, with a sigh, he pushed it back across the table.

'This is exactly why we're trying to keep it quiet,' he said irritably. 'The Chinese, well – I'm generalizing, of course – they put up with things, they have no choice, but when they can't take any more they explode. Like these killings. Imagine how they feel: women are getting killed but no one's talking about it, no one's reassuring them about what's being done to stop it, so it bursts out in the form of demonstrations or protests. But protests against the government aren't allowed here; the government has no problems, however, with protests directed against some foreign power. So if there's even a suggestion, and I mean a suggestion, that a British man raped a Chinese woman, or that he killed Chinese women . . . well, there are Brits all over China these days, and if there were revenge attacks . . . If I were you, I wouldn't want to be responsible for spreading the news that there's a British man in custody. Whatever you know of any communication between the embassy and Zhuli Sumner is entirely private. Anything I have shared with you is similarly confidential. If you start shooting your mouth off I can't stop you, but you'll be putting Britons in harm's way. Can you live with that, Ms Ballantyne?'

CHAPTER 11

It was late afternoon now, but it felt like mid-evening, with the sky darkening and light spilling from windows and shops onto the snow that had settled on roofs, on the ground and on top of cars. Song elbowed his way through the early evening crowds towards his office. He was home and dry, Detective Chen off his back, no one chasing him with an arrest warrant, just the small matter of the kid to deal with. He should, he thought miserably, be feeling euphoric.

His mobile rang and he pulled it from his pocket, peering at the screen, fearing a call from Lina or from her father, but it was his sister.

'Thank goodness I've reached you,' she said, and he could hear that she was flustered and excited.

'What is it?'

'Are you still in town? Can you come to the hospital?'

'I have things to do . . .' I have a child to catch, he thought.

'You have to come, there's a man who wants to meet you. He's given us all the money that we need for medicine, and it's because of you.'

'He's given you money?' Song ran his hand over his face, then stepped sharply out of the path of a bicycle.

'Ten thousand *yuan*, for Pa's treatment, and he'll hire a nurse for him too.'

'Who is this man? What does he want from us?'

'He says he wants nothing, only to speak with you; he says he admires you, and wants to talk to you about your work.'

Song rubbed his hand over his face again as though this would wake him up. He did not know what to think.

'Give the money back to him,' he told his sister and he heard her cry out in horror. 'It must be a con trick. You have to say we won't take the money.'

The heavy red gate to the courtyard stood ajar. Song walked through it, the snow crunching under his feet. Wolf was there, in the yard, rinsing out a metal rice bowl under the tap. He looked up, startled by the noise of the gate banging.

'You're back,' he said. 'What happened?'

'How many times do I have to tell you to lock the gate?' Song snapped at him, bolting the metal gate shut. 'If we lose our files, we lose everything.'

Song pulled open the rickety door to the office and stomped inside, scraping the snow off his boots as he crossed the threshold. Wolf hurried in behind him.

'What happened?' Wolf asked again. 'Last I knew, you were leaving town.'

Song sat down at his desk. He ran his hand over his laptop's silver surface and lifted the screen, turning it on.

'Psycho Wang met me at the station,' Song said, watching Wolf's face. Had Psycho Wang just got lucky, had he guessed that Song would try to leave by train, had he followed him, or had Wolf betrayed him?

Wolf swore under his breath. He sat down hard on the leather sofa that they'd managed to salvage from a rich friend's apartment.

Song lit up, inhaled, then coughed. He stubbed out the cigarette in an ashtray that was already deep in dog ends.

'Detective Chen doesn't want me, he wants the boy,' Song told Wolf.

'What do you mean, he doesn't want you? People saw you there, your car . . .'

'He's buried all the evidence that I was there, he knows I didn't do it, he wants the boy because he's a witness.'

'So give him the boy.' Wolf stood up excitedly. 'What are you waiting for? Go get the kid and hand him over.'

Song turned away, avoiding Wolf's gaze. He reached for a flyer that had been placed on the desk, pulled it towards him. It was a notice to quit, addressed generically, to whom it might concern, delivered no doubt to every residence in the street. At the bottom was the local government stamp. Water and electricity would be cut off first, demolition would follow within a month. Song crumpled the paper into a ball and dropped it in the ashtray. He had expected it. It was time to move on. At least this time his office would have a proper address. In the middle of this maze of alleys with no names, clients had to hire a detective just to find the office.

'I need a shower,' he said. 'I'll get the kid later.'

'Don't tell me you're not going to do it.' Wolf all but jumped up and down in frustration. 'Don't tell me that, because I can't bear to hear it. If you don't get the kid for him, he'll come after you again.'

Song thought about the child and his beggar gang, and then he thought of his father and the medicine the money could buy. He thought of the rich man who wanted to meet him. He looked around him. The courtyard house was falling apart, but the rent was cheap compared with the new apartment buildings. He'd worked night and day to build his business from scratch. From two rooms and a courtyard, with peeling paint and a broken window, a tap in the yard and the toilet twenty yards down the road. He hadn't spent much of his father's money on the office, knowing it would be torn down within a year. Apart from some cheap furniture and a coat of paint, his only real spending went on technology, on broadband and wireless and scanners and cameras, because these were the tools of his trade, and because when the time came to abandon ship, they could go with him. His private quarters consisted of a bedroom next to the office, and a shower.

'Why's the place such a mess?' Song demanded. 'Why hasn't Xiao Meng cleaned up?'

Wolf grinned, but nervously.

'She says I'm too untidy and she's not coming to work until you're back.'

There were files piled high on both desks and on much of the floor. Paperwork had spilled from the files, fanning out onto every surface, photographs of clients, records of phone conversations, the intimate details of people's lives, information worth money. Information worth stealing.

'Has there been an earthquake?'

'I don't think so.'

Song stood and hurled a file in Wolf's direction.

'What have you been doing in here? Clear the place up and get Xiao Meng back. I'm going out.'

Wolf crouched down, gathering papers as fast as he could. He looked up at Song from the floor.

'But everything's all right, you're going to do what he wanted, aren't you?'

Song gazed at him. He could still feel the pain under his ribs from the electric baton, and his burned arm was throbbing.

'Everything's all right?' he echoed softly. 'You have got to be kidding.'

At the hospital he made his way through corridors of patients in pyjamas and families waiting anxiously or stretched out asleep on the benches.

One man lay flat out, his trousers unzipped to ease his belly, his head on his wife's lap, a kid crawling over his legs. There was a faint smell, a bitter mixture of antiseptic and bleach and toilets and blood. Song nodded a greeting to the nurse on duty and found his sister by his father's sickbed. Three years older than Song, she too was tall. In her twenties she had broken many hearts. She had put on weight around her hips and there were fine lines around her eyes, but she was still a handsome woman. Her long hair was pinned back from her face, but she would never have dreamed of cutting it. She looked up when he appeared, then angrily turned her face away from him.

Song stood by his father, who lay asleep, his mouth gaping open. There was a drip by the bedside, and a tangle of plastic tubes vanished into the bandages around his wrist. But, Song saw with relief, he was no thinner. Perhaps there was still hope.

'Did you tell him we don't want his money?' Song asked her.

She ignored him, pretended she hadn't heard.

'You didn't tell him, did you?'

'I couldn't.' She turned, her voice low but her eyes blazing.

'How can I turn him down before you've so much as heard what he has to say?'

'Do you even know his name?'

'Do you know how much time I spend here nursing Pa? He said he'd hire a nurse.'

190

'It's a con,' Song muttered.

'How can it be a con?'

'How can it be a con? Have you got eyes and ears? There are con men everywhere. Which one of them doesn't say he'll give you something for nothing? No, someone's found out about our situation and they're taking advantage. Have you asked around? Has he approached other patients?'

'Just talk to him,' his sister insisted. 'His chauffeur's waiting for you in the corridor.'

'His chauffeur? I'm supposed to get into a car with a con man's chauffeur?'

Her eyes ran over him for the first time, taking in the dirt that Wolf's coat had accumulated from his time on all fours at the feet of Psycho Wang. 'You look like a tramp,' she said. 'No one would give you any money if they took a look at you.'

Song pushed his way out between the curtains that enclosed his father's bed and went back into the corridor. A man who was wearing a blue suit, and who might have been a chauffeur, was sitting reading a newspaper. Song remembered seeing him on the way into his father's ward. The man's knee was jiggling up and down as though he was bored. He looked up and caught Song's eye.

'Are you ready to go?' he asked.

'Who sent you?'

'Nelson Li. You know who he is?'

Song stared at the man for a moment, then he nodded. 'I'm ready,' he said. 'Let's go.'

★　　★　　★

191

Song climbed into the clean luxury of Nelson Li's limousine. He tried stretching out his legs. He closed his eyes. He had slept so badly the night before in that cell of a room, the cold seeping through the thin bedroll which barely cushioned his bones from the concrete floor. He had not showered for forty-eight hours, he had not shaved. He could smell himself, the oily ointment on his arm, stale sweat mixing sourly with the chemical sweetness that emanated from a green perfume dispenser on the dashboard. He opened his eyes, looked down at his thighs, his dirty jeans against the cream leather upholstery, his scuffed running shoes shedding flecks of filth on plush burgundy-red carpet.

He thought about Nelson Li. Song had often thought that a man like Nelson Li, a man with fingers in so many pies, must need a private detective. Song had watched Li from his early days, from the first nightclub by the lake. He'd watched how Li's 'Fashion Club' had flourished while others around it closed, how with his first profit he had opened a second club in the western suburbs then, with loans from who knew where, two more clubs in the city centre. Questions, hassle from police, from the tax authorities, from neighbours angered by noise, all of these had arisen and somehow Li had silenced them all. Then from nightclubs to property, to apartment blocks and further up-market to villas, construction sites that sprang up wherever there were slums or empty ground. Nelson Li had all the wit and all the luck a man needed, Song concluded enviously, but with his good fortune came enemies.

The heating purred, the softness of the seats was like a womb, the tinted windows cut the glare of the winter light, and Song's last conscious thought, before sleep claimed him, was that if this was treachery he might learn to like it.

He came to when the chauffeur shook him, and in his sleepy confusion he nearly hit out at the man.

Another man, a man whose face he recognized from magazines and television, stood by the car, peering in with some concern.

'Are you all right?' Nelson Li asked.

Song clambered out of the car. He nodded at Li, red-faced, still tongue-tied by sleep. Then, behind the man, he saw the mansion. It was, in its proportions, not unlike its owner, broad and squat, its mirror-glassed windows like blank eyes, the whole impression reminiscent of nothing so much as a toad. Song knew, because he had read about the building in a lifestyle magazine, that it was supposed to be a copy of Versailles, which was a palace in France. But whereas in France there was only one of these palaces, Li had built a series of them, twenty in all. His Versailles hunkered down next to another Versailles, and to another, only a sliver of light between one and the next. They had no gardens, but were built shoulder to shoulder around an ornamental lake, now frozen over.

'I found you,' Li said, turning away. 'I should be the detective.'

Song followed him into the house, speeding up to keep up with the smaller man, whose feet seemed to skim the snowy ground. The double doors, which were twice as tall as Nelson Li and as wide as ten men, opened into a cavernous lobby two storeys high, floor intricately tiled, walls muralled, with a vast crystal chandelier hanging like an overburdened fruit tree between twin sweeping staircases, one of which Li ascended, Song following on behind.

'Fifteen hundred square metres of space,' Li sounded bored, as though the information was necessary but tedious. 'The marble is imported from Italy, the furnishings are French, there is nothing here that is Chinese. This is the pinnacle of European living.'

Song had an impression of servants, of faces behind heavy doors, of hushed conversation at the end of seemingly endless corridors. The staff would not be imported, of course, Song thought. A man like Nelson Li would spend a fortune on a Savile Row suit, but he would not waste his money on an English butler.

They entered what appeared to be a study. It was thickly carpeted, one wall was lined with bookshelves, and although there were windows they were so heavily draped that very little light

194

entered. Li ignored the vast leather office chair behind the dark wood desk, and instead chose a sofa, indicating that Song should sit opposite him. Song had never been in a room like this. It looked like a room in a magazine, one in which either a beautiful woman in an evening gown or a man in casual golfing wear, or perhaps a riding habit, should recline. There was a marble table at his elbow, and he turned to look at the silver-framed photographs on top of it. All of them featured Nelson Li, and in most he was shaking hands with an important politician, or a banker, or a high-ranking bureaucrat. In one picture a young man stood next to Nelson Li, and although their faces were not the same, and the young one was dressed in casual sports clothes whereas the elder wore a business suit, their expressions were so identically circumspect as to suggest they must be father and son. Song had heard of this son . . . something about his name. Then he remembered. When Nelson Li's son was four years old, in the early 1990s, his father had given him the American name Nixon. The father had told the newspapers then that it was a celebration of China's importance in the world.

'So, Song Ren, I've heard of you by reputation,' Li said.

'Likewise,' Song said.

There was a moment's silence as Li digested Song's impertinence.

'You think your reputation compares with mine?'

195

Li leaned forward, eyes gleaming, voice politely interested, and Song thought: this is how he speaks when he goes in for the kill. Li continued, his tone cruel, putting Song in his place. 'You specialize in photographs of cocks and cunts.'

But Song, who had spent all day being pushed around by Psycho Wang, was in no mood to be bullied further.

'You have a cock you need photographing?' he asked quietly. 'Or is there some other reason you came looking for me at my father's sickbed?'

Li sat back. His eyes travelled over Song, from long face to swimmer's shoulders, to powerful legs.

'You are a filial son,' he said.

'How did you find my father?'

'If I did not know how to ask questions, and how to find out what people need, then I would still be sweeping streets,' Li said.

'Then why? Why me?'

'Two nights ago I had business that took me to the lake,' Li said. His eyes sought out Song's. 'It is not important what my business was. The part that concerns you is that I was nearby when the watchman's tent caught fire that night. I saw you emerge from the tent with the child in your arms.'

Song opened his mouth to protest, but he could not formulate the words he needed.

'You were blinded by the spotlight,' Li continued, 'you could not see the faces of those of us who approached you. You turned and ran in panic because you feared you would be held responsible

196

for whatever violence had happened there. And as a witness I can tell you, you looked crazed. I myself would have believed you capable of anything . . .' For a moment he paused. 'After you had gone, I asked the others who had crowded around if anyone knew who you were, and there was a young woman who recognized you and told me where you lived; from there it was not difficult to find your office, to speak to your neighbours. They didn't know where you were, but they told me of your father's condition.'

'So you used him as bait. What do you want from me?' It occurred to Song that it was the second time he had asked that question in one day.

'I want . . .' Li hesitated. 'I need the boy. I assume you know where he is.'

Song made a noise, half bark of laughter, half grunt of surprise. The boy, for the second time that day.

'What good can he do you?'

Li licked his lips.

'No one can do me any good,' he said softly, and then, louder, 'but this murder happened on *my* land. I want to know what the boy saw. I won't let it happen again.'

'Why should it happen again?' Song asked. When he got no reply from Li, he said, 'I don't want the police to get their hands on the boy.'

'They won't. I'll see what he has to say and then I'll make sure his needs are met.'

'You have no responsibility for the boy,' Song said.

'It is not your place to tell me what my responsibilities are or are not,' Li said. 'Your place is to invoice me for your fee and look after your father.'

Song ran his hand over his face.

'What happens to the boy then?' he insisted. 'I don't understand. I won't hand him over unless you can tell me clearly.'

Li's mouth twisted in an acid smile.

'A private eye who worries about the fate of a ragged child? You can't be much of a businessman.'

'Tell me what will happen to the boy,' Song said again.

'For heaven's sake,' Li's voice resonated with exasperation, 'I have staff, and I have money – for the moment he can stay here. There are a dozen empty rooms. I'll never have to set eyes on him. I'll make sure that he is clothed and educated. It is not the first time that I have taken financial responsibility for those who have encountered harm on my premises. I bend the rules but I understand my responsibilities.'

Nelson Li looked away, and Song saw that his hands were balled in fists on his lap. Song did not know whether to believe what Nelson Li had said. It seemed preposterous to expect that this man would take the beggar boy into his house, but these days anything was possible. Nelson Li had so much money that the upbringing of one child could not dent it. Song had read about a few rich entrepreneurs who had become philanthropists. They were using their fortunes for charitable purposes, sponsoring the school fees of rural children, and paying medical bills for families facing great difficulty. What Nelson Li was suggesting was entirely possible. Nevertheless, behind Nelson Li's words Song could hear evasion and something like desperation. Song told himself he was imagining things. An association with Li would bring many advantages.

'What about my father?' Song asked. 'You have been very generous.'

'I will continue to pay for his care as long as you work for me. Let us call it a retainer,' Li said, more calmly now. 'If this goes well, the money I spend on your father's treatment is my investment in your social welfare. Otherwise . . . well, I have taken the risk and it's my loss.'

'You are very generous,' Song said.

'So it's agreed?'

For a long moment Song gazed at Li's hand, stretched expectantly towards him.

'There's a problem,' he said.

Li's hand dropped.

'The police want the boy too. It's possible they will punish me for keeping the boy from them,' Song said. 'Detective Chen has information that he can use against me.'

'I can make Detective Chen go away,' Li said.

Song thought about the file on his hard disk that showed how Detective Chen had chased his dirty money around the country. It was not enough on its own to protect him from a charge of murder. But that disk in combination with Li's influence . . . perhaps that could silence Detective Chen. Again Li held out his hand, and this time Song reached out and took it.

Deep in thought, Song followed Li down the stairs towards the marble lobby. The door opened and a young woman walked in. She was slender and very tall, she wore a linen trouser suit with an open-necked white shirt and carried a leather bag slung over her shoulder. Her hair, black and shining, hung loosely around her face. She must have thought herself alone. She heard their footsteps before she saw them, and Song saw her start in fear. She looked up, saw the two of them, and tried to cover her alarm.

'Pa!' she said, 'I thought no one was in.'

'Pearl,' Nelson Li greeted her in English, then turned to Song. 'She just returned from Harvard Law School and now she works with me. She will be my enforcer!'

'Pa, don't flatter me.' Her eyes met Song's directly. She was Chinese, of course, and yet Song would have said she acted like an American, like an ad for jeans, unfussy, like a boy.

That thought made him blurt out, 'I thought you had a son.'

'I do,' Li said curtly, 'he works for me in a different capacity.'

There was a moment of uncomfortable silence.

'What about you?' Pearl asked. 'Do you work for Pa?'

It was a question that Song was asking himself, and he didn't know how to answer.

'No . . . yes . . . that is . . .'

'He's a security consultant. I have a project for him,' Li said.

Song delved in his shirt pocket, found his business card and handed it to Pearl. It was slightly battered, possibly sweat-stained. And too cheap, now he saw it in these luxurious surroundings. He should have gone for the raised lettering and paid someone to design a logo. He could feel himself sweating, he could smell the stale odour from a night on the floor in his unwashed clothes, smell the rot of his arm where the balm lay thick on peeling flesh.

She glanced at the card, then raised her eyes to him again, and his face burned.

'I may need you too.' Her eyes swept over him, from top to toe, assessing him, and her look was so direct it felt as though she'd run her hand the length of him.

In the stretch limousine he could not relax. It was nearly midnight, but he must go and pick up the boy at once. The sooner he did it, the sooner he could stop worrying about it. He was confused. He had heard unhappiness and evasion in Nelson Li's voice, but did it matter what Li's motives

really were if the boy was fed and clothed? Song
tried to silence the doubts that clamoured in his
head. The boy would be safer with Nelson Li than
in a cell with Psycho Wang, at least. How many
beggar boys, after all, ended up living in a
European palace? But the moment he had thought
it, he doubted it. He believed what Nelson Li had
told him about his financial support for people in
difficulty And yet – although he had no evidence
– he knew that Nelson Li had not told him the
whole truth.

Well, it was best to get it over with. He leaned
forward and instructed Nelson Li's chauffeur to
take him to the road where the beggar gang was
lodging. He remembered how the boy had clung
to him on the night of the fire, and then how he'd
fought to escape, hurling himself at the door. It
was likely that the boy would not come easily. It
would be easier to seize him while he slept.

CHAPTER 12

After Sean Benton had told me about the Briton who had been detained for attempted rape, my mind was racing. Besides, my body was settling into a jet-lagged pattern of late-night wake-fulness. So instead of going back to my hotel I went in search of Angus Perry. Zhuli had told me that he lived in the Rainbow Hotel, and I found him in the hotel bar, which called itself The Tortoise and The Hare. From the name I expected a kitsch copy of an English country pub, complete with roaring fire and quiz night, but once I walked through the door I saw it had more in common with Bangkok than with Berkshire. Trance music vibrated through the room, setting my nerves on edge. Eyes glanced hungrily in my direction, then jumped away again. It took me a moment to realize that I was not part of the food chain. Young Chinese women in skin-tight jeans straddled bar stools, flirting with middle-aged Caucasian men, whispering in their ears, squeezing their thighs, rubbing their backs.

I spotted Angus Perry drinking beer at a table

with a couple of men I didn't recognize. Last time I'd seen him had been three weeks earlier, in the offices at Kelness. He'd been wearing a suit, and he'd given me the interview which had turned out so disastrously for him: he'd tried to tell me that Sumner had been misquoted, and then had to admit he wasn't at the banquet so he had no way of knowing. I knew he had returned to Beijing the day after our interview to work with Sumner on the negotiations with Nelson Li. Two weeks later, Sumner was dead.

Perry was a bulky man with carrot-red hair and freckles and his green eyes gave him a surprisingly attractive face, but right now he didn't seem to be having a good time. His shoulders were hunched over, his eyes were on his beer, and his mates were talking around him. I approached the table. He didn't recognize me until I was right there, standing in front of him, and then something made him look up and his jaw dropped and he tried, with no success, to pretend he hadn't seen me.

'Angus, good to see you.' I had to yell to make myself heard over the electronic music. He got up awkwardly. He was dressed for an evening out, in a leather jacket and jeans. His face flushed red, and his open-necked shirt meant that I could see the colour spread right down to his chest.

'What are *you* doing here?' He glanced nervously at his drinking buddies, who were watching us with open interest, waiting to be introduced.

Now that he was standing right in front of me, I shouted into his ear, 'I thought perhaps we could have another chat, off the record.' Off the record – those words again. I hated to hear myself say them every time they came out of my mouth. But none of these people had any vested interest in speaking to me, and I had to work on that before I had any hope of an interview on camera.

His eyes darted anxiously around the room. He leaned forward, his mouth so close to my neck that I could feel his beery breath.

'Not here,' he shouted.

'Not here,' I agreed, shouting back. All this mouth and ear stuff was way too intimate for me. 'I'll meet you in the lobby.'

I was pushing my luck. I'd have told myself to get lost. But either he had an unnaturally courteous bent or he was afraid I'd make a scene. Whichever it was, he just nodded his head and sat back down with his friends, and I mimed a farewell then left the bar.

I went to sit in the lobby and waited to see if he'd turn up. I kept an eye on my watch, fearing that he would not come. Then, from the direction of the bar, he appeared, chin thrust forward, his face troubled. I got to my feet.

'I've got nothing to say to you,' he said. 'You've got no right to track me down and embarrass me when I'm on my private time with friends. That's called stalking.'

'You spoke to me before, in Kelness.'

205

'And that was a mistake, I never should have.'

'It wasn't your fault. Your bosses were using you, encouraging you to lie to me about what Sumner had said. But you told me the truth in the end, you told me you weren't at the banquet so you didn't know what he had said. I appreciate the fact that you were straight with me.'

He jerked his head away from me at that, his eyes roving around the lobby.

'You told me Derek Sumner was your friend,' I went on. 'Was that bit true?'

He cleared his throat. His face was more purple than red by now. He grunted, 'Derek was my friend.'

'I saw Zhuli this morning, and she told me you were one of the group who ate with Sumner at the Lotus Pool. She wanted to know why there was no one with her husband when he died. Can we talk about that?'

The mention of Zhuli's name wrought devastation on Perry's face as it had on Karen's. Still he made a stab at bravado. 'Why does she think?' He gave a nervous bark of laughter.

'You need to sort some things out,' I told him, 'if not for me, then for Zhuli's peace of mind.'

I turned away and started walking towards the exit, afraid I'd lost him, but he followed me, his head sunk onto his shoulders.

We walked down the street outside, a broad avenue bordered with skeletal poplars. Fresh snow was falling and settling on the pavement. I could sense Perry pulling away from me, thinking about turning back.

'Zhuli is upset because Derek felt you were freezing him out,' I said.

'It was our jobs at stake,' he muttered. 'What did he think he was doing?'

'Did you think Derek wanted Nelson Li to give him a job?'

'What's the bloody difference? Start talking like he did at that banquet and he might as well have been working for Li anyway.'

I hadn't expected Perry to be well disposed to me. I could tell that his humiliation during the interview I'd conducted for television three weeks ago still rankled. But I was surprised by the strength of his hostility to Derek Sumner.

'Derek Sumner was your friend, and he's dead,' I said. 'Why are you so angry with him?'

But the question stopped him mid-stride and struck him dumb. His fleshy lips pressed close together and his head turned one way and the other in distress. I thought he was going to start crying on me there and then. Or else, I thought, he's going to turn around and walk away. Somehow the slow fall of the snow seemed to hold us in suspended animation.

'I know Derek was your friend,' I said gently, trying to draw him out. 'I'm not out to get anyone, him or you, I just want to understand what happened.'

There was silence, except for the heave of breath

in and out of Perry's lungs. I could hear a rattle there, from cigarettes or sickness.

'Everyone keeps telling me how close Derek was to Nelson Li,' I said. 'Isn't it possible he handed over the memo about the radioactive contamination because he genuinely thought Nelson Li should know before he paid good money for Kelness?'

Still he wouldn't say anything. If we stayed like this too long, I thought, we would both freeze solid. I had forgotten to put on my scarf, and the cold air was like a tourniquet around my scalp, squeezing tight. My eardrums were hurting and my jaw was aching in the sub-zero temperature.

'He got too close to the man,' Perry finally leaned in towards me, his expression fierce, 'that's all I'm saying. The memo doesn't matter, it's just a crappy piece of paper. Toms is running the mill into the ground. He never bought the new radiation detection units. That's how little respect he has for the workforce. If Toms covered up something like that, you know what I think? I think he should end up like Derek did. They should shove him into the furnace.'

I flinched, repelled by the violence of his words.

'A container-load of scrap from Russia – and just because it's not actually glowing, they let it through,' he continued bitterly. 'It should never have got through the gate without an alarm going off. It should never have got to the scrapyard. It wasn't until they carted it off again to be melted down, when it had been sitting there a week with men walking backwards and forwards past it, that they found it. Finally the one functioning monitor in the whole bloody place raised the alarm.'

'How do you know all this?'

'It doesn't matter, don't you understand that? What matters is the negligence that's going to give men cancer.'

'What did they do when the alarm went off? Did they inform the authorities? Was there a clean-up?'

Something stopped him dead then. His eyes grew wide and wild and then he leaned forward again and spoke into my ear like he had inside the bar.

'Just stay out of the way,' he said, his face inches from mine, 'and you won't get hurt.'

Involuntarily, I took a step back, trying not to show my fear, the air making a white cloud of my breath. We were all alone on the broad street, and the traffic had thinned to almost nothing. I was shivering. Still I persisted.

'Why was Derek by the lake that night?'

Perry glanced behind him. He was finished with me, I could tell, he would be gone in seconds.

'Why was he there?' I wanted him to look at me, not at his escape route. 'Where was he going? Who was he going to see? A man? A woman?'

'A woman,' he snapped, twisting his face back towards me angrily, 'maybe he wanted a woman. Don't tell me you didn't think of that? How about

Nelson Li's daughter, Pearl? Would that be the one? She'll do. They worked together, spent late nights in the office, she was always hanging round him, and who would turn that down?' He shook his great head like a bull about to charge. 'Is that what you want to hear? That's right. You tell her. You try telling that to Zhuli. You do that.' His voice cracked, and he turned away from me. He started to jog back through the snow towards the hotel. I called after him, but he kept on running.

It was one in the morning by the time I got back from my confrontation with Angus Perry. In my hotel room, the chambermaid had drawn the curtains. The lighting was dim, and the room felt dark and claustrophobic. I collapsed onto the bed and wrapped the duvet around my shoulders, eased my shoes off my aching feet and massaged my toes until the blood started moving, and then they hurt even more. The cold had gone deep into me and I wasn't sure I would ever feel warm again. I ran a hot bath, and soaked. Then I pulled on the white towelling gown, looked at the clock and realized it was nearly two in the morning on Monday, which meant it was Sunday evening in England. I picked up the phone to find out how Finney was doing, and when he answered I could hear hysterical giggling in the background.

'I did have to go into the office as it turned out,' he said. 'Tanya and Pat came to take them out to a funfair in Battersea Park with their lot.'

'That's good,' I said. My sister Tanya has great kids, and I was pleased to think of the twins spending the day with their cousins. 'It's a lot more peaceful at work than at home, isn't it?'

'It certainly is.' I could hear him smiling, and I liked the fact that now he understood how I sometimes felt on rainy weekend days when I was trying to entertain children fed up with being cooped up inside, or when they were sick and unable to go out.

'They came back with candyfloss in their hair, and face paints all over them and their clothes,' he grumbled, and I thought with amusement that he was sounding like a weary disgruntled mother. 'Now I'm trying to get them in the bath to scrub it all off, but they're bouncing off the walls.'

I didn't want to tell Finney how Perry had threatened me, I didn't want to talk to him about my work at all, I just wanted him to keep on talking about what was happening at home.

'What took you into the office?'

'One of your lot.'

'One of my lot?' I was confused. I thought I could hear 'my lot' in the background, shouting and laughing because they didn't want to get into the bath.

'I mean a journalist, that lot,' he said. 'One of your lot paid one of my officers to pass him information about a case we've been working on. An online sleaze by the name of Reese, who we've been tracking for months. He's been picked up in your part of the world.'

'You mean here, in Beijing?'

Finney didn't answer. He must have heard the quickening of interest in my voice.

'He's been picked up in Beijing?' I asked again. 'On suspicion of rape? Reese? Is that who it is?' I pulled the hotel memo pad towards me and scrawled the name 'Reese' on it. 'I just had dinner with a man from the British embassy, and he told me a man had been arrested. He's worried in case this man is linked with the murders I told you about . . . if so, it's diplomatically sensitive, obviously.'

I suppose, in my excitement at putting two and two together, I came on a bit strong.

'Whoa,' Finney sounded defensive, 'hang on, Robin. I've spent all day setting up disciplinary procedures against my officer who's been selling information to the press and undermining our investigation. You have any questions, you go through the press office like anyone else.'

I don't know why I snapped. He was being perfectly reasonable. But I was tired and stressed, and he'd hit a nerve.

'You want me to go through the press office?' I snapped back, regretting it even as I heard my voice rising. 'I'm on the other side of the world. We live together, you trust me, remember? You're looking after my kids. And you're going all coy on me? Go through the press office?'

'Exactly.' His voice rose to meet mine, at the end of his tether. 'We live together, *I'm* looking after *your* kids while you're . . . while you're over there. I'm letting you get on with your business, let me get on with mine. I cannot afford to let information leak out that can prejudice an investigation.'

It didn't escalate any further, but a telephone line halfway round the world wasn't much good for making up, either. Instead he handed me over first to Hannah and then to William, and I could hear how tetchy and tired they were after their day of fun and sugar, and how much trouble they were going to be to get to bed, and I didn't want to be on the other side of the world escaping from the tantrums and the tears. I wanted to be there. I wanted to put my arms around Finney and say that I was sorry. Of course, I also wanted to find out what else he knew about Reese.

I called Damien then. He was annoyed that I hadn't been in touch, and not at all mollified when I told him it was two o'clock in the morning. He did sound impressed, however, when I told him what Angus Perry had told me about the radio-active contamination at Kelness. While I was speaking to him, I was making notes to myself on the hotel pad, still afraid that something would slip my memory if I didn't write it all down while I had the chance. Unfortunately Damien returned to his former irritated state when I told him I'd got none of this on tape or film or even on the record. It was knowledge, but apart from using it to prod and probe in Kelness itself, it was of no immediate use to us. Put simply, we couldn't put it on the telly.

When I'd got off the phone I should have gone to bed, but my defrosted brain was now zipping around as though it was broad daylight. I dragged the curtains open again and sat looking out over the city while I logged onto the broadband connection, searching for the name Reese, and finding it in a Sunday tabloid. The piece was (from Finney's point of view) mercifully short, reporting simply that a fifty-three-year-old man named Terry Reese, who'd been under investigation by the Met, had been arrested in Beijing on suspicion of attempted rape. The piece made no link either with the serial killings in Beijing, or with the death of Derek Sumner, so presumably Sean Benton was still sleeping soundly.

It did, however, give further details of Terry Reese's alleged crimes in Britain, which included bringing women into Britain for use in the sex industry. According to the tabloid's 'police source' (who I was pretty sure would soon be suspended), Reese used the internet both for distribution of his pornographic output, and for making online contact with women who had signed up to inter-national dating agencies. He would travel to meet them, convince them of his affection, and they would then be brought into Britain under the illu-sion that they were to be married. Instead, the police were convinced, Reese was part of a network of men who were installing women in private premises around London and operating brothels.

I Googled, and instantly found Asian brides, Asian women, Asian girls, Asian dating, Asian personals, Asian singles, page after page of women. Many of them were in China, smiling into cameras, many of them divorced or widowed with young children, all looking for a husband, promising that they would look after him and cherish him, and explaining that they wanted to see the world. Then there were the men, Gerald from Manchester, Bernie from Oklahoma, Jorge from Spain, all fifty-something divorcees who seemed to be genuinely looking for love. They wrote about how they loved hiking and fishing and reading and good movies, and their kids had grown up and moved away, and now they just wanted someone to share all that with. I wondered what had happened in the lives of Gerald, Bernie and Jorge that they wanted to look as far afield as Thailand and the Philippines and China for good company.

I dug around for the name Reese, and eventually came up with a comment a man named Terry Reese had logged on one of the matchmaking websites: 'A Western woman has several fundamental problems that will never go away and that will get much worse a few years after she is married,' he had written. 'They have general mental instability and psychological disorders, using sex as a bribe to get things. A Western woman has an inherent anti-male bias and preoccupation with fairness that has been drilled into her by the media. Marrying a Western woman simply does not make sense.'

I felt sick and sad and tired. I couldn't read any more. I turned the computer off and lay down, and my head was filled with the images of the lonely, needy, mixed-up men and the hopeful, smiling women who believed that one of these unlikely princes could transform their lives. I pitied any one of them who had met Terry Reese.

CHAPTER 13

As the limousine drew closer to the beggar gang's lodgings, Song thought how the boy had sat hunched and shuddering beside him before dawn that very morning in his outsize clothes. He thought about the boy's left sleeve hanging empty, his right hand gripping the door handle as if he was about to leap out. Then he thought about how the boy had grovelled on the floor at the feet of the gang leaders, keening and stammering out the story of his sister's death. The boy's life was already so screwed up, Song surely couldn't make it any worse.

'Pull in over here,' Song said to Nelson Li's chauffeur, 'and wait for me, I won't be long.'

He'd eaten almost nothing all day, and his bones were stiff from two nights on the frozen floor. He wanted a shower, a full belly and his own bed. But if he was going to do this thing then he knew he must do it at once or he wouldn't do it at all. He would go in while they were all sleeping, he'd carry the boy out and take him straight to Nelson Li. Then he could go home to bed.

The chauffeur pulled into the side of the road

and Song stepped out of the car onto the icy pavement. Quietly he made his way through the entrance. There was a dim light on in the shack on the other side of the courtyard. He opened the door to the room where the children were sleeping in their bunks. It was pitch-black in there and silent. He had not come equipped with a torch. How was he to tell one child apart from another? He could feel for the boy's shoulder stump, of course, but he would wake them all up with his prodding and poking. Better to turn on the light. He'd still be out of there with the boy by the time they realized what was going on. He must move quickly.

His hand found the cord and pulled hard, poised to seize the boy from his bunk and carry him away. The light bulb burst into life, illuminating the room. He blinked around him, taken by surprise himself. The wooden pallets were bare of bedding. There was no one, nothing, not a shred of clothing to show the beggar gang had been there.

Behind him there was movement and he swung round, arms raised defensively, anticipating a metal rod swung against his head. But it was not the block of a woman, nor her husband. It was an old man who shuffled towards him, his toothless gums fudging his words.

'You want to rent the room? There's electricity and water in the yard.'

'There was a boy . . .'

'Filth and scoundrels every one,' the old man

218

grumbled. 'All cleared out by the time I finished my breakfast, creeping away like thieves in the night. If you're a friend of theirs you can pay me the rent they owe.'

'You're out of luck old man,' Song backed away, 'I'm no friend of theirs.'

Slowly, ignoring the old man who ranted at him about the crooked beggars, Song walked back to the limousine and got in.

'There's no delivery for Nelson Li tonight,' he told the chauffeur. 'Just take me home.'

He stretched his legs. This, then, was likely to be the last time he'd ride in the chauffeur-driven car. Perhaps, he thought, they'd taken the one-armed boy back to his village, as he had told and paid them to do. The whole gang would not have gone back to the village, of course, that would have incurred too heavy a financial loss. Perhaps the gang had split. Perhaps the man had taken the boy back to his mother while the woman had taken all the children to fresh begging grounds well away from any police investigation.

Whatever had happened, his fantasy – Nelson Li gets beggar boy; boy gets new life; Song gets rich, important client; Detective Chen's career collapses – now seemed to exist only in reverse. Nelson Li wouldn't get the beggar boy; the boy would stay on the streets; and if anyone's career was in tatters, it was Song's. Yes, he thought, that was probably how it would go. The boy, toughened by life on the street, would become beggar-turned-billionaire and Song – ever victim to what Lina would call his 'excessive sensitivity' – would join the new but growing class of 'failed entrepreneur'.

His mobile phone rang, and he answered it.

'Investigator Song?' A woman's voice, faint against a throb of music, and for a moment he thought that Lina was calling to harass him. 'This is Pearl Li.'

'Hello,' he said, distracted, thinking that he knew why Pearl sounded like Lina. It was because they were both daughters of powerful men and the confidence of that rang in their voices.

'I want to see you,' she said.

'Of course.' Song tried to marshal his thoughts. 'When would suit you?'

'I mean, I want to see you now.' It was more order than request.

Song looked at his watch. It was past midnight. Discreetly, hoping that the chauffeur couldn't see him in the mirror, he sniffed himself. He did not smell good, but there was no time for him to return home and shower.

'Where are you?'

She named a club near the Workers' Stadium, which he recognized as one of her father's.

The bouncers were as big as Song, dressed in black, standing legs braced apart like soldiers, hands clasped behind their backs, eyes hidden behind sunglasses even in the dark lobby. Inside,

220

Song pushed his way through the crush of bodies, looking for Pearl. Light flared and died, pink then yellow, lightning sparks flashed across the ceiling, the walls were giant screens showing images like drug-induced hallucinations, dry ice shrouded the dance floor. The pounding music filled his head, making him uneasy. He could see people's faces, he could see their lips moving, but he couldn't hear their voices.

His phone rang again – he felt its vibration in his pocket rather than heard it – and he pressed it to one ear, covered the other ear, strained to listen.

'Turn around,' she said.

He turned and saw her sitting in a booth on a leopard-skin sofa, mobile phone to her ear. She was still wearing the linen trouser suit and the white shirt, long legs stretched out in front of her, flat shoes. She looked out of place here.

She raised her head, waved him over.

He didn't know how to greet her, so he put out his hand. She took it, held it briefly but firmly, and released it. Her hand was cool, like her eyes. He took a seat next to her.

'You should have checked your coat,' she said.

It was true. He was sweating profusely. He unbuttoned his coat, shrugged it off and sat awkwardly.

'Order something,' she told him, and beckoned the waiter. Watching her, the way she raised her hand so casually, flicked her wrist, index finger extended, Song imagined that she had emerged from the womb like that. He was born watching and listening. She was born beckoning waiters.

Song ordered a draught beer. After that, he didn't know what to say to her, so he looked around. A fat man in an orange shirt sat at the bar, smiling, with three bottles of Scotch whisky and a row of shot glasses in front of him. There was a foreign DJ, a big balding man, head moving in time with the music. The beer arrived and Song drank some. He turned to Pearl. He had to lean in close to talk over the music. His mouth was almost touching her ear.

'Do you come here often?' he asked.

'You're wondering why I called you so late.' She eyed him appraisingly. 'I'm thinking of hiring you. I want you to tell me about yourself.' His ears were getting better at separating out her voice from the noise, but still they had to huddle unnaturally close in order to converse.

'I'm an ex-swimmer.' He caught her eye and once more he had that strange sensation that she had stroked him with her hand. He noticed that she had slipped her narrow feet from her shoes. She wore stockings, her toes flexing against the nylon. 'I was picked for the national team but I wasn't patriotic enough to keep sticking a needle in my ass.'

She didn't find that funny. He took a deep breath.

'The agency is doing well, we're growing fast,

I'm going to take on more staff. Perhaps we'll do some international work. I have some testimonials I can share with you, refer you to some previous clients. I can assure you our reputation—'

'Where are you from?' she interrupted.

'From Daxing County. My parents were teachers, my mother died when I was a child.' She was killed, pushed from a window, but he never told people that. It was a political thing, better to leave the skeletons buried where they were; the same with his father's problems, the years of disgracc. 'My father . . . hasn't been well . . . My background isn't like yours.'

'My father never went to school,' she said, and shrugged. 'He joined the Communist Party and he got a low-paid job in a factory, but he made something of himself.'

Those words – but *he* made something of himself – as though she could not imagine why everyone did not do as her father had done, as though it was a form of peasant idiocy not to have become a millionaire.

'Well, he joined the Communist Party,' Song said slowly. 'It's not surprising he made something of himself. Joining the party is like having a gold card in your wallet.'

She smiled and gave another shrug.

'You can buy anything, go anywhere with one of those,' he said softly, 'as long as you sign yourself "liar" on the bill.'

She recoiled at his impertinence, but they were

223

struggling to hear each other over the music and she seemed to think maybe she had misheard.

'What did you say?'

'I said my father is an honest man who lives simply.' But Song heard the sharp way it came out and she took offence anyway. He cursed himself. The implications of the boy's disappearance kept nagging at him, distracting him. With the boy gone, his commission from Nelson Li had vanished. That meant his father's medical bills would go unpaid. He needed to make some money, he needed work from this woman, but with the boy gone he had lost the protection of Nelson Li, and Detective Chen could come after him again. What was the point of this job interview when really he should be attempting to flee town all over again?

'You are very close to your father,' he said to her, in a last-ditch attempt to salvage their conversation.

'I hardly know him, I have spent no time with him. We spent our childhood with relatives and in boarding schools. He was always working or entertaining clients.'

'What happened to your mother?'

'That is a good question . . .'

She broke off, distracted, and Song followed her eyes. A young man with long sideburns was making his way towards them, and Song recognized him from the silver-framed photograph in Nelson Li's house. This, then, must be the famously named Nixon. He sat down next to Pearl, pulling his chair closer to hers. Abruptly, Pearl stood and indicated that she would be back in a few minutes. Left on his own with her brother, Song held out his hand and the young man grasped it. For the first time Song saw how young he was, a boy with the eyes of a clever man. Almost instantly, Song pulled his hand away from the boy's, distrust coursing through him. He broke out in a cold sweat. Nixon had noticed him flinch, Song saw that immediately. Again Song cursed himself. These were the people he needed, the people who had money enough to hire him. Why did their wealth provoke disgust in him, when it could be his salvation?

'Do you work for your father?' he asked Nixon, making an attempt at normal conversation.

'I'm going to go to America to study, or to England, I haven't decided which.' Nixon leaned in close and Song tried not to recoil as the boy's breath brushed his neck. 'But my father insists that I stay here and learn how to do business first. So I am my father's apprentice. I model myself on him. I've told him there will soon be nothing more for me to learn. If he wants to annoy me further by refusing to let me go abroad that's up to him, he can take the consequences.'

Nixon smiled, as if to take the sting out of his words, but the smile – which was without humour or warmth – only served to deepen Song's malaise.

'Your father has been telling me about his philanthropic work,' Song said, as Pearl returned. 'Does he involve either of you in that side of things? It must be satisfying to distribute charity to the poor and needy.'

'What do you mean?' Pearl spoke nervously.

'Your father told me he had paid medical bills for people injured on his construction sites even where there was no legal requirement for him to do so. He is a very generous man.'

Nixon stared at Song, then got to his feet. He scanned the dance floor for a moment before setting off towards it. Song watched him go. He had found their brief exchange disturbing. Song found it rare, in conversation, that no connection whatsoever was made. But in this case Song felt that he might as well not have been there, that Nixon would have said exactly what he had said, or thought exactly what he had thought, with or without him there.

'My father . . .' Pearl said, turning to Song, her face distressed, 'feels responsible for the consequences . . . of things that happen.'

'What sort of things?' Song asked. He watched Nixon as he moved across the dance floor. The young man slipped effortlessly through the crowd, then seemed to manufacture a collision with a woman. As Song watched, he realized Nixon had been aiming for this woman through the crowd. The woman turned towards Nixon in confusion and Nixon bent his head to speak to her, smiling. An instant later, his hands were on her shoulders

226

but she was shaking her head and pushing him away. Quickly, he turned and went on his way.

Song glanced at Pearl and saw that she was watching Nixon too. 'What do you mean? What sort of things does your father take responsibility for?' Song reminded her of his question.

'A few months ago,' she said, 'there was an accident outside the gates of one of his sites. A car ran over a worker, it was a hit and run. My father paid compensation to the family.'

Song remembered the case. It had not reached the newspapers, but as usual there had been talk, rumour, speculation. Workers on the site said they had caught sight of the car as it ran down their colleague, and that it was Nelson Li's car, that he was at the wheel. They had demonstrated outside the gates of the construction site, demanding that the CCTV video film be given to the police, but Nelson Li's site manager told them the cameras had been empty. Song thought that perhaps Li's generosity – he had given bonuses to all the staff to get them back to work – reflected the man's pragmatism rather than a selfless sense of duty to his fellow man. In which case, what was the pragmatic motivation for finding the boy?

'I want to hire you as a bodyguard,' Pearl said. Song was taken aback by the abrupt change of subject. 'Beijing is not as safe as it was. I move around the city a lot on my father's business. People can see that I am rich. I hear terrible tales about what can happen to women on their own.'

'But still, all in all Beijing is not a dangerous place, the risk is tiny.' Song tried to reassure her, teasing her gently. 'You were more at risk in America than you are here. In a city of fifteen million you have a good chance of survival. Unless you think having a bodyguard will enhance your status.'

She frowned, and he could see that he had made a mistake by teasing her. Still, he felt sorry for her, and relieved that she was capable of vulnerability.

'I want a bodyguard,' she insisted like a child. They were still taking turns to talk in each other's ear.

'I don't do that kind of work. You need one of those guys.' He nodded in the direction of the bouncers.

'I thought you said you do security work.'

'Your father didn't put it well. I'm a detective. I deal in intelligence gathering, I don't do the fighting.'

'Why not? You have the muscle for it.'

'Because I don't like getting beaten up,' he said, and for the first time she laughed properly, her face relaxing, dimples appearing, creases at the edges of her eyes, as though he'd made a really good joke, as though she liked him for it. It was a lie, of course. He had tried doing bodyguard work, and he wouldn't do it any more because he scared himself. If he started fighting he thought he might not stop.

Song felt his mobile phone vibrate. He pulled it from his pocket and answered it with his eyes still glued to Pearl. He strained to hear, covering his other ear.

'This is Detective Fang,' a voice from the past said faintly. 'We want to speak to you.'

'Who's we?' Song raised his voice so that he could hear himself.

'It doesn't matter. You and I are old friends, and I have something to talk to you about.'

'I can't hear you,' Song bellowed, and hung up. He and Detective Fang were not friends, even if they were old allies against Detective Chen. Song had no desire to get dragged back into their quarrels.

Pearl had stood up and was reaching for her bag.

'I should go,' she said, her voice reaching him over the music.

Song nodded, grabbed his coat, and followed her. In the lobby she retrieved her coat from the cloakroom and he stood waiting for her, digging in his pocket for a cigarette. She pulled on her coat, and together they walked out into the cold. The snow had stopped falling and the air was clear and still. A chauffeured Audi purred to a halt at the kerb. Her driver opened the door for her, but she hesitated.

'Thank you for coming to meet me,' she said, softly. 'Please don't mention to anyone my desire to have a bodyguard. You are quite right, it is unnecessary. It was a silly idea.' Now, without the boom of the music, Song had the strange sensation that he could hear her unhappiness separating itself into different colours, as though he had dropped her blood onto a sheet of chromatographic paper. There were red peaks of bitterness and purple troughs of loneliness. Awkwardly, he extended his hand in farewell. With a small smile, Pearl reached out and took it, and then she turned and stepped into her car.

CHAPTER 14

When I pulled back the curtains in the hotel room on Monday morning the sky took my breath away. It was clear blue with luminous wisps of cloud. A scarlet flag danced in the wind and the advertising hoardings were splashes of vibrant colour, as though they had been washed clean overnight. The thin layer of snow that remained in places looked bright white. Even the traffic seemed clearer and faster, as if some vast, putrid obstruction had been expelled from the city, and everything was now moving as it should. With the departure of the smog, the skyline had lost its ominous murk. The tower blocks were an architect's delight, powder-puff clouds reflected in their mirrored walls so that the buildings shimmered like an illusion in the sky. I had overslept, it was past eight o'clock already. I felt a surge of energy.

I dialled Karen Turvey's number, glad that she wouldn't be able to see I was still in my pyjamas. She said hello grudgingly, and I thought she regretted her rudeness to me the day before, but not much.

'I'm afraid I have another question, but it's really quick,' I told her.

'Shoot.'

'Did you ever hear Derek talk about a man called Terry Reese? He might have met him here or in England.'

'No. Never,' she said, after a moment's thought, sounding sure. 'Why?'

'It was just a long shot,' I said evasively.

'For God's sake, if you can't be straight with me don't call me again,' she said, and hung up. I thought, as I put the phone down, that something must have happened to make her angry even before my call.

I rang Angus Perry then, steeling myself, expecting that he would hang up on me too. But he let me ask my question and quickly gave me the same reply as Karen Turvey. Then, immediately, he changed the subject.

'I'd had a few drinks last night,' he said, in a cheery tone that rang false. 'I talked a lot of rubbish about the radioactive contamination business. Lucky you didn't have your notebook on you or you'd get in trouble with your bosses for reporting fantasy. I expect it sounded so far-fetched you knew it was just the booze talking.'

'It didn't sound so far-fetched,' I said, 'and I'm not sure you'd been drinking all that much. I'd really like to sit down with you and talk through it again if you have time. We can protect your identity on film either through the camera angle we use, or blurring your face. We can even change the sound of your voice.'

But there was a click on the line and I realized I was talking into dead air.

My freelance cameraman, an American Chinese by the name of Larry Mak, was waiting for me in the lobby with Blue. We hailed a taxi, piling Larry's mountain of gear onto the back seat between us and into the boot, and holding it on our laps. As we pulled out into the traffic I turned to Blue.

'Did you find out anything by the lake yesterday afternoon?'

'I met one of the men organizing the protest. He will telephone us if there's any news. Also I was in a coffee shop and I listened to the staff chatting. One of the waitresses has a brother in the police force, and he said that the woman who was in the lake was killed on Nelson Li's construction site, in the night-watchman's tent, which burned down. They found her blood there on the ground.'

I remembered the knot of people we had encountered that first day by the lake, and the police car. The subsequent horror of the discovery of the woman's body had pushed it from my memory.

Larry pointed out of the window. 'If you look straight ahead of us, due west, you can just see the mountains through the haze? That's where we're headed, it's a district called Shijingshan.'

233

The road was thick with traffic, and the driving astounded me. No one ever seemed to stop or slow down unless they absolutely had to, so cars accelerated into impossible gaps, careening back and forth across the road. For most of the journey my foot was braced on an imaginary brake. There were cars reversing down exit roads, cars in the emergency vehicle lane, cars in the bicycle lanes.

To distract myself from imminent death I asked Larry where he lived, and about his life in Beijing. He made it sound like a lot of fun, as though with a little cash in one's pocket one could spend every night of the week at a different party. His friends were Chinese and Japanese and Russian. He had a local Chinese girlfriend, an artist who had set up a small gallery in the embassy district.

'What do you know about Nelson Li?' I asked.

'He has a different car for every day of the week, a private jet, you name it,' Larry said, 'mansions here, and in Hong Kong, and at Huanghuashan, at the Great Wall.'

'Derek Sumner spent time with him at his house at the Great Wall,' I remembered. 'Blue, can you write down the characters for that place for me?'

She took my notebook and pen and bent her head over to write.

'And,' she looked up and fixed me with her gaze as though she was about to impart very important information, 'Nelson Li is very short, only one metre fifty-five.'

'But he's rich,' I said. 'I thought you said short people can't get rich.'

'He joined the Communist Party many years ago,' she said, 'so of course he is successful. The Communist Party is not there to help the ordinary people, it is there to help the Communist Party.'

'She's right,' Larry chimed in, unperturbed, 'the party is just like the mafia.'

'They should all be lined up and shot,' Blue muttered, glaring out of the window.

We continued on our way in silence, and I used the time to look through my collection of news clippings about Li. One of the profiles made mention of a son and a daughter, but not of their mother.

'Either of you know what happened to Nelson Li's wife?' I asked.

'I heard she was a peasant,' Blue said. 'He only married her for political reasons because she was the daughter of a local party official. He divorced her when the children were small. When he started to do business in Beijing he was embarrassed by her because she could not even read and write, and he would not let the children see her any more.'

As we proceeded the air got palpably worse, and soon it became clear why. To our right, blackened apartment buildings with grimy windows were built up into the hills. To our left, behind high walls, there was a vast industrial complex, and

235

Blue informed me that this was the Capital Iron and Steel Works, the huge state-owned steel mill that the government had identified as a major polluter, and that was to be gradually moved out of the city. Right in the middle of the plant a steep hill rose above all the industry, and on its top was a pagoda whose walls were cracked and black with dust. Down below, at the perimeter, railway tracks criss-crossed the road, and vast pipes ran overhead. As we reached the crest of a hill, the landscape stretched below us, peppered with chimneys and cooling towers, all pumping white clouds into the sky. The surrounding hills were a spider's web of power lines and forested with grey pines.

Nelson Li's company, Sunrays Steel, was nestled close to Capital Iron and Steel Works, but it had its own imposing gate, its own pagoda-like roof on top of its gatehouse, and armed guards to man the entrance, one of whom stood to attention in front of us, stopping us dead. A woman, swathed in layers of clothes against the cold, emerged from the guardhouse, and we climbed out of the car.

'I am Jade, Nelson Li's secretary,' she said, smiling. 'He is looking forward to meeting you.'

We were led into a meeting room furnished with sleek Italian office furniture. One wall was covered in enlarged prints of Nelson Li shaking hands with Chinese men in suits. In one of the photographs, standing next to Nelson Li, was a young man I vaguely recognized.

I was expecting Nelson Li to be all bombast and charm, but the man who strode into the room, shook my hand (ignoring Larry and Blue, who was in any case flattened against the wall as though she thought she could melt through it and find herself on the other side), sat down on the chair opposite mine and adjusted his position for the camera lights was simply businesslike. His suit was immaculate, his cufflinks were gleaming gold. He was not much taller than Blue, with a solid torso and plentiful jet-black hair that was slickly oiled.

'Thank you for seeing me,' I said. I glanced back at the photograph of Li with the young man, trying to remember where I had seen that face before.

'I am doing international business,' he said, his English fluent if accented. 'I understand that we in China must start to do things in a more open way, at least when we are dealing with our foreign friends.'

It was the boss from the nightclub, the young man I'd seen reclining on a sofa with his white-sneakered toes jigging up and down.

'Do you know the Fashion Club down by the lake?' I asked Nelson Li.

'I own it,' he said, 'it was one of my early ventures.'

'Does your son work there?'

For a moment Nelson Li did not answer, and I thought he must be annoyed by this diversion from the matter in hand.

'He's learning about management,' he said

shortly. He has a lot to learn, I thought to myself, remembering the empty dance floor.

Larry gestured to me that he had started filming, and I gathered myself.

'You have just described to me your wish to do things in an open way,' I said to Li. 'In the same spirit, can you clear up for me the confusion about your plans for the Kelness steel mill?'

'But it is not me creating the confusion,' Nelson Li replied. Larry's lights illuminated the severity of his expression, the furrowed brow, the down-turn of the lips. 'It is the management of Kelness. What kind of negotiation is this, where radioactive contamination is kept from the buyer? This is vital information. The cost of a clean-up, of potential lawsuits from millworkers who may have been exposed? All these factors will affect my decisions, that is only natural.'

'Can you tell me exactly how you learned of the radioactive contamination?' I asked. 'Did you see an internal Kelness memo, and if so, who gave it to you?'

'You are a journalist,' he jerked his head towards me, 'so you would protect your sources. So will I.'

'If you won't give me a name,' I persisted, 'can you at least tell me whether this information came to you in the form of an internal memo? Because if it's just word of mouth, how can you evaluate its accuracy? Kelness management is continuing to deny there is any proof that contamination took place.'

'I trusted my source.'

I paused, nonplussed. Nelson Li was not a native English speaker, but he had used the past tense. Was I reading too much into it to think that maybe his source was no longer alive?

'Derek Sumner was a personal friend of yours.'

'I was delighted to know him and do business with him. He understood China very well. I invited him into my home as a guest. I cannot tell you how angry I am about his murder.'

I thought it an interesting choice of word, but angry was exactly how he looked. His jaw was tensed, his brow heavy. I noticed that his hands had clenched to fists on his lap.

'Do you think that Derek Sumner's death had anything to do with the Kelness negotiations?'

Nelson Li did not hesitate.

'That is ridiculous. I can think of no reason. It is too farfetched.'

'Did Derek Sumner ever pass internal Kelness information to you?'

'My dear lady,' Nelson Li leaned forward, gripped the arms of his chair, then launched himself upright, his polished shoes landing on the floor with a snap, 'I agreed to an interview, not to an interrogation. I am a busy man, I have no time to appear on *People's Court.*'

I glanced at Larry, and he nodded at me, grinning. I didn't smile back. It's always great tabloid television when an interviewee walks out on an interview, but I wasn't in the business of tabloid television. We would not be able to use that last piece of film. I had no evidence beyond a hunch that Derek Sumner was the mole in Kelness, and Sumner could not defend himself from the grave. If I aired that film, I would be – as Karen Turvey would no doubt put it – fucking with Derek Sumner's reputation. Larry thought I'd intentionally provoked Nelson Li on film. The truth was I just wanted to know the answer to the question.

Nelson Li swept out of the room. Jade, his secretary, thoroughly flustered but still desperately polite, herded us out the way we had come. I had the feeling that she felt her boss had been unnecessarily rude, and that she wanted to please us.

'Why did Nelson Li set up his offices so close to Capital Iron and Steel Works?' I asked her as we hurried along a cold corridor. 'After all, Kelness will be his first mill, he doesn't produce steel here in Beijing.'

She said in English, 'It is because Capital Iron and Steel Works will move away from this site to reduce pollution in the city, and when they vacate the plant Mr Li will buy some of the equipment from them. There are pieces of machinery that they will not need any longer and that Mr Li can use. So he will buy it from them and move it to the site of his new steel mill. Mr Li is new to the steel business. He likes to be close to Capital Iron and Steel Works to talk to his contacts in the plant, to learn how to run the machinery, and to discuss with engineers which parts of the mill will be of use to him.'

'Like a magpie,' said Blue out of nowhere. I looked at her in surprise. She seemed proud of her English simile.

Jade looked impressed too, and repeated, 'Yes, yes, like a magpie.'

'Or a vulture,' Larry muttered under his breath.

'It is convenient for Mr Li to have his office here, and he has an apartment here also in case he or his son or daughter works late on this side of town.'

'Where is the site for Mr Li's new mill?' I asked, trying to sound offhand. I felt Blue, at my side, pay attention. She was no fool.

'Outside Dalian,' the secretary said. 'Mr Li has secured a large area of land there.'

'Dalian is a port city in the north-east,' Blue murmured beside me.

'So that is where the Kelness plant will be moved to after it is dismantled,' I said. I swear Jade had started to nod and say yes, before it dawned on her that she had spoken out of turn.

'I think I am mistaken.' She looked shaken. 'Yes, I am mistaken.'

'But there is a plot of land outside Dalian?' I persisted.

'I don't understand,' she said, looking at me with frightened eyes. 'I don't know what you mean.'

'Mr Li has bought a plot of land for a new steel plant, that's what you told her,' Blue tried to help me out, but Jade just shook her head, and when Blue spoke to her in Chinese, she shook her head again.

She sped up so that we were racing to the exit. Even then she didn't stop until we were beyond the gate. Avoiding our eyes, she shook hands with each of us and turned and rushed away.

'She's frightened,' Blue told me, 'because she should not have told you about the land in Dalian.'

'Come on, let's go before we freeze,' I said.

We hailed a taxi and climbed in.

'How do I prove it?' I asked Blue. 'He must be intending to dismantle Kelness and move it to Dalian, but how do I prove it?'

She screwed up her face. It was hopeless, of course. Even if I took a trip to Dalian my foreign face would make me an object of suspicion. Besides, proof that Li had secured land that belonged to the city would not necessarily be easy to come by. Evidence would be lodged deep in local government offices.

'When someone gets land use rights is that information made public?' I asked Blue.

She seemed reluctant to respond. 'I don't think this information is published,' she said eventually, 'but perhaps if someone knew the appropriate official and requested the information in a polite way . . .'

'If you rang the local government offices . . .'

'I could try, but . . .'

'So try,' I said.

Larry had said nothing so far. But now he twisted round from the front seat.

'Give her your phone,' he said.

'What?'

'A call like that can't come from her mobile,' he said, his expression disapproving. 'You can always leave the country, Robin. She can't.'

'It's just land use rights,' I said. 'It's not a state secret.'

He held my gaze.

Silently I handed Blue my mobile.

I listened while she made a call to get a number, watched while she jotted it down in her notebook, and then listened again as she tried to get through to Dalian's local government offices.

'Who should I say is asking?' she said.

'The Corporation,' I said firmly. 'Let's be straight with them.'

'Don't give them your name,' Larry instructed her. 'If they want a name give them Robin's, she can be straight with them if she wants.'

Blue was passed from the switchboard to a man, and although I understood no Chinese I could hear the surprise and suspicion in his voice, and I could hear the tremor in hers. I recognized Nelson Li's name, and the word 'Kelness'. Then I heard the man's voice again, this time agitated and hectoring. Blue mumbled something, and then the line went dead.

'He said he'd never heard of the Corporation.

He wanted to know my name; he said I had no right to ask the question.'

The silence from Larry in the front seat was resounding.

After a few minutes, Blue's mobile phone rang. She spoke, and I heard excitement on the other end of the line.

'Robin,' she said urgently as she folded her mobile away, 'that was the man I spoke to yesterday. He wants us to know there will be a protest outside the local police station at the lake in one hour. He says there is a foreign man in custody and the people are angry because they think the police might release him in order not to offend other countries.'

I looked at my watch. It was five in the morning in London, but I needed to talk to Finney. I dialled his number, and he answered blearily.

'What's happened? Are you all right?'

'I wanted to say sorry for yesterday.'

He groaned.

'Robin, you still have to go through the press office. I can't give you anything on Reese.'

'There's going to be a protest here because the locals think he's the serial killer, and they're demanding that he's charged. Reuters will get hold of the story, and then the newspapers will get hold of it and they'll speculate about a link with Derek Sumner, because it's the obvious question.'

Finney groaned again.

'All I want to know is,' I persisted, 'did you come across anything in your investigation that might suggest he knew Derek Sumner?'

There was a long silence on the line, and then Finney said, 'No.'

'Or that he had any link at all with Kelness?'

I heard Finney breathe heavily.

'Reese grew up in a small town ten miles from Kelness,' he said, 'his mother still lives there. That's all, it's as good as nothing.'

Then I dialled Sean Benton's number at the embassy.

'I have some information for you,' I said, 'but I have a question for you first.'

'I'm not promising I'll answer, but let me hear the question,' he said.

'This Reese character—' I started, but he interrupted me.

'How do you know his name?'

'The press had it yesterday,' I said, and heard him swear softly at the other end of the line, 'the arrest, and his activities in England. The paper didn't make the link with the serial killer, but they will. The embassy must have been trying to find out more about him. Have you come across any evidence that he knew Derek Sumner?'

He hummed and hawed, and then he said, 'I'm probably allowed to answer that because the answer's no.'

I thought for a moment about how I still wanted Benton on my side. 'Sean, I've heard there's going to be a protest outside the police station at the lake in a few minutes. The locals have heard there's a Westerner in custody.'

'Damn!' Benton said, and then, 'Damn!'

'You owe me,' I reminded him, before he put the phone down.

I put my mobile away and stared out of the window at the bleached landscape, the sepia residential apartment blocks and the busy shops and restaurants at street level. I had been wrong to write Reese out of the equation. That one small link – a childhood spent ten miles from Kelness – could lead to greater and more sinister connections. I thought of the people who lived near the lake, and how frightened they must be that the killer would strike again. Just like me they were clutching at straws, at insubstantial rumour and unreliable hunches. How could anyone blame them for assuming Reese's guilt in the absence of any other information? I asked Blue to redirect the driver to the lake, where the protest would soon begin. Sometimes it's only when people get angry that you begin to learn the truth.

CHAPTER 15

Song found the metal gate to the office locked. That should have pleased him, but he was distracted. Inside he registered, as if from a great distance, that the office was tidier, and Wolf was not there. He walked through the office to the door which led to his private quarters. It was bitterly cold, but he stripped off his clothes and stepped into a hot shower, and stood with his head bowed as the water purged the grime and sweat from him and steam filled the room.

He did not understand what had happened in the past few hours, but he knew that Pearl and Nixon were not like him. They came from different worlds. He was not sure whether there was a set of values in their world, or a standard by which behaviour was judged acceptable or unacceptable, and if there was, what it consisted of. He sometimes wondered what exactly his own values were, and even whether he had any. The government had been trying ever since liberation to dictate standards of behaviour for the entire population, the first of these was always patriotism, loving the country, by which they meant submitting to the

Communist Party. But the pendulum of politics, swinging ceaselessly forwards and backwards, had produced only confusion and a desperate clinging to self-preservation. Song had a sense of something that pushed him to do some things and stopped him doing others, but he had never attempted to codify or define what that thing was, and much of the time he felt as though he was floating in a choppy grey sea, buffeted by waves and not sure which way to swim to find land.

He rubbed himself dry and dressed hurriedly, and then he went to the place where Wolf had hidden the knife. He reached up to the top of the wardrobe and, behind piles of papers and books, he found it still there, a cardboard box, and inside he could feel the knife, wrapped in the boy's jacket. He pulled the cardboard box towards him, and as he did so the lid came loose and the knife and jacket fell, parting company as they tumbled to the floor, the knife narrowly missing Song's foot, the jacket landing separately, something small and black bouncing away from it and disappearing again under the wardrobe.

Song swore. He bent and gingerly picked up the knife, checking that it was still in one piece, placing it on top of a towel on the bed. Then he bent again and looked under the wardrobe for the object that had fallen from the child's jacket. He could see it, small and flat, with some kind of white string or wire attached, and just beyond his reach. He looked around him for a suitable implement, picked up a plastic fly-swatter, and, on his knees, prodded the thing out towards him. It emerged at last. He picked it up, sat back on his heels and inspected it, then shook his head in puzzlement. What was the beggar boy doing with an iPod? His fingers explored it, and a tinny beat emerged from the headphones. He fiddled with it, muttering in frustration until he found how to turn it off.

He placed it on the bed next to the knife and stood back, staring down at it. It told him nothing. The child might have stolen it, he thought, or been given it, or found it. Only one thing was certain, and that was that he had not bought it. Still staring at the knife and the iPod, he fumbled for his mobile phone and dialled Lina's number.

'Tell your father I'll meet him at your place in an hour,' he told his ex-wife. 'I have something for him.'

The orange dog started yapping, backing away from him, as soon as Lina opened the door. Song walked past her, shrugging off his coat, ignoring the dog, and found Detective Chen sitting slumped on the sofa. He looked worse than the last time Song had seen him, eyes bloodshot, skin with an oily sheen. There was an ashtray at his elbow, a thin trail of smoke rising from a cigarette.

'Where's the boy? Lina said you were bringing the boy.' Detective Chen pulled himself up to stand and face Song. Then he seemed to regret the decision, because in the small space Song loomed over him. Detective Chen collapsed back onto the sofa and reached for his cigarette.

'Something else, not the boy,' Song said, holding up the bag in which he had put the box which contained the knife.

Detective Chen muttered an obscenity then spoke sharply to his daughter, waving her away, the cigarette between his fingers describing an arc in the air: 'Leave us alone.'

Lina bent to attach a chain to the dog's collar. She glanced up at Song, who saw the worry on her face.

'Where's Doudou?' he asked her.

'I've sent him away to be with my aunt in Tianjin for a rest,' she said, her eyes going nervously to her father.

Song watched her lead the dog from the apartment, his heart heavy. If Doudou had been sent away to relatives, then the threat of disgrace must not be far away. He wished that Lina had gone too, so that Doudou had his mother with him, but she was too close to her father. If Detective Chen fell, then Lina would have to run further than Tianjin to escape trouble.

When the door had closed behind Lina, he turned back to his ex-father-in-law, who was glowering at him from the sofa.

'There is a problem,' Song said, sitting at the other end of the sofa, placing the plastic bag on the floor at his feet. 'I can't find the boy, I don't think he's in Beijing.'

'You witless idiot,' Detective Chen spat the words out, scattering spittle over Song's face, 'you let him go, and now you're going to ruin me.'

'You've ruined yourself,' Song muttered, 'but be that as it may, I have something else for you.' He picked up the plastic bag, taking out the box and lifting off the lid, producing the knife. He had sluiced it under the shower, washing it clean of everyone's DNA so as to avoid confusion. Then he had wrapped it in clean paper, and now it looked as good as new, gleaming in the light from the window.

'What is it?' His ex-father-in-law's eyes ran over the blade.

'It's what you think: the murder weapon. I lied to you, I didn't drop it in the woods. I've cleaned it because it had my blood on it and that would have misled your investigators, but it should be examined.'

Detective Chen lowered his head, inspecting the knife intently, but he did not touch it.

'We think the same knife killed the foreigner and the women,' he said. 'We could learn more from this. It's foreign, it looks expensive. We may be able to discover where it was sold, and even who to. It's likely to have been sold in a high-class department store.'

'Or in a foreign country,' Song said, because this was something that had occurred to him more than once.

'Or in a foreign country,' Detective Chen growled, 'in which case we're finished. You've heard there's a protest by the lake this afternoon, people upset about the killings, accusing us of dragging our feet, failing to protect them? They've found out we've detained a foreigner, they want to think he did it all, the women and the British man.'

'Did he?'

'He had a knife, but not like this, a small pocket knife. It was blunt and he used it to terrorize the woman he was with, but it would not sever a man's neck.' His eyes went back to the knife, and he shook his head. 'If I give this to the forensic pathologist, questions will be asked, he'll want to know why it's so clean.'

The two men sat and thought.

'Perhaps you could find it in the lake,' Song suggested.

Detective Chen wiped his hand across his lips, his eyes still fixed on the knife.

'There's been an attack since then,' he said, thinking aloud. 'The wound is different, it's obviously a different knife, so it would not be strange if this one's found elsewhere, people will think the murderer dumped it with the body in the lake.'

'What happened this time?'

'Another prostitute. This time she's not dead so we know what happened. She's a scrawny thing, but she's worked in the fields and she's as strong and stubborn as a mule, brought here from

Shenyang with a gang, lodging in a hostel, ten to a room. You know how it goes, her boss distributes business cards in the better hotels, and when a hotel guest feels in need of a woman there is a mobile number, and a girl is dispatched to the hotel to service him. There was a phone call. Her boss took it, but he's scarpered now. Anyway, the girl was dressed up like a tart and dispatched to the Waimao Hotel, room 518. When she got there it was about eleven at night, the door was ajar and she went in. She closed the door behind her, assuming he was inside, and that he'd want privacy once she went in. The room was empty, but a man's voice called to her from the bathroom saying he'd be out in a minute and she should make herself comfortable. She got bored and started to look out of the window. She heard the bathroom door click, and then he grabbed her and put a knife to her throat, and started to paw at her and tear her clothes. He pushed her face down on the bed, grabbed her hair, pulled her head back and started to cut her neck, but she kicked up with her foot, she had high-heeled boots on, and she must have caught him, because he cried out and half rolled off her. She managed to get free, and to run as far as the lift. She made it to the lobby and collapsed. Within minutes, a member of hotel security went into the room, but he was gone out of the window.'

'From which floor?'

'Fifth floor; he dropped two floors to a lower roof, then from there to the ground.'

'Is it the same man?'

'We can't be sure. This woman said her attacker wore a surgical mask, and that is consistent with the other woman who was attacked in Shijingshan two months ago. But if this British man killed the women by the lake then he cannot have done this too. He has been in detention. In that case, there must be someone else.' His voice dropped to a bitter, anxious murmur, thick with contempt. 'Maybe the so-called serial killer squad knows something I don't. I see the way they look at me. They hold meetings without me . . . they've got Detective Fang investigating me. He's been waiting for this for years. He's demanded the paperwork for my affairs . . . bank accounts, apartments. You know Fang, you know how inflexible he is. He's got a list of questions for me . . . I'm refusing to cooperate.' He gave a yelp of laughter and shook his head hopelessly. He pushed the knife across the sofa, and drew his sleeve across his nose, and then his eyes.

'These women who've been knifed and survived,' Song said, 'did any of them say the attacker wore earphones, like for an iPod?'

'A what?' Detective Chen frowned.

'For listening to music,' Song explained, describing it with his hands. 'It's a very small device, with earphones.'

Detective Chen looked baffled.

'No,' he said.

Song did not want to be asked why he was

254

asking. He felt strangely protective of the iPod. It had been in the beggar boy's jacket, but perhaps it had nothing to do with the murder of his sister. Perhaps he had stolen it or been given it. If he found the boy he would give the iPod back to him and he would ask him about it then.

'Keep Lina out of it if you can,' he said gruffly to his ex-father-in-law. 'She doesn't deserve to be pulled down with you.'

He picked up his coat, opened the door, then thought of something and turned back to Detective Chen, who was gazing at the floor.

'Let me know about the knife, let me know if it killed the foreigner.' Song closed the door behind him.

On Alley Number 7, outside the walled police compound in a small square at the junction of several alleys, Song joined the people who were gathering. He stayed on the edge of the crowd, an observer not a participant. He scanned the faces, recognizing many of his neighbours. He was dismayed but not surprised to see the crowd was dotted with thugs, men who were paid trouble-makers. The thugs could dispense the beatings that the police could not. They each wore a black leather jacket. They would be able to identify each other quickly, no matter how messy things got. He saw a man with a news camera propped on his shoulder, and knew his presence would antagonize the police. There was one foreign face in the crowd, a pale-skinned woman, thin and beautiful, who was tugging her scarf over golden-red hair, but Song could not understand how she thought she could disguise the fact that she was a foreigner. The foreign woman was leaning down to listen to a short Chinese woman, and Song thought that the smaller woman must be a tour guide, or a translator.

In front of the gate to the compound, half a dozen police guards watched impassively as a middle-aged woman shouted at them, sobbing, 'I have lived here all my life but now I'm afraid to go out to the market to buy vegetables in case someone cuts my throat and leaves my child motherless. Why don't you police protect us? Is it because the killer is one of you?'

There were cries of support from women in the crowd. Song glanced up at the windows of the police station and saw faces looking out, watching. Several officers were levelling cameras on the crowd. There would be an offical record. They would not let this go on.

Then a man pushed his way to the front. Instead of shouting at the guards, he turned his back on them and addressed the crowd instead. Immediately they fell silent and listened, watching as he jerked his thumb back towards the station.

'There is a foreign rapist in there,' he shouted, 'and the police are hiding him.'

Even before he had finished speaking, the mood of the crowd had changed. Another man screamed.

'The foreigner is a diversion. The killer is a cop. They're trying to put us off the scent,' but he was howled down.

Some of the women melted away then, or stood silently watching as a hard core, mostly men, ran at the gates. One man kicked wildly at a police guard, and a pile of scuffling bodies fell to the ground. A voice from inside the compound came through a megaphone. 'Go home, you are impeding traffic, we must maintain stability, go home.'

Again and again the voice rang out, the words never changing. But far from dispersing, the crowd seemed to turn into a tidal wave, and Song could see the pale foreigner and the short Chinese woman being buffeted back and forth as the crowd gathered itself and then made a second onslaught on the gates of the police station. She should not be there, he thought, she stood out too much, she was too much of a target. She would get hurt. Song saw the thugs in the crowd exchanging glances, and knew they would soon disperse the protesters with violence. Song pushed slowly through the crowd towards the pale woman, wincing as people moved and banged against his burned arm.

When he reached them, he bent down and spoke in the ear of the short woman.

'You have to get the foreigner out of here,' he said.

'I know that,' she shouted back up at him,

straining to be heard over the noise of the crowd, her face angry. '*You* try to make her go, I can't.'

There was a swell of excitement, then shrieks of alarm, and Song saw, over the heads around him, that the thugs had, at some pre-arranged signal, swung into action, breaking up the crowd with their fists and their shoulders and their feet. Mostly people scattered, trying to keep out of the way of violence. But some had been whipped into even greater fury, and fist fights were breaking out. As bodies pressed against Song, he saw that some people were scrabbling up and over the walls, into the courtyards of the houses beyond. The pale woman had started pushing her way through the crowd towards the cameraman. Two black-jacketed men wrestled the camera from him. One of them held him in an armlock while the other ripped the film cassette from his camera. Next to Song, the tiny Chinese woman was having trouble standing upright. He bent and lifted her, placing his hands under her arms, and she gave an astonished cry. She was as light as a feather, and he lifted her over his head, and she hovered there, above the crowd, her hands clutching at his wrists. If he could reach the courtyard wall, she could climb down the other side to safety. He waded through the crowd, shouting at her not to wriggle, to let him carry her, he was trying to help her. Then, at the last minute, with the wall just out of reach, someone grabbed his right arm, and the pain tore through him; he lost his grip, she slid from his grasp, and he huddled over his arm, clasping it to him, head bent until the agony passed.

When Song looked around him again, the girl was pushing her way through the crowd towards the pale foreign woman, who had almost reached the cameraman, slumped on the ground with his head in his arms. He saw them all seized at once, the cameraman yanked roughly to his feet, the tiny woman scooped up as easily as a puppy, fists flailing, the pale woman giving as good as she got, elbowing the thug in his ribs. Song moved through the crowd towards them.

Down one of the alleyways, he saw that police in riot gear were emerging from a white van and moving towards the crowd. The pale woman twisted to look behind her, but she was bundled up and into the van, and the cameraman was thrown in after her. He could see that the small woman was already lying inside, on the floor of the van, curled in her coat, shaking like a broken bird.

'You!' An officer yelled at Song and ran towards him, stopping just short, intimidated by his size. 'You get in the van.'

'Why me?' Song was confused.

The officer seized Song's right arm. It was a simple reflex. Song's left fist struck out at the man who was still attached to his burned arm, swiping him across the face with such force that the police officer fell to the ground.

Then four of them grabbed hold of him. One of them kicked him hard in the groin and then, when he was doubled over, they opened the door of the van and pushed him inside. For a while he huddled over, shoulders heaving. The van shuddered and moved away, and when Song raised his head he saw the small woman had rolled herself into a corner, all green padding, her face hardly visible. The cameraman seemed to be trying to bash his way out of the van. The pale foreign woman was glaring around her. She said something to him in English, and Song shook his head and looked away, finding a small window in the side of the van. Outside, the crowd was reduced to the wounded and the thugs and a few diehards. Up ahead, helmeted officers were hauling open the gates to let the van pass inside the high walls of the police compound.

CHAPTER 16

They bundled me out of the van and through a dark corridor, and it was in a room with pale green walls and fluorescent lighting that I finally lost it.

'Get your hands off me,' I yelled at the man who was gripping my upper arm. He looked about seventeen years old and the belt of his uniform was tight around a thin waist, but his bony fingers were like claws. I twisted away from him but he squeezed harder.

All the frustration of the past few days came bursting up out of me. If they had been able to understand English, they would have known just how I felt about a country where protesters were set upon by thugs, and where the police grabbed you for filming in the street.

After a couple of minutes, an older uniformed man came in, and I started to tell him too. He began to look immensely irritated, which was fine by me. He barked an order at one of the young recruits, who hurried from the room. A moment later Blue appeared, escorted, head bowed. She gave a nod of deference in the direction of the

261

police officer, and then she raised her head and gave me a look that told me to keep my mouth shut.

'You are being very dangerous,' she hissed at me, 'and very stupid.'

I shut up mid-sentence. I followed Blue's lead and lowered my head. We were made to sit on metal-framed chairs next to each other in front of a large desk, and behind that desk sat the senior officer who looked at us as though his day had already been very bad. He wore a heavy green coat over his uniform, and as my temper cooled a great chill came over me. In part it was physical. This room had seen no sun, and it was bitterly cold. But the larger part was a frigid realization that I had indeed been dangerous, not just to myself but to Blue. Why had I assumed my escorts did not speak English? Why had I not assumed that everything I said would be recorded for later translation? I had cursed China, I had cursed China's police force, I had ranted and raved about the freedom of the press. The press . . .

'Where's Larry?' I turned to Blue, but she ignored me. The officer snapped at her. She unzipped her coat and dug in a pocket for a plastic wallet that she handed over.

'Give me your ID,' she said to me, her voice harsh. I took my passport from my bag and handed it over, my heart thumping as the officer spent forever thumbing through it, staring at the visa stamp that I'd got at the Chinese embassy in London.

He looked up, and there followed an exchange in Chinese. The officer fired questions at Blue – I supposed the questions were as much about me as about her – and she answered with no reference to me. Once I tried to interrupt, to insist that she translate the question and give me a chance to speak for myself, but she gave me another from her gallery of murderous looks, and I shut up again.

That was when my mobile phone rang. I pulled it from my pocket, glanced at the screen and saw that Finney was trying to reach me. I hesitated.

'Turn it off,' I heard Blue spit, but this time I ignored her.

'My children,' I whispered to her. 'I have to take it in case there's an emergency.' I looked away from her, feeling the officer's eyes on me. I expected Finney's voice on the line, heard Hannah instead.

'Mummy, Mummy, why didn't you call us?'

I cupped my hand around the phone, turning my face from the officer, who was watching me stonily.

'Hannah, is everything all right?'

'You said you'd call us, why didn't you call us?' Her voice was a howl, and it seemed to spread through the interrogation room and grow louder.

'I'm sorry my love, I can't speak to you right now,' I said, and then the howl grew louder. I looked at Blue. Her face was appalled.

'Tell him it's my kids,' I told her weakly. 'I'm

263

very sorry, tell him my daughter hurt herself, that's why she's crying.'

Perhaps, I thought, my lie would earn sympathy points. Finney came on the line.

'Why's Hannah crying?' His voice was wearily protective of the child in his care. I had never heard him speak like that before.

'I can't speak to her now,' I could barely control my voice.

'You said you'd ring them before school to wish them luck in the school concert. They've been waiting for you to ring . . .'

'I'm in police custody. I'll call you back as soon as I'm out . . .'

There was a moment's double take, and then he got it, his voice changing.

'What can I do? Can I ring someone at the embassy?'

'No,' I told him. 'Right now I just need to be off the phone.'

He hung up. Just like that. And I loved him for it. I stared at the slip of plastic in my hand. I had been there, with them, half in this room, half somewhere across the world. I switched my phone to its silent setting.

Behind me I became aware of Blue's voice. I turned back towards her, saw her there, still pleading my case, and suddenly I wanted to cry. She should have left me to fend for myself. Without me, none of us would be in this mess. She was trying to dig me out of a hole, and she would dig herself in deep.

'Stop,' I found myself muttering to her, 'please stop, it's all right, I'll take care of it,' but she just kept right on going, talking over me.

The telephone vibrated in my hand. Damien's number appeared on the screen. Blue glanced at me anxiously, but I shook my head, reassuring her I wouldn't take the call.

As the conversation washed around me, only its texture was accessible, a roiling wave of apology and censure, penitence and castigation. Even through my anger I found myself responding to the officer's tone, beginning to feel that we must have done something terribly wrong. Blue was mostly calm. Then at one point she dipped her head and I thought that she was crying, but when she turned her face slightly towards me I could see that her eyes were dry and full of anger.

Outside, dusk was drawing in, the thin rays falling through the window increasingly faint, until I could see a yellow-grey sky outside. Eventually, when I had lost all sense of time passing, the officer pushed back his chair, got to his feet and left the room.

'What's going on?' I asked Blue, but she shushed me, and we sat there silently waiting for what felt like forever, under the eye of a young officer who looked more scared of us than we were of him.

The officer returned, took up his seat behind the desk and spoke severely to Blue. She bent her head subserviently, murmuring what I guessed must be apologies. The officer jerked his head in acknowledgement of Blue's servility, then threw her ID card and my passport skidding across the desk towards us. Again he pushed his chair back, again he stood, and this time Blue stood too, and I saw her hand dart out and sweep her card and my passport from the desk into her pocket before he could change his mind. I stood, my legs stiff from the cold, feet almost numb against the floor. I took my lead from Blue, waiting for the officer to leave, and then I followed her out of the room and into the long corridor.

Outside it was dark and a bitterly cold wind was screaming through the alleyway.

'Shit,' I muttered, 'where's Larry? What have they done with him? Did you see him in there?' She turned a stare on me, then shook her head.

I swore again, pulled out my mobile and started to dial, but Blue snatched it from my hand.

'You've already done too many stupid things,' she snapped at me. 'If he's with the police when you call him, then they'll find out you know him.'

Now I gazed at her, befuddled.

'They don't know I know him?'

'If he will tell them, then he would be stupid like you.' Blue's English tenses went astray in her anger.

'So . . . what did you tell the police?'

'I told him you're a tourist, I'm your guide, and that we came upon the protest by chance, and that you saw Larry hurt, and that was why you went to him, to help,' she said. 'He told me it is my

266

responsibility to keep you away from unpredictable situations like this afternoon that could give you the wrong impression about China, and will cause negative consequences on the international stage, and that I should take you to the Great Wall or the Forbidden City, which are more appropriate for foreign visitors.'

I cursed silently under my breath. It was standard Corporation procedure to get tourist visas for countries where regimes dictated that there was no other way to get in and get the news. But it was another thing for Blue to lie on my behalf to a police officer sitting across a table from me.

'Don't you think that's ridiculous? Doesn't it strike you as paranoid?' It came out of my mouth like a challenge. 'Saying foreigners can't see what happens in public on the streets of the capital?'

'Of course I think it's ridiculous,' she rounded on me. 'Do you think I am some Communist Party—' she searched for the word – 'some Communist Party fan? What should I do about it? I wish I could see the Statue of Liberty, I wish I could have that freedom. You have a vote, I do not. It doesn't matter what *I* think.'

We stood for a moment, both of us shivering, barely able to think, let alone speak. If Larry was still inside I didn't want to walk away from him, but we weren't doing him much good out here, risking frostbite and insulting each other.

'Come on,' I said, 'let's walk. I should be

thanking you. Tell me everything you said. I'm sorry I shouted at them.'

'When you shouted, he doesn't understand, but he knows you're not their friend, so he is suspicious. He says that foreign journalists and spies like to seek out the tiny handful of dissatisfied people so that they can write negative things about China's conditions. He said that I would bear responsibility if there were unfortunate consequences to your visit.'

Unfortunate consequences . . . I thought of Larry's battered camera, his life, his Chinese girlfriend. Then, as she walked so silently beside me, I thought of Blue. She'd lied to save my neck, she'd lied to the police.

I glanced behind us, at the dark bulk of the police station to check that we weren't being followed. A tall man emerged from the gate. I remembered how he'd knocked down the police officer, and how he'd been kicked and hurled into the van. Yet here he was, walking free.

I put my hand on Blue's arm.

'Is that the man who tried to help us?'

'I think so,' she said.

'Let's wait,' I said. 'Perhaps he can tell us what happened to Larry.'

'But we don't know who he is.' Her rebellion was still simmering.

'For God's sake,' I turned on her, 'he tried to help us. Don't you trust *anyone*?'

Blue's unspoken recrimination was as loud as

the wind that whistled through the alleyway. I had endangered her, and now I was putting her in further jeopardy, waiting here for a man she did not trust. I was like a time bomb around her neck, seconds counting down to my escape and to her ruination. But how could I let her go? Without her I was speechless, useless. Without her I did not exist, not here at least. The tall figure loped its way along the street towards us, head lowered, shoulders hunched.

We waited there in bitter silence, ahead of us the lake where I had seen the woman's body in the water, the wood where Derek Sumner's body was found. The bloody deaths, the protest, our detention and interrogation were not random happenings, the lines between them could be traced, but I could not do it on my own.

CHAPTER 17

Inside the police station, Song let himself be led by his good arm. He heard the foreign woman in the distance. He wasn't sure why she was shouting, but he knew that it would achieve nothing, just as the protesters screaming outside the gates would achieve nothing. Tomorrow they would nurse their bruises and they would count their missing – organizers spirited to jail for days or weeks or more – and their bitterness would grow.

He thought they would not hurt her. When he was growing up it was drummed into him that no foreigner could be trusted. Most foreigners, indeed, were spies for foreign governments, conspiring to topple the People's Republic, if not by armed force then by feeding Chinese with 'spiritual pollution'. For the few foreigners visiting China, that meant an internal exile that looked like extravagant courtesy: the foreigner shall eat behind a screen; shall be allowed only to travel in prosperous areas; shall be ushered to the front of the queue; shall have his own currency; shall live separated, behind a wall; he shall make love only with his own kind. Now foreigners roamed China as freely as they roamed their own countries. Foreigners could no longer push to the front of the queue, but they could sleep with whoever they pleased, live wherever they pleased, could imagine they were living entirely like a Chinese. But still the foreign woman would be treated better, probably she would not be hit.

When he entered the duty officer's room, Detective Fang looked up at him with no surprise. There were great bags under the man's eyes, as though he had not slept, and he observed Song mournfully.

Song shook off his escort and sat down without being asked. Fang gestured with his head that the young officer should leave the room.

'So, what is your interest in this, Song Ren?' Fang asked. He spoke dolefully. Not once had he raised his voice against Detective Chen, not once stood against him, although Song had seen in his face how much he despised his boss.

'Why did they bring me in? You know I have no interest in organizing activities like this.'

'You wouldn't come to me so I had to come to you. I knew you would be here, I looked for you on the surveillance camera, I seized the moment.' In his own downbeat way Fang seemed pleased at his inventiveness. Song remembered him as a straightforward man not given to political games. 'A dozen people saw you hit that officer, so they know why you're here, and now we can speak frankly.'

Song scanned the room. If there was recording equipment, it was unlikely to be visible, rather it would be lurking in a light fitting or taped to a chair.

'Detective Chen is about to fall,' Fang continued, glancing towards the door. 'They've taken all his responsibilities away from him, he can't last more than a week. They'll take him away. There's a special investigation team working on the serial killing. The leadership can't afford this kind of social instability. You heard them out there, there's word that Detective Chen's covering up for a police officer.'

'One of your colleagues,' Song said, intending bravado.

'Maybe not a serving officer, maybe someone who was on the force who had access to police plates, someone who's left the force.' Fang hesitated. 'Someone like Psycho Wang, or someone perhaps who has family or business connections with Detective Chen, some reason for him to protect them.'

Song cleared his throat.

'You have a foreigner in custody, that's what they say, they say he'll be charged with the killings.'

'We have no evidence to use against him, the outcome of his detention is still unclear . . . and it is irrelevant to the case against Detective Chen.' Fang paused, then said almost apologetically, 'Detective Chen says that if he falls he'll take you with him.'

Song's throat grew dry. The smoke from the fire seemed to smother him again. Fang's voice went on, relentless, low, like the hum of electricity. 'The investigating team is double-checking every witness interview, they're sending people out into the provinces to find anyone who's left town. Some of the things they discovered have led them to establish a second investigation, a tangential one, touching on Detective Chen's business dealings, on family use of official funds.'

Fang leaned across the table, eyes gloomy.

'Tell me, Song, can Detective Chen do it, can he bring you down with him?'

The two men stared at each other. If this was being recorded, Song thought, it could be the end of one of them.

'Are you part of the investigation team?' Song's mouth was so dry that he had trouble articulating the question.

'I am assisting in the clarification of Detective Chen's affairs.'

What was it he had thought – that he wanted to be there when they led Detective Chen away in handcuffs? Well, he likely would be, although not in the way he had intended. He could almost feel the metal on his wrists. And what of Lina and Doudou, would they have to hide their faces in shame? Song knew Fang to be a decent man, but he did not trust Fang's superiors. Song thought of Doudou, fat chin wobbling in humiliation. Then he said, 'What do you want from me?'

'You know all Detective Chen's dealings. You can bring him down and save yourself, save your son.'

Song stood, the chair fell behind him, clattering on the concrete floor.

'The man's my father-in-law,' he said.

'Ex-father-in-law,' Fang corrected, sadly, 'and I can assure you *he* has no affection for *you*.'

'I have to think,' Song said.

'You misunderstand me. This is not an offer,' Fang shook his head. 'You can save your skin by providing us with documentation. Or I am afraid you will go down with Detective Chen. I cannot protect you, although I would like to. There is talk that you helped him trace dirty money he had lost; they say he is covering up for you.'

Song thought of Wolf, whose mouth sometimes swung as wide open as the office gate, information running out of it like diarrhoea. How else could Fang have known of Song's work for his former father-in-law?

'You must think hard about your situation,' Fang said slowly and heavily. 'Tonight you may go. If Detective Chen's spies are out their suspicions must not be raised. You may not leave town. You may not communicate with Detective Chen. If you do, I will know about it. In fact, if you fart tonight, I will know about it. Tomorrow you must bring documentation, diaries, any information that you have to central police headquarters. It's the best that I can do for you.'

★   ★   ★

Song, head buried in his collar against the biting wind, mind turned inwards, did not even see the women until the tiny Chinese one accosted him. He didn't hear her question at first over the whining of the wind. He had to ask her to repeat herself, and he bent his head to listen. The other one, the foreign one, stood close to the short woman, as if she wanted to take part in the conversation and was frustrated that she couldn't, and he understood without being told that she could not speak Chinese, and that the short one was her translator. The question was about a man, a friend of theirs, someone who had been detained by the police. He tried to pretend he still couldn't hear, or that he didn't know the answer – he was too preoccupied with his own problems to get involved in the difficulties of a foreigner – and he started to walk on, but the short one ran after him and grabbed his arm.

'He was filming,' she said, pleading with him. 'We are worried about him.'

Song stopped and shook her off, but gently.

'He's still in there,' Song found himself saying, shouting over the wind, despite himself. 'I saw him on my way out.'

He was going to walk on again, but something – perhaps it was the agitation of the foreign woman as the short one translated – changed his mind. Then the short one asked, 'How did he look? Was he all right?'

Song saw that they were both shaking with the cold. He shrugged. 'He looked fed up,' he replied.

His phone rang. The number was Lina's but when he took the call the voice was Detective Chen's.

'The knife's the same,' his ex-father-in-law said. 'There's a kink in the blade that tears the flesh and makes marks on the bone where the cuts have reached the spine. Also the tip of the blade has been chipped off.'

'In all the victims?' Song demanded, needing absolute accuracy, and forgetting about the women who were listening. 'Are the cuts the same in the foreign man and in the woman in the lake and in the prostitute on the rubbish dump by the lake?'

'They are.'

'And the woman who was attacked two months ago and survived in Shijingshan?'

'The cut wasn't so deep, but it is likely that it was caused by that knife, or one like it.'

When Song ended the call, he realized that the Chinese translator was staring at him.

'Who are you, what do you do?' she asked him.

Distractedly Song dug deep in his jacket pocket. He found another battered business card and handed it over with an impatient nod of his head.

She peered down at the card in the half-light. The foreign woman was frowning, looking from one to the other of them, clearly not sure what was going on.

'Song Ren. You call yourself a consultant,' she said. 'What does that mean?'

'I'm a private detective,' he said, wishing that he could escape. But the Chinese woman persisted.

'I'm sorry to eavesdrop, but I could hear that you're investigating the deaths of the women who have been murdered near here.'

Song looked for words to deny it, but she had heard what she had heard, there was no getting out of it short of a downright lie, and something stopped him lying to her.

'That's right, I am,' he said.

She seemed to be making up her mind about something. Her face twisted and then she spoke. 'My employer is a foreign journalist. I think the two of you should talk to each other. I would like to invite you to dinner. We are all cold and hungry.'

Song shook his head in an instinctive refusal. His head was churning with the things that Fang had said to him. He did not need the further complication of a foreign journalist. He glanced behind him and a figure retreated into the shadows.

'I think it would be to your advantage,' the woman said to him. 'She is investigating the death of the foreign man, and I think that she may be able to help you in your enquiries.'

The restaurant was full. The noise of conversation rose up to meet them together with a wall of garlic-infused heat, and the air was thick with a

fug of smoke from cigarettes and steam from caul-
drons of muddy soup. Song glanced back at the
doorway, and saw that two of Detective Fang's
plainclothes officers were following them inside.
Song looked for the waitress, who was rushed off
her feet. He beckoned her over.

'We want a private room,' he told her.

She hurried them between tables of red-faced
diners to a corridor that led away from the main
dining room, and which was lined with doors. She
opened one of these and led them into a private
booth with plain grey walls, a bright white light
over their heads, and a table with a disposable
plastic cover. Song ordered rapidly, without asking
to see a menu, and the waitress left, the door
banging shut behind her.

The Chinese guide was speaking rapidly – Song
had noticed that the foreign woman called her
Blue, which was a word Song knew, although he
thought it a strange name. Song could tell that
they were speaking English, but he could not
understand what was being said. He was interested to see that the foreign woman's skin, which
had a blue tinge when they entered the restaurant,
was recovering a pink hue in the heat, with two
spots of red high on her cheeks where her skin
was freckled. She was staring at him, and then she
started to fire questions at Blue, who translated
them.

'She wants to know who hired you to investigate this.'

278

'No one hired me,' Song said. 'I have my own reasons for investigating.'

'She says she is looking for links between the death of the British man and the deaths of the Chinese women.'

The waitress returned, with a large metal bowl of liquid which she placed on top of a gas flame, a plate of thinly sliced raw meat, and others of raw vegetable. The soup began to bubble.

'I want to hear what she knows first,' Song said.

'She thinks the British man was killed because of his work here. She thinks it's possible the British man who has been detained killed him. The man who has been detained grew up in a town not far from where the victim worked.'

Song thought that this might be nothing more than coincidence, but he did not say so.

Seeing that the foreign woman did not know how to eat, Song picked up the plate of raw sliced meat and tipped half of it into the boiling soup, along with dark green leaves and raw mushrooms. He waited a few moments, then fished in the soup with his chopsticks and drew out a piece of the lamb, now cooked to a dull grey with veins of white fat. He dipped this into a bowl of sesame paste, into which he had mixed coriander and chilli sauce, oil and garlic, and then placed the meat on the woman's plate. He balanced his chopsticks against his plate and waited while she lifted the slice of meat to her mouth with her chopsticks. After a moment she nodded and smiled to let him know that it was good.

'I can tell you that the police have the knife that killed the British man and the two Chinese women,' he said.

This was translated, and immediately the foreign woman started asking more questions. What kind of knife was it? Were there fingerprints or blood on the knife? Where had they found it? Song watched her, and observed her rising excitement. She was smart and hungry for information. She was like him. The questions she was asking were the questions he would have asked.

She fell silent, noticing how he was looking at her. For an instant they stared at each other as though each of them was looking in a mirror. He gestured at her that she should eat.

Awkwardly, the foreign woman picked up her chopsticks and tried doing as he had done, fishing for cooked meat, dunking it in sauce, putting it in her mouth, chewing. Song poured Yanjing beer into her glass. She drank. Briefly, she closed her eyes, but the tension did not leave her shoulders. He could tell that she was anxious about her friend.

He started to answer her questions through Blue, but in sanitized form. He made no mention of the fire in the tent, or of the boy. He told them that the police had found the knife in the lake, that it had been washed clean of DNA, but that markings on the blade had left traces in the cuts on the bodies. There had been knife attacks in Shijingshan as well, he said, although it was not clear that they were linked.

'Shijingshan is where Nelson Li's offices are,' Blue said. The foreign woman started to speak again, and Blue struggled to keep up. 'Everyone keeps telling her how close the British victim was to Nelson Li, suggesting he saw his future here in China, not back in the UK. She thinks it's possible he passed confidential Kelness information to Nelson Li, or that he helped Nelson Li draw up plans to move the Kelness plant to Dalian, and that one of his colleagues knew what was going on and saw him as a traitor and hated—'

Song raised his hand to stop her, and gestured to Blue that she needed to translate for him.

'What is Kelness? What does Nelson Li have to do with this?'

For a moment the foreign woman stared at him, open-mouthed. Kelness, she said, was a bankrupt British steel mill that employed the man who had been beheaded in the woods by the lake. The murdered man had been negotiating the sale of the Kelness plant to Nelson Li. She – the foreign woman – believed that Nelson Li was preparing to move the Kelness plant to Dalian. Did he, Song, know any way to secure proof of this?

'Proof of an intention?' Song sounded dubious. He was too busy worrying about the fact that Nelson Li's name had come up again to listen to what she was saying. Was this coincidence too?

Nelson Li had admitted that he was there by the lake when the tent burned down, the night the girl was killed. He had given no explanation for his presence there. Nelson Li wanted the boy, the witness to her murder. Now this direct link to the foreign victim raised disturbing questions about Li's involvement.

'I need proof that Nelson Li has secured land use rights in Dalian,' the foreign woman said urgently. 'Surely a local government document would say what the land was to be used for.'

'It might be possible,' Song said slowly, trying to concentrate. Wolf had contacts in Dalian, an uncle who worked for the local government. Wolf had asked favours of him before, and Song had allowed Wolf to expense a generous banquet for his uncle's family. Much of the information that Song gathered came to him through friendly contacts in exchange for what they liked to term 'a token of thanks'.

'I am going to go to Shijingshan tomorrow,' Song told Blue, making up his mind as he spoke, 'to find out more about the attacks on the women. I can't take her, she's too conspicuous.'

She started to translate this too, but he could wait no longer, this incessant to and fro was driving him up the wall. He thought of Detective Fang's men waiting for him in the main dining room and of how he must escape them if he was to go to Shijingshan the next day to find out whether Nelson Li might be implicated in the murders. He pushed back his chair and stood up. The two women looked at him in surprise.

'Call my mobile tomorrow at seven, and I'll tell you where to be,' he said to Blue. 'If you're not there I'll go without you.'

He turned to the waitress, pulling her aside, and pressed fifty *yuan* into her palm. 'I want you to show me a way out of here that isn't through the dining room,' he said. 'Anything, a door or window, that gets me out the back way.' She hesitated, but only for a moment, and then she gestured that he should follow her.

CHAPTER 18

When the detective, Song, left in such a great hurry, I was afraid that we had put him in danger, or that we had alarmed him with our suspicions of someone as powerful as Nelson Li. As soon as the door banged shut behind him, my mobile phone rang and I heard Larry's voice.

'Do you need to see a doctor?' I asked him.

'I'm just a bit bruised, I'll be fine,' he said, but his voice was agitated.

'What happened?'

'I had to write a self-criticism. It's Cultural Revolution crap, like a confession. I confess I shouldn't have been in the wrong place at the wrong time, I confess I shouldn't have been filming on a public street, I promise I'll never fucking breathe without asking permission.' He took a deep breath, calming himself down. 'I didn't bring you into it. They rattled off their bullshit about how I'd been endangering state security, and how they'd be watching me from now on, and then they let me go.'

'They'll be watching you? Do they mean literally, will they put you under surveillance?'

'Who knows what they mean? I'll keep my head down. But I have to tell you, they ripped out the film.' He sounded wary, now, as though he didn't know how I'd react.

'You changed it after the interview with Nelson Li, right?' I checked. It was standard practice, in sensitive situations, to get valuable film out of harm's way as quickly as possible.

'You didn't say I should, so I didn't.'

I closed my eyes and breathed deeply, in and out. I counted to ten.

'So we've lost the interview with Nelson Li,' I said, frustrated. It was all I had.

'No, you don't get it,' Larry said. 'The film shows you interviewing Li. It tells them you're a journalist. If they look at the film, then we're all screwed.'

I slumped back in my chair.

'Then we're all screwed,' I echoed. Larry, Blue, all of us screwed. Song had been right to leave. I was poison, contaminating everyone I came in contact with. Sal had warned me. It would not be me who bore the brunt, it would be those I associated with.

Blue was waiting for me to finish the call, her eyes fixed anxiously on me.

'The police have Larry's film,' I told her as calmly as I could. 'If they look at it they'll know that I'm a journalist. You already told them that you're working for me and that I'm a tourist. Now they'll know you lied.'

Her face blanched.

'You have to stay away from me from now on,' I told her. 'I need to get your money to you somehow . . .'

'It doesn't matt—'

'Of course the money matters. I've put you in danger, the least I can do is pay you. The money's sitting in the hotel safe, but you shouldn't come back with me tonight. I'll leave it for you at the desk in an envelope, you can collect it tomorrow.'

'Tomorrow,' she said, 'I will go with Song.'

'No,' I countered, 'you go shopping, or you go to the cinema, or you go for a walk in the park . . .'

'I'm the one who will decide,' she said. 'You cannot tell me what to do with my own time in my own country.'

I threw up my hands in exasperation. At least, I rationalized, if she went with Song, she would not be with me. She would be safer with him. Instinctively, I trusted him.

We left the restaurant together and she hailed a taxi for me. I shook her hand, and it felt as light and insubstantial as on the day I had met her.

'Thank you for your help today . . . not just today,' I said, feeling hopelessly inadequate. 'I hope I haven't caused you too much trouble.'

'It is no problem,' she said with a tight smile. I climbed into the car and raised my hand in farewell.

When I got back to the hotel I rang Damien, who – to do him credit – tried to sound supportive rather than frustrated at the loss of the Nelson Li interview. I decided to alert him to the possibility that the police might yet look at the film, rumble me and throw me out – I didn't want to be accused later of keeping him in the dark. 'Well, let's see what tomorrow brings,' he said, in an unusually philosophical mood. I knew it was an act, knew he'd be tearing his hair out as soon as he put the phone down.

I rang Finney too. I'd spoken to him earlier, to tell him I was out of police custody, but now I just needed to talk over what had happened with him, to decompress. He tried to make time for me and I could tell he needed reassuring too that I was all right. But I could hear his other line ringing constantly in the background, and after a while I told him that I would let him go, and would speak to him the next day.

I slept fitfully, expecting at any time a knock on the door. When I awoke in the morning and I was still there, I felt the stirrings of hope. Perhaps the police had not looked at the film. Perhaps they would not look at the film. Perhaps pigs would fly.

I went down to the breakfast buffet, but I could only face black coffee. I rang Larry and asked him to call me at once if the police contacted him, and he said he would. He sounded subdued, as though he was waiting for the axe to fall. When I hung up I sipped my coffee miserably. If the police threw me out the worst that would happen to me would

287

be a premature return to the arms of my children – something I actually yearned for – whereas Larry had a girlfriend and a job here, a whole life to lose.

I returned to my room, went online and checked the news.

> Embattled Kelness CEO Richard Toms yesterday denied allegations of radioactive contamination at the bankrupt steel mill, calling the leaked memo 'a work of malicious slander'.
>
> Protests outside the steel mill have reached fever pitch as workers have demanded the truth about the alleged incident, fearing the potential health impact of unmonitored radiation at the plant.
>
> According to the memo, a shipment of contaminated Russian steel entered the steel mill three months ago, and was left in the scrapyard undetected for a month, during which time personnel moved around freely in the immediate vicinity.
>
> The Health Protection Agency yesterday said it would conduct an urgent investigation to confirm the status of the plant. During this period, a skeleton staff will operate at the plant and the area which was allegedly contaminated will be sealed off. Richard Toms said he was satisfied that no contamination had taken place, but agreed than an inspection would 'clear the air'.

Industry analysts say that even if no evidence of radioactive contamination is found, the allegations have further disrupted negotiations with potential Chinese buyer Nelson Li.

I stared at my screen. The details of the memo were exactly as Angus Perry had described to me on Sunday night. At what stage had he seen the memo or heard of its contents? He seemed to think that the allegations were genuine. I couldn't work out why Sumner would have faked it either. He might have thought that Nelson Li could use the allegations to knock a few million off the price of the plant, but if the allegations were false he was bound to be found out, and the price advantage would be lost.

I rang Nelson Li's secretary, Jade.

'Is there any way Mr Li could spare me a few more minutes of his time today?' I pleaded with her.

'I'm very sorry,' she said, 'Mr Li is not available. He has a meeting at his house.'

'You mean,' I glanced at my notebook, 'at Versailles Villas?'

'Not there,' she clearly didn't want to give me too much detail, 'he's in the countryside.'

Jade had hung up before I could pin her down. Frantically I thumbed through my notebook until I found the page where Blue had written down the name of the place where Nelson Li had a log cabin under the Great Wall. I grabbed my MiniDV camera, checked its batteries, and stuffed it into my bag.

Then I remembered Blue's money. I retrieved it from the safe, placed it in an envelope with the hotel logo on the front, and wrote her name on it in English. At reception, I gave it to the woman at the front desk and told her I didn't know when Blue would call by. I extracted a promise that the envelope would be kept safe for her, and that it would be given to no one else.

Ten minutes later I was in a taxi in front of the hotel and my friendly doorman was trying, with the help of Blue's exquisite line of characters, to help me explain where I wanted to go. Eventually the driver seemed to get it. As we pulled out into the traffic he turned on the radio and started to sing along. I sat in the back seat trying to formulate my questions for Nelson Li.

We encountered gridlock at one suburban intersection, where a vast hole was being dug in the ground and traffic had become a lawless tangle of cars and trucks. Here, outside central Beijing, trucks of all sorts were thick on the road, with metal rods protruding dangerously behind them, or piled high with precarious loads, or sieving coal dust onto the road. Around the intersection, a dozen or so cranes worked over the rubble of a construction site as big as a town. Everywhere were construction gangs, bashing away with picks at the tarmac or digging ditches or straddling pneumatic drills. The sound was deafening, but not one of the men that I could see wore ear protection. For the most part the labourers had sun-darkened, leathery faces. But here and there I saw young, boyish faces and quick, nervous movements.

I knew that these must be migrant workers, peasants who had lost their land or abandoned it, and had come to the city to earn wages of three or four pounds a day. I had never before seen so many people engaged in active labour, in the brutal, back-breaking creation of a modern metropolis.

It took us half an hour to extricate ourselves from this nightmare of a suburb, and then we were on the open road, flat fields of dry yellow earth around us, the stubble catching wintry sunlight and flashing gold. The pace of life slowed. People dawdled along the streets, chickens pecked in the dust, children chased around mounds of bricks and sand, and scrawny dogs skulked in the gutters. We climbed into mountains, along the edge of a ridge, the land falling away to our right. There was still snow on the hillsides. The sun had thawed the ice from the road, but come dusk it would freeze over again.

Once, the driver pulled over, wound down his window and asked for directions. He drove on, but the singing had stopped. He asked again, and then again. I sat impatiently, unable to express my questions about where we were, or whether the driver had the slightest idea where he was going.

At last we came upon it, a modern construction of stone and wood. In the photograph in Sumner's apartment it looked like a cosy log cabin. In reality it was vast, as though the builder had misread the plans. It sat above a dried-up stream, and in the shadow of a peak along which, like a jagged line drawn in charcoal, ran a wall. The wall ran down the hillside next to the house and would have crossed the road, but it vanished there, then re-appeared on the opposite hillside, where it rose again to a precipitous height. It was an awe-inspiring sight, and for a moment I forgot all about Nelson Li and just gazed at it in wonder.

The house had picture windows through which the view of the valley and the range of hills behind would be breathtaking. What I had not expected was the guardhouse at the end of the driveway, the wall around the property. Netting had been placed across the river bed so that too was blocked off.

The driver pulled in just beyond the guard-house. I mimed that he must wait for me, then got out and approached on foot. There was no one to be seen. I called out. Still no one came. Tentatively I pushed at the gate and found it unlocked. I slipped inside. At once a storm of barking broke out, and I turned to see two dogs, chained but straining at their leashes, mouths wide. I took a step back. One was an Alsatian, the other looked more like a husky, its white eyes narrowed above its yellow teeth. Their restraints seemed strong enough to hold them. Slowly, attempting not to alarm the dogs further, I made my way towards the front door, which was high and wide. There was no bell, so I knocked my fist against the wood, and when that brought no one, I shouted too.

To the right of the door was a window, and I peered inside. The space – too large to be called a room, more like a hall – was furnished with sofas stiffly placed against the walls. A large fireplace was dark, and the whole effect was gloomy.

Something made me raise my head. A black object protruded from the wall, and I realized that I was looking into the eye of a CCTV camera. Slowly I turned. I counted three more cameras, mounted unobtrusively on lamp posts and aimed variously at the driveway, at the path that ran along the front of the house, and at the area to the side of the house. My skin crawled. I started to walk rapidly, back down the path, away from the obese cabin with its empty lifeless rooms and its silent mechanical eyes. The dogs were still howling, the husky throwing itself against the chain.

I heard a shout and thought at first it was a challenge. I stopped and looked around. I could see no one on Nelson Li's land, but from my vantage point I noticed activity on the opposite hillside, and for a moment I lingered, watching. There was an imperial watchtower part-way up the hill, and a man had emerged onto the path shouting to a group of people further down. They too became excited, talking among themselves, and then the group split, the men hurrying up the hill, the women running back down and slipping on the path. I watched and frowned. The scene – their alarm, the urgency – reminded me of the day I'd seen the girl in the lake.

I made my way back down the driveway, crossed the road and scrambled up the path opposite, in the direction of the watchtower. I was amazed to see Angus Perry appear from around a bend, rushing down the path towards me, stumbling on the uneven ground, dislodging small stones and lumps of snow. I stopped in my tracks as he approached. His gaze, wide-eyed, was fixed on the ground under his feet.

'Angus,' I said, as he reached me, and he stopped abruptly, jerking his shoulders back, head rising in panic, wide eyes staring. My greeting died on my lips.

'Are you all right?' I said instead.

He opened his mouth, but no sound came out.

'Why are you here?' I asked him. 'Are you visiting Nelson Li?'

He drew away from me, taking an unsteady step backwards.

'Don't go up there, there's been an accident.' He was using his hands to gesture wildly. 'I warned you!'

His voice, hysterically high-pitched, sent great tremors of fear along my spine, and I turned away from him and hurried up the path. When I got to the ruined watchtower I clambered up precariously balanced stones, rocking wildly as I moved from one to the next. Inside, a knot of men were clustered, their bodies reeling back from something on the ground, paralysed, a tableau of shock. Carefully, I edged around them. They paid me no attention, their eyes were fixed, staring at the ground. First I saw a mess of cigarette butts, dried faeces, discarded condoms. Only then did my brain manage to register what lay on this carpet of degradation, red-black blood pooled around, face blue-cold, eyes dead, throat obscenely severed. She was young, like the other one, and fully dressed, limbs thrown wide in deadly abandon, front teeth prominent, hair loose and long.

An instant was all it took to engrave this in my memory, and then involuntarily I looked away. I found myself gazing through an ancient window enlarged by time and nature, my eyes scanning the valley. In the window of an upper room in the bloated cabin opposite, I saw movement. Was I imagining it or was there a face? Could Angus Perry have got there so quickly, and what was he doing in Nelson Li's house?

I could hear a siren, still some way off. A black car – a dot in the distance – moved along the road towards us. I set off, hurrying down the steep path, my feet slipping on the dust, searching for rocks and sure footing, desperate to get away.

★   ★   ★

My driver was asleep, his seat reclined, a paper bag screwed up next to him, scattering crumbs from his lunch. I climbed into the car and shook his shoulder.

'Go back,' I said loudly, 'go back.' He raised his head sleepily, blinking. I pointed furiously to the way we had come. 'Beijing.'

Slowly, reluctantly, he sat up and adjusted his seat. Blearily he gazed out of the window at the men and women running from their homes and scrabbling up the path towards the murdered woman. Ignoring me, he rolled down the window and said something to a group of women passing the car. When he heard their reply, he turned towards me and gestured that I should wait for him. 'No,' I said urgently, 'no, we go now,' but he got out of the car and wandered towards the line of people climbing the hillside.

I got out and grabbed him.

'No,' I shouted in his face, 'now or no money.'

Just then the first police car arrived, a black sedan full of uniformed men. They spilled out, looking as though they too had been disturbed mid-nap, pink-cheeked, shouting questions at the peasants, starting their own scramble up the hill. One of them, a young man with a digital camera, hung back, looking at me. He lifted his camera and took a snap of my face before I could turn away. He started walking towards me.

'Come on!' I shouted at my driver, pulling on his arm, and this time he gave in and came with me.

We were pulling out into the road when the

young policeman shouted after us. I twisted in my seat, watching the crowd, the police, the hillside all shrink and disappear behind us. No one gave chase. I closed my eyes.

I saw the dead woman then, and in stark detail: the staring dead eyes, the open surprised mouth with its ugly front teeth, obscene quantities of blood mingling with the faeces and the trash.

Suddenly the car veered left, into the oncoming lane, and then swung violently right. The driver swore. I opened my eyes as I was flung to the side, bashing my head against the window. We plunged downwards, my stomach lurched in fear, and I caught a fleeting glimpse of the rear end of a black jeep that accelerated away from us. There was a sickening crunch, and we were both thrown forward again as the taxi crashed into the mountainside. I raised my head, clutching at the side of my face, fumbling for the door handle. I got out. From where I stood at the side of the road the scale of our danger, and the good luck of our escape, was clear. On the far side the hillside fell away in a sheer drop. Another few inches, and we would have fallen. Instead, the driver had managed to pull us back to the right side of the road, but had overcompensated. The taxi had driven off the road, down a ditch, and into the mountain-side, where its nose was buried.

'Oh, my God,' I murmured.

The driver had got out of the car too, and was gazing, stunned, at his vehicle. The front of the car was all snarled up, with glass scattered in the ditch like confetti. I held my palms out to him in a dumb show of my confusion about what had happened. He started to jabber, then gestured with his hands: his left hand our taxi, his right another car coming up fast behind the taxi, nudging forward, trying to overtake on the inside, pushing the taxi out towards the edge of the road, the taxi swinging back in, overcompensating, losing control, going boom – fist punching against palm of hand – into the mountainside.

Then, shouting in agitation, he pointed towards the bottom of the hill, and I could see the black jeep winding down the narrow roads, still moving away from us at high speed.

CHAPTER 19

Song told Wolf to slow down as he approached Dazhanzi.

'Can you see her? She looks like a caterpillar,' Song said.

'Over there? Short woman, big green coat?'

'That's her.'

'A pretty caterpillar.'

Wolf cut in front of a truck, and pulled into the side of the road, leaning over and pushing open the passenger door. Blue bent down, casting a startled look at Wolf then, when she saw Song in the back seat, she scrambled in.

'Wolf is my legal consultant,' Song explained to Blue, who nodded a nervous greeting at Wolf, her eyes lingering on his silver hair, and the partly visible tattoo.

'Give her the envelope,' Song told Wolf.

Wolf stuck his hand inside his jacket and pulled out a long white envelope, which he handed to Blue. She looked down at it in confusion.

'What's this?' she said.

'Last night after I left you, our agency made enquiries about the matter that the foreign woman

299

raised. This morning we received this from sources in Dalian.'

'The land use rights,' Blue exclaimed. She pulled a folded sheet of fax paper from the envelope, running her eyes over the closely printed characters.

'As you will see,' Wolf said, 'Sunrays Steel has secured the land.'

'There will be a fee,' Song warned, thinking of the meal he'd have to buy for Wolf's uncle. 'Our agency has incurred costs.'

'She has money,' Blue said.

'Of course she has money,' said Wolf, 'she's a foreigner.'

'What's she like?' Song asked. He noticed that Blue had pinned her hair back today, so that her face was not hidden. She looked different – younger and older all at the same time. Still she sat like a child, hands clasped tightly in her lap, knees pressed together. She was a funny, nervous thing. Sharp and bright, like a blade, something you didn't want to brush up against. He wouldn't have pegged her as Wolf's type.

'She's very capable,' Blue said slowly, 'and she's very polite, most of the time. She's impatient, she wants things too quickly, and she doesn't understand China . . . Why do you keep looking behind you?'

She was observant too, Song thought.

'I want to make sure no one's following us,' he said.

300

'Who?' she asked, twisting in her seat, as though the culprit would make himself known, waving, perhaps, through the rear window.

'Song never picks small enemies.' Wolf grimaced. 'It's something you should know about him. He looks for the nastiest guys around and then he annoys them. Then he can't go home for days. Where were you last night, brother Song?'

'I shared a room with my nephew in Wangjing, and he snored like a pig.'

They had slowed to a stop, and they were hemmed in between buses on either side of them, with taxis to the front and rear. Somehow three lanes of traffic had become five. Wolf got out and stood on the road, straining to see up ahead, then got back in the car.

'A lorry shed its load. They're blocking off a lane.'

'Why is she in China if she doesn't know anything about it?' Song thought that trying to investigate a man's death in a foreign language was laughable, but he didn't want to be too rude about her employer. He recalled how frustrated the woman had looked when he and Blue spoke together in Chinese, and the effort on her face as she had tried to salvage some meaning.

'When she arrived she told me she doesn't think it matters, because I can translate for her, and she thinks people are pretty much the same all over the world.'

Wolf was stunned into silence by this philosophy,

but Song remembered the connection that he had felt with the foreign woman in the restaurant, that moment when they had looked at each other with mutual recognition.

'Is that possible?' Song asked Blue after a moment. Until now he had steered clear of cases involving foreigners. To be an investigator, he felt, you had to understand how people acted, and why, and to be able to read the vibrations that people gave off like smells. Among Chinese, he was able to feel his way through a problem in the same way he swam, his muscles responding instinctively to the ebb and the flow of the water, working with it rather than against it. He could look up at the sea of bored, weary faces in the bus next to him and know more or less what was going on in their heads. But foreigners, surely, were an alien life form. He knew of course that they had feelings – indeed their emotions seemed dangerously close to the surface – but he had no instinctive knowledge of how they might act and this made him wary of them. Although, he thought again, there had been that moment in the restaurant. It had been nothing more than that, just a moment of connection, and yet in some way it changed his whole perception.

When Song was a child, isolation was easy, the default setting of a nation led by a party of paranoia, fearing contamination. Then contamination, blossoming like disease, had come anyway – a narcissistic regime driven to obsession and slaughter, then rallying to uneasy stability and corruption. The foreigners had come later, eating away like insects at the rotting bamboo curtain, and now they were crawling all over everything.

Young Europeans set up cafes on the pavements, the Americans put stern-eyed marines at their embassy gate, Filipinas sang in hotel lounges, the French collected antiques, the Italians shopped for textiles, the British opened schools for the children of the rich, the Germans ran five-star hotels, the Russians bartered furs, and Mongolian women worked in the brothels, the Koreans opened barbecue restaurants and the Japanese ate raw fish and refused to apologize for history. Confronted with such an invasion, Song knew he could not afford to live in isolation for much longer. He had already turned down one case, in which a consignment of textiles had vanished overnight on a train to Moscow, and another in which a Korean business-man's wife had disappeared.

But Song had been able to pick up signals from the British woman although he could not understand a word she said. He had been able to read her intensity when she shot questions at him, her concern for her cameraman colleague, her exhaustion. He knew that she was trying to do her best in this city that was not her home. He knew that the foreign woman was brave to the point of recklessness just as he knew her Chinese guide, Blue, possessed the same quality.

'Is she married?' he asked Blue.

'She lives with a man,' she replied. 'She has twin children by another man.'

Song grunted in approval. The complexity of this arrangement sounded familiar. He imagined fat twins who looked like Doudou, except that they were blonde.

'How much is she paying you?' Wolf wanted to know.

'A hundred US dollars a day.'

It wasn't bad, but it wasn't a fortune. Eight hundred *yuan* or so a day, depending on the exchange rate, the same as a blue-collar worker's weekly wage, more per day than Beijing's monthly minimum wage. But then, Song calculated, she might work only one day in five.

'I keep telling Song we need someone who speaks English so we can earn some dollars from foreigners,' Wolf said. 'She should come and work for us, shouldn't she?'

There was a moment's awkward silence.

'Wolf just wants dollars so he can go to Disneyland,' Song attempted a jokey response. 'He thinks he'd feel at home there among the freaks.'

'You're so full of crap.' Wolf was grinning.

'Anyway, I have plenty of work,' Blue said stiffly.

They would split up, they decided. Song and Wolf would find out what they could from the hotel in which the prostitute had been attacked, and Blue would strike up conversation with women in the markets in the narrow streets of shabby housing that ran away from the plant.

When they reached the Waimao Hotel Song gave Blue some advice.

'Pretend you're out shopping. Have you got some cash on you? Good. Carry around a plastic bag with some groceries in it. Buy something here, something else there. Talk to the stallholders, talk to other shoppers, say you've been offered a job around here, make up the name of some company and say you want to know about the area. Ask how safe it is for a single woman, that kind of thing. Ask if they know anyone who's been attacked.'

Blue gave Song a look that told him she did not need schooling in common sense, and he shut up. He could see that she was still brooding over what Wolf had said, the job offer that wasn't a job offer. Perhaps that remark about having plenty of work was a lie to save face. Well, she was too prickly to have around the office and so small he'd trip over her.

The manager of the Waimao Hotel, a man in his forties named Hu, was called out to the reception desk to talk to them. He wore a brown leather jacket, and a pair of sunglasses was folded into his top pocket next to a walkie-talkie. Often, when he interviewed people, Song lied about who he was. He had a stack of name cards in the office describing him variously as a journalist, a teacher, several sorts of businessman, a doctor and so on. He had never pretended to be a serving police officer or a government functionary, because that could end in a lengthy prison sentence.

In this case, he chose to tell Hu a partial truth. He was a private investigator working for a provincial insurance company with whom the injured woman had taken out a personal injury policy a month before.

'You're telling me that young tart spent her pay on an insurance policy?' Hu's eyes narrowed and he studied Song's face suspiciously.

'Her parents aren't too badly off,' Song lied smoothly. 'They were worried about her coming to the city, so they bought the policy for her. They thought she was working as a waitress.'

'Crazy waste of money,' Hu grumbled.

'Well, in the circumstances it was a wise choice,' Song said softly, holding out a pack of cigarettes, then a lighter as Hu extracted one and lifted it to his lips. 'It's all routine, we just need to tick the boxes, say we've seen you, so they can sign off on it. It's difficult for them to make enquiries in the capital. I'm ex-police, so they know I know what I'm doing.'

'Ex-police, are you?' Hu echoed, smoke escaping from his mouth. 'Me too. Serious crime squad. Did you know Jiang Dehua?'

Song shook his head.

'Long Ruihuan?'

'I heard the name.'

'He's on the run now. He's my buddy.'

'Why's he on the run?'

'You work too long with crooks, you get like them, you take your opportunities,' he said, 'and he was never careful, never watched his back.'

'I'll bet you knew Wang Rong?'

'I do,' Hu said, his mouth curling in a small, unpleasant smile. 'Everyone knows Psycho Wang.'

'I hear he's gone into business for himself,' Song said, to establish himself as a friend of a friend.

'I do a little business with him myself,' Hu said, and winked, 'when he has requirements. Look, let's not talk here. You guys want to sit down and have a cup of tea?'

Hu led them to an empty dining room. It smelled of stale cooking oil, and there were stains on the tablecloths where they had been inadequately laundered. A grubby red satin curtain hung across one wall, with a cardboard dragon tacked to it, its tail hanging limply to the floor.

'This thing with the girl was no big deal,' he said, lighting up another cigarette and waving it at a waitress, who hurried over with an ashtray. 'She got out alive, didn't she? There are sickos all over the world, we're bound to get some in here.'

'It happens a lot here, does it, prostitutes visiting your guests?' Song asked, although he already knew the answer. The place had that kind of feel to it, as though if you scratched the surface the sleaze would ooze out like pus.

Hu smirked and rubbed his fingers together in a gesture that suggested cash.

'That way everyone gets satisfaction,' Hu said, 'including me.'

'Did your reception staff recognize the man who took that room?'

'He didn't go through reception,' Hu said. 'The rooms on the fifth floor are being renovated, we're not using them. Either the sicko knew that and made straight for them, or he wandered around the hotel hoping he'd find a room left unlocked by mistake.

'Which do you think it was?'

'I think he knew.' Hu pulled on his cigarette and scratched his groin absent-mindedly. 'I think he paid a member of staff. No one has reported seeing anyone wandering around the building trying the doors. But one of our barmaids didn't come back to work the day after the tart was attacked. I think she knew she was in trouble.'

'Perhaps your barmaid was in danger.'

'They haven't found her body in the quarry yet, have they?' Hu grinned.

'In the quarry?'

'Behind the steel mill.' Hu gestured in a roughly south-east direction with his cigarette. 'You want to dump something, that's where you go. The peasant women will tell you . . .'

'The barmaid who's gone missing,' Wolf said, 'you have a copy of her ID, of course? You must have taken one when you took her on.'

'I do,' Hu said, 'in accordance with regulations.'

'I'm sure you'll make a copy for us,' Wolf requested.

Hu raised his wary eyes to Wolf. 'What for?'

'We've been given sheets of questions,' Wolf said vaguely. 'It's very tedious, just paperwork, for the report; they want the ID numbers of possible witnesses, just for the record. We don't need to chase her up, I can guarantee that, and even if we do it won't impact on you – she's gone, hasn't she?'

Hu gave Wolf a long, hard look, then spoke into his walkie-talkie. After a few moments a duty manager brought a photocopy of the barmaid's ID to their table. In her photograph, the barmaid had a sullen look. There was an address for her family, in Shanghai.

'I'd like to see the room where she was attacked,' Song said. Hu began to look as though he'd had enough, but he accompanied them in the lift to the fifth floor. The corridor was stripped of wall-paper and carpet. Electric wires hung from the ceiling. Two men in overalls were squatting on the floor drinking tea from glass jars.

'This will be our executive floor when we're done,' Hu explained. He pushed open a door and they stepped inside the gloomy room, its wallpaper coffee-coloured, the carpet beige and purple. It stank of stale cigarette smoke. The bedcover was creased, and there was a newspaper lying on the pillow. Song recognized the headline, 'We Are Creating a New

Socialist Countryside', from two days before. Song thought that this room was used more than Hu had suggested. Rooms closed to guests might be popular with offduty staff, or even with on-duty staff. Wolf went to the window, unlatched it and pushed it open. Cold air rushed in as he leaned out.

'It's a big drop,' he said. Wolf moved aside so that Song could look out onto the roof two storeys below. Song turned to Hu.

'You're sure he went this way?' he asked. 'It's a big risk to jump that far. What about the fire exit?'

Hu shook his head. 'We keep it locked for security reasons.'

'He might have gone down in the lift, walked out through the front door,' Wolf suggested. Song thought that a man of Nelson Li's age could not have made that jump.

'My staff would have noticed a stranger,' Hu said. 'I train them to do that.'

'Who said it was a stranger?' Wolf murmured, and Song caught his eye.

'I think,' Song said, 'we've seen enough.'

They shook hands.

As they left the hotel, Wolf muttered, 'I feel like my hand is crawling with germs.' Song did not respond. He was thinking about the fact that Manager Hu knew Pyscho Wang and wondering how well Wang knew the hotel.

Blue was waiting by the car. Song thought she looked shaken.

'The women are all full of stories,' she told them. 'I can't work out what's going on, whether it's one woman who's been attacked, or two or three, but no one feels safe any more.'

Behind the plant, they found a dirt track that ran parallel to the perimeter wall, across a patch of land with villages to the right. To their left was a river bed where a man herded scrawny sheep to patches of vegetation, and where bright orange ducks pecked among frozen puddles for sustenance. Above it all, beyond the wall topped with barbed wire, the plant rose like a city, its white breath gathering in the sky.

Song looked towards the villages. Between the path and the traditional grey-brick houses was a gash in the earth that must be the abandoned quarry. He pulled the car onto the dirt at the side of the road, and all three of them got out and walked towards the rim of the abyss. As they approached, an acrid stench filled the air. Blue pulled her scarf over her face and Wolf mimed a retching action, only half acting. Silently, they stood in a row at the edge and looked at the reeking devastation spread before them. The villages on the other side of the pit were using it as an unofficial dump. Waterfalls of detritus tumbled down the sides of the ravine, and smoke rose, curling into the air, where refuse had spontaneously combusted, so that it looked as though the earth's crust was about to erupt.

'What is that stink?' Wolf's face contorted.

'That's not just trash. Someone's dumping something here. Shit, my eyes are burning. I can't take it.' He turned and jogged back towards the car.

Song spotted ghostly outlines in the brume. Two children, perhaps three or four years old and padded against the cold, walked hand in hand across the bottom of the quarry along a track that meandered between smouldering piles. At a fuming heap three figures bent, spines doubled over their task, scavenging, pulling themselves upright only to load something onto the handcart that was parked there. Song turned, looking up and down the length of the quarry, and saw that the whole area was populated with figures who had all but disappeared into the reeking garbage.

'Look at those poor kids,' Blue murmured.

'Their parents are over there.' Song nodded towards the scavengers. He was guessing, but sure enough the children came to a halt by the scavengers' cart. Song felt the toxic air catch in his throat, and he bent over in a spasm of coughing. Blue started down the track towards the scavengers, her head bent, face covered in her scarf.

Song watched for a moment as the haze washed around her tiny figure. Then he followed, his stride catching hers easily. They walked in silence, so as to save on breathing, but Song could feel Blue's fury from the way her feet hit the ground. They reached the scavengers.

'Your children will die if they breathe this,' Blue confronted them.

The scavengers, two women and one man, looked at her in blank surprise. Only their eyes were visible over the cloth masks they had improvised to cover their faces. The children, unmasked, one sitting on the other's lap on top of the handcart, stopped their chattering and stared too.

'We're here for information,' Song muttered at Blue,' not on a health-education mission.' Extracting information was always an exercise in making friends, not enemies. Blue looked away from him angrily, but she shut up.

'What are you doing here?' The masked man's voice was unfriendly, protective of his territory and his family.

Song pulled his business card out of his pocket and handed it to the masked man, who looked at it vacantly. A business card always impressed with its authority, especially when the recipient was illiterate.

'I'm an investigator,' he told them, hoping that would sound official. 'I'm investigating the assaults on women here.'

They exchanged glances, and then the young one, more girl than woman – spoke up. She spoke with a heavy accent, and the mask muffled her words further, so that Song had to ask her to repeat herself.

'My cousin disappeared,' she said.

'Disappeared . . .' the man echoed, pulling the mask down from his face and speaking as clearly

313

as he knew how, trying to make it easier for them to understand. 'She was working here in the summer at sunset, and she never came back. She was gone. Do you understand? Vanished. At first we thought she'd gone off with a friend, but nobody had seen her. Then we thought maybe she took fright at something and went home. So I contacted my sister, but she wasn't there either. My sister cried and cried . . .'

'You reported it to the police, of course,' Song said, thinking that it would not be a bad thing if they thought he had been sent to check up on the officers who had responded.

The scavenger spat into the dust and muttered.

'They treated us like stray dogs,' the older woman said. 'They told us people come and go in this city, and we shouldn't be surprised. They asked if we'd checked the whorehouses.'

'Had she made any new friends, talked about anyone you didn't know?'

They both shook their heads. The man indicated the younger woman.

'She's my other sister's child. She's come to replace the one that went missing.'

The girl nodded shyly. She looked about fifteen.

'She never leaves our side,' the man said.

'Your children . . .' Blue said again. The children, filthy and cheerful, gazed at her, and at the tall man at her side.

'We don't let them out of our sight.'

One of the children said something.

'What did your daughter say?' Song asked the scavenger, but the man just shook his head.

Song squatted down next to the cart and tried to speak to the child, a girl whose jacket would have been red, but for the soot that clung to it and turned it black. She grinned, her mouth wide under a nose heavy with snot, but she would not speak.

'She said she found a dead cat a few weeks ago,' the scavenger said, coming to his daughter's rescue.

'Ah,' Song said. He stood up, uninterested.

'A skinned cat,' the man added, 'with its tongue cut off and its eyes gouged out.'

Song frowned.

'You get many of those?'

'A few.' The scavenger looked at the ground, kicking his foot in the dirt.

'All cut up like that?'

'Not so much recently.'

Song scanned the landscape.

'Show me where you found them.'

After a moment's indecision the man turned and headed across the uneven ground, Song and Blue following. They reached a gully, at the bottom of which was some rotting vegetable waste. 'They were in plastic bin bags down there,' the man said, pointing. 'Someone must have chucked them in from the top.'

'Did you see anyone?'

The scavenger shook his head.

Song looked up at the sheer side of the quarry. This side of it was away from the villages, nearer the dirt road they had driven along to get here. Whoever had thrown the butchered animals into the quarry could simply have got out of a car and tipped them over the edge. At night or in the very early morning, whoever had dumped the bags would have disturbed no one.

'Was there anything else in the bags?'

'Once there were some yellow high-heel shoes, very beautiful, but the heels were broken, and they were dirty from the cat meat.'

'Do you still have them?'

But they were long gone, stuck back together, cleaned up and sold on to a used-clothing market.

Song turned and looked towards the village.

'Has anyone else disappeared?'

The scavenger seemed to consider the question.

'Not disappeared, no . . . but a woman was attacked.'

The village seemed deserted. The scavenger led them through a maze of narrow grey-walled alleys with houses to either side, until they reached a front door which he pushed open, calling out as he stepped inside. They followed him into a dark room. There was a coal brazier, and a thermos for water, and a small calendar hanging from the room's only decoration, which was a mirror on the wall. A sleeping platform ran the length of one wall, with a grubby quilt rolled on top of it. There was a bent woman in the room, and on the sleeping platform a girl sat cross-legged, her face in shadow. The old woman regarded her visitors with some surprise.

With all five of them in the room it was crowded.

'He's an investigator,' the scavenger told the old woman. 'He wants to know about the attack.'

At this, the girl cringed back, but the old woman went to her and took the girl's chin in her hand, forcing her to face them.

'You see?' the old woman said, her voice rising in outrage.

'You see what he did to her? Two months ago, and still so red and raw, so ugly.'

In the dim light they saw that the right-hand side of the girl's face was grotesquely disfigured. A great chunk had been carved out of her face between her eye and her chin, the eye pulled almost shut by the great scar, the mouth pulled downwards in an obscene grimace. The scars were, as the old women had said, still red and inflamed.

Blue stepped sharply backwards, but Song bent close to examine the wound, and spoke softly to the girl.

'Who did this to you?'

She would not speak. She pulled her face from the old woman's grip and hid herself in her arms.

'She said she couldn't see his face,' the old woman said.

Once more Song tried to persuade the girl to speak, hunkering down so that he didn't loom over her, but she whimpered and drew away from him, and so he was reduced to questioning the old woman, whose answers were so excited and delivered in such a strident tone that it was difficult to make any sense of them.

Eventually Song understood that the girl's attacker had been wearing a white cloth mask, like a nurse or a doctor, and like the scavengers themselves. That he had attacked the girl in the quarry, grabbing her from behind and cutting her. Somehow, blood pouring from her wound, she had managed to wriggle free and had run back towards the village, clambering quickly up the steep sides of the ravine.

Perhaps her attacker had not known the terrain, perhaps he had stumbled in the dirt. At any rate, he had not caught up with her. The police had taken a statement in hospital, but the girl had been too frightened to be cooperative, and the police did not seem to take her story seriously. She was, after all, still alive.

'In hospital,' Song echoed, thinking: how had they afforded it?

'Someone . . . a well-wisher paid her hospital bills.'

Behind him Song became aware of people entering the room. He turned and saw that a group of men were pushing inside. He felt Blue shift uncomfortably next to him as she was shoved against the sleeping platform.

'She was beautiful, and now she looks like a

monster.' Tears were running down the old woman's gnarled face, and her voice was becoming louder over the increasingly plaintive sobs of the girl. Song glanced round again, saw stony faces. 'Who will marry her now?' the old woman wailed.

A man elbowed his way to the front and stood in front of Song, his body fairly shaking with officiousness.

'Are you a journalist?' he demanded, and the room fell silent. 'Why are you here?'

Blue and Song exchanged a glance. Village chief or Communist Party secretary, or both, it didn't much matter, this man was trouble.

'Show me your ID,' the man insisted. He put out his hand, palm upwards, to receive their documents.

'Thank you,' Song addressed the girl, who was huddled on the sleeping platform, 'we won't trouble you any more.' He turned and started to make his way through the crowded room to the door, Blue following in his wake. They emerged from the house, and started to walk quickly away from the village, skirting the quarry and heading for the car. The scavenger who had brought them here had disappeared. But the official who had accosted them inside the house strode behind them, his posse of three behind him, all of them shouting, asking over and again who they were, their voices increasingly shrill.

As Song and Blue approached the car, still pursued by the gang of men, a teenage boy ran up alongside them. He wore a peasant's padded clothing. He thrust a piece of paper towards Song, and as Song reached out to take it from him, the boy seized his wrist, pulled him close and spoke into his ear.

'We saw the car, me and my father.' He spoke quickly, gulping for air. 'This is the licence number. My father showed it to the police and they beat him up. I saved the piece of paper. This is it.'

The boy released Song's wrist, and turned and ran across the open land. Behind him, two men broke from the official's posse and gave chase.

Song and Blue broke into a jog, and when they reached the car they climbed in quickly. Song reversed the car off the dirt, his foot down hard on the accelerator.

'Hey!' Wolf protested, rudely awoken from sleep, his head jolting hard against the window.

'Watch to see if they follow us,' Song ordered Blue. She twisted in her seat and watched the road behind. A few moments later a black unmarked sedan with no licence plate bumped onto the road. It settled in fifty yards behind them.

'There is a car,' she told Song, 'but I don't know if it's following us. I think there are two men in it.'

They drove on in silence in the direction of the city. Somewhere inside the fifth ring road the unmarked sedan disappeared from the rear-view mirror.

'Either they've lost interest or they know all they

need to know,' Song said quietly. He shifted in his seat and pulled from his pocket the piece of paper the boy had handed him, passing it to Blue.

'It's just a number.' She held it in front of Song, and he glanced down at it.

'It's a police licence plate,' he said simply. He did not say, and I have seen it before, on a car parked on the road by the lake, on the night the girl died. He thought of the Waimao Hotel manager, Hu, and his friend Psycho Wang, and he wondered what business the two of them got up to. Song drove on silently, back towards the city. Inside the car, the stench of the quarry hung around them like evil.

CHAPTER 20

I was still deeply shaken, less by what had happened on the road than by what might have happened. I kept looking from the taxi, with its snarled-up nose, to the abyss on the far side of the road. The taxi driver walked round and around his vehicle, scratching his head and mumbling. Then he looked over at me and said something I could not understand. I shrugged helplessly at him. At that moment, I would have given a great deal to have Blue at my side.

He helped me hitch a ride in the only vehicle that came down that road, a truck fit for the scrapyard and driven by a teenage lad who looked about sixteen. I left the driver waiting despondently by his bashed-up car, presumably hoping for a tow. The lad cheerfully hurtled down the increasingly precarious roads and then, once on the flat, drove at the truck's maximum speed, which was about thirty miles an hour, back into Beijing.

Every painful, jolting minute of the way, I thought about the crash. I tried to put out of my mind the thought of the twins orphaned. It had not happened, and I could not afford to torture myself. Instead I racked my brains to try to work out what had happened, and why. Angus Perry had staggered down the hill ahead of me, and had seemed on the edge of a breakdown. Did he have a black jeep? Had he been so shattered by the sight of the woman's dead body on the Great Wall that he had lost his mind, or did he have some reason to try to kill me? The darkest thought that occurred to me on that long journey was that his reason for trying to kill me was simply that I had witnessed him there, on the wall, leaving the place where the woman had been killed. Had a serial killer been in my sight all along? Had Sumner discovered a terrible secret about his colleague that had required him to be silenced?

By the time the driver had pulled the truck to a shuddering halt in the hotel forecourt I felt as though every bone in my body had been dislocated, and my head was screaming with tension.

I paid him handsomely, and he departed. I nodded in greeting at my friend the concierge, but he looked away, and I thought that I must be lowering the tone of the place, walking into the lobby with a bruise the size of a fist on my forehead and my clothes covered in dust.

In my room I turned on every light that I could find so that there were no dark shadows, and then I sat on the bed and I stared at the phone, fighting the urge to call Finney. If I spoke to him now it would feel as though I was calling because I needed him to save me.

I went into the bathroom and stared in the mirror at my bruise. I stripped off my dusty clothes and took a shower, thinking that perhaps the water would wash away my deep sense of unease, but it did not. I pulled on a white hotel dressing gown and boiled the kettle on top of the minibar, thinking that perhaps a cup of tea would put everything right. Wrong again.

The phone rang and I snatched it up, desperate to hear Finney's voice. With my senses screaming and adrenalin coursing through my veins, the click on the line sounded like a small explosion. They were listening. This was it, then, they had watched the film and they would come for me.

'Robin? I am downstairs. I have something for you, I will leave it at reception.'

'Get off the line. Get out of the hotel.'

'I think you will be pl . . .' Blue's voice trailed off as she digested what I had said.

'Get off the line,' I said again. 'It's for your own good. I'm really sorry, I can't explain now.'

I hung up. I closed my eyes, then opened them again, in case I saw the woman in my head, her big white teeth in that gaping mouth, red blood pooling amid the trash.

I pulled on a sweater and jeans then took the lift down to the ground floor and scanned the lobby. There was no sign of Blue.

I walked over and addressed the woman at the reception desk.

'I think someone left something for me,' I said.

She took my name and room number. With my heart pounding I watched her shuffle papers, frowning, and I thought: they have taken it already. Then, to my surprise, she held a long white envelope towards me. I snatched it from her and crossed my arms, as if trying to keep myself warm, hiding it next to my chest. I nodded my thanks and moved away. I caught the eye of my friend the concierge. Again, he looked away.

When I had returned to my room I sat down on my bed and opened the envelope. From inside I pulled a sheet of fax paper, folded in three. I stared down at it, at lines of Chinese characters. I hadn't a clue what Blue had handed to me. It looked official. With mounting excitement I realized that somehow Blue had managed to get hold of a document that proved – what? Could it possibly prove what I suspected, that Li was preparing to move Kelness to Dalian?

The phone rang again and I snatched up the receiver. I realized, too late, that I had a crossed line, and that two women were already speaking in English. I was about to hang up when my blood ran cold and I knew that I was listening to my own conversation.

'Robin? I am downstairs. I have something for you, I will leave it at reception.'

'Get off the line. Get out of the hotel.'

'I think you will be pl . . .'

'Get off the line. It's for your own good . . .'

Then a loud click, and the line went dead.

I replaced the receiver. I picked up the handset again, holding it to my ear, and the dial tone burred blandly. I hung up. I tried to think calmly about what had just happened. Someone was listening in on my telephone, and the calls were being recorded. There was no reason for anyone to have replayed my own conversation to me, unless someone wanted to warn me. More likely it was a mistake, I thought, a quirk in the eavesdropping system. Someone or something had mistakenly caused a machine to dial my room and to replay the conversation I had just had.

I picked up the folded fax paper Blue had left for me, and I held it on my lap. I thought of Larry trying to protect Blue when I had asked her to make a phone call to the Dalian local government offices. I had no idea what the paper was, or whether it was in any way secret, but I was infected now with Larry's paranoia. I folded it again and again, until it was about three inches square, and placed it inside my bra where it rubbed uncomfortably against my skin. I took the hotel copy of the *China Daily*, and with a blunt pair of scissors from the hotel's sewing kit I snipped out a bland article about steel production figures, folded it and placed it inside the envelope, then placed the envelope in my jacket pocket. The butchered newspaper I folded and slid deep under the bed, where I knew the cleaners would not venture. Then I packed.

*　　*　　*

When they came, I was not yet asleep. How could I have been? I was lying curled, fully dressed, on my bed. To give them their due, they didn't barge in. They rang the polite hotel buzzer that sounded softly at the console by the bed. I pulled myself upright, and sat on the edge of the bed and waited again, unwilling to engage in this last, inevitable confrontation. Then someone knocked.

I got to my feet. I went to the door and peered through the spyhole. Outside there was a delegation of three men, fronted by the hotel manager, who looked distinctly uncomfortable, and I thought perhaps this was his first time, as it was mine. I opened the door and tried to rally myself.

'Can I help you?'

'Miss Ballantyne, I am afraid your visa . . .'

The two men in uniform who accompanied him looked impatient at his politeness and one of them spoke sternly.

'Please come now.'

I turned to collect my bags and the hotel manager, by now in an agony of embarrassment, leaped forward to take them from me. As I was closing the door behind me, the phone started to ring. Without asking for permission, I stepped back inside the room to take the call.

It was Blue, her fear and fury burning down the line, 'They will tell you I wanted to go away . . .' She was talking rapidly, breathlessly.

'What's ha—?'

But she spoke over me.

327

'. . . but don't believe them, I didn't want to go, I don't know where they are taking me . . .' And then there was an angry exclamation, and Blue screamed, not in pain but in anger, words in Chinese, and with a clatter the line went dead. I put down the handset. Slowly I turned to face them.

'What have you done to her?' I demanded, shaking with fury. 'She has done nothing. Nothing. What law has she broken?'

The hotel manager looked distraught, but the two police officers regarded me impassively. One of them stepped forward and spoke to me woodenly. I had failed to abide by the terms of my visa . . . undertaken activities harmful to the People's Republic . . . endangered stability . . . first available plane . . . The timbre of his voice, the rhythm of his words transported me back to the police station just the day before, to Blue ordering me not to yell at the police, hissing, 'You are being very dangerous.' The greater the noise I made on her behalf, the greater was her peril.

They drove me to a run-down hotel near the airport where we seemed to be the only guests. We would wait there, they told me courteously, until the British Airways flight in the morning. They rummaged very thoroughly through my luggage, sifting papers, confiscating notebooks, snatching away the demonstrators' flyer, removing the card from my digital camera. Meanwhile, they had questions for me. They took me to a meeting room, and we sat on opposite sides of a table. Terrified of implicating Blue in what should be my crime, and mine alone, I said as little as I could. Their English was good, but without Blue to navigate the interrogation I struggled to contain the damage. They did not shout at me, nor did they lay a finger on me. And yet I found myself reduced by their assumption of utter authority and by their tone of contempt. I had to fight to maintain any sense of myself.

'She delivered an envelope to your hotel,' the older one said.

I frowned, as if it had been such a minor thing that I was having difficulty remembering. I could feel the folded fax paper crumpling when I moved, and thought maybe they could hear it.

'This evening,' he said impatiently, 'she left it at the front desk. You picked it up.'

I pretended enlightenment, took the envelope from my jacket pocket and handed it to him, and he removed the *China Daily* article from inside.

'This?' he said.

'She thought I'd find it interesting because I'm reporting on the steel industry.'

He looked disappointed, then pushed a pad of paper across the table towards me, with a pen.

'You will write a self-criticism,' he ordered.

'You mean, like a confession?' I remembered what Larry had told me.

'To acknowledge your mistakes,' the young one

said, and I thought I saw a shadow of apology on his face.

'It's medieval,' I snapped.

'You must bear the consequences of your actions,' the older one chimed in.

That was when I realized I could use the self-criticism to deflect blame from Blue and Larry.

I set pen to paper. When it was finished, it read like this:

> I came to China on a tourist visa and, whilst in Beijing, in contravention of the terms of my visa, conducted illegal reporting activities. I am told by the police that my actions have endangered state security and brought the reputation of China into disrepute. While in China, I hired a translator, Blue Tang, and a cameraman, Larry Mak. I told neither of them the true purpose of my visit, nor did I explain that my reporting activities contravened the terms of my visa and were therefore illegal. We came upon the street protest by accident. I instructed Larry Mak to film it. When the police detained us, I told Blue Tang to lie about my reason for being in Beijing. I deeply regret my deception of the Chinese authorities and of Blue Tang and Larry Mak, neither of whom were aware of my illegal status as of my ulterior motives in coming to China.
>
> Signed, Robin Ballantyne

I handed it over, and thought how proud Blue would have been of me. I didn't shout, I didn't yell. I had played their game, just as she had the day before inside the police station. They looked satisfied, even pleased, as they read my statement. The younger officer went off to photocopy it, and gave me a copy which I folded and put in my pocket. Later, I thought, I would burn it. They took me to a room and turned the key in the lock behind me. I went to the window, and found that was locked too. There was no telephone. I sat down on the hard bed, and found that I was shaking. I watched Chinese television until the small hours of the morning, and then I fell into a shallow sleep.

I arrived at Heathrow, and still I did not ring Finney. I had a strange idea that I would simply join the queue to get back on the plane, and that I would return to Beijing and somehow I would achieve Blue's release, and that Finney would never know of my detour. Finally I came to my senses. My visa had been revoked. I would not be allowed back on the plane.

As I stood in the taxi queue, the moisture in the air seeped into my lungs and into my skin. Still I did not ring Finney. All the joy I thought I would feel on my return had been turned on its head, and I didn't know how to explain to him.

We drove through the afternoon traffic, stopping and starting. In the taxi, I pulled out a notebook, and I sketched out a timeline, but without knowing the dates of all the murders by the lake I could not know whether Perry had been in Beijing at the time. In frustration, my pen tearing through the paper, I scratched two black lines through my timeline, crossing it out. I gazed out of the window at the shoppers. They were still buying for Christmas, as they had been even before I left. I felt as though I had been in a time warp, I had gone and lived a whole life, and I had come back and no time had passed. It occurred to me that, from this far away, I could let Blue recede until she was nothing but a point of guilty darkness on my clear horizon. She was an option, nothing more. I could choose to care, and I could choose not to because I was no longer there.

When I got home it was ten to four, and the house was empty. Still I did not ring Finney. He was at work, the twins on their way home from school with the babysitter, Carol. I paced around, impatient for company. It wasn't my intention to inspect the house, but I wasn't blind, and my eye kept catching on things. In our bedroom, the curtains were still closed, Finney's discarded clothes were on the floor, the bed was unmade.

Downstairs in the kitchen the remains of breakfast were still on the table and ants were busily carrying off crumbs from the floor. The door to the tumble dryer was open, spewing clothes onto the kitchen floor as though some item of clothing had been retrieved in panic. I transferred the clothing from the floor into the laundry basket, picked up the brush and started to sweep.

Then there was the sound of a key in the lock, and the next few minutes passed in shrieks and yells of surprise, and solid little bodies flung around mine, hugging so hard I could hardly breathe, pushing me over so that I sat on the stairs with both of them on top of me.

'Hi,' I greeted Carol over their heads.

'Hi,' she smiled, 'we weren't expecting you yet.'

Then William said, 'Mummy, Mummy, Mummy . . .' and Hannah said, 'I want, I want, I want . . .' and for what seemed like an hour the twins talked at me, one taking over when the other stopped to take breath, the narrative going in two wildly divergent directions, punches exchanged when one took my attention from the other. I watched as they gabbled. They looked well, I thought. It was only a few days since I'd left, but they both seemed taller and more grown-up. They hadn't starved, their little bellies pushed greedily against their school shirts. Hannah's dark curls were tangled and wild, and William's eyes were huge with exhaustion, but that was how they always looked by the end of the school day. Neither of them had anything one could describe as a haunted look in their eye. They even looked some-what cleaner than they ever did on my watch.

'Daddy, Daddy, Daddy . . .' William started, and I stared at him.

'You mean Fin—' I started to correct him.

'Daddy made me late for school this morning,' he said. 'He looked at the clock and he said a bad word. Sod. He said sod. I told Miss Taylor, and she said it was a bad word and I must tell my daddy off, and I said he's not really my daddy, I just call him that because he sleeps in the bed with Mummy. Sod, sod, sod.'

'No,' I said, alarmed, 'no more. That's enough.'

'Sod,' William repeated, in a satisfied tone.

At which point, quite suddenly, the twins lost interest in me. They hurled themselves into the sitting room, and I could hear a burst of sound from the TV. I buried my head in my hands, exhausted by the flight, and overwhelmed.

Hannah reappeared, curls bouncing.

'Mummy,' she said, settling back on my lap, 'Finney is a policeman but he said a bad word. Sod. Does that mean he has to arrest himself?'

'No,' I said, 'it was a . . . a mistake, and I'm sure he won't do it again, and neither must you.'

'Because,' she dragged the word out, 'if he arrested himself, he'd have to put himself in prison.'

'He would indeed,' I agreed. 'It would be very awkward.'

'Silly Mummy.' Hannah grinned, happy to have turned the tables. She kissed me, and ran off.

I went into my bedroom and sat on the edge of the bed. I reached for the phone and dialled Finney's number.

'It's me,' I said.

'They told me you'd checked out, where the hell—?'

'I'm at home.'

'At home?'

'They deported me. That doesn't matter, but they took Blue away. Oh, God . . .'

'Are you all right?'

Tears were running down my face.

'I want you here.'

'You don't mean to say you need me?' His voice was low, as though he was afraid someone might overhear him, and gently sarcastic.

'I need to talk to you,' I said, wiping my tears away, and then, sharply, in response to his silence, 'Unless you'd rather I went through the press office?'

'I'll come home,' he said.

When he arrived Hannah and William fell upon him with hugs, just as they had welcomed me. Stranger still, Finney succumbed to them, asking them whether they'd brushed their teeth (yes), and whether they'd washed behind their ears (no). Part of me was intrigued – when had this happened? – and part of me flinched. Who was he to butt in on bedtime? When I put them to bed they begged me to get him to come and say goodnight to them, and he went without complaining and a few minutes later came back to the kitchen without comment and reached into the fridge for a beer.

'The kids . . .' I said, 'William, anyway, he called you daddy. Did you coach him?'

'You're jealous.' He grinned.

I couldn't bring myself to match his smile. 'I'm jealous.'

'What does Hannah hate more than anything else in the world?'

'Hannah? The dark? Monsters? Me being away?'

'Bad bananas,' he kissed my neck, 'black on the outside, and brown and squidgy inside. She calls them badanas. What's William's . . .'

'They're my children – don't forget it,' I said. 'I just lent them to you for a bit.'

'William has bad dreams about supermarkets,' he murmured in my ear. 'He's been left alone in the fresh fish section and—'

'Stop it!' I protested. 'Why on earth would he tell you, not me?'

'You're one crazy mother,' he said, and I kissed him then with all the urgency that was inside me. I brought it all to our bed that night, the images of violent death etched on my eyes, a woman dragged unwilling from her home, another widowed, a killer stalking a dark lake. I thought that love could purge it from me, but in the middle of the night my eyes opened and I saw it all still there.

CHAPTER 21

Song had dropped off Blue at the hotel where the foreign woman was staying. Then he stopped by the side of the road to let Wolf out, to go back to the office. They had agreed that Song would take Wolf's car for the next few days. It was an open-ended arrangement, neither of them could be sure how long Song's exile would last.

'Detective Fang will come looking for me,' Song warned Wolf, as he got out of the car. 'Lie, tell him you haven't seen me.'

'Where are you going?' Wolf leaned on the car door, bending down to look in at his friend.

'I don't know,' Song said. It was only half true but he thought that Wolf would laugh at him if he told the truth, which was, 'I'm going to find the boy.'

First, though, he stopped at a cafe, and ate a bowl of noodles to sustain him for the drive ahead. He pulled the piece of paper from his pocket and put it on the table next to his bowl and, as he ate, he stared at the licence plate number. Now that Song knew Psycho Wang had

337

contacts in Shijingshan he wanted to know whether that number had ever been registered to a car used by his former police colleague. It was a long shot, but the man's cruelty and violence were not in question.

Song pulled his mobile from his pocket and dialled Detective Chen's number, but a woman's voice informed him that his ex-father-in-law's phone was switched off. He dialled Lina's number, and when she answered her voice was high-pitched and distraught.

'They've taken Daddy away . . .'

Song stood up, glancing around him, knowing that he could not have this conversation inside the cafe, with other people listening in. He made his way outside, with Lina sobbing in his ear.

'Who? Who's taken him away?'

'Detective Fang came with his men. How can he do this? He's worked with Daddy for years. I begged him, pleaded with him, I said, "Daddy's your friend, how can you do this?" I—'

'Detective Fang has been waiting to do this for years,' Song interrupted coldly, becoming impatient. 'I warned you of this, and you wouldn't listen.'

'You are going down too,' she screamed at him. He held the phone a little way from his ear, and still he could hear every word. 'They're going to take the flat from me, my home, Doudou's home . . . Detective Fang said he gave you the chance to keep me out of this. He said if you had cooperated I would have kept the flat, and instead you run away like a dog, leaving a trail of shit behind you.'

'Did Detective Fang tell you how he wanted me to cooperate?' Song demanded. 'Did he tell you he wants me to destroy your father? Is that how I should be a role model to our son?'

He hung up on her, not waiting for her reply.

Song drove through the night with the window cracked open so that the icy air kept him awake. On the way out of Beijing he'd passed queues of trucks lined up waiting to be allowed to enter the city, but now he was away from the city and on the toll roads he was on his own on a six-lane highway. Still, he tried not to let the darkness and the tedium of the drive get the better of him. A man he knew had died on a night like this, on a road like this, just six months before, when the dark hulk of alorry had lunged out of the black sky roaring the wrong way down the fast lane.

The land around him was black flatness, the sky unrelieved by stars. His phone beeped to tell him that text messages had arrived, and he reached out and checked them.

Nelson Li: Where is the boy?

His sister: Pa doing well on new medicine. He wants to see you.

Eventually, when sleep would wait no longer, he pulled off the highway and got a room in the least filthy establishment he could find. Still his room smelled of the en suite bathroom, which had matted long hair blocking the drain and a damp grey towel hanging on a rail. The singing of drunken revellers leaked into his room from the karaoke bar. He lay down fully clothed on the musty bed and reached out to turn off the bedside light.

In the morning, Song was woken by his mobile phone. He grabbed it from the bedside table and held it to his ear, his eyes still closed.

'Who's this?' an older male voice asked.

'Shouldn't I be the one asking that?' Song replied, fully awake now.

'We found your number on our daughter's phone, we don't know who . . .'

Song glanced at his phone to check who was calling him. The number was Blue's. Logically, then, this was her father. Song pulled himself upright.

'Okay,' he said, 'I understand who you are now but I don't really know your daughter. We just . . . our paths crossed.'

'I . . .' the man's voice faltered, 'excuse me, who am I speaking to?'

Song took pity on the man.

'I'm a . . . a legal consultant . . . What's the problem?'

'They've taken her away – the police, I mean. We don't know why. She's always been a good girl. What could she have done to bring this trouble on herself?'

Song ran his palm over his face, listening to the man speak. If the police wanted evidence of wrongdoing, they would be recording these calls from her family's house, but Blue's father seemed too naive to know that. He thought of the document Wolf's uncle had faxed to the office, and that Wolf had handed to Blue. Did she have it on her when she was arrested? Song closed his eyes. That prospect was too horrible to contemplate. The sensible thing now would be to hang up, or just to say he was sorry, he had made a mistake, he didn't know this woman after all, had no idea how his number had got onto her phone. But then there was this poor man.

'I hardly know your daughter,' he repeated. 'Perhaps a foreigner she was translating for has led her into trouble. Foreigners don't know about our laws, and they can get people into trouble very easily. I'm sure the police will realize your daughter is an innocent victim.'

He thought of the British woman with the golden hair, and cursed her. He had not sensed malice in the woman, only a determination to get to the truth, but to blunder around like this . . .

There was a long pause on the line, and Song thought that Blue's father had perhaps read between the lines, and that he had perhaps even realized why Song was not speaking frankly. Blue's mental acuity, after all, had come from somewhere.

'What should I do?' the man said, in a sad voice.

'There was no opportunity for her to pack. They dragged her away from us.'

Song remembered holding Blue high above the crowd, remembered the tension in her muscles, and thought that he would not like to be the one to remove her when she did not want to be removed.

'I have no knowledge of your daughter's situation,' Song said slowly, 'but speaking as a legal consultant, I would advise that you go to your local police station and ask politely for information. They may allow you to send her some provisions, perhaps you will learn where she is being held. Then . . . well, then you wait . . . see whether she reappears in a day or two . . .'

'I see.' Blue's father sounded further diminished by the prospect of waiting. 'And if she doesn't come back?'

Song exhaled slowly. It was unlikely, of course, that she would come back, not in a day or two.

'I have no knowledge of this particular case, of course,' Song thought he might scream if he heard himself say this again, 'but I may be able to put you in contact with a lawyer.' As an option it sounded better than it was. In most cases, only money or connections could make the system bend, but he doubted Blue's family had any. The man's voice did not sound like money, there was no privilege or pride about it, and no assumption that this thing could be made to go away.

The man thanked him graciously. Song thought

that this man would have done all these things in any case. He would have sought out a police officer, he would have been polite but firm in his enquiries about his daughter. His wife would have wept at his side. They were of the generation who knew what it was to vanish into police custody, who knew that tears might conceivably help but outraged protest would only make things worse. In that sense, Song counted himself among the old and disillusioned. He'd been old enough in 1989, when the army opened fire on demonstrators calling for democracy, to count those who vanished, himself escaping narrowly from the tanks that roamed the streets. It was the youngsters, those born in the eighties, who got taken by surprise when the system snapped its jaws shut around them and took them down into its belly.

Back on the road, Song started his search in earnest. He remembered the name of the village the beggar boy came from, Xiaoshanzi, and had assumed that people in Longhua county town would know of it. But now, after asking half a dozen people, it seemed that there were at least two villages by the name of Xiaoshanzi. Lower Xiaoshanzi was just ten kilometres outside the county town, Upper Xiaoshanzi high in a mountain range. Wolf kept a book of provincial maps in the car, but they were pretty useless, good maps being, like so much else, a state secret.

He headed first to Lower Xiaoshanzi, a tiny

collection of ancient tile-roofed cottages set around a square. Song parked in the square and got out of the car. He glanced around. There were grasses growing on the ancient rooftops, and fallen statuary by the road. His was the only car. He would have thought himself stepped back a couple of hundred years, except for the electricity pylons and the slogans about the virtues of birth control painted in red on a concrete shack that declared itself to be the village clinic. It had a poster tacked to the door, showing a woman's reproductive organs in pink and yellow. He didn't want to go anywhere near the clinic. Those places unnerved him, with their metal spittoons and their white coats, and their middle-aged women with a fetish for menstrual cycles and the insertion of copper coils.

He approached the village shop, a building that appeared to be about to crumble into the ground. Its windows were so thickly grimed that one could not see the tins and packets on display, and the doorway was covered with an army-issue piece of quilting. He pushed the grubby fabric aside and walked in to find two women, one of them ruddy-cheeked, behind the counter. They carried on talking, pretending not to have noticed him. Song waited politely until they deigned to pause.

'I'm sorry to interrupt. I'm trying to find someone,' Song said. 'A family, with a teenage daughter and a younger son. Both of the children were sent to Beijing to get work.'

The women shook their heads in unison. Their

instinct was suspicion, but Song awed them both with his height and his courtesy and they were inclined to be helpful, even to impress him with their wisdom.

'That way lies tears,' said the ruddy-cheeked woman. 'Anything and everything goes on there, there's no safety for a child even in our great capital. School is the only safe place for a child.'

'I'm afraid you are quite right,' Song told her seriously. He bought a Coke from her, then asked, 'Is there a school here?'

'In the next village,' she told him. 'There's a bus that comes for the children.'

Outside, Song found two village boys examining his car and thought they should have been in school. He put the same question to them, about the children sent to Beijing. But they shook their heads too, and watched solemnly as he reversed and did a U-turn in the dirt road.

He rose higher and higher into the mountains, precipitous drops first to one side and then to the other, alert at every bend in the narrow road for a truck hurtling in the opposite direction. The road here was icy, the bare bones of the trees that clung to the steep mountainsides had become frosted confections. As he inched forward, his mind was on Blue. He could not help her, he feared, without further endangering himself. And by suggesting to her father that he would help to find a lawyer, he had entangled himself even further in the web of obligation.

Upper Xiaoshanzi had a Ming dynasty wall and cypress trees at its heart. This was a larger settlement than its cousin in the foothills, but the rough streets seemed empty of life. Either people were huddled inside against the cold, or it was deserted. Song parked inside the wall, under a notice board on which had been painted the instruction, 'Tell Good from Evil!' in red characters. He got out of the car and walked down the street. He felt eyes upon him, but still he saw no one. A padlock hung heavily on the door of the village shop.

At last, in the distance, a man appeared from a side alley. Song approached him and asked whether there was such a family here, a boy and girl both sent to work in Beijing.

'Why do you want to know?'

'The family is owed money,' is all that Song had to say, and the man agreed to lead him there.

Song had never seen anywhere as poor as the hovel where the boy's mother lived. There was a coal-fired stove, which had blackened the walls, but no electricity, no curtains at the window, no glass in the window. There was a flaking gilt bust of Chairman Mao on a shelf.

'I'll get you something to drink,' the woman said. Her eyes saw them, and her response was hospitality, but she didn't seem to register the fact that this large man was a stranger.

'Her name is Cao Liming,' the man who had guided him there said. The man did not attempt

346

to introduce Song to the woman, did not even bother to ask his name, and Song did not volunteer it.

Song watched Cao. She might have been different when she was young, but all that shone from her now was incompetence. Her movements were slow as she poured water from a blackened kettle into a stained cup. There were no tea leaves to flavour the water. Song made a show of sipping, but he didn't let his lips touch the rim of the cup. The man who chaperoned him accepted water too, and did not drink.

'Where is your son?' Song asked Cao, and she looked at him with blank eyes.

'My son's a naughty boy,' she said.

'You sent him to Beijing,' Song said, 'with his sister. Have you heard from them?'

She gave a quick uncomprehending glance at the man who had brought Song there, and Song began to realize that this woman was not just slow but inadequate.

'You said she's owed money,' the man said.

'She is, that's right.' Song pulled his wallet from his trousers, and pulled out five one-hundred *yuan* notes. He handed them to Cao, who took them in her hand and held them, frowning at them. Then, darting a look of suspicion at Song, she fell down to her knees and pushed them underneath her bedding.

'That's all?' The man was disgusted. He drew Song aside and spoke in a low voice so that the woman could not hear. 'You came all this way to give her that? Two children gone for months and now . . . we heard what befell the girl – word came through another family.'

'Does she know?' Song looked at the woman, who was sitting humming on the bed and rocking gently to and fro, apparently unaware of the whispering that was going on in the same room.

'No one knows how to tell her, or how to make her understand. Her husband is in jail, he'll not be back for years, never if he has sense. The children ran wild, they got in trouble . . . She didn't know what she was doing when she let them go. Look at her, look at how she lives. You come from the city, you can afford to give her more.'

'If she can tell me where the boy is—'

The man interrupted him.

'If that's all you want, I know where they are. Another kid went with them, he telephoned his mother to tell her what happened to the girl, and to say the gang had left Beijing.'

Song delved in his wallet, retrieved another five hundred *yuan*, made to hand it to the man, who shook his head and indicated the woman.

'Her children, the money's hers,' he said.

Song handed the notes to Cao, and again she fell to her knees, and again secreted them under her bedding. The man watched approvingly, but when he turned back to Song his face was dark with suspicion.

'She can't lose both her children. You won't harm the boy?'

'No,' said Song.

'They've moved on to Shanghai.'

Song laughed nervously.

'It's a city of twenty million people . . .'

The man shook his head.

'He'll be on the street in the city. If you have cash, he'll find you.'

CHAPTER 22

I pushed through the revolving doors of the the Corporation and nodded at the security man, Simon.

'ID, love?' he asked, holding up a hand to stop me. I glanced down, and realized I'd forgotten the laminated card that should hang around my neck on ribbon. I'd never forgotten it before, it was so automatic: get dressed for work, pull ID on over my head. But today, jet-lagged and disorientated even in my own home, I'd managed to leave the house without it.

'I know you, love, but you'll have to sign in or I'll get the axe,' Simon said, pushing the visitors' register towards me, 'just in case you've had a face transplant – you know how all the terrorists are having them these days.'

I signed my name, then looked up to find his grin fading. He'd made a joke, and I hadn't even noticed.

'I think I've had a brain transplant,' I said, and then he smiled.

None of it seemed real. The carpeted corridors were too quiet, too empty of people. Colleagues hailed me, but I kept my head down and hurried on. I headed straight for Sal's office – I wanted him to hear about Blue from me, and face to face. But he wasn't at his desk. I sat in his chair and called his mobile, thumbing through the pile of magazines on his desk while I waited for him to answer. Someone had taken down several messages from a Dr Cox reminding Sal about appointments he'd made and missed. He needed someone to look after him.

'Goldilocks,' he greeted me, and I could tell just from his gleeful tone of voice that he was on the road. 'I'm in Bosnia. What is it?'

'I wanted to tell you before you heard it somewhere else. Blue was arrested.'

There was an instant's silence, and then a hail of invective, directed at the universe, rather than at me.

'I'm sorry,' I said. 'I feel terrible.'

'Why? Were you the one who threw her in jail?' His voice was fading in and out, as though he were up a mountain or underground.

'Of course not, but—'

'Then stop being sorry.' I closed my eyes, straining to hear what he was saying. 'It's the system, stupid. The question is, what are you going to do about it?'

'Either scream blue murder or shut up, I can't decide.'

'Scream blue murder,' Sal said.

'The more fuss I make, the more trouble she's in.'

'Not so, Goldilocks . . .'

Then I lost the connection, and when I tried to ring again, he was no longer reachable.

I found Damien in the *Controversies* office, a large open-plan space on the third floor, with windows overlooking the Strand. He was standing staring at one of the three television screens that were suspended from the ceiling. A couple of junior reporters and Damien's assistant, Heather, were watching too.

The screen had a dateline in the corner that read Beijing, and the picture was of an angry crowd of Chinese people shouting and chanting outside a high wall topped with barbed wire. It was night, but the scene was illuminated by police spotlights. Some of the demonstrators carried placards in English, and I saw the words 'Reese' and 'rapist'. A bottle was thrown by someone in the crowd, and it smashed against the wall. Damien glanced over and saw me.

'See the story we haven't got?' He addressed the room, but I knew it was aimed at me. 'Riots outside the British embassy, a major diplomatic incident, but we missed the story because our correspondent was on a plane flying out of the country at the time.'

'I didn't have much choi—'

'For fuck's sake, it's the story of the week, and we've got sweet fuck all.'

'She was deported, Damien,' one of the junior

reporters, Maya, came to my defence. 'Be reason-able.'

'Reese had a knife, you know that, Robin?' Damien picked up a newspaper and shook it towards me, as if he expected me to read it half the way across the room. 'Look at this. Sumner disturbed Reese trying to rape another woman, that's what they're saying. Sumner, walking past, hears a woman shouting from the woods. Being a gentleman he goes to her aid, confronts Reese, gets killed for his trouble. It's that simple, and we haven't got it.'

'It's speculation,' I said, 'and I don't believe it.'

'*You* don't believe it?' Damien echoed sarcastically. 'Well they seem to believe it in Beijing.'

'A woman was killed after Reese was arrested. I saw her with her throat cut.'

He stared at me, then recovered.

'A copycat crime,' he said.

'Maybe,' I said, trying to contain my temper, 'but I don't think so.'

'Well, don't let's forget your one achievement, which was to get your interpreter arrested.'

'Damien,' Maya protested again, 'it's not her fault.'

I gave Maya a grateful look, although I wasn't sure that she was right. Then I turned and walked into the glass cubicle at the centre of the room that was Damien's office, and after a moment he followed me.

'Don't you dare do that again,' I hissed at him.

'If you've got something to say to me, you say it in private.'

'But we've got – *you've* got – fuck all,' he said again, gesturing at the screens through the glass, still showing the riot in Beijing. 'I'm looking like a fool.'

'They're all wrong,' I said. 'They're leaping to conclusions, they're the ones who'll look like fools.' Through the glass I could see Maya and Heather casting glances in our direction and whispering. I sat down on Damien's couch, sinking into the cushions, leaving him to pace furiously. He'd run his hand through his hair so much it was standing on end.

'Nelson Li is going to move the Kelness plant to Dalian,' I said. 'He's going to box it up and ship it off to Dalian and rebuild it.'

Damien was still staring out through the glass at the TV screen. Abruptly he turned to look at me.

'Do you have proof?'

'I have a piece of paper,' I told him. 'I need to get it translated. I don't know what I've got yet.'

Damien collapsed back onto his chair.

'Well, that's just brilliant,' he said.

'Send me back to Kelness,' I said. 'Nelson Li arrives tomorrow, and both the Kelness reps from Beijing – Karen Turvey, Angus Perry – will be there for the negotiations. I think that perhaps all or some of them knew about Li's plans to ship the plant out, that someone hated Derek Sumner for backing the plan, and killed him because of all those men who're going to lose their jobs.'

'You do?' he asked nervously. 'You think that?'

'I told you I saw another woman's body,' I said slowly. 'Well, Angus Perry was there too, and he was in a total state.'

Damien was staring at me, frowning.

'You think a Kelness employee killed the women as well?' he asked.

I hesitated. It was an outrageous accusation, and it was not one I was ready to make in public. If it was not true, it was a terrible slur against Perry. On second thoughts, I didn't trust Damien with my suspicions.

'I think,' I said, 'that if we find out who leaked the memo, we find out who killed Derek Sumner.'

He puffed his cheeks out, ran his hands down over his face, then back through his hair, and I thought then that for all his achievements so far, Damien's career was taking a terrible toll.

'You have to get me some bloody pictures this time,' he said hoarsely, waving his hand in dismissal.

I hesitated for a moment. I'd come here to talk to him about Blue, about how we – by which I meant the Corporation – could help her. But when I looked at Damien sitting there with his head in his hands, I knew he was incapable of helping anyone.

CHAPTER 23

Song had spent much of his adult life avoiding Shanghai. He had never met a Shanghainese he trusted. They were, as all Beijingers knew, hustlers, obsessed by money, cold-hearted commercial creatures with no sense of personal space. They had no soul, or else they'd sold it long ago to the foreigners who'd colonized their city. And they were arrogant – their women, they boasted, were more beautiful, their buildings taller, their dumplings more delectable than those anywhere else in China. They thought their Beijing cousins sluggish and brainwashed by politics.

Song took a taxi from the airport, and already he sensed the restlessness of the city in the way the traffic moved, the shifting, racing speed of it. In Beijing drivers elbowed their way through traffic. Here in Shanghai they might as well have fired a starting pistol at every junction.

'Where are you going?' The driver's question was barely intelligible, the Shanghai dialect lumpy and slurred.

'Where are your beggars?'

'We work for our living here in Shanghai.'

Meaning, unlike you Beijing-party-coddled boys up north.

'I mean the beggars who come from out of town.'

'Try the Bund,' the driver suggested. 'There's low life of all kinds there.'

Along the Bund, the promenade on the Huangpu River, colonial buildings lined the west bank. On the eastern shore modern skyscrapers had sprung up, a TV tower like an alien killer spider rising above Pudong. Song leaned on the balustrade for a few moments and judged it brash and unsightly. Unlike the crowd, who looked across the water in awe, Song now fixed his eyes closer to the ground, searching for the boy. Commerce seethed around him. He was besieged on every side by hawkers offering him toys and souvenirs and food. He fought them off, battled through the crowds, then turned and looked back across the sea of heads. There was not a beggar to be seen.

He tried the Yuyuan bazaar, criss-crossing the maze of shopping alleys outside the gates of the Yu garden, increasingly impatient with tourists, salesmen, the whole damned population of this beehive of a city. And nowhere did he see a beggar.

What he did see was a cat, a scrawny kitten being chased across the road by a child who nearly got run over. It stuck in his mind, that cat, leading him to think of the skinned carcasses thrown into the quarry, and of another thing that had been nagging at him. Detective Chen believed that the

357

killer filmed himself torturing cats, and had posted that film on the internet.

When Song saw a sign for a cyber-cafe he went in, and climbed up the stairs to the first floor, to a room full of computers and boys and young men playing video games. He went online and accessed a search engine, typing in 'cat torture'. The censors tried to bar access to politically dubious material on the internet, but they were less interested in sex and violence. The list that appeared did not, at first, offer him anything that sounded likely. But Detective Chen had implied that the pictures were available on the internet, so Song persisted. He looked at some images of kittens who seemed more pampered than tortured, and then, leaning in close to the screen, to shield it from the young eyes around him, he worked his way through images of torture, not one of which involved cats.

Then, all at once, there was a video frame in the centre of his screen, a kitten's face looking up at him. He clicked on play and the camera panned out. The cat, a tabby kitten, mouth pitifully opening and closing, was lying with its stomach flat to the carpeted floor, skewered by a woman's stiletto heel that twisted to and fro. The woman's foot was broad, bulging from between the straps of the sandal, toenails painted purple. A man's hand reached into the frame, holding a knife.

'Hey,' a voice said. In an instant Song clicked to close the image. He turned his head to look behind him. The 'hey' had been addressed to someone else – a teenage boy was slapping another on the back, they were both laughing. Song turned back and sat staring at the screen, waiting for his thundering heartbeat to return to normal. Song was not an animal lover, but he had no stomach to return to the picture. Nor could he risk discovery. He closed the connection and left the building, head down.

He had recognized two things. First, the flooring to which the kitten was flattened, a beige and purple carpet such as he had seen in the Waimao Hotel. This linked the cat torture with the attack on the prostitute in that hotel. Second, the knife. It was not the knife he had seized from the tent on the night of the fire and that he had handed over to Detective Chen. But it was a smaller version, roughly fifteen centimetres long, the same elegant shape, the sweeping curve from point to handle, the same brand name and logo clearly visible on the blade. It could be a coincidence, of course, but he did not believe it was, and if those two knives belonged to the same person, the cat torturer was linked to the murders by the lake. Since the cat carcasses had been dumped in the quarry where women had been attacked, he was inclined to think it was reasonable to link all three phenomena – the cat torture, the murder by the lake, and the attacks on women in Shijingshan.

Song flagged down a taxi and showed the driver the missing barmaid's address. He found it down a narrow alleyway, in a dark labyrinth of staircases and corridors, and he asked directions from an ancient woman who sat outside the house chopping vegetables. The air was thick with the smell of cooking.

'I'm looking for Zhao Aiwen,' he called, knocking on the door. His eyes had not yet adjusted to the gloom.

'Why do you want her?' A woman's voice, aggressive and suspicious.

'I just want to talk to her. I work in the personnel department of the Waimao Hotel,' he had not prepared the lie, 'and she put this address on her records.'

'Well, why come here?' the voice snarled, and a woman moved out of the shadows. 'You said yourself she's in Beijing, so why come here to look for her?'

Song thought fast. Should he alarm the barmaid's family by telling them that their daughter had not returned to her job in the hotel, or should he hope that his hunch was wrong and that she was simply lying low? He had no way of telling what kind of relationship she had with her family, but he knew that if this dark dank room was his family home, and this snarling woman his mother, he would not return here even if he was in trouble.

'You're right,' he said, deciding on the latter course of action, 'but I should be straight with you. I have a friend who's in love with her. He's too embarrassed to approach her directly. Since her family is here, and I am here, he asked me to enquire whether she already has a boyfriend.'

The woman screeched with laughter.

'He's such a gentleman that he can't approach her directly?' she cackled. 'Where would the likes of her meet such a man?'

'Don't say such things!' From the shadows came an old man's voice, and now Song's eyes could just make out a shape huddled in a wheelchair.

'There's already a man who is courting her,' the voice, reedy and weak, continued from the shadows, 'and he has a good job. He's a police officer. He comes to take her out in his car. He buys her presents. He'll ask her to marry him, and they'll have a bright future together.'

'Do you know this man's name?' Song asked. 'Or his rank? Do you know what kind of car he drives?'

His mind had immediately gone to Psycho Wang, who knew the manager of the Waimao Hotel and may therefore have been known to this woman.

'A Santana,' the mother had remembered this important point, 'a black one. He has use of an official car. After all the trouble she had with the police in Shanghai, all the lies they told about her, she goes to Beijing where no one knows her and straight away she finds a police officer to look after her. Look what he gave her. She sent it to show us how well she's doing there.'

The woman snatched something up from a table

and shoved it at him. Song reached out and took it, a small flat piece of plastic, like a smooth pebble with a circle set into it. He ran the flesh of his thumb over the sleek line of it. An iPod, black, just like the one that had skittered out of the boy's jacket and under his wardrobe.

'That's wonderful,' he said quietly. He returned it to the woman's waiting palm and bowed slightly in the direction of the elderly man. 'I will tell my friend that your daughter is spoken for. You must be very proud of her.'

He took a name card from his pocket. It was a card from his stock of false cards. This one described him as Personnel Manager, Beijing Personnel Solutions, but it gave his correct mobile number. He placed it in the woman's hand.

'Just in case her situation changes,' he said, 'please get in touch.'

When his mobile rang, he saw that it was Blue's father again. For a moment he didn't answer, and then he cursed and lifted the phone to his ear, taking the call.

'She still hasn't come back,' her father said. Song noted with relief that this time the man did not introduce himself, or refer to his daughter by name. He thought that the man must have been advised by friends to be more cautious with his daughter in police detention.

'Do you have news of her?' Song asked. 'Do you know where she's being held?'

'They say that she is being well looked after,' the man said hopelessly, 'and they have allowed us to send a package of toiletries and clothes, but they will not tell us where she is. They say we will have news of her soon.'

'She hasn't been charged?' Song clarified.

'They say not.'

'That's good,' Song said, although he knew that he was exaggerating to comfort her father. 'I'll try to put you in touch with a lawyer, someone I was in college with. His surname is Yang. If he agrees, I'll give him your number.'

The man murmured his gratitude. Afterwards, Song found a public phone box and called his friend Yang. He did not want to use Wolf on this, it would bring Blue's case too close to the agency, but Yang was a fine lawyer and a good man.

'I'm going to ask you for a favour,' he told Yang.

'I'm glad,' said Yang. 'I've been in your debt for five years now.'

Song smiled.

'I'm going to give you a telephone number,' he told Yang, 'ring it and give your surname to the old man who answers, and arrange to meet him somewhere outside his house. See if you can help him.'

'All right,' Yang replied, and took down the number as Song read it from his mobile phone.

'One more thing,' Song said, 'they have no money.'

'Of course they don't,' Yang said. 'Or it wouldn't

be a favour. Don't worry, I like the ones who have no money.'

Song made Yang agree that they would meet for a meal soon, and then he hung up. He knew that Yang would not be afraid to speak to the police about Blue, and that he would steer her father away from further trouble.

Song ate supper in a modest restaurant that specialized in *xiaolongbao*, traditional Shanghai dumplings. The waitress brought him a bottle of Tsingtao beer and a bamboo steamer full of tiny silvery dumplings, which he picked up one by one, dipping them in soy and vinegar and then popping them into his mouth, where his teeth sliced through the paper-thin skin and hot soup exploded onto his tongue. While the steamer of *xiaolongbao* lasted, Song toyed with the idea of extended exile in Shanghai.

Before leaving the restaurant, he asked the cook where he would find the city's beggars, and the cook gave him directions to areas where foreigners and the rich Shanghainese ate and played. With his belly full, he walked through the night-time city. Although the temperature was higher here than in Beijing, the moisture conducted cold air through his clothes and deep into his bones. Nevertheless, commercialism seemed fiercely active – the population was not huddling by a fire at home, many of them were pursuing a sliver of the prosperity that seeped from the neon lights and the restaurants, the karaoke clubs and bath houses. For the beggars, who had come out from their hiding places, that meant approaching diners on their way into and out of these establishments. Where there were children, Song scanned their faces, and some of them approached him, asking him for money. He did not see the boy and he walked away.

He found himself back at the Bund. Now, at night and in the cold, there were dwindling crowds drawn by the neon lights of the east bank, the Martian TV tower illuminated in pink, skyscrapers on whose massive sides gigantic advertisements played. On the west bank, the colonial buildings topped with Chinese flags looked like wedding cakes, decked out in lights. Song headed for the group of buildings near the Peace Hotel which had been turned into exclusive restaurants. It was eleven o'clock, and the rich had finished eating and were emerging from the gilded doors. The women, in furs or cashmere, their shining hair elaboratedly plaited and pinned, platinum and diamonds glinting in the glow from the restaurants, looked like movie stars, their male companions like sleek capitalists from the 1930s. The couples hurried through the cold towards their cars, where chauffeurs had the engines running and the heating on, and they played a game of bluff and double bluff with the beggars who attempted to intercept them.

Song stood in the shadows and watched. There

was a girl with no legs, who pushed herself on makeshift wheels towards the ankles of these women, tapping her forehead against their shins. Mostly the beautiful women sidestepped her. Some dropped coins and notes into the bowl she had strung around her neck. One woman tripped in her attempt to avoid the beggar girl and slipped half to the ground, twisting her ankle. Her companion aimed a polished black toe towards the girl and kicked her wheels from under her.

There were ragged women with sleeping children in their arms, and a woman who pushed an older boy in a wheelchair, his mouth agape and drooling. Song spotted a boy, the right size and shape, lopsided, one shoulder falling away, the sleeve formless. The boy darted back and forth, grabbing a well-clad arm, dropping to his knees, head jerking and bobbing in servile desperation, palm outstretched. Song watched him, trying to get a clear look at his face, waiting for the boy to emerge from shadow into light. Unlike the other children, the boy muttered constantly. Song could not hear what it was that he said, except that it was a drone of misery. And then he saw the boy's face, his restless troubled eyes, the wind-roughened skin, the mouth that was never still, and in the same moment he saw the twisted slip of a man who had swung the metal rod at him.

Song hadn't admitted to himself that he was ashamed of returning the boy to the care of the beggar gang, but now that shame receded. The boy was alive. Song stepped forward and grabbed the wrist of the boy, who cried out and looked sharply at him, then recognized his assailant and shut up.

'You're coming with me,' Song hissed at him, and pulled the child further down the street, lifting his free hand for a taxi. A cab eased into the kerb and Song grabbed the door handle, swinging himself and the child into the back seat. The boy was so light. Every time, the child surprised Song with his lightness. Behind them, Song could see the twisted man giving chase on foot, and then their taxi had turned a corner and accelerated and the man disappeared from view.

CHAPTER 24

I pulled off the road, manoeuvred the hired car so that it nestled against the hillside, and killed the engine. I got out, wrapping my scarf around my face, and looked out over the land where it fell away, streaked with snow. A shaft of wintry sun cut through the early morning moisture like a handful of glitter released into the air. A mushroom cloud rose from Kelness, which hugged the shoreline way below me, a vast industrial mass of warehousing and chimneys, tangled walkways and great blast furnaces. A ship was slowly coming into port, laden perhaps with iron ore or coal. The town fanned out behind the steel plant, the rows of tiny houses reduced by distance to a faint spidery web.

I knew the fate of Kelness. It was in my pocket, a translation of the fax that Blue had left for me. This community below me would either die or refashion itself. But the fabric of the place, the bricks and metal, would form the heart of a new community. While the families of Kelness were plunged into desperate insecurity, halfway around the world the plant would raise thousand of others out of grinding poverty. It felt inevitable that morning. I hadn't warmed to Nelson Li, but I couldn't blame him – Kelness was dying before he ever set eyes on it. The men who would be laid off when the plant closed down would be only the latest of the thousands who had already gone. Better that the plant be recycled than it be left to rust.

I thought of Karen Turvey sitting in Starbucks in Beijing and asking where my jeans were made and by whom, and how much they were paid per hour. She'd made her point well: we all used cheap labour. In a couple of years' time the families of Kelness might be delighting in low-priced cars imported from China. That was if they could afford to buy a car at all.

When I had rung Karen Turvey the day before, I'd expected her to refuse point-blank to see me. Media speculation was seething around the steel plant, and the Kelness public relations machine had battened down the hatches. I could see the gates of the plant, and a speckling of colour where vans belonging to broadcast journalists or demonstrators were parked. No journalists were getting in, nobody was talking. So when Karen said yes, she would see me, I was prepared to agree to anywhere any time, and that had turned out to be this deserted hillside at dawn.

I saw a car winding up the road towards me, and for a moment felt uneasy. The sight was too reminiscent of the black jeep after it had forced my taxi off the road. That jolt, the sickening crunch as my taxi buried its nose in the rocky mountainside, had returned to me repeatedly in the night, and I'd woken in a panic, my heart pounding, my head full of What Ifs? What if the driver had failed to turn the car into the mountainside? What if we had plunged from the road and into the abyss?

Karen Turvey raised a hand to me as she approached, and pulled in next to my car. She got out, zipping up her jacket, rubbing her hands together as she came to stand next to me. For a moment she stared out over Kelness, her long curls lifting like a halo in the wind. She pulled up her hood.

'Look at it all stretched out like that, it's like an iron giant fallen on its back and dying.' She paused and turned to me. 'We've all been given an order to turn down all interview requests, not to respond to questions. I can't be seen talking to you.'

'Karen,' I asked, 'does Angus Perry own a black jeep?'

Her brow creased.

'I don't know. He's to and fro to the UK so much I can't imagine he'd want a car in Beijing. We all use taxis.'

I nodded. Even if he'd owned a jeep, it wouldn't have been conclusive.

'I'm going to ask you again about Derek,' I said. 'I know the two of you were friends, and I know you were angry when I suggested he might have leaked information to Nelson Li. But I need to go over it again.'

I'd half expected her to explode with fury, like she had in Starbucks in Beijing, but she did not. I glanced at her face. She was biting her lip, but she caught my eye and gave me a nod.

'There were other leaks,' she said, 'in the month before Derek died. Not big ones, just bits and pieces, figures, statistics that Nelson Li shouldn't have had access to. It was frustrating. Li's daughter was brilliant at using the information to haggle down the price.'

'Was it information Derek had access to?' I wrapped my arms around me, leaning in close to get every word.

'It was information we all had access to, and the figures were real enough. They were the reason Kelness was bankrupt. It was all stats we'd have had to disclose anyway if they'd asked us the right questions. What was frustrating was that they hadn't asked us much at all, but they got handed the information anyway. Then, after Derek said that stuff about dismantling Kelness at the banquet, a lot of people in the company assumed that it was he who'd been leaking to Nelson Li. And that seemed to drive him crazy. I mean I think he actually went a bit mad.'

Her hair was escaping from her hood, whipping around her face, and she paused to push it back, away from her mouth.

'What do you mean, he went crazy?'

'On Sunday, after we spoke, I was kind of worked up. I went back to the office and I took a look at Derek's computer. We all knew each other's passwords, we were all coming and going so much, I was always ringing up the office and asking whoever was around to check something in my computer. Anyway, I opened up Derek's computer.'

'Had anyone else touched it since he was killed?'

'I didn't see anyone touch it.' She frowned. 'We were all too shocked. But I can't promise no one else had turned it on. Anyway, I might as well tell you, I was looking for this memo. I didn't want to, but I thought maybe you and Angus were right, that Derek was the one leaking. And so I looked for it, not expecting to find it, but I did.'

'You found it? Where did he get it from?'

She shook her head, her mouth twisting in remembered disbelief.

'He made it up,' she said. 'It was all sitting there in Word. There was an earlier draft too, with notes to himself about things to change, ways to put things. Why would he do that?'

She broke off, then after a moment she resumed. 'I suppose he thought, if he was going to leak to Nelson Li, he might as well just start making things up that would help him. I can see how he got the idea. Kelness hasn't got the radiation monitors it needs, that's true. That's a scandal in itself. It was a decision Toms made, to risk it, not to spend the money: the monitors cost tens of thousands. That's why none of us leaked it to the workforce then, we all knew we should have the monitors, but if he forked out for the detection system, we were all out of a job. Either the plant would close down or it would be sold.'

'But there were no incidents,' I said. 'Was there radioactive Russian scrap?'

'Who knows?' she said, her mouth turned down. 'Perhaps there was. We wouldn't have known about it. Probably not. The odds were on our side.'

I heaved a breath, and the air chilled my throat.

'I need you to say all this on film,' I said to Karen. 'Will you do that?'

She shook her head.

'I can't,' she said.

I turned on her impatiently.

'Why did you agree to see me? You know what I need. Why do you want to keep these secrets?'

'It would kill Zhuli to know what Derek did,' she said. 'You'll have to find your pictures another way. But I want to tell you there's someone else you need to see. Colin Liscombe.'

I struggled to remember where I'd heard the name.

'He ate at the Lotus Pool with us that night,' she said, 'he was with the visiting delegation. He lives here in Kelness. You should hear what he has to say.'

'What . . . ?'

But she shook her head. 'You've got to hear it

from Colin,' she said, 'and keep me out of it. Like I said, I'm not supposed to be talking to journalists. If he knows I talked to you, and if he tells management, I'm out of a job, if I'm not already.'

I agreed, and she pulled her mobile phone from her pocket, speaking while she searched for the number. 'The poor guy is killing himself with worry. He may take some persuading. He hasn't talked to anyone except me.'

Karen insisted on leaving before me, so that we weren't even seen driving one behind the other. Once she had driven off I tried calling Colin Liscombe, but he wasn't answering his phone. After a few minutes, I drove down towards the plant, past the golf club and the social club, the Kwik Save and the Jobcentre Plus, the business park, the lap-dancing club and the beauty salon called 'Tan Ya Buns'.

A roughly spiked metal fence defined the perimeter of the plant. Inside, the blackened pipes were like a tangle of giant intestines. Yellow earth movers stood like great animals set in stone. Patches of unmown grass and weeds were scattered with rusting metal, a heap of rubber sheeting folded like a broad ribbon of pasta. In the distance, workers in orange and white suits moved slowly around the plant.

I followed the perimeter fence until I found the

main gate where the press was camped out, and where a knot of demonstrators was huddled, miserably nursing cups of tea. I parked behind an outside broadcast van with the Corporation's logo on the side. I sat in the car and tried phoning Colin Liscombe again, but there was still no answer. Someone knocked on the window and I looked up. A Corporation producer I had worked with a couple of years earlier was mouthing something at me through the glass. I wound down the window.

'Hi. What's going on?' I said. I couldn't remember the guy's name.

'Not a lot, as you can see,' he said. 'Nelson Li's expected later today, and that lot say they're going to block him from the plant.'

I thought of the protesters outside the police compound in Beijing, and how they'd been dispersed. Nelson Li was not used to facing anything like this.

'Robin,' I realized the producer was saying my name, and I wished once more that I could remember his, 'I saw the Reuters copy this morning about your interpreter.'

I stared at him.

'The Reuters copy?' He registered my confusion. 'Okay, you haven't seen it. Come on in the van and I'll show you.'

I clambered into the van with him, and in among the mountains of kit he found his laptop and brought up the Reuters copy for me on the screen. I squatted in the mess and read it.

Police in Beijing refused to confirm or deny that they had detained Tang Lijiang, a free-lance interpreter nicknamed Blue, who has been working for Robin Ballantyne, the correspondent for the Corporation's *Controversies* series.

Ballantyne was deported two days ago after she was discovered reporting illegally from the Chinese capital.

The report of Miss Tang's detention came from Larry Mak, a freelance cameraman, who said he had tried to contact her but had been told by her father that three police officers had come to their house and taken Blue away.

'I want to get the word out,' Mr Mak said, 'or everyone will forget about her, and she'll just be left to rot in jail.'

'That is you, isn't it?' the producer said. 'Weren't you just in Beijing?'

I stood up. Larry had unilaterally ended my attempt to keep quiet about Blue. There was no point now in pretending nothing had happened, and perhaps that was for the best. I was surprised no one had called me about the Reuters story, but maybe it was just the calm before the storm.

'That's me,' I told the producer.

He was about to say something else, but I shook my head and dialled Damien's number. Damien's greeting was brusque, but I thought he was angry at himself for cracking under the strain, not at me.

'You've seen the Reuters,' I said.

'I have. I'm just off to the editorial meeting. We'll be discussing how to deal with it. If we don't comment maybe the story will go away.'

'It won't go away,' I said, 'and we'll look heartless.'

'I'll let you know what the line is,' he said.

'No,' I said firmly. 'I'm telling you what the line is. I'm in an outside broadcast unit at Kelness, so if anyone wants to interview me down the line, they can. I'm going to get calls from agencies, and I'm going to talk to them too. I'd have preferred to keep this quiet, but it's impossible now, so we go with it.'

I hung up, and Damien must have delivered my message because twenty minutes later the phone started ringing. For the next hour, I answered questions for radio and for television. I tried to keep the message simple, and I tried to keep it cringingly diplomatic, so that if Blue's Chinese jailers were watching on a satellite feed it wouldn't make things worse for her. I deeply regretted that my reporting visit had brought such trouble on Blue Tang, I said. I took full responsibility for working in China illegally. Blue had done nothing that warranted imprisoning her. If she'd violated any laws it was my fault, not hers. Then, at the end of each interview, I said, 'It's such a pity that the Beijing police feel they have to do this, because it spoils all the goodwill they're building up around the world.' I tried to sound sad about it, not angry, and hoped that someone in Beijing would listen, and would let Blue go.

When I had finished I felt drained. I could almost feel Blue with me in the outside broadcast van. I could feel her anger and her tension, and now I felt I understood her for the first time, because somehow she had known that this would happen, or at least that this could happen to her. She was angry even at the possibility, angry at the way she knew the system worked, and that it was waiting to ensnare her.

Outside, I tried calling Colin Liscombe again.

'Hello, who's this?' he answered.

'My name is Robin Ballantyne, I—'

'Did you try calling me before?'

'I did.'

'I don't know you. How did you get this number?'

'I'm sorry,' I said, 'I can't . . . Mr Liscombe, I work for the Corporation. I'd really appreciate the opportunity to sit and chat with you about Derek—'

'Don't call me again,' he instructed, and hung up.

I swore softly and nearly pressed redial, then thought better of it. I closed my eyes, then opened them again and looked at my watch. It was lunchtime and my stomach, now doubly confused by jet lag, was screaming for its food.

I found a pub, sat down at a table next to an empty fireplace, and ordered cottage pie from a grease-spattered menu. It was just me, a reluctant waitress, and a long-faced barman who kept disappearing. Paper chains drooped along the bar and criss-crossed the ceiling. I realized I had made no preparations for Christmas.

After a few minutes contemplating the dismal scene I got up and walked around a bit, attracted by the notice board. There were ads pinned up – kittens for sale, a quiz night, a snooker tournament, regular Thursday evening darts. Something caught my eye. A poodle puppy, chasing a ball, above a name, Nicola Liscombe, and a home telephone number.

I ate what I could of the cottage pie, and waited until I was outside to ring the number. Nicola Liscombe answered, and soon I had an appointment, at six-thirty that evening – just before supper, Nicola said. The purpose of my visit would be to view a black standard poodle called Ziggy that had been owned by her uncle and was now in need of a new home.

It was a modern semi, red brick, with space to park a car in front. I rang the doorbell and heard the dog barking. I heard voices, then footsteps, and a woman opened the door. She had a child on her hip and another clinging to her skirt. She looked flustered and worn, and for a moment she looked as though she couldn't remember who I was or why I was there.

'I'm Robin Ballantyne. I telephoned.'

'Oh, yes, of course, come on in. Ziggy's through here.'

'I heard him barking,' I said, not knowing what else to say. I had hoped that Colin Liscombe would be in evidence, but at this rate I was going to end up without an interview, and with a dog.

'Ziggy likes visitors,' she said, leading the way into a kitchen that was as chaotic as mine. The dog was a big puppy, gambolling around the kitchen, a child's sock in his mouth. He flung himself at Nicola, and then at me.

'My uncle bought him a few months back, but then he had a stroke and was gone just like that. He's a lovely dog, and lovely with the kids, but I can't cope with anything more right now. My husband's away half the time, so I'm on my own with the kids, and he needs training and time, and some boundaries. Have you had a dog before?'

She looked at me expectantly, and the kids looked at me expectantly, and Ziggy looked at me expectantly, and I wanted the floor to open up and swallow me.

'I'm sorry, I didn't really come here for the dog.'

She looked scared then, taking a step back, clutching her children closer. I wished it wasn't dark already; she'd have trusted me more in the daylight.

'I'm sorry, I'm a journalist . . .'

'Get out of here,' she ordered.

I took a step towards the door. I should never have crossed the threshold. I didn't know what had possessed me.

'I needed to speak to your husband,' I said, 'and I saw your ad up in the pub . . . I am so sorry to intrude.'

'Out!' she shouted.

Well, I'd have done the same, and called the police to boot. I retreated. But as I reached the front door it opened and a man came in, wearing a long coat over a business suit. He had a receding hairline and an aquiline nose, and was wearing spectacles.

'Colin,' I said, 'Colin Liscombe?'

He halted in surprise. His wife burst into the hallway, one child still on her hip, the other trailing, Ziggy dancing at their heels.

'This woman lied to me.' Her voice was shrill with fury, and then she directed herself to me, shrieking, 'Get out of my house!'

'What's going on?' Liscombe's face creased in a frown. He looked at his wife and moved to block the door. 'Tell me what's going on? If she lied her way in here, we call the police, we don't let her get away with it.'

'She's a journalist,' Nicola said. 'She wanted to talk to you, she saw the ad for Ziggy, and she telephoned me . . .'

'You rang to see the dog?' Colin Liscombe turned

381

to me in outraged perplexity. Then he worked it out. 'It's you, the one who kept calling,' he said.

'I'm so sorry,' I said. I'd never lied my way into a house before, the next thing I knew I'd be sticking a camera zoom inside someone's bedroom window. 'I really need to talk to you about the night Derek Sumner died, and you wouldn't see me, and I was desperate.'

He and his wife were staring at each other, some kind of message seeming to pass between them. I opened my mouth, then shut it, deciding to leave them to their silent dialogue. Ziggy scampered over to me and circled me, sniffing.

'I'll make a pot of tea, then,' he said to his wife, as though they'd been having a conversation out loud instead of with their eyes. 'I'll bath the kids later.'

'I'll do it,' she said, and cast a mutinous glance in my direction before heading upstairs.

In the kitchen, Colin said, 'I said tea, I meant beer. You want either?'

'I think I need a beer,' I said. I was still reeling from the abrupt change of atmosphere. Ziggy, who had followed me into the kitchen, went to lie in his basket, his head propped on the rim, watching me.

Colin pulled open the fridge door, took out two cans and handed me one, then found glasses in the cupboard.

'Best drink of the day,' he said. He sat opposite me and pulled off his tie, then filled his glass, his eyes on the liquid.

'Does anyone know you're here?' His eyes moved to my face.

'No.'

'Well,' he said softly, raising his glass to me, his eyes shadowed, 'ask your questions.'

'Tell me about that night at the Lotus Pool restaurant.'

'It was very informal,' he said. 'Owen and I got there first, Karen arrived almost at the same time as us. We'd booked a private room, and it had a TV, so we had a couple of drinks and watched some football. Angus and Derek arrived a short while later.'

'Together?'

'Yes,' he answered quickly, as though he had given this some thought. 'Together. I got the impression they'd both come from the office. Thinking back, they both seemed . . . I don't know . . . hyped up about something. I don't know how to explain it. Perhaps I'm imagining it. Angus was making jokes, bad jokes . . . as if he was nervous. Once everyone was there, we ordered and the food came quickly. Karen switched the TV off.'

'What did you talk about?'

'Football, until Karen stopped us.'

'And then?'

'What you'd think. We're in the middle of a

takeover, we'd been negotiating all day, so we talked business. Derek was quiet, on edge. He'd taken a lot of flak about what he said at the banquet. There'd been things said that it was hard to unsay. A lot of bad feeling.'

'His wife told me she thought you were all freezing him out.'

'No one exactly froze him out, but there was no group hug either.'

'Is there anything that now sticks in your mind about the conversation?'

'No,' he said. 'I've thought about it, gone over everything, and there's nothing that was wrong or out of place. Nothing that was said, that is. Like I said, the atmosphere was edgy.'

'When the meal was over did you see Derek walk towards the lake?'

Colin placed his glass of beer carefully on the table and gazed at it, twisting it round and round in his hand.

'Ask it in a different way,' he said.

I frowned. Upstairs I could hear a child shrieking, water splashing.

'A different way . . . Who did you see head for the lake?' I asked.

'All right.' He nodded in approval of the question, then replied, 'I saw Angus walking towards the lake.'

'Angus?' I echoed.

'I assume Derek had gone on ahead. I mean, I assume that now, because his body was found there. But I didn't assume that at the time, because I didn't know where Derek had gone. I didn't give it a thought.'

'So, when Angus says Derek had some kind of rendezvous there . . .'

'Maybe they both had a rendezvous. Maybe they'd decided between themselves that Derek would go first and Angus would follow.'

'Or perhaps Angus decided to see where Derek was off to? Have you told this to anyone else?'

I heard footsteps on the stairs.

'I've been waiting for Angus to say it himself.' Colin looked at me over the top of his spectacles. 'He keeps telling everyone he went straight home. I don't understand why.'

'Would anyone else have seen him apart from you?'

Nicola came into the kitchen. She went to the fridge, got herself a bottled beer and a glass, and pulled out a chair to join us. Liscombe glanced across at her with an unspoken question.

'They're in bed,' she said.

'No,' he said, turning back to me. 'I've thought about it, and no one else would have seen. We waited outside for taxis. Karen took the first one. Then Owen and I shared one. We were going back to the hotel. Angus told us he'd get the next taxi. At that point, I don't know where Derek was. I'd probably have said he'd got in the taxi with Karen. Anyway, the moment I was in the taxi I realized I'd left my briefcase in the restaurant. So I told

385

Owen to go on – we'd only driven a few yards down the street – and I walked back towards the restaurant, and that was when I saw Angus.'

'How do you know it was him?'

'He has a down jacket we all rag him about. It's got reflectors on the back. There aren't many of those around. There's a lane between the restaurant and the lake, and he was heading up that way. I thought it strange at the time, because it didn't lead to anywhere.'

I reached for my beer and took a sip, thinking about what he'd said.

'Did you tell her?' Nicola asked her husband.

He gave her a warning glance.

'What?' I demanded.

'You have to tell her,' she said, then turned to me. 'He's worried that there's some innocent explanation, so he doesn't want to be the one to spread suspicion, but I keep telling him someone else has to decide that.'

'What?' I demanded again.

'He had scratches,' she said, her eyes pleading with her husband, 'didn't he? You should tell her.'

'Nic . . .' he said. She sent him an imploring look, and he rolled his eyes, but after a moment he went on speaking. 'The next day, none of us knew immediately what had happened to Derek. It took a while for them to inform us after they'd found the body. Before they did that, I was in a meeting with Angus. They had the heating turned up high in the meeting room and we both had our sleeves rolled up. There was a bruise above his wrist. Not scratches, love, a bruise, black and blue. As though someone had grabbed him hard, or hit him.'

'Show me,' I said.

Liscombe rested his arm on the table, and unbuttoned the cuff, then described an uneven circle, about five centimetres in diameter, just above the wrist, on pale skin that was thick with black hair.

The three of us sat in silence for a moment, all staring at Liscombe's wrist. I felt something on my lap, and started with surprise, then realized it was Ziggy's head. He looked like an ageing rock star, with shaggy hair hanging around his face and doleful eyes. This was not the time to fall in love with a dog. I looked away.

'Did you ask him about it?'

Liscombe nodded, jaw tight.

'He said he'd had an accident in the gym, a weight—' Liscombe broke off. 'He said a weight had fallen on his wrist . . . I suppose I pulled a face or something in sympathy. And then, a few moments later, I saw him pull his sleeves back down, and do them up again, and I thought: why would he do that? What's to be ashamed about a stupid accident?'

'Did you ask him?'

'I was embarrassed. I thought maybe he'd got in a bar brawl, or he'd been in some clinch with a woman,' Liscombe glanced apologetically at his wife, 'but Angus would have boasted about that, not covered it up.'

My mobile rang, startling Ziggy. I pulled it from my pocket, cursing its timing. It was my cameraman, Robert, who had driven up from London that afternoon.

'Get over here,' he said. 'Nelson Li is twenty minutes away, and they've called the protesters out of the pub. It's getting lively.'

CHAPTER 25

Song thought that on the plane at least the boy could not escape. And then he thought that he might try. The boy was wild, there was no holding him, anything was possible.

'You open the door, you'll fall out of the sky and break your neck, you understand?' he hissed in the boy's ear in the departure hall. He thought it had to be said, but he didn't want to attract even more attention. The boy looked at him, head cocked to one side, eyes wide, whether with innocence or calculation Song could not tell. They'd bought him clothes in Shanghai, and now he wore corduroy trousers, a woollen sweater and a down jacket, but there was no concealing his dark peasant skin, or his facial expressions, which changed, undisciplined, with the thoughts that flitted through his head. Or his lack of an arm. He drew attention wherever he went, even before he opened his mouth and the halting, stuttering speech fell out.

They queued to board, and the boy did not understand even that, trying to push to the front, Song grabbing him back. They stepped inside the shell of the aircraft, handing boarding passes to the stewards, and the boy's eyes fastened on the cockpit, the panel of lights, before the door closed on the pilot. They found their seats, and the boy twisted and pressed his nose against the window. He had never travelled with his own son, Song realized, never shown him anything, or taken him anywhere. It was no wonder Lina had not believed him when he said he would take Doudou skiing. What on earth did you do with a child? The engines roared, and the boy looked alarmed, then flattened himself against the seat as the plane taxied and pushed into the sky.

Song closed his eyes. At his side he could feel the boy wriggling against him, playing with his safety belt, clicking and unclicking it.

He'd interrogated the boy in his hotel room, laying out a banquet on the coffee table: fizzy orange and chocolate and peanuts from the minibar. Song had sat on the edge of the bed, and the boy had sat on the sofa, so small that he'd been swamped by it. The boy had watched Song warily, his jaw working on a mouthful of peanuts.

'Where did you get this?' Song had shown the boy the iPod that had fallen from his jacket pocket. He'd thought the boy might try to snatch it, but the boy had pulled back from it and jerked his head away so that he did not have to look at it.

'Gave it to her,' the boy had said, his voice high with panic.

'Who? Who gave it to her?'

'No face.' The boy had shaken his head, then gestured with his one hand that the gift-giver had covered his nose and mouth with a face mask. This was in itself not so unusual, some people wore them in the winter as a barrier to infection and dust. But Song had remembered the quarry, and the woman whose face was so disfigured. Her attacker too had worn a face mask.

The boy had fidgeted on the sofa. He'd pulled a cushion onto his lap and plucked at it.

'Where did you meet him?'

'The lake,' the boy had said. Then the story had started to pour out of him, his strange, stumbling speech a rocky torrent, his eyes huge, his whole body moving nervously, tics and twitches taking him over. 'He's talking to her. I can see him, No Face. No Face goes away. My sister shows me what he gave her. A present. No Face says he'll give her five hundred *yuan* if she goes to the tent. Five hundred *yuan*. She cries. I'm walking with her. I'm playing with the thing he gives her. I'm hiding in the tent, under the bed, she's scared without me. She says I can have the thing, but I mustn't look. She sits on the bed. Waiting. I mustn't look. She's changed her mind, she wants to go. But then he comes . . . I'm not looking . . . it's too noisy . . . crying on the bed . . . She screams, he does something to her, but I don't look . . . I'm not looking . . . I'm scared, I'm crying . . . His legs, he's pulling her off the bed and she's on the floor and she doesn't move. She's all bloody. She's got no clothes on. I don't want to look. I close my eyes. He's moving, pulling her out of the tent. I lie there. Something's burning.'

'Then I arrived,' Song had said softly.

'The knife's right there by my hand,' the boy had said. 'I pick it up. I think that he's come back.'

'How did you know I wasn't him?'

The boy had stared at Song.

'You're big,' he'd said, 'he wasn't so big as you. He wasn't old. He was young like her.' Song thought he had been stupid to have suspected Nelson Li. No one would mistake him for a young man even if he was wearing a face mask. He was energetic, but still, he moved like a middle-aged man, not like a youth. Psycho Wang was younger, and could perhaps be mistaken for someone younger still, especially with a mask over his ugly face.

They arrived in Beijing. They had no luggage apart from what they carried, and soon they stood in the taxi queue, Song's hand firmly on the boy's collar in case he made a break for it.

'Where?' the boy asked.

'I'm taking you to a friend's house,' Song said. He wanted to explain, even to reassure, but did not know what to say.

He pushed the boy into a taxi and told the driver to take them to Nelson Li's mansion. There had been a heavy snowfall while Song was away, and the traffic moved slowly.

The heater was on, the air inside the car warm and smelling of the day's passengers. Within moments the boy was asleep, his head knocking against the window, his one hand clasping a packet of peanuts that he'd taken from the plane.

Song gazed at the sleeping boy, then forced his eyes away. He cursed and ran his palm over his face. What was to become of both of them? He was sweating, and a point of pain was pulsating in his forehead. He told himself it was the overheated taxi. He wound the window down, and the cold air rushed in and froze the sweat on him. He wound the window up again. Nothing made him feel better.

The suspicions he harboured about Nelson Li had faded to a vague disquiet. He would turn the boy over to Nelson Li, and Nelson Li would continue to pay his father's bills. Nelson Li would put more work Song's way, and Song could rent himself a new office. Next winter he would take Doudou skiing. As the taxi drove them along the long flat expressway into Beijing, Song realized that during his absence he had also come to a decision about Detective Fang's demand. He would supply Fang with the file which documented Detective Chen's pursuit of his corrupt millions. It would finish Chen, but it would protect him and Lina and Doudou. He could not justify condemning himself, his former wife and his child to untold trouble. Besides, the man deserved it, and it would prove his point to Lina.

When they reached the gates of Versailles Villas, the guard stopped them. Song spoke with authority – Nelson Li was expecting him – and the guard did not ring ahead, just waved them in, and they pulled in beside the frozen ornamental lake. Song paid the taxi off.

The boy was sleeping soundly, and rather than wake him Song picked him up and carried him out of the car, through the snow to the front door of Li's house. In his sleep, the boy wrapped his one arm around Song's neck. The feel of the shoulder stump, of the child's body pressed against him, made him remember the night he'd saved the boy from the burning tent. Perhaps saving his life gave Song the right to dispose of the boy in any way that he saw fit. He rang the bell. He fancied he could feel the boy's heart beating through layers of clothing, then thought it was his own.

A maid in white tunic over black trousers answered the door, her eyes going from Song to the boy and back again.

'I'm here to see Nelson Li.'

'He's not here, he's gone to England.'

'Pearl? Is she here?'

'She's in England too.'

She started to push the door closed, and Song stood there, dazed. This was the only time, he knew that much. He could not walk up to that door again. All the way here, he'd been handing the boy over in his head. If he walked away with the boy, that would be it, Song would be stuck with him. He stuck his foot out, to block the door, and found it opening again, this time to reveal Nelson Li's son. When Nixon saw the sleeping boy a smile flitted to his face, and then away.

'Your father told me to bring him, but he's not here to receive him,' Song said, irritated at the position he found himself in, as though he was a delivery boy with a consignment of groceries. 'What am I to do with him?'

Nixon Li looked down at the child, his eyes running from the sleeve that hung from the shoulder stump to the new shoes on the boy's feet.

'Do whatever you want.' A heartbeat's pause. 'Leave him here.'

Song hesitated, and saw Nixon watch him hesitate. Nixon called for the maid to return, and when she appeared he said to her, 'Take the boy and find a bed for him. Look after him until my father returns.'

The maid looked from him to Song, and to the boy. She was reluctant, Song could see that; she did not understand what was going on, or what the repercussions would be for her. But then she took the child from Song and said softly, 'He's so light.'

Song said, 'He needs to eat more.'

He watched as the maid turned away with the boy in her arms, and as she retreated into the house, until he could see her no longer.

'Are you waiting for money?' Nixon asked. 'My

father will settle up with you. I can't pay you – he's the one who fixed a fee.'

Song took a step back. 'No,' he said, 'you're mistaken, I'm not waiting for money. I was just . . .'

But what, after all, was he doing there?

He nodded a farewell and walked away.

CHAPTER 26

When I left the Liscombes' home it was fully dark, and by the time I reached the steel plant the drizzle had turned into a full-fledged rainstorm. The protesters were full of tea and beer; they'd dressed themselves in yellow rainproof capes and brought striped red and white umbrellas from their houses, but even they retreated to huddle under a roof and peer out at the sky.

The journalists sat grimly in their vehicles and called each other on their mobiles discussing whether to wait – and if so, for how long – or to cut their losses and retreat to B&Bs until the morning. The rumours were still strong that Nelson Li was on his way, but we were all aware that we might be enduring this misery for nothing.

'If Nelson Li thinks a bit of rain will scare us, or that we're all going to curl up under our duvets while management sells us down the river, well, he's got another think coming,' I heard one bedraggled protester saying bravely to an equally sodden TV anchor.

Robert, the cameraman, was hanging out with

friends in the van. The only company I wanted was Finney. I sheltered in my hired car, huddling up on the seat to keep warm, dialled, and listened to the phone ringing in my house a couple of hundred miles away. It had been strange leaving the twins to come up to Kelness, much calmer than my last departure. Of course, Kelness was in the same time zone as London. But that aside, there was something different now about leaving the children in the care of Finney. William was still calling him Daddy, and Hannah had settled happily on the hybrid Fin-Daddy.

Finney picked up. He said he'd just got in, and that Carol had put the children to bed. He asked how things were going, but I didn't want to talk to him about my suspicions. I knew Finney would say I was not approaching the investigation in a proper way because I had not sent a dozen officers out to talk to every witness, that I was clutching at straws, putting two and two together and getting five.

'Let's not talk about work,' I said.

'If that's what you want,' he agreed, sounding doubtful.

'Do you like dogs?' I asked him. A gust of wind and rain buffeted the car. The lights of Kelness were reduced to a yellow blur as my windscreen was deluged.

'Depends on the dog.'

'I thought I was a cat person,' I confided. We

had not had this conversation before. 'But now I'm not so sure.'

'I see,' Finney said, uninterested, then changed the subject. 'Robin, I know you don't want to talk about work, but it was you who asked me about Terry Reese. The foreign office just informed us he's being deported tomorrow without charge in Beijing.'

The rain lashed down, beating violently on the roof of the car.

'Not even a charge of attempted rape?'

'Some kind of arson attempt was made a few hours ago at the British embassy. It didn't come to anything, but the British are beside themselves. They've demanded the Chinese police disperse the protesters, but the Chinese are reluctant to look as though they're taking orders from the British. I think the Chinese government wants Reese out of the country before they've got a riot on their hands.'

'So he gets away with attempted rape.'

'I'd say he's innocent until proven guilty, but he's got a track record.'

'If they had evidence of murder they'd try him on it and keep the protesters happy.'

'Maybe,' Finney seemed hesitant. 'Robin, we dug up one thing I wanted to pass on, but . . .'

'I know,' I said, 'it goes no further.'

'It probably means nothing. Reese's brother was laid off by Kelness a year ago. He's unemployed now, his marriage broke down, his wife won't let him see his kids.'

Through the rain a figure appeared and rapped on the window. I wound it down, ear still to the telephone. It was Robert, swathed in waterproofs, camera balanced on his shoulder, telling me that Nelson Li's car had been spotted half a mile away. I told Finney I'd call him later.

Nelson Li was driven into the plant through a crowd of steel workers who were all the more angry for standing soaking in the rain. I could just make him out in the back seat, his eyes set on the gate ahead of him, not looking to left or right. For a few minutes, it felt like a huge victory for the protesters as they let rip, but Nelson Li's humiliation was fleeting.

As soon as he had vanished inside, the protesters began to disband. To our astonishment, word came that a press conference was to take place and the gates opened again. A public relations woman led the untidy gaggle of journalists, and security men snapped at our heels. Behind us, the protesters reformed at the gates, so that their chanting accompanied us. The woman led us to a large meeting room, and again we waited, cold and damp, patience running thin, squabbles over positioning breaking out among the cameramen.

Nelson Li entered, his retinue trailing behind him, and a hush fell. He wore a double-breasted suit, buttoned up, with an elaborate tie. He carried himself like a bird, with his chest stuck out, his left hand clutched the strap of a man's leather bag, and his black hair was slicked back. Richard Toms, the CEO of Kelness, was at Nelson Li's side, fussing around him, practically straightening his tie for him. Karen Turvey, Colin Liscombe and Angus Perry were all just yards away, all studiously avoiding eye contact with me. I'd been to many press conferences in my life, but never one like this, where nervous tension crackled in the air like electricity. There was the dull thrum of machinery in the background, and without that I think we would have been able to hear the protesters chanting outside.

'Thank you all for being here.' Richard Toms had taken the microphone. 'I'm not going to pretend to you, the past week has been tough for Kelness, and important decisions have yet to be made that will affect this community. That's why, even at this sensitive point in our negotiations, we've decided to take the unusual step of holding this press conference to show that we are open . . .' Toms paused to take a deep breath, making it sound as though this was the last thing he wanted, 'to public scrutiny. I hope, now that Mr Li has made time for us in his busy schedule, rapid progress can be made towards a solution that is to everyone's long-term benefit.'

Toms stepped aside and Li approached the microphone. 'Everything that Richard has said, I agree with. So far. Maybe for the last time today.' That got a laugh.

The floor was opened to questions, and a sea

of hands rose. Richard Toms pointed to a woman I knew who worked for a national tabloid.

'Mr Li,' she said, 'the workforce here is split between those who believe their jobs are more secure with you, and those outside the gates, protesting because they believe that their future livelihood is in jeopardy. Now that you're here, can you give workers some specifics about your plans for Kelness?'

'Your question is premature,' Nelson Li barked, and Richard Toms gave a weak smile at his side, nodding. 'We are here to negotiate, and I cannot tell you anything final. But I tell you this, it is too noisy in Kelness, so it is hard to reach a deal.'

'How did you see the Kelness memo?' another journalist shouted out. Li refused to answer, and when the next questioner also asked about the memo Richard Toms forced his way past Nelson Li to get to the microphone.

'These talks are all about looking to the future,' he said, 'to the potential for cooperation . . .'

I found myself watching Angus Perry's face. He was listening to Richard Toms with an expression of bare contempt. I saw him turn to leave. I stuck my hand in the air. I saw Nelson Li's eyes settle on my face, saw him turn to Richard Toms to tell him not to call on me, but it was too late.

'Robin Ballantyne for the *Controversies* programme,' I said loudly, waiting for cameras to train on my face. If I was about to blow my exclusive wide open for the public good, I might as well get some publicity for my programme.

'Mr Li, isn't it true,' I asked, 'that you have reached agreement with the government of the port city of Dalian, on the use of an area of land roughly equating to the size of Kelness, and that there is a document in existence which describes the land use as an integrated steel plant, and that the document further goes on to state that the equipment will be imported from Britain, and that the government will waive import duty because the equipment is second-hand?'

Silence had fallen on the hall.

Li's jaw dropped. He stared at me for a moment, as a buzz of excitement spread through the room, then shook his head.

Toms turned, stunned, from Li to the press corps, and back again. His face looked ashen but he was smiling weakly, and I was afraid that he was about to attempt a joke. The entire room held its breath.

'If such a document exists, I'd really like to take a look at it,' he said, and stepped back from the microphone.

The room exploded in questions, but I was already pushing my way to the door.

Outside, night was falling fast. The wind surged, then dropped and surged again, carrying rain with it. Through the semidarkness I could see Angus Perry in the distance, walking quickly, head bent

403

against the weather, hands in pockets. My footsteps, splashing onto wet concrete, gaining behind him, sounded like depth charges. But Perry did not look back. Around us, the vast industrial flues and chimneys, and railway containers and conveyor belts became monstrous shapes in the dark.

'Hello, Angus,' I said as I drew alongside him, and he turned to face me angrily. A yellow spotlight overhead threw his eyes into shadow.

'What are you doing here?'

'I have some questions about the night Derek Sumner died.'

'Get out of here. You've no right to be here.'

'I'll ask someone else, then. Like how you got the bruise on your wrist.'

He ignored me and started walking again, and I stuck at his side.

'I have a witness who saw you follow Sumner towards the lake the night he died.'

We came to the base of some steps, gleaming, slippery, wet.

'You're going to follow me up, are you?' He challenged me.

I raised my head, realizing for the first time that we were standing in front of the blast furnace. The narrow steps formed the base of what became a ladder with a handrail which wound up and around the blast furnace, leading to metal platforms further up. At the summit, there was a platform on the very ridge of the furnace, where cart loads of iron ore, coke and sinter were tipped over the rim into the burning oxygen below.

I could not follow him. I could not climb up there, so very high. My knees began to give way underneath me. As I hesitated Perry swung himself up, his hand gripping the rail, feet lifting, coming down on the next step up, one after the next. The ladder made a dull clang with every step he took. I watched him climb away from me.

'Come back down,' I shouted. 'Talk to me down here.'

Still he climbed. I ran my hand over my face and a helpless sob escaped me. He was getting away. I could sit at the bottom of the steps and wait, on the principle that what goes up must come down, but sooner or later someone was going to spot me and call security. In my desperation, my suspicions became hardened fact: the man who had decapitated Derek Sumner and who had tried his damnedest to kill me on a Chinese mountainside was getting away. A red rage came over me, overwhelming reason. I looked up at him, and saw that he was slowing. His bulk was working against him, putting strain on his heart and lungs. This was not a man who climbed these ladders every day. I was fitter than him, I knew, and more agile.

I delved into my bag. If I tried to film him, he would surely kill me. But if I was going up there, I was going to get incontrovertible evidence of what he had done. I grabbed a digital recorder out of my bag, stuffed it in my pocket and hurriedly ran the microphone wire up inside my jacket to the collar, where I thought he wouldn't see it.

I left my bag on the ground, grabbed the handrail, and started climbing. After the first ten rungs, I paused to pull off my gloves, which were impeding my grip, and grabbed the cold wet iron with my bare hands. My boots – flat, rubber-soled and flexible – meant my feet didn't slip, or I would have plunged to the ground. I began to catch up with him. He saw me climbing, gave a bellow of anger, and carried on up.

Halfway up Perry stopped, breathing hard, and there I was, clinging on for dear life in mid-air, my skull just inches below the soles of his shoes. I didn't look down.

'You don't know what you're messing with, you nosy bitch.' His voice, breathless, came down to me.

'How did you get the bruise?' I called up, but he was already climbing again, pulling ahead of me, setting up vibrations that arrived in my hands like a purr of danger. Above me, he hauled himself onto the platform, into the yellow glow of another spotlight, and moments later I did the same. I was panting, my legs threatened to give way, and my heart was pounding as though it was going to break my ribs. He turned to me, on the attack although he was in a worse state than me, gasping for breath, his face puce, dripping with sweat and rain.

'We had a man fall off here . . .' he panted, 'broke

406

his back, now he's in a wheelchair. They said he was lucky not to have died. Someone could easily slip in this weather.'

I glanced down. The rain was splashing off the metal slats which formed the platform, but I could see the ground far below, and I felt giddy. The ground seemed to recede even as I looked. I'd seen a woman fall to her death once, I'd seen up close what happened to her when she hit the ground, and that had been in the rain too. My head began to swim, and I felt sick, as though my stomach and my head were churning all at once. Through all that, I heard the quiet voice of common sense whisper to me: I must not be seduced by the edge, I must not look down, I must stay out of Perry's reach.

I took a step away from him, and from the edge. The bulk of him could swipe me off the platform if he came after me.

'What the witness said – it's all on tape,' I lied, shouting through the wind and rain. 'You killed Sumner, didn't you? You followed him when he took the document to Nelson Li's daughter. You followed him and killed him. Did you kill the women too? Did you kill the woman on the wall?'

He launched himself at me, and pushed me hard against the rail, and I heard my mobile phone fall from my pocket and clang as it hit the metal platform. For a moment he held me there, with his arm across my throat, and then his fingers found the microphone.

'You bitch,' he said, 'you fucking bitch.' He yanked the microphone wire from its socket, and pulled the recorder from my pocket, hurling it against the side of the blast furnace. I heard the plastic smash against the brick.

'I didn't kill anyone,' he screamed in my face, and I knew as I saw the fury in his eyes that he was telling the truth.

Then, horribly, he clutched at his chest and staggered, collapsing onto the platform.

I knelt next to him, my cold fingers struggling with the wet fabric and the buttons at his neck. His face was contorted, but he was breathing. I scrabbled around for my mobile phone, but I couldn't find where it had fallen. I rushed to the barrier, leaning over the side. I could see figures in the distance, and guessed that the press conference had come to an end.

'Help!' I yelled. 'I need help up here!'

They turned to one another in confusion, looking around them. I shouted louder and louder, until my lungs ached and my throat burned. At last three figures broke away and ran towards me.

'We need an ambulance,' I yelled down at them. One of them pulled a phone from his pocket. The others started climbing up the ladder towards us.

I looked down, terrified that I would find Angus lying dead, but he was trying to say something. I knelt and cradled his head, trying to make him more comfortable.

'Please,' I begged him, 'please don't speak.'

But he only became more agitated, and so I put my ear close to his mouth. He struggled to form the words.

'*He* followed *me.*'

The rain splashed over our faces, so close together. His eyes, full of pain, were fixed on mine.

'*You?*' Then I saw it clear as day. I remembered the look of contempt on Perry's face as he listened to Toms speak, his anger about the decision not to buy radiation monitors. '*You* were the one leaking to Nelson Li, and he was getting blamed. Sumner faked the memo to smoke you out.'

'Tricked me, gave me a printout . . .' He paused, breathing heavily. Again I pleaded with him to say no more, and again he carried on: '. . . Li waiting . . . Derek . . . grabbed my wrist to get the briefcase . . .'

'Don't talk,' I said into his ear. 'Tell me later.' He shook his head.

'. . . the kid pulled a knife . . . couldn't believe it . . . kid held a knife to Derek's throat. Derek's face . . .' Angus turned his head away, closing his eyes at the memory.

I stared at him, unable to speak. The kid – he'd referred to him as Li. He must mean the son, then, Nixon. A series of images flashed through my mind: a white running shoe, tapping in time to the music in the Fashion Club; the teenage boy walking behind me by the lake, getting into a

409

Hummer and revving the engine; the photograph on his father's office wall. Angus was looking up at me again, his lips moving, and I leaned in close once more.

'I shouted . . . "Derek, give him the briefcase." I ran . . .'

'Did you see what happened?'

'I ran . . .'

I could hear footsteps on the ladder, getting nearer. I could imagine what had come next. Angus returning home, unable to sleep, trying to call Derek, getting no reply, trying to reassure himself there was no way Nixon would have used the knife. Then the discovery of his friend's decapitated body, panic setting in, self-preservation, greed. He must have gone to find Nelson Li in his great log cabin on the Great Wall to blackmail him.

'You told Nelson Li his son's a killer?' I asked, and Angus closed his eyes in confirmation. 'His son killed that woman in broad daylight – why? To taunt you both? Is that it? When I saw you, you were terrified. That's it, isn't it? You'd miscalculated. Even when Sumner was killed you didn't realize you were up against a psychopath. Who was it who nearly ran me off the road? Nixon?'

He closed his eyes. His agitation was gone. I could hear the air rasping in and out of his chest. And then they reached us, their excited voices shouting something, trying to tell me something. I staggered to my feet. I heard a great beating noise

410

come from the sky, and I looked up, a great wind whipping my hair. Above my head a helicopter hovered like a great bird shifting in the currents of air, a rope descending.

CHAPTER 27

Song left Nelson Li's mansion and headed towards the ornate gate that separated Versailles Villas from the road. The boy was, quite literally, off his hands, but he felt no relief. The muscles in his shoulders and his neck were aching, perhaps the boy was heavier than he seemed. He tried to put the child out of his mind and formulate a plan. He would hail a taxi. He didn't know where Psycho Wang lived these days, but he would find him. And if he found him in the middle of the night, that was all the better, for Song could take him by surprise.

Song had questions that needed answering: did Wang know the barmaid who had vanished from the Waimao Hotel? What did Wang know of the car with police plates that had been seen at the quarry in Shijingshan where the women had been attacked, and which had also been seen where the women were murdered by the lake? If Wang resisted, so much the better, Song's fist would welcome it. He could feel hot tension coiled inside him seeking release.

Song's mobile rang. He could not fail to recognize

the scratchy voice. The woman from Shanghai, the mother of the barmaid who had gone missing the day after the attempted rape and murder in the Waimao Hotel.

'Hello?' she screeched into his ear, as though she was shouting all the way from Shanghai.

'It's me, it's Song.' He stopped short of the gate and turned back towards the lake to speak to her. The guards had swept the road clear of snow, but by the lake it lay thick.

'I have a message for your friend,' she said, 'the wealthy one who fancies my daughter.'

'Where is she? Is she with her policeman boyfriend?' Song demanded.

'No,' the woman sounded agitated. 'Don't tell your friend about her boyfriend. They've split up. My daughter rang her father to say that she has left her boyfriend, she's frightened of him, he's a cruel man and she has gone to stay with friends to get away from him. You must tell your friend that she's free, so they can meet.'

Song gazed out across the ornamental lake then turned to look back towards Nelson Li's villa. Lights blazed throughout the house. He could see them from the shoreline, great chandeliers and lamps in shadowed corners of vast rooms. The light spilled out of the house, reflecting off the snow.

'My friend wouldn't want to pick a fight with a policeman,' he said.

'No, no, don't worry about that, he fooled her.

My daughter was crying, crying on the phone. He told her he was a policeman, he had a police plate on his car and police equipment, but he was not. He made her do all sorts of things, and she did them because she thought he was . . . but don't you tell your friend that.'

'Was her boyfriend called Wang?' Song asked.

The woman's voice wavered.

'Why are you asking me that?'

'Was his name Wang?' Song insisted.

'She never told me his real name,' the woman grumbled. 'She called him by his foreign nickname. But what does that matter? I thought your friend was interested in my daughter.'

'What was his nickname? Come on, woman, what's his nickname?'

But she had hung up. Song frowned. A foreign nickname?

Behind him, he thought he caught a flash of movement at a window. Instinctively Song stepped back, away from the shore of the lake, into the cover of undergrowth, out of sight from the house. He hurried, swearing at his own stupidity, away from the lake, in the direction of the gate. But before he reached the gate he turned quickly into the driveway to Nelson Li's mansion and ducked through the door to the garage.

Inside, it was pitch-black. Song felt his way along the wall until he found a switch, praying that it was not an alarm. Bright white light flooded the garage and Song blinked, then almost laughed out loud. It was like a showroom. Gleaming cars, a sporty silver Mercedes, a yellow Hummer, a black jeep, a green Land Rover, a red Ferrari, a fleet of black Audis, all with number plates full of lucky 8s . . . then, like the runt of the litter, something else, its dusty nose hiding shyly at the end of the line. Song moved towards it, his fingers brushing the shining metal as he hurried by, Mercedes, Hummer, jeep, Land Rover, Ferrari, Audi . . . a Santana. Song stopped and stared, noting that it had ordinary blue plates. He bent to peer through the shaded window, but he could not see much except that the upholstery was black.

Song reached into his jacket pocket and pulled on gloves. He tried the doors, but they were locked. The boot, however, was unlocked, and swung upwards at pressure from his thumb. He stood back and surveyed a spare tyre, a tool box, a petrol can. With increasing urgency, he seized the tool box, fumbling with the catches that secured it. It burst open, and its contents spilled out into the boot, clattering noisily. Song looked hurriedly towards the external door where he had entered, and then to the other door, which he guessed must lead into the house. No one came, and he turned his attention back to the boot. A car number plate lay face down where it had fallen from the tool box. Gingerly he reached out, flipped it over, and as he had expected it was a white plate with the red character which said 'police'. The number was the same that Song had seen on the car parked on the street near the lake on the night of the fire in the tent, the same as that on the piece of paper he'd been handed in Shijingshan. Still jammed inside the tool box there was a second plate that matched the first.

There were tools too, a screwdriver which fitted the screws in the number plate. It would be the work of minutes to remove the plates front and back, and replace them.

From the far side of the door that led into the house, Song heard voices. Quickly, and as silently as he could, Song returned to the light switch and plunged himself once more into darkness. He waited, pressed his ear against the wall. He realized that he was still clutching the screwdriver.

'You can go home,' a male voice said, young and arrogant. 'I don't need you here.'

'What about the child?' The *ayi*'s voice was uncertain. 'He's woken up. He's hungry.'

'I'll take care of that. Go home.' The male voice was impatient.

There was the sound of rustling just on the other side of the door, where Song thought the *ayi* must be collecting her coat. He heard the front door close. He peered around the door and saw her, padded in layers against the chill, pushing a bicycle away from the house.

After a moment Song gently eased open the door that led from the garage into the house. He found himself in a maid's room, which led into a brightly lit kitchen that was bigger than his office. Electronic music was pulsing through the house, coming from upstairs. He went from room to room, twisting door handles, glancing inside before he moved rapidly on, gaining an impression of yawning emptiness.

When he had opened every door on the ground floor – maid's room, kitchen, utility room, store room, sitting room decorated in Asian style, home cinema, dining room, study, conservatory, a reception room in European style – he ran softly up the stairs. The music masked the sound of his movements, but its relentless beat added to his agitation.

One door yielded Pearl's room to him, and he stepped inside, glancing around him. Tidy, without frills, there were English language books and photographs: Pearl somewhere that looked like America, with friends, some Chinese, some Caucasian, some of them male, an arm carelessly flung around her shoulders. There was a smile on her face that he had seen only once, when she laughed at his joke. He did not linger. With every room that he eliminated, his search became more urgent.

Voices reached him again. He listened, concentrating hard. Nixon's voice, low and friendly, and a second voice, much higher pitched, halting. Song ran softly up the stairs. Nixon was speaking, his voice coming from an open door.

'What's your name?'

Song peered through the crack where the door

was hinged. Nixon's back was to him. He saw the boy, sitting on a bed, head cocked, frowning up at Nixon, saw dawning recognition and, with it, fear.

'Do you want something to eat? Are you hungry?' Nixon held his hand out to the boy. The boy shrank back, terror on his face. He clambered up onto a table by a narrow window and cowered, crouched and curled there like a monkey, pressed against the glass, his hand grasping the handle of the window.

'Come here,' Nixon said again. He pulled something from his pocket that Song could not see, and he held it towards the boy, who cried out and twisted backwards away from him. 'Look, it's a toy, it plays music. See? You put these in your ears. Here, you try . . .' He reached out to the boy.

Then all at once the latch dropped, the window was open and the boy was gone, scrambling, clutching at the window sill with his hand, then body, head, and hand too, disappearing.

Nixon lunged forward, leaned out of the window. He too clambered onto the window sill, balancing precariously like a cat, then dropping down.

Song ran to the window. Ten feet below Nixon had landed on a flat roof. He scurried to the edge then dropped down again, landing without noise in the snow.

A small shape, the boy, moved towards the frozen lake. Nixon pulled himself upright and gave chase, his longer legs closing the gap.

Song looked at the window, then the door, but there was no time for stairs. Wincing, he seized the window frame and squeezed his body out sideways, struggling to maintain his balance. He looked down at the roof below and closed his eyes then jumped, curling his long legs under him. When the impact came, knocking the breath from him, he rolled and ran to the roof's edge, and jumped again.

The figures moved ahead of him, the child, and then the taller figure, onto the ice, and moments later Song was there too, stepping out on the frozen surface of the lake. He heard the ice crack beneath his feet, felt the suck of the water, the shifting of the surface. Where the lake was open to the sky the daytime sun had thawed the ice and it had become treacherous. It groaned and creaked below him, but Song ignored it. A shriek came from the child, and he lay fallen, crumpled, on the ice, and Nixon was reaching into his clothing, bringing out something that glinted in the moonlight. The boy screamed, 'No . . . Don't hurt me!'

Song hurtled forward and threw himself upon Nixon, and as he did so the ice gave way, and the three of them were submerged in the arctic water, limbs flailing, tangled, clutching. Song grabbed a body so thin it had to be the boy's, and pushed it towards the surface. Something sliced through Song, and he thought that it was Nixon's knife, then knew that it was the temperature of the water. He felt a hand grip his arm, and Nixon clawed him down, tugging and scratching and trying to drown him. Below the ice, bubbles escaping too fast from his mouth, Song's hands met flesh, his fingers probed a mouth and eyes, a head that strained away from him. Song felt his mind slipping away, short of oxygen. Which way was up and which way down? His limbs had abandoned him now, they were not his. Blackness closed in. He had lost. Everything was extinguished. There was no boy, there was no Nelson Li, no Nixon, no Pearl, no mission accomplished, nothing . . . And then a point of light at the centre of it all, a pinprick of memory cutting through the anaesthesia, and suddenly his body knew how to move, how to flex and push and use the weight of water, how to move with water, not against it. His fingers found hair, dug deep into the scalp, pushed down. Fingers scrabbled at his, first hard, then weaker, losing strength, and Song's lungs screamed, but still he thrust down until the fingers loosened from his own, then let him go, drifted away and down. Song kicked up to the surface, exploded into the air, hauling oxygen in.

He heaved himself out onto the ice. He could barely move, but knew that if he did not he would become frozen to the surface. He forced himself, gasping at the raw pain, to stand upright. At his feet, Nixon's body was swallowed by the water. By morning the ice would be frozen hard again, even this deep chasm they had created would be iced over. The body would not be found for days.

420

Ten yards away, the boy was spread-eagled on his stomach on the ice, shaking and staring at Song with wide eyes full of fear.

Song's eyes scanned the shoreline. Where were the security men? Were they so useless, or so drunk or fast asleep that they had not heard the shouting, or so deaf they could not hear his heart pounding and his lungs heaving? The shoreline was silent, the row of mansions empty, their windows blind, the skeletal trees still. There were no servants, no Pearl, no Nelson Li. All that had been possible was still possible, opportunities to be seized, good relationships to maintain, prospects and prosperity. There were no witnesses, except the boy.

CHAPTER 28

That night, after Angus Perry was winched up into the helicopter and flown to hospital, I had tried to reach Nelson Li to confront him with what Angus had told me. I'd driven straight from Kelness to the hotel where Li was staying, deep in the countryside. But security was tight and I'd been stopped at every turn. In the end I'd retreated to my B&B and curled up, shaking, on the bed.

I didn't sleep. I couldn't bring myself to talk to anyone, least of all Finney. I lay awake and stared at the ceiling. I had confirmed all his fears. I had taken a stupid risk. It wasn't reason or good sense that had driven me to climb those steps and challenge a man who might have killed me, it was red rage. Worse, I had been wrong. It was one thing to risk one's life challenging a guilty man, another to accuse someone who's innocent. I had pursued Angus Perry up those steps, I had charged him with multiple murder. No wonder the man had a heart attack. I could not see one thing that I had done right. Behind me I left a young Chinese woman detained and a middle-aged man fighting for his life in hospital. I had the answer to my riddle, I knew who had killed Sumner, I knew who had killed the women all over Beijing, and yet there was nothing that I could do about it. I had not a shred of evidence.

As dawn broke on Christmas Eve, I fell asleep. By the time I woke up, Nelson Li and his daughter had already left the country.

On Christmas Day, with two overexcited children and one overexcited poodle hurtling around the room, I sat on the sofa with my head in my hands and quietly confessed to Finney what had happened in Kelness. I told him everything, and I told him how bad I felt.

'I don't trust myself to do this job any more,' I said. 'I blundered around, I got Blue in trouble, and God knows what I've done to Angus Perry.'

'Don't waste your pity on Perry,' Finney said. 'He doesn't deserve it.'

'That's not the point,' I said.

On Boxing Day, Angus Perry was discharged from hospital. The first thing he did was to call me and to threaten me with all manner of lawsuits if I ever repeated anything he might have said that night. I responded with silence. I didn't trust myself to speak.

Later that day, they found the body of Nelson Li's son drowned in the ornamental lake outside his home. It would have stayed hidden deep in

423

the ice but for an unseasonal thaw. Over the next few days the discovery led first to a flurry of newspaper headlines in the British press and then to a strange silence. The storm that had raged over Kelness for nearly two months was quelled by Christmas, and by the death of Nixon Li. The demonstrators seemed to lose all heart for further protest.

There was no evidence – or if there was, it was not reported in the desert that was the Chinese news machine – of wrongdoing in Nixon's death. He fell, the reports said, through ice that was dangerously thin, and at night. The column inches that accompanied these reports in the Chinese newspapers concerned the danger of walking on thin or thawing ice, and gave statistics for the number of people who died each year like this.

'Nelson Li must have had something to do with it,' I told Finney.

'Or the boy committed suicide,' he said.

Either way, the death of the psychopathic teenager took a weight from my shoulders. If he had lived, I could not have stopped his killing spree.

Damien wanted me to make a film for *Controversies* about the secret plans to dismantle the Kelness plant and rebuild it in Dalian. In January, Nelson Li bought the plant for the price of scrap, and within months the entire staff was redundant, Angus Perry included. Weeks later, teams of Chinese workers arrived to dismantle the plant. It would have made a great documentary, but I couldn't bring myself to make it. As a journalist, I had often only been able to tell one part of a bigger story. But to tell only a fraction of what I knew felt like a lie.

My refusal to make the film led in the short term to a row with Damien. I did not know what it would mean in the long term for my career. Privately I continued to feel that my professional life must change direction. I had loved being a journalist, loved its possibilities, but now I saw only the dangers. If Finney had been happier at work, I might have discussed it with him, but as it was I kept my unhappiness to myself. It was only one part of my life, and I would have to find my way through on my own.

One day in mid-January, the phone rang. Ziggy raced to answer it, put the brakes on at the last minute and came to a sliding halt with perfect precision, his head landing on my lap.

'I am Blue,' the woman on the other end of the line announced herself.

'They've let you go!'

'They sent me home last night. They told me to stay away from foreigners.'

I felt tears of relief running down my face.

'Are you all right?' I asked, wiping my sleeve across my eyes.

'I am all right,' she said, and I thought that she would not be Blue if she sounded happy. 'Our friend helped.'

'Who?'

'The man who helped you with your research,' she said cautiously, and it struck me then that the police might be listening in to her call. 'The tall man,' she said, becoming impatient when I didn't respond. 'He has a friend who is a lawyer, and he helped my family.'

I remembered then the burly man who had loped out of the police station after us, and who had gone to dinner with us and then abandoned us. Was his name Song? My memory for Chinese names was short. I thought that I must owe him a fee for his research on the land use issue in Dalian, then thought that this phone line, with its parasites, was not the place to discuss payment for services rendered.

'The killings have stopped now that the British rapist has been deported,' she said.

What should I say? Not the truth, not on this telephone line, and if not the truth, then nothing.

'I hope we'll meet again one day,' I said simply, 'so we can talk about it more.'

CHAPTER 29

The room was dark and cold, there was no heating. The evening's cooking smells emanated from the kitchen next to the office. Two dozen children had scrubbed their faces clean with water from an enamel bowl, and had brushed their teeth, and were now asleep in dormitories. This abandoned soy sauce-processing plant on the edge of town was not built for children, and it would be taken over by developers sooner or later, but at least for now it was a refuge from the street.

The elderly man switched on a desk light, and Song ushered the boy forward into the circle of light. He couldn't stand still, of course, he shifted from foot to foot and jerked his head around, blinking. The elderly man and his wife, both bespectacled, inspected the boy from the far side of the desk.

'My father has always respected your work,' Song said nervously to the elderly man. 'I know your school does not have much money, but it provides a service that is badly needed by society.' He didn't know how to ask what he had come to ask.

427

'Your father and I worked together for thirty years,' the man said. 'I have heard that he is ill.'

'You argued, I know, over a minor thing, but he still talks of you . . . When I sit with him, he likes to talk about the past—'

'I've heard your ex-father-in-law is in trouble,' the old man interrupted him to say.

'He has been detained on suspicion of corrupt use of government funds,' Song said. 'The investigation is ongoing.' He had said it so often recently that it tripped off his tongue. The last time he had seen Lina and Doudou they were huddled together miserably in Lina's aunt's house in Tianjin, waiting for news. The investigation would take several months. Song was still hoping that Detective Fang would have enough evidence against Detective Chen without his dossier. He was afraid that Detective Fang did not have enough influence to deliver what he had promised, which was protection for Lina and Doudou.

'Why are you here?' the wife asked. She had a round face, and soft grey hair.

'The boy,' Song said, gesturing to the shoulder stump, 'he has no arm . . .'

'Yes,' the elderly man said drily, 'we can see that.'

'I know you have other children here with similar handicaps.' Song tried to gather up his thoughts. 'Anyway, that's one problem. Also, his father's in jail.'

The boy turned and shot an angry look at Song, and Song sighed. This boy, whose entire life had been made up of humiliation, was ashamed of only one thing, and that was his father's criminality.

'His mother can't cope and she has no money. He can't read or write . . . He looks like an imbecile but he's sound in the head.'

'You want him to stay here?' The elderly man sounded concerned.

'I can pay.'

'He has a mother . . .' the grey-haired woman said doubtfully.

'He cannot go back to her . . .' Song started, then stopped and began again. 'He had a sister. She was murdered.'

As one, the husband and wife took a sharp breath.

'Is the boy in danger too?' The elderly man was agitated. 'We can't let killers loose among our children.'

'Not from . . .' Song hesitated, 'not from the same quarter. That has been dealt with.' It was like a physical pain for him to trust these people, although his father had assured him that it was safe to do so. 'But he is safest hidden. There are those who want to find him because of what he's seen.'

'What has he—' the elderly man whispered, then broke off at the warning in Song's eyes.

'It's a risk, then . . .' His wife spoke in a formal tone. 'Our position, as you know, is delicate. We are – our school is an embarrassment to the authorities, who would rather believe these children did not exist. We could be closed down in an instant, any excuse will be seized on, questions raised about our funding. Any suggestion of impropriety, and we will be closed down.'

Song stood silently, head lowered, and the couple scrutinized the boy, who tried his hardest to stand still but seemed to vibrate with energy. He darted a look at Song over his shoulder. If these people didn't take the boy, Song thought, he didn't know what to do. He could not keep the boy with him any longer. In the five weeks since Nixon's death the boy had been holed up in a peasant's house in Tongxian, but this could not go on. In a village he would be noticed as soon as he went outside. In a school he would be one of many boys, and in a city he would assume a certain anonymity.

So many times, Song had relived that night. He could not be sure, but he assumed the *ayi* had told Nelson Li that he, Song, had come to the house on the night of Nixon's death, and had brought the boy with him. Yet in the weeks since his return, although they had met several times, Nelson Li had never raised the issue of the boy with Song. Nor had he asked where Song himself was on that night. Nixon's funeral was arranged with speed and efficiency, and since then Nelson Li had not mentioned his dead son.

That silence made Song feel, perversely, that in killing Nixon he had done Nelson Li's bidding. Well, he was Nelson Li's man now. Li and his daughter kept him busy. But he did not believe for a moment that Nelson Li had forgotten that somewhere there was a one-armed boy who had witnessed Nixon commit murder, and who could still ruin him. Of course the boy had also seen Song kill Nixon. And although Song suspected that this would not come as a shock to Nelson Li, it was something – and he had tried to impress this on the boy – that must never, ever, be spoken. Even Wolf did not know the truth.

Song did not know where to take the boy, apart from this school for the children of prisoners, which ran on the charity of the elderly couple and their supporters, people who were good and discreet. The boy could be traced back to his mother's village either by Nelson Li, or by the police, who were still mystified by the spate of serial killings. The police, the serial killer squad, had noted that the killings seemed to be on pause, but they could not be sure that they were over. They gathered data still. They worked on identifying the boy's sister.

No, the boy could not go back, and in any case his mother's hovel offered him nothing in the way of education or advancement. The mother had received a letter. Song hoped one of her neighbours would read it to her. There was no return address, and it was clean of any identifying marks, including fingerprints. But inside the envelope he had placed a photograph of her son, all cleaned up and well dressed, and there was money. One day, when it was safer, her son would visit her.

Song became aware that the elderly man and woman were talking softly, and he waited with resignation for dismissal.

'For your father's sake, we will take him on a trial basis,' the elderly man said wearily. 'We'll see if he fits in.'

Song thanked them both profusely and laid on the desk an envelope that was thick with banknotes. It would feed more than one mouth, for many months to come. He touched the boy's shoulder.

'Don't run away,' he said. 'Stay still for once. You're safe here.'

AUTHOR'S NOTE

Beijing is constantly changing. A building may be here one day, gone the next, and in another blink of the eye a tower block has taken its place. So I don't feel too bad about taking some liberties. The location at the heart of the story is Anjialou, once a village but now surrounded by city. Anjialou has changed even since I started writing; it may or may not exist in its present form by the time this book is published. I invented Nelson Li, his construction site and all his other business interests, as well Orgasin beauty salon, the Lotus Pool restaurant, Song's detective agency, the Rainbow Hotel and other locations. Shijingshan exists to the west of the city and is the home of Capital Iron and Steel, which is being moved out of the city in an attempt to reduce pollution. The scavengers and beggar gangs exist, as does the quarry turned dump, although it's been cleaned up a bit. The specific crimes and characters between the covers of this book are entirely fictitious. The only character based on a living thing is Ziggy the dog, and I want to thank Joanna for letting me steal his identity.

If you want to read more please visit my website.
www.catherinesampson.com

ACKNOWLEDGEMENTS

In Yorkshire, Lorraine Clissold fed me delicious home-made Chinese food and Tim, the author of *Mr China*, shared his knowledge of steel plants and of the pleasures and pain of doing business in China. In Beijing, another friend, James Kynge, wrote the excellent *China Shakes the World*, which describes – among much else – the story of the Dortmund steel mill which was dismantled and rebuilt in China. Another former journalist, Matt Forney, who has written extensively about serial killings in China, generously discussed his experiences with me. Cece Hayes, who set up the Wisdom Springs sanctuary, introduced me to former street children brought to Beijing from the countryside by gang leaders. Joey, Ruth and Nicholas – these are their English names – told me stories of great hardship, and of their relief at finding a home at Wisdom Springs. From Germany, forensic biologist Mark Benecke patiently answered my gory queries. In Shanghai, Kirsten Thogersen shared insights on criminal psychology. Any mistakes, on any subject, are my own. My former editor, Sarah Turner, was extremely supportive as I thought this book through. Later Anna Valdinger edited with great vigour and enthusiasm. I want to thank Amanda Preston, my wonderful multi-tasking agent. I am hugely grateful to Martha Huang, Kathy Wilhelm, Lucy Cavender and Jen Schwerin both for their encouragement and for their criticism. Alistair, Rachel and Kirsty were cheerfully tolerant of my labours, and my parents Joan and John Sampson lent me long summers of support. This book is dedicated to my husband, James, in his Chinese incarnation. James and I met in 1988, when we were both journalists in Beijing. We have been watching China's transformation together ever since.